A
Week in
Winter

———

A
Week in
Winter

Marcia Willett

Thomas Dunne Books

St. Martin's Press ✠ New York

THOMAS DUNNE BOOKS.
An imprint of St. Martin's Press.

www.stmartins.com

ISBN 0-312-28785-2

First published in Great Britain in 2001 by
Headline Book Publishing,
a division of Hodder Headline

First U.S. Edition: May 2002

10 9 8 7 6 5 4 3 2 1

To Rachel

Prologue

The lone walker on the hill shivered a little. The sun had set long since, sinking gently down, received by plump cushiony clouds above a fiery sea. The glow was all about him, transforming these bleak moorland heights with a golden, heavenly light. Far below, where lanes and tracks weaved and curled their secret ways, shouts and laughter drifted up into the clear air. He paused for a moment, dragging his gloves from his pocket, watching the small figures of men as they prepared to stop work for the day.

The old house was being renovated. Even from this distance he could see the evidence of it in the yard: piles of timber, a small bonfire still smoking, ladders and scaffolding. A schoolmaster, recently widowed, he'd walked these paths for years, during holidays and half terms, and could remember when the cream-washed walls had been bare granite and the yard full of cows. He'd heard the voices of children as they'd clambered on the swing beside the tall escallonia hedge and seen smoke rising from the chimney on cold autumn evenings.

Now, an agent's board bearing green and white lettering leaned at an angle against the low stone wall which bordered the narrow lane, and the workmen were ready to go home. A pick-up idled in the yard whilst someone opened the farm gate, shouting to his companion who came hurrying from the barn. The truck was driven slowly through the gateway, waiting whilst the gate was shut and the man safely aboard before disappearing behind the shoulder of the hill.

The walker drew his collar more closely about his throat and walked briskly onwards, his face to the west. The house, built at the moor gate, in the shadow of the hills, always reminded him of a poem he'd known from childhood. He murmured it aloud as he trudged onwards.

> 'From quiet homes and first beginning,
> Out to the undiscovered ends . . . '

A sudden gust of cold wind came snaking over the moors. He bent his head against it, still trying to remember the next lines. A handful of chill rain made him blink and he began to hurry, the verse forgotten, his mind now on supper: his landlady's warm kitchen, hot, strong tea and the comforting smell of cooking.

He did not see the muffled figure crossing the moor below the house, pausing within the shadow of the thorn hedge, climbing swiftly over the dry-stone wall.

The clouds gathered overhead and the rain began to fall steadily.

Part One

Chapter One

Maudie Todhunter poured herself some coffee, sliced the top neatly from her egg, and settled herself to look at her letters. A rather promising selection lay beside her plate this morning: a satisfyingly bulky package from the Scotch House, a blue square envelope bearing her step-granddaughter's spiky writing, and a more businesslike missive stamped with an estate agent's logo—which she placed at the bottom of the pile. She slit open Posy's card with the butter knife and propped it against the marmalade before plunging her spoon into the rich golden yolk of her boiled egg. Posy's writing required concentration, decorated as it was with tiny drawings and exclamations, and often heavily underscored.

'Don't forget,' Posy had written at the side, so that Maudie had to turn the card to read it, 'that you promised to think about Polonius. Mum's saying that he'll have to go to the Dacres. Pleeeze, Maudie! . . .'

Maudie shuddered. The idea of housing the boisterous Polonius, a large English mastiff, rescued by Posy during the Easter holidays, filled her with horror.

'I am *not* a dog person,' she'd told Posy severely. 'You know that quite well after all these years.'

'Well, you should be,' Posy had retorted. 'Taking Polonius for walks would keep your weight down. You've just told me that you can't get into half your clothes. Anyway, it's only for term times. I've made Mum promise I can have him at home for the holidays if I can find a home for him during the term. Mind you, she'll be spitting nails if she knows you've agreed to have him . . .'

Maudie chuckled appreciatively to herself as she spread marmalade on her toast. Selina had fought hard to prevent the alliance between her step-mother and Posy, but their mutual affection had been too strong for her. As soon as she was old enough to be independent Posy had spent as much time as she could with Maudie, ignoring her mother's sulks, fielding her accusations of disloyalty, bearing with her ability to make life extremely tiresome. Posy was quite bright enough to know that Maudie might well house Polonius simply in order to irritate Selina and she was ready to go to any lengths to keep him.

Resisting such a temptation, Maudie opened the next envelope. Soft squares of tartan tumbled on to the table. Distracted from her breakfast, her coffee cooling in the big blue and white cup, Maudie caressed the fine woollen samples. She examined them closely, reading the descriptions written on the white labels which were stuck to each square: Muted Blue Douglas, Ancient Campbell, Hunting Fraser, Dress Mackenzie. They slid over her fingers and lay amongst the toast crumbs. Miss Grey at The Scotch House had done her proud as usual.

'Something different,' Maudie had pleaded. 'Not dull old Black Watch. Have you still got my measurements?'

Maudie had been a customer at the Scotch House for many years, and her measurements were kept on file, but it was a while now since she'd ordered any new clothes. She'd been assured, however, that her file was at hand and that her order would be given immediate attention. Meanwhile, samples would be sent at once. Tall, with a generous, low-slung bosom and long legs, Maudie remembered with regret the good old days when clothes could be made to measure without costing the earth. She had a passion for the texture and colour of fabric: supple tweed in earthy shades, nubbly raw silk the colour of clotted cream, fine lawn shirts, crisp white cotton, soft, comforting cherry-red lambswool.

'You're so . . . so *understated*,' Hector had said once, fumbling for the word. 'Not like Hilda . . .'

No, not like Hilda who'd loved bright floral prints and fussy foulard frocks with pussycat bows; not like Hilda who held it an article of faith that a woman should make the best of herself at all times; who considered it an almost sacred duty to be good-tempered and forbearing at any cost. After a while, when Patricia and Selina made it painfully, cruelly clear that she would never replace their dead mother, Maudie had made it almost a point of honour to be as different from Hilda as it was possible to be.

'Be patient,' Hector had pleaded. 'They're so young. It's still raw for them and Hilda was such a wonderful mother.' Everyone had wanted her to know it, voices lowered respectfully, eyes alert, eager for her reaction: a wonderful mother, a wonderful cook, a wonderful wife, a wonderful friend. Even now Maudie still struggled against the resentment which had festered intermittently for thirty years, corroding and insistent, clouding happiness, destroying peace—and now Hector was dead too.

Maudie gathered up the scraps of material and thrust them back into the envelope. Outside the window, on the veranda, sparrows pecked at the crumbs she'd thrown out earlier, whilst two collared doves balanced together on the bird table. She swallowed some lukewarm coffee, grimaced and refilled the cup with hot black liquid from the pot. The rain which had swept up from the west during last evening had passed away to the north and the sun was shining. From her table beside the French windows she could see cobwebs, glinting and sparkling, strung about the high hedges which protected the long narrow garden. A few leaves, golden and russet, were scattered on the lawn. The sun had not yet risen high enough to penetrate the dark corners beneath the trees, or pierce the shadowy waters of the ponds, but the big square living room was bright and cheerful. Soon it would be cold enough to light the big wood-burning stove; soon but not yet.

Maudie took up Posy's card again. It was odd how the child's personality flowed out of the thin spiky letters which carried the usual messages of affection, cloaked beneath sharp observations and teasing remarks; odd and comforting. She refused to allow any concessions to Maudie's advancing years—'I'm seventy-two, child!' protestingly. 'So?' impatiently—and was now suggesting that Maudie should drive to Winchester to see her new quarters, meet her fellow students and share a pint or two at the local pub.

We're in this old Victorian house, *she wrote*. It's really fab. You'll like Jude. He's doing theatre studies with me and there's Jo, who's doing art and stuff. She's cool. I've got this really big room to myself on the top floor. It's great to be out of Hall and independent. You've got to come, Maudie . . .

She laid the card aside and looked almost indifferently at the last letter bearing the Truro postmark. Far too early, surely, for the agents to have a buyer. Moorgate still had the workmen in, although they were at the clearing-up stage as regards the house itself. Hector had always insisted that she should have Moorgate. The London house should be sold and the proceeds divided between Patricia and Selina; Maudie would have an annuity and Moorgate—and, of course, The Hermitage.

Here, in this colonial-style bungalow built at the end of the nineteenth century on the edge of woodland a few miles to the north-west of Bovey Tracey, she and Hector had spent their summers ever since he'd retired from the Diplomatic Corps. Maudie's father, widowed early and a rather solitary man, had bought it for his own retreats from his desk in Whitehall, and Maudie had always declared that she would live in it in her turn if anything happened to Hector. Her friends had not believed her. 'Extraordinary,' they said, now, to one another. 'Oh, haven't you heard? Maudie's gone native in a wooden bungalow down in the wilds of Devon . . . I know. I couldn't believe it either. Mind you, she was always a bit odd, didn't you think? Super fun and all that, oh, absolutely, terrific fun, but underneath . . . Not *quite* cut out for the motherly bit and I wonder if she didn't give darling Hector a bit of a hard time. Well, we all *adored* Hector, didn't we? Of course, you never really knew Hilda, did you? Oh, she was a *brick*, my dear. An absolute *brick* . . .'

Maudie knew what they were saying and revelled in it. Once married to Hector she'd acquired a reputation for tactlessness, for laughing at quite the wrong moment, for a worrying lack of respect for the hierarchy, whilst on the domestic front she was naïve. Dinner parties for twenty diplomats and their wives, organising bazaars, the children's Christmas party were out of her ken. The men liked her—though some feared her—despite these failings. Those years she'd spent at Bletchley Park during the war and her subsequent appointment as assistant to a well-known research physicist in America lent her an odd glamour which some of the wives resented.

'And that's what attracted Hector,' murmured Maudie, picking up the long white envelope. 'After Hilda's perfection in the home he couldn't resist the opportunity for fun. And we *did* have fun when the girls weren't around to disapprove and make him feel guilty.'

There had been more disapproval—especially from Selina—when they learned that Moorgate was to be left to Maudie.

'My whole childhood is wrapped up in that place,' Selina had declared dramatically. 'We always spent the summer at Moorgate with Mummy.'

'But what would you do with it?' asked her husband, trying to suppress his embarrassment. 'It's been agreed that Maudie should sell the house in Arlington Road. What more do you want?'

Maudie had appreciated his partisanship but had no wish to be made out as a martyr.

'I wouldn't want to stay in London without Hector,' she'd said abruptly. 'But you and Patricia will get far more for that place than you will for an old farmhouse on the edge of Bodmin Moor.' She'd smiled grimly. 'Or do you feel that you should have *both* houses, Selina?'

'Of course she doesn't.' Patrick had been horrified. 'For heaven's sake! Hector is being scrupulously fair . . .'

'To me? Or to the girls?' Maudie had looked innocently enquiring.

'I meant, well, given the circumstances . . .' Patrick had grappled with his confusion until Maudie released him from his misery.

'I shall have my father's house in Devon and an annuity. Moorgate is my insurance policy. Hector knows that neither Patricia nor Selina would ever use it or afford to keep it without a tenant in it. He believes that the money you'll get from the sale of the house in Arlington Road will be enough to give you plenty in reserve for almost any emergency. Well.' She'd shrugged, preparing to leave. 'Shall I tell your father that you're unhappy about his plans?' She'd warded off Patrick's protestations and beamed into Selina's sulky face. At the door she'd paused. 'Of course, there's always the possibility that you might die first and then all your worries will be over. So *taxing*, deciding what other people should do with their belongings, isn't it?'

Remembering the scene, Maudie chuckled again, briefly, then grew sober. What *would* Selina say when she discovered that Moorgate was about to be put on the market? The elderly tenants had died and Maudie had brooded long as to whether she should relet it or sell it. Expediency forced her hand. The bungalow needed a new roof and her car should have been replaced long since. She would sell Moorgate and give herself a buffer; it would be a comfort to have a cushion between herself and the sharp realities of life.

As she slit open the envelope and drew out the sheet of paper, Maudie wondered again what had happened to those investments of which Hector had told her years ago. She hadn't taken much notice at the time but he had been scrupulous in showing her the extent of his portfolio. He wasn't wealthy, but she knew that even after the purchase of her annuity there should have been certain shares and investments which had not, after all, been mentioned in his will. Could he have changed his mind and given them to the girls much earlier? As usual she dismissed this recurring thought. Even had he bound them to secrecy, surely Selina could not have resisted displaying her triumph to her stepmother? Yet it seemed impossible to imagine Hector having financial problems which he had hidden from her. She pushed the nagging question aside and read the letter from the agents in Truro.

. . . the work inside the house is almost finished and we have already erected a board to tempt any passer-by. However, Moorgate being in such a remote location, we shall mainly be relying on advertising and sending out the particulars . . . There is some problem about a key to the office, storeroom and cloakroom. This is the area which is approached both through the kitchen and from outside and, whilst it is not a particularly important selling feature, it will be necessary to allow clients to view it. Mr Abbot has been intending to contact you about it since he is unable to renovate this part of the house . . . Perhaps you would be so kind as to contact me.

Maudie frowned. Surely she'd given Rob Abbot the full set of keys, having kept one spare front door key for herself and one for the agents? Rob wasn't the sort to mislay keys. Aged about thirty-five, tall, tough, with a keen sense of humour, he'd appealed to her at once. He'd looked over Moorgate, making notes, cracking jokes, telling her that he'd given up his engineering job in London after promotion had made him more of an administrator than an engineer.

'Boardroom politics aren't my scene,' he'd said cheerfully. 'I like getting my hands dirty. So I've come West to make my fortune.'

'Well, you won't make it at my expense,' she'd answered tartly. 'I can't afford to spend too much.'

'You'll be a fool if you don't do it properly,' he'd said seriously. 'People throw money away. They refuse to spend a few pennies on a run-down cottage and they sell it to a builder who moves in and makes a killing. She's worth doing up properly, this old place. You'll get your money back twice over, believe me.'

She'd listened to him, making tea for them both with an old kettle in the huge, bare kitchen, and then they'd gone from room to room whilst he showed her what might be done. His ideas were simple but good and she decided, with one or two restrictions, that she'd allow him to go ahead if his price were reasonable. He'd encouraged her to visit two other properties he'd renovated and she was privately impressed.

He'd grinned at her. 'Wait and see. When I've finished you won't want to sell her.'

'Then you won't get paid,' she'd answered. 'Send me an estimate and I'll think about it.'

That had been at the beginning of the summer. Perhaps it was time to make a visit to Moorgate; to meet Rob again and to check out his work for herself. She'd made one visit and meant to go back but the right moment had never yet arisen.

Maudie decided that now it had. She would drive down to Cornwall, see Moorgate and Rob, sort out the problem of the key. She removed her spectacles, collected her post together and, rising from the breakfast table, went to make a telephone call.

Chapter Two

Listening to the enthusiastic voice of the young agent in the office in Truro, Maudie was able to imagine him quite clearly—although she had never met him.

'It's an absolutely super property, Lady Todhunter, quite my favourite. I can't wait to start marketing it properly. It's just this thing about the keys to the office . . .' His voice, rather breathless, rattled on in her ear as she visualised the clean, floppy hair and scrubbed, fresh complexion; imagined the leather Filofax whose leaves she could hear rustling as he flicked through the pages; envisaged the head at an angle, shoulder hunched so as to grip the telephone receiver. In her mind's eye she saw his tie; silk, of course, and decorated with some cartoon animal: Daffy Duck, perhaps? Of course, he would also own a mobile phone, a laptop and a small hatchback: the necessary toys of his profession.

'I quite understand, Mr . . . ?' She peered at the name typed beneath the scrawled signature on the letter she held in her hand. 'Mr Cruikshank, is it . . . ? Oh, very well, then, Ned,'—she hated the modern informality but could never resist the young—'I understand that the keys have gone missing but I don't have a spare set for the office and the side door. What does Mr Abbot say about it?'

'Well, you see that's the whole point.' Ned's voice was confiding, now, inviting her to share his bafflement. 'He can't remember ever having them.'

Maudie frowned, cudgelling recalcitrant memory. 'I'm quite certain I gave him the whole set,' she said firmly. 'As I recall, there was only ever the one complete set of keys and I thought it sensible for Mr Abbot to have them until he'd finished. I kept one front door key for myself, in case of emergency, and gave you the other to be going on with. How very tiresome.'

'I suppose,' he suggested diffidently, 'that there couldn't be another set somewhere? You know? Just knocking about at the back of a drawer, or in the bottom of an old vase, or something?'

'I suppose it's possible. The tenants returned the set which I passed on to Mr Abbot. There might be a faint chance that my husband had another set somewhere.'

'Perhaps you could ask him.' Ned sounded hopeful.

'Rather tricky, under the circumstances,' said Maudie drily. 'He's dead and I have no inclination towards spiritualism . . . No, no. Don't apologise. How could you possibly know?' She felt a stab of remorse for her abruptness which had caused his embarrassment and spluttered apologies. 'My fault. You must forgive my bad taste. I'll look about for the keys but I'm not at all sanguine. Everything was sorted out when I moved down from London, you see, but I'll just make absolutely certain. No, not a nuisance . . . Don't give it a thought . . . Yes, I'll be in touch.'

She replaced the receiver and returned to the living room, picking up the big wooden tray and piling up the breakfast things ready to be taken into the kitchen. Pausing to watch a nuthatch, upside down on the nut container which hung from a hook on the bird table, she was distracted for a moment from the problems at Moorgate. She loved these two big sunny rooms which opened on to the veranda and the garden. They were divided from the other rooms by a wide passage, with the front door at one end of it and a box room at the other. An adequate-sized kitchen, a surprisingly large bathroom, a tiny cloakroom and a spare bedroom made up the rest of the accommodation but it was quite big enough for Maudie. Each holiday Hector had chafed at its lack of space, at the impossibility of giving parties or inviting friends for the weekends.

'For heaven's sake,' she'd cry impatiently, 'we're only here for a few weeks. Surely you can survive without them? Isn't it nice to be on our own for a while?'

He'd smile repentantly. 'Withdrawal symptoms,' he'd say. 'Give me a day or two . . .' But he'd never been able to hide his pleasure and anticipation as the day for their return to London drew near.

Maudie took the tray into the kitchen and unloaded the contents on to the draining board. Hector had always been at his best surrounded by people—selected people, if possible, but almost any people were preferable to his own company. Maudie was happier in a more intimate setting, one friend at a time so that she could concentrate upon them, rather than the bustle and noise of large parties. Nevertheless, they'd managed pretty well, given that Maudie had never entertained more than six people at a time before she'd met Hector. Naturally, Hilda had been the perfect hostess . . .

The sudden jet of hot water, splashing against the back of a spoon, sprayed Maudie's jersey and she cursed sharply, turning off the tap. How foolish, how utterly *pointless* it was, to feel such antagonism against a woman who had been dead for more than thirty years. The irritating thing about dying young—well, forty-four was fairly young—was that it immediately hallowed the dead with a kind of immunity. They were always ahead of the game, one point up, they didn't play fair. Maudie bashed the dishes about in the hot soapy water with a splendid disregard for their welfare. Even now, with Hilda and Hector both dead, she still felt the frustration of what she called 'second-wife syndrome'. Perhaps it would have been easier to deal with if Patricia and Selina had been prepared to meet her halfway. To be fair—did she want to be fair?—Patricia had been tolerant enough. She simply wasn't interested in her new stepmother, too immersed, at sixteen, in her own growing-up to make any efforts to make Maudie feel part of the family. Selina had demanded her sister's partisanship in her battle, however, and Patricia, through loyalty or indifference, had added her weight to Selina's resistance.

Drying the dishes, putting away the marmalade and butter, Maudie struggled for rationality. It had been difficult for Hector to remain unmoved by his daughters' hostility. Patricia's attacks had been spasmodic, distracted as she was by boyfriends and parties, but Selina had waged a determined, unflinching war. At twelve she'd missed her mother terribly and had no intention of sharing her father with this stranger. It was perhaps unfortunate that she'd started at boarding school in the autumn following the wedding so that, although it had been arranged for years, she could always blame Maudie for packing her off to school in true wicked stepmother style.

'Absolute rubbish!' Hector had shouted irritably, driven to distraction by Selina's tears and recriminations. 'You knew quite well that you'd be going away to school next term. Patricia went at thirteen and you were perfectly happy about it until . . . until now. You know that I've been posted to Geneva and that Mummy would have wanted you to be settled with Patricia at school by the time I leave. It has absolutely *nothing* to do with Maudie.'

He'd slammed himself into his study leaving Selina, tear-stained and furious, outside the door.

'Look,' Maudie had said awkwardly, 'I know it's hard to understand but he feels it too, you know.'

Selina's face was as stony and unyielding as granite. 'I hate you,' she'd said—but quietly, lest Hector should hear and come storming out—'and I wish it was you who was dead.'

'I expect you do,' Maudie had answered cheerfully. 'But while we're waiting for that happy event can't we try to be friends?'

Selina had not bothered to reply but had gone away to her room, locking herself in, refusing to come down to lunch, and the house had been wrapped in an atmosphere of gloom and ill-feeling until the term started. Oh, the joy of being alone with Hector, ghosts and guilt banished—only temporarily, however. Both would be resurrected with monotonous regularity at half terms and each holiday.

'We must be patient,' Hector had insisted—also with monotonous regularity. 'After all, at least we get the term times to ourselves.'

Hanging up the dishcloth Maudie smiled secretly to herself. What fun they'd had; careless, selfish, glorious fun.

'I must say,' he'd admitted, just once or twice, after afternoons of love, or an extra brandy after a particularly good dinner party, 'I have to admit that it's rather nice not to be worrying about the girls all the time. If Hilda had a fault it was that she used to fuss about them. Know what I mean? I felt that I was a father and provider first and husband and lover second.'

She'd learned that it didn't do to make a little joke about such criticism. 'What's this heresy?' she'd asked once, laughingly. 'Come now! Can it be true? Hilda wasn't perfect, after all?' It had been mild enough but he'd descended at once into self-criticism and remorse, rehearsing a catalogue of Hilda's attributes, singing her praises, mourning her passing. No, it didn't do at all to hint, even light-heartedly, that she felt the least bit inadequate in the face of such perfection. Instead she'd done what she was good at; she'd made him laugh, made him feel young, sexy, strong. Responsibility, grief, anxiety would slide away from him and he'd respond in such a way that her own esteem would soar again and she'd feel needed, desired, witty, vital. It hadn't been easy, after all, to give up her own career, to become a diplomat's wife and stepmother to his ungrateful, tiresome daughters.

Although, at the start, she had to admit that it had been only *too* easy. She'd been on her way home to England for leave following the retirement of the physicist for whom she'd worked for more than fifteen years. Part of her life was at an end. It was Christmas and the airport was closed by snow. Disgruntled passengers huddled together, complaining, whilst Hector . . . 'hectored', as Maudie had said to him afterwards. 'You hectored the staff and bullied them into finding us accommodation.'

'Perfectly reasonable,' he'd said. 'You didn't refuse a nice warm bed, if I remember rightly.'

It was odd—odd and altogether delightful—how she and Hector had so quickly drawn together. Laughing, sharing his hip flask, making light of the difficulties—the brief episode had been romantic, unreal, fantastic, yet afterwards they'd refused to be separated. Maudie had given up her career and Hector had risked the surprise and disapproval of friends and family so that he and Maudie could be married twelve months after the death of his wife.

'It might be tricky,' he'd admitted anxiously as they'd driven to meet Hilda's mother and the girls. 'It'll come as a bit of a shock. Everyone adored Hilda . . .'

It was only then that she'd realised that their life together was to be a delicate balance, a seesaw of emotions. There was the Hector that she knew, lover and companion, and the Hector who was the responsible elder son, the adored father, the admired friend, the respected colleague.

'I feel that nobody really looks upon me as Hector's wife,' Maudie had once said to Daphne. 'It's the oddest sensation, as if there's something illicit about the whole thing; that Hilda was his official, legal wife and I'm regarded as his mistress.'

'Sounds good to me,' Daphne had replied. 'Much more fun.'

Daphne had been the one who had welcomed her, done her best to make her feel at home, eased her path: Daphne, who was Hilda's oldest friend and Patricia's godmother.

'You might have a problem with Daphne,' Hector had warned as they'd waited for their guests at the official cocktail party in Geneva. 'She and Hilda were at school together. They were like sisters.'

He'd been clearly uneasy at that first meeting, awkward during introductions, quite without his usual urbane ease, but Daphne had taken

Maudie's hands readily, smilingly, although her gaze had been very direct, searching.

'How clever of you, Hector,' she'd murmured. 'How very clever.' And she'd leaned forward to kiss Maudie's cheek.

Even now, more than thirty years later, Maudie could remember the warmth she'd felt at Daphne's brief embrace. There had been a genuine liking, discernible even in such an artificial setting; a warmth that had thawed Maudie's wariness.

'I like Daphne,' she'd said later, over their nightcap, and Hector had taken a deep breath, stretching as he stood before the fire, clearly relieved.

'It all went off very well,' he'd admitted. 'Very well indeed.'

Daphne had become her closest friend, her ally in the ongoing battle with Selina, her defender against the whispers of Hilda's supporters.

'After all,' Maudie had said, enraged by a snub, 'it's not as if Hector divorced the blasted woman, abandoned her for me. He was a widower, for God's sake!'

'Oh, my dear.' Daphne had looked rueful. 'Can't you see the threat you are to us old wifies? Hector's flouted the unwritten rules which govern our small bit of society. He has found himself a younger, attractive woman who can't cook, doesn't want children, can't tell the difference between His Excellency and the gardener and *he doesn't give a damn.* He's clearly enjoying himself enormously. He looks ten years younger and he's making us question all our entrenched beliefs.'

'But why?' Maudie had asked. 'Why can't people just leave us alone?'

'Research laboratories must be very unusual places.' Daphne had shaken her head. 'Are you only just learning that if someone steps aside from the herd he is likely to be torn to pieces? We're all so insecure, you see. If you behave differently from me, I either have to question my own beliefs and habits or prove that you are wrong. Misguided, stupid, ill-bred, it doesn't really matter how I label you so long as I can continue to feel complacent and safe. You have come amongst us and upset the apple cart. But you must be patient with us, Maudie. Middle-aged wives are very vulnerable people, you know. And middle-aged men are very susceptible.'

'I don't want to be a threat to anyone,' Maudie had cried. 'I just want to be left alone. I don't criticise any of *you.* I don't care what you do or how you do it.'

'That's the problem,' Daphne had sighed. 'You're so confident, so sure, so indifferent. You'll find that some people will simply not be able to cope with it.'

'You make it sound as if my life is one big laugh,' Maudie had said crossly. 'I promise you it isn't. Being a second wife and a stepmother can be hell. I'm not nearly as confident as you imagine.'

'Ah, but you're not admitting it. You're not confiding in all those wives who would love to advise . . .'

'And gloat, privately together, afterwards.'

'Well, there you have it. So why do you admit it to me?'

'Because you're different,' Maudie had said, after a moment or two. 'I trust you.' And Daphne had laughed then, laughed until Maudie had felt almost uneasy.

'I know it's odd that I should trust you,' she'd said almost defensively, 'you being Hilda's closest friend and all that. But I do. So now *you* can go and gloat privately.'

'No, I shan't do that. But I agree that it's odd. I loved Hilda, I really did. We started at boarding school together, you know, and I spent a great many holidays with her family whilst mine were abroad, and we had a lot of fun. But she was always a serious girl, rather prim and proper, and as she grew older this developed into a kind of complacency which, if I'm honest, could be very irritating. There, how's that for disloyalty?'

'Not a bad effort for a beginner,' Maudie had answered, grinning, 'but I'm sure you could do better if you were to try harder.'

Daphne had hesitated—and then laughed. 'You are a wicked girl,' she said. 'Hector's a lucky man. He's clearly a very happy one.'

Had he been happy? Maudie took her jacket from the peg inside the door and rummaged in her bag for the car keys. What about those endless rows over Selina? Those accusations he'd hurled at her: that she was unsympathetic, cold, selfish? What about those times that he'd gone alone to see his daughter and her children because Selina complained that Maudie was so critical, so unaffectionate that the boys were frightened of her? What about the pain when she realised that Hector was beginning to take Selina's word against her own?

'Over,' Maudie said loudly, as she stepped outside and slammed the door. 'Over, over, *over!*'

So why, asked the insistent small voice inside her head, *why* are you still so angry?

'Shut up,' said Maudie. 'I will not do this. I am going to enjoy myself. Go away and leave me alone.'

She opened the door of the large shed which housed the car, drove slowly down the long moss-covered drive and headed westwards, towards Bodmin Moor.

Chapter Three

The farmhouse stood in a small hollow beside the narrow lane. At the end of the garden, by the dry-stone wall, two granite pillars—the moor gate—leaned either side of the cattle grid, beyond which the lane climbed steeply to the open moor. Maudie parked the car by the gate to the yard and climbed out. A pick-up stood in the shelter of the open-fronted barn and a bonfire smoked sulkily. It was a soft grey day, the distant farmland veiled in mist, and a brooding quiet lay over the countryside. The place looked deserted, the house closed up, empty. In the stand of trees to the west, across the lane, a party of rooks rose suddenly, noisily, into the damp air, and the faint clopping of hoofs penetrated the silence.

Maudie looked with approval at the sturdy cob which now appeared round the bend in the lane. Its rider raised his crop to his hat and jogged onwards, bending to unfasten the small gate beside the cattle grid. They passed through, the cob waiting quietly whilst the gate was shut, and began to climb the moorland road. Presently they were out of sight and Maudie turned her attention once more to the house. In this land of granite and slate the cream-washed walls struck a warm note. The roof was Delabole slate, the front door solid oak, and the old farmhouse had an air of permanency and safety; a place of refuge in an inhospitable environment.

On a hot summer's day, with the tall escallonia hedge in full flower and the larks tossing high above, it was an idyllic place to be but in winter, with the storms lashing the uplands and the wind screaming from the west, it was harsh and bleak. Left empty, the farmhouse would become damp, icy-cold and uninhabitable. It needed to be lived in, kept dry and warm, used as a home, not bought for a holiday retreat.

'Mummy adored Moorgate,' Selina had been fond of repeating. 'Her family owned it when she was a little girl and she used to stay with the farmer and his wife. Then, when they retired, we kept it as a holiday home for years. We went there every summer, Mummy, me and Patricia. Daddy joined us when he could. We must never get rid of Moorgate, there are so many memories.'

Even after the sale of the London house Selina kept a watching brief from a distance.

'Pure dog-in-the-manger,' Maudie had observed crossly to Daphne, after one of these sessions down memory lane with her stepdaughter. 'She hasn't been there for years. Sentimental hogwash. I notice there was no problem when it came to selling the house in Arlington Road. Yet she spent much more time there with Hilda than down at Moorgate.'

'I suppose that childhood summers are always invested with a kind of glamour,' Daphne had answered thoughtfully. 'You know the kind of thing I mean? The sun was always shining, wasn't it? The sea was warm and adventure was always round the corner.'

'Thank you, Enid Blyton,' Maudie had said acidly. 'Shall we have a chorus of "Jesus wants me for a sunbeam" before you go?'

Nevertheless, Maudie had not yet told Selina that Moorgate was about to be put up for sale. Now, as she wandered into the yard and stood looking about her, she felt rather sad that the old farmhouse should pass out of the family. Posy loved it too, and for Posy's sake she wished she could keep it. Yet, even for Posy, it would be crazy to hold on to a property which none of them could enjoy. If she kept Moorgate it must be let—so what was the point? Better to sell and be able to help Posy financially later on.

Rob Abbot came striding round the corner of the house and she gave a gasp of surprise. She could see that she'd startled him too. He frowned a little—and then came on towards her, eyebrows raised, a faint smile hovering on his lips.

'Come to check up on me?' he asked lightly.

Maudie grinned at him. 'Thought I'd catch you slacking,' she said. 'Mr Cruikshank's been in touch, wittering on about keys. I couldn't get you on your mobile so I thought I'd drive down and see if we could sort this out.'

'He's been here,' said Rob grimly. 'Poking around, rattling door handles, peering through windows. I told him that I can't break down doors without your permission. You know, I'm sure I've never had those keys.'

'It's a mystery.' Maudie shrugged. 'I honestly can't remember now what I did with them. If they weren't on the big ring I gave you then I simply haven't a clue. We'll have to force the locks. As I remember, there's a door from the kitchen which leads into a passage to the office. There was a small cloakroom, I think, and a kind of storeroom which had an outside door.'

'Both doors are firmly locked,' said Rob. 'And the window has a blind or a curtain pulled across it. You can't see in.'

'How silly of us!' exclaimed Maudie. 'Perhaps we can just break the window and get in that way. Why didn't we think of it before?'

Rob looked doubtful. 'It's not that sort of window. I had thought of it, actually, but it's too small to climb through. Anyway, we'll have a look at it now you're here.' He hesitated. 'I shouldn't leave the car in the lane. It's very narrow there and a tractor will probably be along in a minute. Pull her into the yard.'

He opened the gate for her and went away to put the kettle on for some tea. Maudie backed carefully through the gateway and parked beside the pick-up, and by the time she arrived in the kitchen the kettle was boiling and Rob was putting tea bags into mugs. She paused inside the door, looking around. The kitchen faced northwest, stretching almost the whole width of the house, and looked out across the moor, beyond distant farmland to the sea. Empty, except for some built-in cupboards, the sink unit and the Esse range, it looked enormous, cavernous.

'It needs really big, old-fashioned farm furniture,' Maudie said, accepting her mug. 'Huge dressers and a big refectory table. The odd thing is that it doesn't feel as cold as I'd expected. There's a warm atmosphere,' she sniffed at the air, 'and what's that smell . . . Bacon?' She shook her head. 'I'm imagining things.'

Rob was looking at her oddly. 'It's funny you should say that. I've had the same impression once or twice. I'm on my own here now, tidying up, and the lads have moved on to the next job, but I sometimes get the feeling that I'm not alone.' He chuckled, almost embarrassed. 'No stories of ghosts or hauntings, are there?'

She stared at him, watching him as he turned away, sipping his tea, staring out across the moor, and felt a twinge of uneasiness. Rob Abbot was the last person in the world to let his imagination run away with him but he seemed rather distant today, unresponsive, not at all his usual joking self.

'Of course not,' she said briskly. 'What nonsense. Anyway, ghosts don't cook bacon. Are you absolutely certain that none of your men could have taken the keys, Rob? I have this feeling that there were several keys on a smaller ring, attached to the big one. Could you have taken them off and put them down somewhere?'

He turned back to her, frowning. 'Don't think I haven't thought it over. It's possible, of course. A lot of keys pass through my hands, and I'm usually very careful, but I suppose it's possible that I may have taken them off and left them lying about. But why should anyone take them? I've asked the boys, of course, and they're all as puzzled as I am. I certainly can't imagine any of them having any use for them. The house is empty, nothing to take, and it's clear that nobody's squatting in it. At the same time . . .'

'It's odd, isn't it?' She grimaced. 'Rather creepy. Come and show me the sitting room—I haven't seen it since it was finished—and then we'll decide what's to be done about the office. How annoying it is. Not that it will take long to get it decorated. I hope you won't abandon me before it's done.'

'No, I shan't do that.' He put his mug down on the draining board. 'It's always good to have some indoor work as the winter comes on and I wouldn't want to leave a job unfinished.'

'It's taken rather longer than you thought, hasn't it?' Maudie asked as they passed into the hall and she paused to look appreciatively at the oak staircase, restored now to its simple, natural state. 'You've done well, Rob. It looks right. Not like some tacky conversion. It's retained its dignity.'

He looked about him. 'She's like an elderly countrywoman,' he said affectionately. 'Strong, kindly, sheltering. She's not some passing fad for a pseudo townie who wants to pretend he's living the good life.'

Maudie glanced at him, touched by his warmth. 'The trouble is, now that the farmland has been sold off, Moorgate isn't really a farmhouse any more. And she's right off the beaten track. I'm not certain exactly who would buy it.'

'No offers yet, then?' He led the way into the sitting room. 'Mr Cruikshank seems very keen.'

She laughed. 'He's young,' she said tolerantly. 'He'll get a lot of interest from the type of people you've just described but it's too big a house for a second home and it's a long way from London. Lots of people work from home these days so maybe it'll attract a young family who can afford to ferry their children about and pay the heating bills. This warm wet climate can do such harm.' She paused. 'Have you been lighting fires in here, Rob?'

The square sitting room faced southeast and the natural stone walls had been washed with cream paint. Built into the alcove to the right of the inglenook fireplace was a glass-fronted cupboard, the oak floorboards had been stripped and polished, and the original wooden shutters were folded back on each side of the sash windows. In the fireplace, on the big, central slate, was the remains of charred twigs and a few half-burned logs in a pile of soft grey ash.

He glanced at it indifferently. 'I had a trial run after the chimney sweep had been in. I did the same in the other room just to make sure the fires were drawing properly. There's a pile of logs out in the barn so it seemed a good idea. Apart from anything else it doesn't do any harm to give the place a warm through. Actually, I was going to suggest that we might light the Esse and have some background heat if she hasn't sold in a month or two. I can pop over and keep an eye on her until you get a buyer.' He hesitated, shrugged. 'If you want me to . . .'

'That would be very kind of you,' Maudie answered. 'If it isn't a trouble. It's not a bad idea to light the Esse. Better to pay for a bit of oil than have damp coming in. Should we have put in proper central heating, I wonder?'

'Too late now,' Rob said firmly. 'And it would have been very expensive to lift these slate floors. Natural fires are best in these downstairs rooms and the Esse runs two radiators upstairs and heats the kitchen. It's more than adequate with the night storage radiators in the other bedrooms. Don't fuss.'

She grinned at him. 'Are you married?'

'No,' he answered shortly. 'What's that got to do with central heating?'

'Nothing,' she answered, feeling another twinge of uneasiness. It was unlike Rob to be so—she tried to define his mood—so *preoccupied*; as if half of him were off somewhere else. Perhaps he had woman trouble and her question had touched a nerve. Certainly he was not on his usual cheerful form. 'Nothing at all. I'd better look at these firmly locked doors, I suppose. Are you OK, Rob? Plenty of work coming in?'

'Too much, if anything.' He led the way back to the kitchen. 'I've fallen a bit behind schedule here, I'm afraid. The truth is, it's been an unusually dry summer and I've been giving the lads outside work on another site while I carried on inside here.'

'That's not a problem,' she said quickly, anxious lest he should think that she was criticising him. 'People can come and view, after all. You've done splendidly.' She watched as he indicated the door to the office, turned the knob, put his weight against it and pushed. 'Yes, well, that's not going anywhere, is it?'

'It's a lovely old oak door and I don't want it broken,' he said. 'Come outside and see the other door. It's sturdy but not particularly worth saving. That's the one I'd go for, I think. No point in smashing windows.'

Outside, on the path which ran along the side of the house, Maudie tried the unyielding door and attempted to peer through the grubby window. A fold of cloth obscured her view and she shook her head as she stepped back, dusting her hands.

'I take your point. What shall we do?'

'Better leave it to me,' he said. 'I'll get it opened, now I have your permission. We'll do as little damage as possible but I'll need some time to get it sorted inside.'

'That's fine,' she said. 'I'll tell Mr Cruikshank. There's one thing, though. If it's been locked up since the tenants left there might be things which need sorting out. I suppose you could try to break it down whilst I'm here. If we're going to have a new door it wouldn't make much difference, would it?'

He frowned thoughtfully. 'I'd rather not leave the house with a broken door,' he said. 'Anyone would be able to get in, wouldn't they? I wouldn't want to arrive tomorrow morning and find the house full of New Age travellers. There's a party of them up on Davidstow, so I've heard. Give me a chance to think about this. I want to be able to leave the place secure, whatever I do.'

'Sounds reasonable. Telephone me when you've done it and if you need me I'll come down.'

'I'll do that.' He looked at her, smiling a little. 'I promise not to sneak off with any treasures I find.'

She was pleased to see him relaxed again, less touchy. 'In that case,' she said, 'why don't we go down to the pub and have a pint and a sandwich before I go home?'

He laughed. 'Now there's an offer I can't refuse. I'll lock up and be right with you.'

Chapter Four

Driving back towards Launceston Maudie found herself rehearsing different ways of telling Selina that Moorgate was to be sold. Her fear was that, in a fit of misguided nostalgia, Selina might insist that she and Patrick should buy it. Despite the injection of cash from the sale of the London house, Maudie knew that her stepdaughter was not in a position to attempt such a quixotic act; not unless they intended to sell up and move to Cornwall. The idea of Selina living on the edge of Bodmin Moor made Maudie snort with laughter; childhood holidays were one thing, real life another. Selina's smartly shod feet required a pavement; her love of entertaining and being entertained demanded delicatessens, theatres, restaurants. No, it was unlikely that she and Patrick would make any such sacrifice. The real problem was that Selina might insist that Moorgate should be kept as a place for holidays; that she might try to persuade Patrick that it was their duty to save it.

Looking out at the bleak moorland landscape, the black, twisted thorn, the dying, rusty bracken, Maudie suddenly felt all the melancholy of the season. She knew that she was, once again, to be cast in the role of wicked stepmother. Patricia and Simon, happily settled in Australia, would receive letters and telephone calls reporting this latest calumny, and Selina's boys—Chris and Paul—would be prevailed upon to add their weight of disapproval. As she slowed to allow a sheep to meander across the road, Maudie shrugged. Patricia was too far away to lend more than a token support; as for the boys, they didn't give a damn about Moorgate and were too busy with their own lives to take action. For once, however, Posy might be on her mother's side.

Rain misted the windscreen, drifting across from the sea in thick vaporous clouds, smothering the granite outcrops in its clammy embrace, obliterating the road ahead.

'Damn,' muttered Maudie, switching on the car's sidelights and turning the windscreen wiper to intermittent. 'Damn and blast.'

Driving carefully she cast her mind back to brighter, sunnier days; a glorious summer twenty years before, when she and Daphne had spent the holidays at Moorgate. Daphne's daughter, Emily, had been unwell and Selina, committed to assisting with the boys' school trip to Venice, had been let down by the au pair who was supposed to be looking after Posy. It was Hector who had suggested that they should all go to Moorgate: Maudie and Posy; Daphne and Emily. The sea air and walks on the moor would be good for them, he'd said and, somehow, it had all been arranged—although Selina was clearly unhappy at the plan. Hector and Philip, Daphne's husband, appeared at intervals—punctuation points in the long, slow, hot days which slid seamlessly past. By day the house had been filled with sunshine; the flagged floors shockingly cold to hot, bare feet; by night the bedrooms were washed by moorland air and moonlight.

Slowing the car a little, peering into the mist ahead, Maudie remembered the old wooden swing in the shade of the escallonia hedge where Emily would sit, idly pushing herself, dreaming about her forthcoming wedding, whilst Posy splashed about in the paddling pool, squealing with delight. Daphne would lie, recumbent on the old plaid rug, her book open across her chest, her eyes closed, as Maudie poured iced lemonade from a tall, frosted jug, the sunshine burning her bare arms. Later they would have an early supper in the huge, cool kitchen; swimsuits drying on the rack above the old solid-fuel Aga; Posy, newly scrubbed, drowsing in her high chair; Emily, bright-faced, chin in hands, describing her wedding-gown; Daphne moving quietly between table and range, cutting new brown bread, placing a bowl of sweet, wine-red raspberries beside a bowl of thick, crusted, yellow clotted cream.

Darling Emily: what an enchanting bride she'd been at the end of that magical summer; drifting up the aisle in cloudy white, with small Posy staggering behind, the train clutched in hot, determined fists, the wreath of flowers askew over her eyes. Darling Emily, slender and fragile beside Tim's tall, broad-shouldered figure. The next summer they'd returned to

Moorgate. Emily was pregnant and Tim had agreed that the country air would do her good. This time, however, Selina and the boys had been members of the party and Maudie and Daphne feared ructions. By sheer good fortune, some of Selina's friends had taken a cottage at Rock and the boys had been loud in their insistence that it was more fun to be on the golden sands with their chums than to be impeded by two old women, one young pregnant one and their small, tiresome sister. Reluctantly Selina had given way before the demands of her sons and her friends so that, once again, the four were left much to their own delightful devices. For a few years the pattern had continued, until Hector had decided that Moorgate should be let on a long lease.

Young though she'd been, Posy insisted that she could remember those summers, had even, once, whilst staying with friends, insisted on being driven over to see Moorgate. The long-suffering tenants had given them tea and let Posy show her friends over the house. Her love for Moorgate was more genuine than Selina's, and Maudie dreaded breaking the news to her. She hoped that Posy was too involved with her friends and her studies to be truly miserable but it would not be a pleasant task. Posy was her darling; the baby who had broken down her defences, shattered her pride and made her vulnerable.

'We all have our favourites,' Daphne had said once, her eyes on Emily's sleeping, peaceful face. 'It's only natural, I suppose. The thing is not to let it show to the others.'

Emily had been everyone's favourite, arriving long after Daphne and Philip had given up hope of having children. She had Daphne's short nose and small square chin, her cornflower-blue eyes and blonde hair. Even if she hadn't been such a miracle child she would still have been special. She was beloved of old and young alike; sweet-tempered, merry-hearted, generous, fun.

'She's such a darling,' people exclaimed—and so she was. Daphne brooded over her with an odd mixture of delight, relief and gratitude that touched Maudie's heart.

'You are besotted with that child,' she'd said—and Daphne had looked almost guilty, defensive.

'She might so easily have been a boy,' she'd answered.

'You'd have loved him just the same,' Maudie had suggested, surprised.

'Yes,' she'd replied quickly. 'Yes, of course. Only I'd always so longed for a little girl, you see.'

How anxious Daphne had been whilst Emily was having her babies; how relieved when it was over.

'It's a girl, Maudie,' she'd cried down the telephone. 'She looks just like Emily. Both quite well. Oh, thank God! Thank God!'

She'd been quite hysterical with joy and relief. The second time round it was another girl, just like her beautiful mother, but Daphne's reaction had been exactly the same. Maudie had teased her about it but Daphne was unrepentant.

'You have no idea how happy I am,' she'd said. 'Darling Emily . . .' and she'd burst into tears.

The third occasion had been quite different—but by then Tim was dead, killed in a car accident—and Emily was left with three children to support. They'd been living in Canada for ten years, by then, and Daphne had rushed out to be with her. This baby was unplanned, the other two already in their teens, and there was no joy in Daphne's voice when she'd reported his premature birth. The long distance call had been marred by crackles and Maudie had suspected that Daphne was crying.

'Daphne. Oh, Daphne, I'm so sorry.' She was almost shouting into the receiver. 'Oh, if only you weren't so far away.'

Hector had been standing beside her, his face creased with anxiety, and she'd shaken her head at him, indicating that she couldn't hear properly. He'd taken the receiver from her.

'Daphne,' he'd said. 'It's Hector. Don't cry, my dear. Try to be calm and tell us exactly the situation so that we can help you . . .' and Maudie had gone to pour herself a drink, comforted by his calm strength, knowing that Daphne would feel it, too, however serious the news.

Emily and small Tim had survived, however, although Maudie had never seen him. There was no money for trips to England, although Daphne and Philip flew out to see them all every year.

'Why doesn't she come home?' Maudie had asked—but Daphne had shaken her head.

The older children were settled in school and Emily was afraid that another upheaval, so soon after Tim's death, would be too much for them. Perhaps, later on . . . Then Philip had died and Daphne had broken the news that she intended to go out to Canada, to make her home with Emily.

Now, as moorland gave way to farmland and small villages and the clouds began to clear away, Maudie recalled the sense of desolation with which she'd listened to Daphne's plans.

'I know it's selfish of me,' she'd said later to Hector, 'but I can't bear it. I shall miss her so much. It was bad enough when Emily went but I can't imagine how I shall manage without Daphne. We must go out and visit them.'

Not long after, however, Hector had become ill and the visit to Canada never happened. Daphne had flown home for the funeral and they had wept together, mourning not only for Hector's passing but for their own pasts, their youth, friendships, hopes. Memories flooded back and they'd talked long into the night, remembering.

'Dear Hector,' Daphne had said at last, swollen-eyed from tears and weariness. 'He was such fun. I'm so glad he had you, Maudie. You made him laugh and Hector loved to laugh.'

'We had some difficult moments over the girls,' sighed Maudie. 'I wish now that I could have been more tolerant but it hurt when he used to take Selina's side.'

'At least you've got Posy,' smiled Daphne, recalling Posy's almost aggressive protectiveness towards Maudie at the funeral. 'What a sweetie she is.'

'She's so like Hector. Black hair, brown eyes, not like her brothers at all, but they look just like Patrick. I think Selina is irritated that none of her children looks like her. Odd things, genes.'

Afterwards, when Daphne had returned to Canada, Maudie had felt truly alone—yet, in another way, strangely relieved. During the eighteen months of Hector's illness he had become withdrawn, difficult, morose. She had struggled to remain cheerful and positive but it had been a strain. In the last few months he had become confused, his memories muddled, and at the end he had not known who she was. It seemed that he was reliving the years when he and Hilda were young and the girls were children. He became querulous, irritable, and occasionally tearful. When Selina came, he thought that she was Hilda and he'd mumbled, 'Forgive me, my dear. Forgive me,' over and over, until Maudie could bear it no longer and went down to the kitchen to make some tea.

Selina had come downstairs looking smug. 'Poor Daddy,' she'd said. 'Of course, Mummy was his first, true love. I think he felt guilty quite often actually, for betraying her memory,' and Maudie, worn out with disturbed nights, frustrated and unhappy, had lost her frail hold on her temper and had shouted at her. 'Don't be so bloody dramatic!' she'd cried—and Selina had raised her eyebrows and gone away without her tea.

'Don't take any notice,' Daphne had pleaded, when Maudie told her. 'He's away with the fairies. It means nothing. He's far too confused and sick to remember anything sensibly. You simply mustn't let it upset you, Maudie. Selina will make the most of it, of course. Oh, how upsetting this must be. If only I could be with you.'

'He talks about you,' Maudie had said, 'and Emily, too. He remembers everyone but me.'

'Oh, darling.' Daphne had sounded near to tears. 'Oh, Maudie, don't be hurt. I simply cannot bear it. Not being so far away. Please don't.'

'No, no I won't.' Maudie had tried to contain herself. 'It's just that wretched Selina enjoying every minute of it. I'm fine, honestly . . .'

What a comfort Daphne had been, even three thousand miles away, but the fact remained that it was difficult to forget those terrible months, to remember the earlier years with Hector.

'I must not be bitter,' she muttered, turning the car on to the Moretonhampstead road. 'I must try to be balanced about it. If only I could understand his guilt. Why feel guilty about marrying again once Hilda was dead? Of course, Selina was the real problem. The mistress of emotional blackmail. She kept his guilt alive. And what happened to that money? Damn! I will not *do* this.'

Deliberately she brought to mind the happy times before he was ill: dinner parties when Hector was at his sparkling best; holiday foursomes with Daphne and Philip; quiet days at The Hermitage. She delved further back: nights of love; snatched weekends away from the crowd; dinner for two at their favourite restaurant. It had been so easy to distract him, then, to make him laugh, to create a shared intimacy. She'd been confident that she could hold him, that his love could withstand Selina's undermining, and it wasn't until the boys were born that the cracks began to appear. With Patricia so far away, Selina held all the cards in the grandchildren game—and Hector liked children. Selina was quick to take advantage.

'Darling, don't touch Maudie's skirt with those sticky fingers, you know she doesn't like it.' 'Could you hold Chris, Daddy? He'll be off to sleep in a minute and I know Maudie's so nervous with babies.' 'Paul couldn't help spilling his juice on the sofa, Maudie. He's only three, after all. Don't cry, Paul, Maudie's not really cross. She just doesn't understand little boys.'

She wouldn't have minded if Hector could only have seen through it, realised it was simply the latest version of the feud. Her lightest remarks, however, were greeted with a cool silence and the boys, growing noisy, spoiled, demanding, were encouraged to treat Maudie as an outsider. She had few defences, no natural ease with children, no maternal instinct: not until Posy.

It was Patrick who had brought Posy over one Saturday afternoon, whilst Selina and the boys were at a party. He'd dumped her into Maudie's lap and gone off with Hector to look some painting or book. Posy had lain contentedly, crooning to herself, staring up at Maudie with wide honey-brown eyes: Hector's eyes. Her dark hair crisped about her head in peaks, like Hector's when he'd just come out of the shower. She made unintelligible Posy noises and smiled happily.

Sitting there, with the hot, heavy child in her arms, Maudie had felt an extraordinary sensation: warmth radiating from her heart; a breathless wonder; a nameless longing. Carefully she'd drawn the child closer and, bending her head, kissed Posy's cheek. The child had chuckled delight-fully, showing two tiny white teeth.

'Hello,' Maudie had said, feeling foolish. 'I'm Maudie. Hello, Posy. You are beautiful and I wish you were mine.'

'Any chance of tea, darling?' Hector had suddenly appeared, Patrick behind him. 'I'll look after Posy, won't I, my poppet?'

'No,' Maudie had insisted, holding on firmly. '*I'm* looking after Posy. *You* make the tea'—and so it had started.

Maudie stretched herself, shaking off thoughts of the past, easing her shoulders, glancing at her watch; nearly half-past four. She'd made good time and was looking forward to a cup of tea. It was a long drive to Moor-gate, but worth the effort. Rob had made a splendid job of the old place. Settling herself more comfortably, switching on the radio, Maudie found herself wondering what could have happened to those keys.

Rob finished clearing up in the yard and looked about him. The morn-ing had deteriorated into a dank afternoon, the mizzle settling into a steady rain. Soon it would be getting dark. He went into the house and passed through each room, pausing to look carefully about him. In the sitting room he stood for a moment, gazing down into the fireplace, frowning thoughtfully. On a sudden impulse he stepped across to the window and closed the heavy wooden shutters, making them fast. He crossed the hall and went into the smaller living room. It was empty except for the wood-burning stove in the granite fireplace. Here, too, he closed the shutters before returning to the kitchen. He pottered for a while, clearing away the tea things, washing the mugs, and presently he locked the back door and drove away in the pick-up.

Fog rolled down upon the moor, filling the valleys, creeping amongst the trees. It muffled sound and covered the low-lying ground with a thick grey blanket of cloud. No one saw the figure emerge from the darker shadow of the thorn hedge below the house, slip round to the side door and disappear inside.

Chapter Five

Patrick Stone sat at the kitchen table, arms folded, staring at a mug of cooling coffee, listening to his wife talking on the telephone in the room beyond the arch. He'd guessed at once to whom she was speaking. Only to Maudie did Selina use that brittle, cool voice; the almost insolent tone which made him feel strangely uncomfortable, nervous. It was many years now since he'd realised that Maudie was not the cruel, selfish stepmother, the manipulative schemer, described to him by Selina. Well, he'd been young, then; young and passionately in love. They'd met in Winchester when she was nineteen, and at Miss Sprules' Secretarial College, and he, at twenty-four, had just embarked upon his first teaching post at a local school. He'd noticed her first at Evensong at the cathedral and a few days later at the Wykeham Arms. Selina was with a group of young people, one of whom he knew slightly, and soon he'd been integrated into the cheerful crowd. They'd paired off very quickly and before long she'd begun to confide in him: how unhappy she was; the terrible loss of her mother; the arrival of Maudie. How moved he'd been by her plight; how touched by her unhappiness.

Patrick snorted derisively and picked up his mug of coffee. How easy it had been, under the blinding influence of passion, to be moved, shocked by her stories; to long to rescue her. How assured and confident he'd been in convincing her that they were born for each other; how eloquent in persuading her father that he could make her happy. Oh, Young Lochinvar could have taken his correspondence course and learned a trick or two, no doubt about it. How long had it been before he'd learned that Selina was as vulnerable as an armadillo and about as sensitive as an ichneumon wasp? A year? Two, maybe? He shrugged, swallowing back the lukewarm liquid. What did it matter? By the time the truth had penetrated even his stubborn, resisting mind the boys had been born and there was nothing for it but to carry on, working hard, concentrating on his children, hoping for promotion.

Now, he was over fifty years old and the children were grown up and gone. His responsibilities were surely at an end? Selina had lied to him, manipulated him and nearly beggared him with her requirement for amusement, constant entertainment and selfishness for nearly thirty years. Now it was his turn. Now there was Mary; warm, cheerful Mary who suffered bravely, coming to terms and dealing with real hardship. She had an eight-year-old child who had been paralysed in an accident, whose father had abandoned them, and elderly parents who looked to her for a great deal of support. She had worked for just over a year now at Patrick's school as a supply teacher, on those days when her child was at the Care Centre, and friendship had grown up between them. As headmaster he was able to smooth her path a little, giving her extra hours, being as flexible as possible, and soon the friendship had grown into something deeper. It was she who held him in check. He talked of leaving Selina, throwing caution to the winds, seizing this chance of happiness, but Mary refused to let him do anything he might regret.

'Let's give it a bit longer,' she'd insisted. 'You must be absolutely certain. It's such a big step and there's so much to think about. Please, Patrick, don't tell Selina about us, not yet. I know you think she doesn't love you but that doesn't mean that she'll want to lose you. Wait a little longer.'

'There will never be a right time,' he'd said despairingly, putting his arms around her, and she'd held him tightly, anxiously.

Patrick raised his head as the telephone receiver went down with a click and Selina came into the kitchen.

Patrick thought: she walks as if she is subduing the earth beneath her feet. Stamp, stamp, stamp . . .

'You'll never believe this,' she said, her jaw tight with suppressed fury and shock. 'Maudie is selling Moorgate. It's already up for sale, apparently, without a word to me. Oh, this is the end. The absolute end.'

He stirred, straightening his back. 'It's her house, after all.'

'Oh well, I'd expect you to be on her side.' She sat down suddenly at the table. 'I don't think I can bear it.'

He watched her dispassionately, attempting to call up some shred of sympathy. If Selina had ever really mourned the passing of her mother, any genuine grief had been buried long since beneath her almost pathological dislike of Maudie.

'I expect she needs the money.' He tried to introduce some kindness into his voice, along with some reason. 'You haven't been to Cornwall for nearly fifteen years so I expect Maudie feels that it can't be that important to you. She only has an annuity, after all. Let's face it, you and Patricia got the lion's share. To be honest, I think old Hector was in the wrong there. He could have been fairer.'

She stared at him. 'We were his children. Some of the money came from Mummy's side. Why should she have it? Even Moorgate came from Mummy's family, not Daddy's, and now she's going to sell it. What right does she have to sell my mother's house?'

'We've been through this so many times,' said Patrick wearily. 'You'd have preferred Maudie to be left with nothing, wouldn't you? After more than thirty years of marriage you'd have liked her to have been cut out of his will altogether. Good grief! What sort of man do you think your father was? He tried to be fair, despite your efforts, and you can't complain now if Maudie needs some cash. You of all people should understand. You spend enough!'

'What's that supposed to mean?'

'Oh, take it any way you like. Your father left you well provided for, one way and another. Let Maudie do as she pleases with what's legally hers.'

'You know how I feel about Moorgate . . .'

'Do I not!' He got up abruptly. 'I'm going down the pub for a pint. Don't wait up.'

The door closed behind him but Selina remained seated, her face blank, distracted for a moment from her grievance. This going down to the pub after some small scene or other was becoming a regular occurrence. A trickle of suspicion wormed its way into her mind and her eyes narrowed thoughtfully. Patrick had been touchy of late; unsympathetic, uninterested in her problems. Now, with Posy away at college, it was as if something— some commitment, perhaps?—had reached its end and he'd become withdrawn, indifferent. It might simply be that he was missing Posy, of course.

She'd always been his favourite and it was odd—and certainly very quiet—without her. Nevertheless . . . Suspicion, once roused, was not to be too easily dismissed. Patrick had always been careful, alert to his wife's moods, anxious to placate, to soothe. Selina frowned. There had been precious little soothing this evening. Patrick knew very well that Moorgate was her own vital link to the past; the place of happy holidays with her parents.

She shifted restlessly, folding her arms beneath her breast, hunching her shoulders. It was thoughtless of him to leave her at a time like this when he might have guessed that she'd want to talk. Patrick had once been very sympathetic; very ready to try to understand what it must be like for a girl, hardly out of childhood, to lose her mother; and then to have her replaced by a sharp-tongued woman with no maternal qualities or sensitivity. Since there was nobody to observe, to react, Selina saved herself the trouble of tears. Her thoughts were with Maudie again, with Moorgate, and her face grew sullen. Somehow the sale must be prevented. She would speak to Patricia, to the boys; surely, between them, something could be done? If everyone contributed then maybe they could buy the place themselves. Selina brightened, picturing the scene. What fun it would be to own the old house; to use it for holidays and to invite the gang for weekends. Of course it was rather a long drive from London but it could be managed—and how impressed they'd be. It was a pity that Patrick had insisted that part of her share of the house in Arlington Road must be used to pay off their mortgage but there was a little left, enough to put down as a deposit perhaps.

A sound of whining, a scrabbling at the back door, broke into these pleasant plans and her face grew surly again.

'Shut up,' she muttered. 'Bloody animal.' She raised her voice. 'Be quiet!'

The whining ceased for a moment, to be replaced seconds later by a deep-throated bark which rang round the courtyard and echoed up the quiet suburban street.

'For Christ's sake!' She hurried across and opened the door. Polonius barged past her, padding into the kitchen and through to the living room, looking for Posy. He ignored Selina's shouted order to sit until, satisfied that Posy was not at home, he subsided on his rug in the corner, his mastiff's wrinkled face sad.

'You're for the chop,' Selina told him furiously. 'If Posy doesn't come up with something soon, you're going.'

At the sound of his mistress's name Polonius's ears cocked hopefully but, realising that she was not going to appear, he settled, groaning. Meanwhile, Selina had given herself an idea. Posy loved Moorgate. She, too, would be devastated to hear that Maudie was selling it. Perhaps Posy could influence Maudie, persuade her to drop the price, bring pressure to bear.

Selina thought: I must be subtle. Posy loves Moorgate but she also loves Maudie. Perhaps I'll give her a buzz. Tell her that Maudie's put it up for sale.

She went to the telephone, her mind busy preparing phrases, Patrick quite forgotten. She found her address book and leafed through the pages, looking for Posy's Winchester number. Presently she lifted the receiver and dialled.

Patrick was also speaking on the telephone, wedged against the coats which hung in the narrow passage which led to the men's loo, hunched so that he might be as private as possible.

'I had to speak to you.' He pressed the receiver hard against his ear so as to shut out the noise of the busy pub. 'I just had to. I'm missing you. How are you? . . . I wish I could be with you . . . I know. I'm trying to be patient but I'm not certain what we're waiting for . . . OK, OK, but I need to see you . . . No, I don't mean tomorrow at school, I mean properly . . . Really? For a whole weekend. Oh God, that's absolutely wonderful . . . Of course I want to, you idiot. Oh, that's fantastic . . . Let's go away somewhere, shall we? You get so little chance with Stuart, as a rule, and if he's being well looked after and having a lovely time, too, you won't feel guilty or anxious . . . I don't care much, do you? As long as we're together . . . Not too far out of London, though. We don't want to waste too much time just driving . . . Oh, must you go? Is he? OK then. I love you, Mary. See you tomorrow.'

Maudie replaced the telephone receiver and went into the kitchen to pour herself a drink. She needed something a little stronger than tea or coffee after her conversation with Selina, and there was some Chablis left;

more than half a bottle in the pantry. She poured a glassful, shocked to see that her hand was trembling a little.

'I'm getting old,' she muttered. 'I'm getting old when a run-in with Selina can really upset me.'

She took her wine and went back to the sitting room. A series of chill, damp evenings had made up her mind to light the wood-burning stove and the room was cosy and welcoming. The curtains made of heavy Indian cotton, double-sided in rich blues and faded red, were drawn against the dark, and the carved wooden wall-lights, with cream, parchment shades, glowed warmly. Maudie's passion for fabric was evident. The faded, comfortable sofa was partially covered by a velvet, tasselled, garnet-coloured shawl, and a plaid rug in soft lambswool hung on the back of the fireside chair. On the stool beside the chair a mass of multicoloured wool spilled out of a rush basket. Several skeins were rolled together, whilst two sturdy wooden needles were stuck, points first, into a huge ball of the nubbly, hand-dyed wool which had been partially knitted up.

'But will you ever wear it?' a friend had asked, looking cautiously at the first results.

'Oh, no.' Maudie had been amused. 'I knit for fun, for the feel of the wool and the glorious colours. I shall give it to a charity shop when it's finished.'

Books lined the shelves either side of the fireplace whilst the wall opposite was almost covered with paintings, sketches, watercolours which Hector had collected from all over the world. Thick, silky rugs from India were thrown on top of the plain, fitted carpet, and a French clock, delicately painted with pastoral scenes and edged with gilt, ticked throatily from its shelf above the fire.

Maudie sat down and stared at the flames which flickered behind the wood-burner's glass door. It was foolish to be upset. She'd guessed that the news would rake up Selina's grievances from the past, would bring down upon her head the familiar accusations, yet she felt unsettled. It was odd that now, when for the very first time she was in a position to call the tune, there should be no true pleasure in it. Moorgate was her own, to keep or dispose of, as she wished, yet any sense of power was absent. There had been none of the usual pleasure in irritating and annoying Selina; none of the satisfaction in being the victor; only this rather empty, weary depression. Her eye was caught by Posy's card, standing on the shelf beside the clock, and she remembered the plea that she should give Polonius a home. She was filled with horror at the thought of his great form, lumbering about, but she also knew that Selina would carry out her threat of rehousing him. Selina's great strength—and it was this which made her a formidable opponent—was that she never hesitated to implement threats.

Sipping her wine, Maudie knew that it was impossible, now, to offer Polonius a refuge without it being partly a guilt offering. She knew that Posy cherished a dream that one day she might live at Moorgate with some gorgeous man and a brood of children and, however reasonable and adult Posy might be about the sale of the house, Maudie felt sad that she must be the one to shatter her dream. She feared the possibility that Posy might think that the relenting in her refusal to give Polonius a home was a sop to her own conscience. She'd had her own dream—that she'd be able to leave Moorgate to Posy—but the cost of living dictated otherwise and at least she'd be able to invest some money for Posy to help her later on. Meanwhile she could help her out with Polonius and if Posy detected some hidden agenda, well, there was nothing to be done about it. Anyway, she had to be told about Moorgate. Sheer courtesy had obliged Maudie to tell Selina about it before she spoke to Posy but the idea of Selina getting in first with her version sent Maudie hurrying to the telephone again. A breathless Posy answered.

'Hi, babe,' she said warmly. 'Great timing. I've just this minute walked through the door. How are you? Did you get my card?'

'I did,' said Maudie, who still found it difficult to get used to the idea of being addressed as 'babe', 'and I've decided to give Polonius a try.'

She winced as Posy shrieked at the other end of the line, smiling despite her heavy heart.

'That's so great!' she was saying. 'Oh, that's really cool. Oh, Maudie, I'm just so grateful. Mum was being really mean last time we spoke. Listen. Can I bring him this weekend?'

'Well.' Maudie blinked, taken aback. 'Well, why not. But how?'

'Jude is coming down to the West Country for the weekend to see friends in Exeter. I told you about Jude, didn't I? He's doing the drama course too. Well, he's got an old estate car for carrying props about and stuff. We'll be able to fit Polonius in the back. Oh, this is so fab. We can get up to London to fetch Polonius on Friday morning and be with you by about teatime. Jude can pick me up on his way back on Sunday. Is that OK?'

'That's fine.' Maudie swallowed and took a firmer hold on the receiver.

'Listen, Posy, I've got some disappointing news. I'm having to put Moorgate on the market.' Silence. 'I know how you feel about it, my darling, but I simply need the money. I promise you I've done my sums and thought about it long and hard, but The Hermitage needs a new roof and there are other things . . . I'm so sorry, Posy.'

'Oh, Maudie.' It was clear that Posy was struggling to come to terms with it. 'Oh, how absolutely bloody.'

'I know. Don't think I want to do this, Posy. If there were any other way . . .'

'I know. Of course I know that, Maudie. You love it too. Oh, hell . . . Hang on a sec. What?' Maudie could hear muffled voices in the background. 'Oh, OK . . . Look, Maudie, I've got to go. I'll see you on Friday and listen, babe, don't worry too much about Moorgate. We'll talk about it then. Bless you for Polonius. Love you lots. 'Bye.'

In tears Maudie sat down again by the fire.

'Oh, Posy,' she murmured. 'I love you too.'

Chapter Six

It was only after Posy and Jude had left, driving away after tea on Sunday afternoon, that Maudie fully realised the true benefit of having Polonius to live with her.

'I'll get down as often as I can,' Posy promised, hugging her goodbye. 'Honestly. Oh, if *only* I had a car then I could get down midweek sometimes. I don't have any lectures on a Wednesday so I could come down on Tuesday night. That would be really fab. Maybe Jude will lend me his car.'

Jude, a small, slight boy with a sweet smile, shook his head. 'No chance.'

Posy glared at him. 'He's so selfish, Maudie,' she grumbled. 'Don't be taken in by those old-fashioned good manners. He's as tough as cow-hide and wily as a serpent.'

Maudie looked at Jude, eyebrows raised, and he winked at her, jingling the car keys, waiting good-humouredly for Posy to make her farewells.

'You forget,' he said, 'that I saw you arrive at Hyde Abbey Road in your mother's car. I watched that little scene which took place when you attempted to park it and I sympathised utterly with the poor man whose motorbike you crushed.'

'I did *not* crush it!' cried Posy indignantly. 'I barely touched it. Only enough to knock it off its silly support thingy. It wasn't even scratched.'

'She drew a crowd,' Jude said to Maudie. 'Thirteen manoeuvres it took, everyone helping her on with word and gesture, solo and chorus, and even then she managed to bash the bike.'

'Shut up,' said Posy, grinning unwillingly. 'I was planning to ask if I could borrow Maudie's car and now you've ruined everything.'

'Nobody borrows my car,' said Maudie firmly. 'It's too old and capricious.'

'Very wise.' Jude nodded at her. 'Hold fast to that decision. Posy has no sympathy with mechanical things and no patience at all with inanimate objects. She's broken the video, dented Jo's wok, and the microwave will never be the same again since she attempted to cook spaghetti in it.'

'Kill!' said Posy grimly to Polonius, pointing at Jude. 'Kill. Lunch. Go on, savage him.'

Polonius wagged his tail, tongue lolling, and Jude laughed. 'But she's great with dogs. Sorry to break up the party but we really ought to be going.'

'Are you sure you'll be OK, Maudie?' Posy looked anxiously at Polonius. 'I'm certain he'll be good.'

'Oh, he'll be good,' said Maudie cheerfully. 'Don't you worry about that. Off you go. It's been lovely to see you.'

'I'll be back very soon.' Posy was climbing in, reaching for her seat belt, winding down the window. 'No, Polonius. Stay. Good boy. Oh, Maudie, thanks so much for looking after him . . .'

Her cries were lost in the sound of the engine as Jude very wisely cut the farewells short by setting off down the drive that ran along beside the bungalow to the lane. Waving, one hand on Polonius's collar, Maudie suddenly realised that she would see very much more of Posy now. The thought made her feel more tolerant towards the large mastiff with the sad, wrinkled face who stood beside her, watching the car disappear, whining miserably.

'She'll be back soon,' Maudie told him confidently. 'Really she will. And now we're going to have a walk through the woods to take your mind off things. Just let me get my boots on. No, you can't go after her. Come on, old chap . . .'

Talking comfortingly to him, she hauled him back into the house and presently they set out together. Polonius bounded ahead, overjoyed by such freedom after London streets, scattering the fallen leaves. The silence of the woods was broken by the murmuring, ceaseless music of the River Bovey, chuckling its way over smooth, rounded stones and under overhanging, mossy banks, splashing over miniature waterfalls. The hound's lead around her neck, her hands thrust into the pockets of her corduroy jacket, Maudie strode behind him. Twenty-four hours with Posy had renewed her courage. She had been bravely philosophical about Moorgate, sensing Maudie's distress, sympathising with her step-grandmother's dilemma.

'Money's such a curse,' she'd said. 'I can quite see that you have to sell. Of *course* it would have been lovely to hang on to it . . .'

'I'd always hoped that you would have it eventually,' Maudie had answered wretchedly. 'Your mother is terribly upset, of course.'

'Yes, well, she would be, wouldn't she? I'm glad you'd told me before I saw her.' Posy had hesitated, embarrassed. 'The thing is, she's wondering if she can't afford to buy it herself.'

'Oh, *no*.' Maudie had shaken her head. 'Oh dear. This is what I feared might happen.' They'd stared at each other anxiously.

'I thought I'd better tell you. I didn't really want to but I think she's hoping that you might . . . well, back down a bit.'

'Back down?' She'd frowned impatiently. 'Back down how? I can't afford not to sell and I feel quite certain that Selina can't afford to buy it. Even if she could, I wouldn't encourage it. Not unless she and Patrick were prepared to sell up and live in it. They couldn't afford to run it and Selina would hate to have a tenant in. She'd want to use it for weekends and parties. Oh, it would be a *disaster*.'

'I know. I agree with you. It's one of Mum's grand ideas that costs Dad a fortune and just causes trouble. I told her so.'

'Did you?' Maudie had chuckled grimly. 'That must have gone down well.'

Posy had shrugged. 'We had a bit of a row. So what's new? Anyway, I thought I'd warn you. She's ringing round the family for support but Dad thinks the whole thing's ridiculous. Try not to be upset, Maudie . . .'

'It's just that I'd hoped—I shall invest most of it for the future and, once the roof is done and the car sorted out, there might be some spare cash for you for any small thing you need. Oh, dear. I feel so—'

'Maudie!' Posy had interrupted warningly. 'You know we don't used the G-word. It was our new year resolution. Remember? We were never going to feel guilty about Mum again. Or anything else if we could help it.'

'How optimistic we were,' Maudie had sighed. 'It's because the house is not truly mine, I suppose. Perhaps I should move into Moorgate and sell The Hermitage. I wouldn't feel so badly then. No, no, Posy.' She'd felt even more remorseful as she saw the light that briefly rose and fell in

Posy's eyes. 'Even for you I couldn't bury myself on Bodmin Moor. I sometimes wonder how much longer I can manage isolated here, but when I *do* move, it will be into Bovey.'

'I know that. Of course you will. It was just a mad moment. Let's forget about it. When are you coming to Winchester? You'll be able to bring Polonius with you . . .'

As the late autumn afternoon faded gently into shadowy twilight Maudie felt determination and confidence returning. Selling Moorgate had opened too many old wounds, revived painful memories. She must strive to remember Hector without destructive doubts; to simply refuse to allow Selina to wrong-foot her. The money from the sale would ease the financial situation and still her nagging fears of the future. It was a pity that she wouldn't have the funds for a new roof before winter set in but it would be such a comfort to have a sensible sum put by for her old age and for Posy's future.

Polonius appeared, dripping from the river, and shook himself vigorously all over her.

'Wretched animal,' she cried, wiping the cold drops from her face. 'Come on. Home, then.'

She turned back, her boots crunching over beech mast and dead leaves, Polonius loping beside her. A star twinkled high above, tangled in the bare branches of a beech tree, and tranquillity touched her anxious, restless heart. They went together through the garden gate and into the house, and the door closed behind them.

Battling with the endless administrative work that seemed to expand to fill every spare hour, Patrick heard Selina's footsteps on the stairs with a now-familiar dread. It was guilt—what his daughter called the G-word—that caused the pit of his gut to contract sickeningly, made him swallow in a suddenly dry throat. Foolish that part of him longed to shout the truth, have it out in the open whilst the other, more cowardly, part of him feared exposure; foolish and pathetic. Mary was frightened too. What she had now, which was precious little—a tiny, rented ground-floor flat, her part-time job, a place for Stuart at the Care Centre three days a week—was hard-earned, painfully achieved, and she was terrified of losing any of it.

'I simply can't afford to mess it up,' she'd said, anxious that he should understand. 'I know that it makes me sound terribly selfish but I have to be, you see. Because of Stuart. I need to earn money and this little flat is so convenient. The bus picks Stuart up at the door and I can walk to school and to see Mum and Dad. It's so difficult on public transport with a wheelchair and I couldn't possibly afford to buy a car. It's not that I don't love you, Pat. It's just that I can't see how it would work, being together.'

He'd held her hand, looking beyond her to where Stuart sat, immobile before the television set. How would the school governors react if they found out about the affair; if he announced that he was leaving his wife for one of the supply teachers? Would he or Mary be asked to leave? Perhaps they would both he dismissed.

'It's just not that easy, is it?' she'd asked, watching him—and he'd smiled quickly, attempting reassurance, convincing neither of them.

'I've been speaking to Patricia.' Selina was at the door. 'She's furious, of course. Well, I knew she would be, and she thinks it's a brilliant idea.'

He stared at her, puzzled, only partially concentrating.

'Thinks what's a brilliant idea?'

'Buying Moorgate,' said Selina impatiently. 'You know! My idea that we should all contribute and buy Moorgate ourselves. She agreed that it would be great to be able to have holidays there when they come over.'

'Ah, I see.' Patrick turned on his swivel chair so as to be able to look at her properly. 'And how much are they intending to contribute?'

'We didn't go into details. They were in the middle of supper. I just wanted to sound her out.'

'It's out of the question.' He turned back to his desk, too dispirited to pretend. 'Even if Patricia and Simon were prepared to put a bit in, we still couldn't afford it. And anyway, what's the point? It's a hell of a long way down to Cornwall. You might make an effort to get down for weekends in the summer but it would stand empty all winter, getting damp. It's a ridiculous idea and you know it is.'

'You think anything's ridiculous if it's out of the ordinary,' she said bitingly. 'You have no vision. No sense of adventure. You've always been afraid to take risks.'

'I married you, didn't I?' The words were out before he could prevent them and he dropped his head into his hands. 'Sorry,' he muttered. 'I'm sorry. That was unnecessary. But really, Selina, this is just too much. Patricia will agree with you, of course she will. She's thousands of miles away and doesn't give a damn. But do you seriously imagine that Patricia and Simon will sink money into an old farmhouse in Cornwall so that they can have a holiday in it once every three years? Dream on!'

Selina leaned against the door jamb, arms folded, and looked at him thoughtfully. Her instinct warned her that there were other issues involved here and she considered carefully before she spoke.

'I realise that it sounds crazy,' she said. Her voice was friendly, almost amused, and he looked up at her, taken aback. 'But Moorgate really is special to me. OK.' She chuckled a little, holding up her hands as if warding off protest from him. 'I promise I won't go over the past again. After all, you know better than anyone else about my feeling. It's just that I had another idea about it. Look,' her voice was intimate now, almost conspiratorial, 'I utterly agree with you about Patricia and Simon but I thought it was worth a phone call. No, my latest idea was that we should sell up here and move to Cornwall.' She smiled a little at the shock on his face, noting the fear in his eyes. 'Yes, it's quite a mind-bending thought, isn't it? But why not? You're always so tired lately, Patrick. Very edgy. I think your work is getting you down, darling, and I'm worried about you. It would be wonderful to live in the country for a change, wouldn't it? Just there, between the sea and the moor. Wonderful fresh air and peace and quiet. You could get a teaching job locally and we could be together, just the two of us. The kids could come down for weekends. Think how they'd love it.' She watched him, her eyes cool, considering, mouth still smiling. 'I just feel that it's *right*, if you see what I mean. We're still young enough for the challenge of it but old enough to be realistic.'

Silence stretched between them. She raised her eyebrows and he shook his head.

'It's . . . a bit of shock,' he muttered, turning away, unable to meet her eyes any longer. 'I never thought I'd hear you say that you'd want to leave London. We need to think about it very carefully.'

'Do we?' She still sounded amused. 'I don't think *I* do. Still, I can see that I've surprised you. But don't think for *too* long, Patrick, or we might miss the boat.'

She went away, closing the door gently, and he continued to sit, head in hands, fear in his heart.

He thought: She's guessed that something is going on. What shall I do? Call her bluff and take a chance?

An image of Mary—dressed in leggings and an oversized shirt, singing as she fed Stuart—came to his mind. A word from Selina to the school governors and Mary might well be out of a job—and her flat, too, if she were unable to pay the rent. She'd fought hard to get the three-roomed flat with the use of a small garden, so that Stuart could sit outside in summer; it hadn't been easy to persuade the strict, old-fashioned landlord that Stuart would be no nuisance to the other tenants, that she could afford to pay her rent and was not dependent on benefit. Patrick clenched his fists and swore quietly; he could not put Mary at risk unless he could offer her as much or more than she had already achieved for herself. On what grounds could he divorce Selina? Would he be entitled to a share in the house and would he be obliged to continue to support her? Suppose he were to lose his job in the process?

Tired, frustrated, Patrick felt an overwhelming desire to weep. Mary had come into his life at a most vulnerable and dangerous time: missing his children, disillusioned with his career in which the word 'vocation' was now a dirty word; bound to a wife he almost disliked. He'd been attracted by Mary's cheerful, realistic approach; her energy. He felt old and jaded as he watched her with the children, encouraging them, patient but lively. The little ones responded to her enthusiasm and she was clearly in her element. There was no shred of self-pity or resentment when she told him about Stuart's accident, or described the desertion of her husband when he learned that Stuart would be an invalid for the rest of his life.

'He simply couldn't face it,' she'd said, as if this were quite a reasonable reaction. 'He was a macho kind of guy and he just couldn't come to terms with the life ahead. He couldn't bear it for Stuart as much as for himself. He found it simply horrific that he would never kick a ball or swim or be normal in that way. It killed him to see Stuart in his chair. He'd weep. He just didn't come back one evening and then I got a letter. I've no idea where he is.'

'Couldn't he be traced?' Patrick had asked, horrified. 'How could he just abandon you both?'

'I don't want him back,' she'd said, almost fiercely. 'He weakened me. It was terrible, watching him suffer. It was like he was injured too, and I didn't have enough strength for them both. Stuart needs me, Dave doesn't.'

As the weeks passed he'd learned of her joy when she'd been offered the teaching post, her struggle for the flat, the worries about her parents, who were very frail. Her love for her son was wholehearted, practical, vivid. Coming home to Selina was an unfortunate contrast—and he'd fought to resist his growing disloyalty—but the temptation was too great. Mary's courage and vitality warmed him, attracted him, and soon he ceased to struggle too hard against it.

Could Selina possibly have suspected his growing attachment? It was impossible to imagine her living permanently in Cornwall; nevertheless the battle was now joined and he must make some kind of move. But what?

'Lunch!' Her voice echoed up the stair and he instinctively responded, tidying his papers, putting the top on his pen, before going downstairs.

Chapter Seven

Whistling softly to himself, Rob Abbot stirred up the thick paint with a piece of wood and dipped the paintbrush into the gleaming white. The office was empty now—except for the old desk, which was too battered and worm-eaten to be valuable—swept and cleaned out ready to be decorated. The outside door was open to a brilliant, sparkling day, and he worked quickly in the icy, invigorating air, irritated by the thought of the imminent interruption. He glanced at his watch, pressed the lid back firmly on to the can of paint and crossed the small passage to wash the brush out under the cold tap in the cloakroom. Leaving it to dry, balanced on the edge of the Butler sink, he went through to the kitchen, closing the inner door behind him. It was warm in here after the chill of the office and he blessed Lady Todhunter for agreeing that the Esse should be lit. The kettle was singing and he made himself a mug of tea, looking about him critically, pleased with what he'd achieved.

He paused, mug halfway to his lips, imagining that he heard a footstep. After a moment he took a deep breath and drank some tea. The old farmhouse was getting to him, no doubt about it. He often felt that there was another presence in the house with him: steps overhead, a door closing quietly, voices in the garden. Perhaps it was so in all old houses, if one spent enough time alone in them, but Moorgate wasn't just any old house. Moorgate was special. It must be hard to have to part with such a place but he could understand that Lady Todhunter was rather too elderly to up sticks and move into such an isolated situation.

The slamming of a car door alerted him and he set down his mug and passed swiftly through to the sitting room. A young couple were standing in the lane, a sheaf of particulars in their hands, staring at the house. Standing well back he watched them for a moment, noting the new four-wheel-drive vehicle, the smartly casual clothes, the confidence with which they stood together, comparing the photograph with reality. Presently they opened the gate and trod up the path to the front door.

He waited for a moment, composing himself, before he opened the door to them.

'Ah, Mr . . .' The young man consulted his sheet of paper. 'Mr Abbot, is it? I think you're expecting us. Mr Cruikshank telephoned you earlier. I'm Martin Baxter. This is my wife.'

She smiled briefly but her eyes were already glancing past him, trying to see into the hall beyond. They were rather older than he'd first guessed, probably late thirties, and he experienced an odd, irrational desire to slam the heavy oak door in their complacent, well-groomed faces.

'How do you do? Yes, I'm Rob Abbot. Come in, won't you? I often show people round to save Mr Cruikshank the drive from Truro if he can get me on my mobile.'

She was already in the hall, opening the door to the sitting room, exclaiming. Martin Baxter shrugged, smiling, implying that, having let them in, Rob was now surplus to requirements.

'We'll give a shout if we need any information,' he said. 'OK? I imagine it's pretty straightforward, isn't it? Houses are houses. Don't let us hold you up.'

He followed his wife into the sitting room. 'Just *look* at this fireplace,' Rob heard her say. 'It must be positively ancient. Darling! Wooden shutters! Can you believe it . . . ?'

Rob retreated to the kitchen and stood by the open door, listening. He heard their footsteps cross the hall and more cries of pleasure.

'This just *has* to be my study.'

'Darling, have you noticed the beams . . . ?'

When they arrived in the kitchen Rob was washing out his mug at the sink, his back to the door. They stood for a moment, silenced by the sheer size of the room, before Mrs Baxter came across and stood beside him at the sink.

'What an utterly incredible view,' she said.

'Yes,' he replied, without looking at her. 'Yes, even washing up can be a pleasure here.'

She turned her back to the window, leaning against the working surface, barely glancing at him but allowing a faint lifting of the brows to indicate that she had not been addressing him.

'I have a dishwasher,' she said briefly. 'Martin, can't you just see this with the right furniture in it? Provençal farmhouse, would you say?'

Rob stood his mug on the draining board. 'Or even English farmhouse,' he said lightly. 'The Esse heats the water as well as being a cooker.'

'Esse?' She glanced about her. 'Oh, the range. We'd probably want an Aga, wouldn't we, darling?'

'It's probably the same sort of thing.' Martin Baxter sounded slightly embarrassed. 'Is it gas-fired, Mr . . . ah . . . Abbot?'

Rob laughed. 'There's no mains gas piped on to the moor,' he said. 'No, it's oil-fired and just as good as any Aga.'

Mrs Baxter frowned. 'I think I'd prefer it to be electric.'

'Until the first power cut,' said Rob laconically. 'We get a lot of those round here. Then you'd be blessing the fact that you can cook and bath, if nothing else. Assuming the lorry's been able to get up here, that is. It's not always so easy in the winter. Plenty of paraffin lamps, that's what you need. Unless you want to use the old generator. It's still there, out in the barn. That's what they used in the old days.'

'Oh, it can't be that bad,' she said dismissively—but her husband was frowning a little.

'Power cuts? That would be a damn nuisance when you're using a computer. I'd be working a lot from home and I don't want to be sitting here in the dark with a morning's work lost.'

'Oh, darling, it can't be that bad,' she repeated. 'Millions of people live in the country these days and work at home.'

'But you're high up here,' Rob pointed out. 'Look out there. Straight down to the coast with nothing in between. The gales fair whistle up across the moor. It's very exposed. Come and see it on a wet day with a southwesterly blowing. It's pretty bleak.'

Martin Baxter looked at him curiously. 'Not exactly trying to sell the place, are you?'

Rob shrugged. 'It's none of my business, either way. But I've seen people move down here to remote houses that look wonderful on a sunny day, only to sell up a year later because they can't take the long winter months. Have you any idea how much it rains here?'

Mrs Baxter looked at him angrily. 'I was born and brought up in the country. We know all about rain, thank you.'

He smiled at her. 'And where was that?' he asked sweetly.

'Hampshire.'

She turned her back on his chuckle. 'Come on, Martin. I want to look upstairs.' They went out together. 'I've never heard such nonsense,' Rob heard her say. 'Everyone knows how mild and temperate Cornwall is.'

'Well, he might have a point.' Martin Baxter sounded uneasy. 'That's more in the south, I think. It's pretty high up here.' There was the rustle of paper. 'I see that there's no mains water or sewage, either. There's a septic tank somewhere and the water's pumped up from a well . . .'

Their voices grew fainter and Rob listened to them walking about overhead. Presently they returned downstairs and Martin Baxter put his head round the door.

'We're off,' he said. 'Thanks. We've decided to look at a place down in Just-in-Roseland before we make up our minds.'

'Very wise.' Rob beamed at him. 'Beautiful countryside, the Roseland Peninsula. Very mild down there. And temperate, too.'

He followed them through the hall and watched them climb into the clean, new vehicle, reverse it in the yard and drive back down the lane, Mrs Baxter staring straight ahead. Rob grinned to himself, waved cheerfully and returned to his painting.

'The point is,' Maudie said to Polonius, as they sat together before the fire just before bedtime, 'that you are a very large person and very large persons do not climb on to sofas, nor do they sleep on other persons' beds. It is possible, of course, that you imagine yourself to be quite a small person but facts are facts.'

Polonius groaned deeply, settling himself comfortably, head on paws.

'It's no good protesting,' she said firmly. 'I suspect that your partiality for luxurious living was what made you homeless in the first place. I hope you are older and wiser now. Posy's a soft touch, of course. Selina must have had conniptions when she appeared with you on the end of a lead. In fact, I am amazed that she let you stay at all. However, your bed is in the kitchen and that's where it is staying. I want no whining tonight.'

Polonius sighed heavily but he regarded her with a cynical and disillu-sioned eye. He'd learned that the delight and amazement aroused by his size and melancholy expression was generally short-lived and that cries of affection rapidly turned to shouts of rage. Posy was his third owner, and he'd been very happy with her, but he disliked Selina and had been relieved to be brought here to this place of woods and streams and hills. He did not feel that he'd been abandoned to yet another new owner but hoped that Posy would reappear just as she had in the past. Meanwhile, he was enjoying himself. He'd frightened the milkman by barking unexpect-edly and very loudly in his ear through the open window of his pick-up truck, whilst the fellow was rooting about for Maudie's newspaper. Later, he'd lain in wait for the postman; hiding under the hedge by the door, chasing him along the drive, back to his van.

Now, at the end of a busy day, his tail thumped once or twice content-edly and Maudie chuckled too, remembering the incident. The milkman, bred on a farm, once he'd recovered from his shock had simply pushed Polonius aside and delivered the milk and paper, reporting the incident good-humouredly, pulling Polonius's ears and marvelling at his size. The postman, however, was new to the area and he'd already made himself unpopular by complaining about the difficulties of a country round and the distance he was obliged to walk. He'd suggested that Maudie should put a box at the end of the drive and Maudie had replied, somewhat tartly, that he'd probably be a happier, not to mention fitter, person if he occa-sionally took some exercise. To see him sprinting down the drive had reduced her to tears of mirth and she'd had difficulty in remonstrating with Polonius when he'd returned, tail wagging and clearly delighted with himself.

'You're a wretch,' she said, pushing him with her foot. 'And now I shall *have* to put a box at the end of the drive. I'm certain he'll refuse to come to the door again. No more chasing or we'll all be in trouble.'

Polonius yawned contemptuously. He'd taken a dislike to the postman and was looking forward to another encounter. Once outside the bunga-low there was nothing to restrain a dog with brains and initiative and, after the restrictions of a courtyard garden and small municipal park, he had every intention of making the most of his new environment.

Sitting back in her chair, Maudie eyed him somewhat anxiously. Of course it had been madness to agree to have him—yet, if it meant seeing more of Posy, it was worth it. Oddly, she was rather enjoying his company. He was cheerfully companionable, always ready for a jaunt, but there was something intractable and tough about him, a refusal to be dominated and a pronounced liking for having his own way . . .

'In other words, my dear Polonius,' she murmured, 'you remind me of Hector. Except that Hector never chased the postman.'

She took several logs from the big basket, put them on the fire and wrapped herself more closely in the plaid rug. At least the arrival of Polonius had distracted her a little from her anxieties. It was impossible, surely, that Selina would be able to persuade Patrick into buying Moorgate, and, anyway, it was likely, now that Rob had practically finished, that someone would make an offer before Selina could hope to get her act together. Posy had been dismissive, quite certain that her father would prevent it, but Selina had inherited her mother's stubbornness and it would be foolish to underestimate her.

Watching the flames, Maudie remembered how relentless a campaign Selina had waged once she'd noticed Maudie's growing affection for Posy. The child became the weapon with which Selina punished Maudie for attempting to take her mother's place. Though the boys had been brought to visit regularly, Posy was rarely seen; though she and Hector heard of outings with Patrick's parents, of parties to which they were never invited, and were shown tantalisingly delightful photographs of Posy growing up, they were excluded as much as possible. When Hector complained that he rarely saw his granddaughter, Selina made excuses: it was so difficult to find time now, with two growing boys and a baby; that Posy preferred her other grandmother. It was Patrick who had guessed what was happening and tried to put things right; to make opportunities for Posy to be with Hector and Maudie.

It was strange that such maternal feelings should make themselves known so late in life. Patricia and Selina had never given her the opportunity for such emotions and Maudie had been perfectly happy to remain free from the variety of joys and anguish to which Daphne was prey. No terrors for a child's safety kept Maudie awake at night; no anxieties that he—or she—might fail exams, be rejected in love or become unemployed destroyed her peace of mind. For Hector, brainwashed by Hilda's excessive motherliness, Maudie's lack of interest had been refreshing. She'd made no attempt to prevent him from being all that was caring and paternal but she'd made him see that he was not *only* a father and provider, that he could be simply Hector, a person in his own right—and that it could be fun. She'd made it clear that she expected to have a relationship with him which was utterly separate from anything relating to Hilda and her children—and for part of the time she'd succeeded. There were whole periods when they had been united, utterly together, and it was these moments which she strove now to remember.

Those awful scenes with Hector at the end, his begging for forgiveness and Selina's triumph, must somehow be wiped out of her memory. Why should she believe that he'd regretted marrying her—or that Hilda and the girls had, after all, been much more important to him? It must be possible to concentrate on the good times and the fun they'd shared, to stop torturing herself with these doubts, this obsession with how he'd disposed of his money. If only he'd told her what he'd done with it, trusted her. If only it weren't for that peculiarity she might be able to come to terms with the last unhappy year.

Maudie stood up abruptly, disturbing Polonius, who roused himself and struggled up, yawning.

'Last outs,' she said. 'Come on. It's time for bed.'

He followed her out into the clear, cold night and ambled off obediently whilst she shivered, clutching the rug, shining the torch after him. The trees beyond the gate seemed to press closer, leaning over, whispering and creaking gently and, hearing a rustling behind her, she swung round, directing the torchlight into the recesses of the open-fronted woodshed. A feathery ball of wrens, huddling together on a high beam, was caught in the light and she turned away quickly, not wishing to disturb them, smiling to herself.

She thought: Oh, how I wish I had someone to cuddle—and was seized with a sudden and terrible despair.

'Oh, Hector,' she cried aloud, angrily, 'if only you knew how much I miss you!'—and Polonius, thinking that she was calling him, appeared out of the darkness and led the way indoors.

Chapter Eight

The room, with the buffet set out on long trestle tables against the further wall, was full of people. It was a typical pub dining room, rather bare and bleak with all the atmosphere left behind in the bar, but the cheerful chatter and clink of glasses was welcoming. Patrick raised his hand in salute to his host but Selina was too busy scanning the crowd to wave hello. In the normal course of events she tended to avoid school gatherings but Janet was the deputy head and her husband had decided to give a party to celebrate her fiftieth birthday. It would have been churlish to refuse the invitation and, anyway, Selina wanted to make a few investigations. She was quite certain that, if Patrick were having an affair, it would be someone connected with school. He had no time for hobbies and it was quite impossible to imagine that he might be having a fling with any of their own friends. No, it must be a colleague with whom he was involved.

Selina submitted to John's embrace, touched her cheek to Janet's and accepted a glass of wine.

Patrick glanced at her anxiously. Selina was an expert at making people feel inadequate. The coolness of her embrace, a faint raising of the brows at the first sip of wine, the quick, patronising smile that indicated that she was used to better company—it was a masterly performance. She was smart and well groomed: her light brown hair carefully streaked so that she appeared blonde, her clothes fashionably chic. This evening she was wearing well-cut amber-coloured velvet trousers—the only woman present to be wearing trousers—with a long matching tunic and she'd wound a long silk scarf about her throat. She looked sexy, if something of a challenge, and she was enjoying the mild sensation she was making amongst this rather drab and dowdy group. Without the injection of her father's money she would have been unable to make such an impression and this added to the feeling that she was special, out of their league.

Sipping her wine, making no effort to mingle, she looked about her. She knew some of the people present but Janet's personal friends were strangers and there were a few others whom she did not recognise. None of the women seemed likely to have attracted Patrick's serious attention, let alone made him risk starting an affair. To begin with she'd wondered once or twice if she'd imagined the whole thing—if it were simply that she'd become oversensitive because of Moorgate—but his reaction to her test had given her cause for real suspicion. He'd often talked of moving out of London, of applying for the headship of a country school. It had always been she who had laughed at his suggestions and refused to consider such a move. Now, with the children grown, it was a perfect opportunity. The sale of their house in Clapham would more than cover the cost of Moorgate, with enough over to give him time to look about for a position in a local school, yet he had clearly been horrified at the suggestion. Why? Personally, she was deeply relieved. She had no desire to live permanently at Moorgate—although she had every intention of buying it if she could—but she'd taken the chance and seen his reaction.

She smiled rather vaguely as Richard Elton came towards her, arms outstretched. Richard was head of the maths department at the local comprehensive school and the only man in the present company for whom she felt inclined to make an effort. It amused her to go along with the pretence that they were madly attracted to each other—if only because she knew it irritated his wife so much. Angela was a welfare worker and a serious and rather intense woman. To Angela, excessive interest in one's appearance was merely the outward and visible sign of inner poverty, and she regarded Selina with a barely disguised contempt. Nevertheless, it annoyed her to see Richard play-acting so foolishly; kissing Selina's hand and paying extravagant compliments. It irritated Patrick too—he couldn't stand Richard—and Selina decided to play up a little so as to restore her own confidence.

When Richard hurried away to find her another drink, Selina glanced about to see whether Patrick had been watching. She saw him at last near the supper tables. He was standing quite still, slightly behind a group of animated people so that his odd stillness was the more striking, but what made her catch her breath was the expression on his face. He was looking at someone she could not see but his look of longing, a kind of desperate hunger, and his whole attitude of concentrated, unwary love, first frightened her, then unleashed a tide of pure, atavistic rage. The sensation was unnerving yet strangely familiar but Selina was in no mood for self-analysis. Keeping her eyes on his face she began to make her way round to where he stood. He seemed unaware of anything that was happening around him and, as she watched, a young woman emerged from the press of people and approached him.

Selina paused, still some feet away, seeing the warmth in Patrick's eyes, noting the reluctance with which he let go of the girl's hands, which he'd held for a few moments in greeting. He glanced about quickly, nervously, but Selina had taken care to remain well screened by people and he clearly believed himself to be unobserved. Moving slowly, she edged herself round so that she was able to see the girl at last. Short, with an eager face and brown hair cut in a bob, she was nothing special; nothing out of the ordinary. She was certainly neither slim nor elegant, although that bright, intelligent look was attractive enough, but surely there was no serious competition unless it was that the girl was probably a good ten years younger than Selina herself. Somehow this made matters worse. That Patrick might be unbalanced by some gorgeous young dolly-bird type was bad enough but to find him behaving like a teenager over a perfectly ordinary young woman was insulting.

They were talking together but now Patrick had lost the look of intent concentration and his glance was anxious. In that brief unguarded moment he'd betrayed himself but now he was alive with fear and his eyes constantly scanned the crowd. It was pleasant to see him start with terror when she spoke, her eyes fixed on the girl's face.

'Hello, darling,' she said lightly. 'You abandoned me to Richard. I wondered where you were hiding.' She arched her brows, smiling at the girl. 'I don't think we've met, have we?'

His stammering awkward clumsiness might have been amusing if it had been anyone else. As it was, however, her fury made her sick to her stomach and it required all her self-control not to scream at them both.

'This is Mary Jarvis. She's one of our supply teachers. Didn't you meet last Christmas at the staff party? I somehow thought you had . . .'

He was talking for the sake of it and Selina took his arm, feeling it tremble beneath her fingers.

'I didn't go to the party.' Mary's voice was calm. 'I couldn't leave Stuart. My son was paralysed in a car accident, Mrs Stone, and it's not always easy to find someone who is prepared to watch him for me. Patrick's been kind enough to arrange for me to teach when Stuart's at the Care Centre.'

Acid words burned against Selina's closed lips, though her eyes were icy with dislike, but she remained silent and it was Patrick who hurried into speech.

'He goes to school for three days a week. Mary says he's coming on splendidly. It seems that he might be able to use his right hand again . . .'

He stumbled into an uneasy silence whilst Selina continued to smile, managing to convey an air of faint disbelief that either of them should imagine that she should be the least bit interested in the handicapped son of an undistinguished supply teacher. When the silence had stretched to excruciatingly embarrassing proportions, she took a deep breath, still smiling, and her grip on Patrick's arm tightened.

'Well.' It was a dismissal and Mary bit her lip. 'So nice to meet you, Margaret. Now.' She looked at Patrick. 'Shall we go and find something to eat, darling? You know I can't cope for too long at these ghastly bun fights.'

She stood beside him, seething with rage, whilst he mechanically piled food on to two plates, sensing his impotent frustration, wishing that she could smash his face into the bowls and platters of food. As he turned to give her one of the plates Janet joined them with a full plate of her own, but Selina caught a glimpse of the misery on his face before he controlled himself and began to talk to his hostess. Richard was approaching once again and it was with some relief that she greeted him, relaxing just a little, letting him talk and joke, pretending to eat some supper whilst she planned a future course of action.

'Thank God that's over.' Selina flung her coat on a chair and filled the kettle. 'I need some decent coffee. Want some?'

Patrick shook his head, not trusting himself to speak. Somehow, now that he had seen his wife and mistress standing side by side, the true ghastly reality of the situation was borne in upon him. Until this moment his time with Mary had been something apart, special, existing in a different world;

he'd managed to compartmentalise his life but now he saw that he could no longer keep them separate. Ever since they'd left the party he'd been waiting for Selina to speak. Fear quaked inside him, his gut churned and he swallowed nervously in a dry throat—but still she had remained silent. He knew that she'd guessed but he did not know, yet, how to react should she accuse him. He must protect Mary, that much was clear in his mind, but how? So he waited.

Making the coffee, Selina willed herself to be controlled. When she spoke again her voice was light—if brittle.

'Well, I have to say you have my sympathy. Most of your colleagues could bore for England and they were certainly in good form tonight. How *do* you cope with them all day long?'

Patrick remained silent. He was used to this kind of thing and had long since become inured to it. Selina had only ever managed to tolerate his colleagues and he'd given up attempting to defend them. She was sipping her coffee now, leaning against the sink, but he would not meet her eyes. He pretended to be looking through some papers, glancing at the telephone bill, waiting for the blow. She laughed and he could imagine the accompanying shrug.

'You've got into a rut, darling. I really believe that you don't even notice it any more. I tell you what, though. This evening has really convinced me that Moorgate is the place for us. It's our last chance to break away from this mediocrity. Surely you can see my point?' She paused. 'No? OK. Well, give me one good reason for staying here.'

Patrick shifted his weight, putting down the bills and letters, turning, bracing himself to look at her at last. It was impossible: impossible to meet her eyes, to exchange any kind of glance with her. It was as if she had become a stranger—and, what's more, a frightening stranger. He felt ill at ease, embarrassed and, in that moment, he realised that he would be unable to share a bed with her. The mere thought of performing the familiar, intimate actions of simply undressing or cleaning his teeth, whilst she padded around in close proximity, filled him with revulsion. In his present mood he might as well strip in public. The comfortable indifference brought about by thirty years of marriage had been stripped away in a moment and he was seized by panic.

'I really don't want to discuss it now,' he mumbled. 'To tell you the truth, I don't feel too good. I feel rather sick. Perhaps it was that salmon. The sauce was very rich.'

'Perhaps.' She'd put her mug on the draining board and had folded her arms under her breasts. 'Or perhaps it might be something else altogether.'

He refused to rise to the bait. 'Possibly. There are the usual Christmas term bugs going round at school. I think I'll sleep in the spare room so that I don't disturb you if I have to get up in the night.'

'Oh, nonsense. I don't mind being disturbed, you know that.' She sounded amused. 'Much better to be in your own bed if you don't feel well. The spare isn't made up and it's far too late to fiddle about finding sheets. Come on. Let's go up. The sooner you're in bed the better. Thank God we haven't got to worry about Polonius any more.'

He climbed the stairs racked with self-disgust, emasculated by fear. He knew that any kind of resistance would be equivalent to declaring war; knew that Selina was waiting for precisely that to happen. She followed him into the bedroom, watched him whilst he undressed.

'You're shivering, poor darling.'

He felt her hand on his back and shrank away from her, seizing his pyjamas, struggling into them, hearing her chuckle. He leaped beneath the bedclothes, hauling them up, rolling away to his own side of the bed whilst she took off her clothes. Hugging himself, eyes clenched shut, he felt her climb in beside him, felt her arm slide over him and knew with a sick shock that she was naked. So this was to be the test. Well, they'd made love since Mary, so why not tonight? If it lulled her suspicions, gave him a breathing space, why not? He knew the answer almost before his brain had formulated the question. Tonight it would be impossible to feign affection, let alone passion; tonight, he knew, his body simply would not respond. He caught her roving hand and held it fast, rolling on to his back, pretending rueful disappointment.

'Sorry, love,' he said apologetically, feeling her stiffen into immobility. 'It's simply not on, tonight. Too much of everything, I think. Damn! I need the loo. Hope I shan't be long.'

He swung his legs out of bed and hurried out, leaving Selina staring into the darkness.

Maudie woke suddenly and lay quite still, listening. Presently she relaxed, smiling to herself. The noise which rumbled along the passage and echoed round the walls was merely Polonius snoring. Knowing that sleep had now deserted her, she struggled up in bed and switched on the light.

Half past one. Maudie sighed and muttered various oaths which were not complimentary. Polonius had ceased to whine and scratch at the kitchen door at night but his snoring was almost worse. Packing herself about with pillows she recalled how often a sharp jab in the ribs had been the answer to Hector's snoring. He'd rarely woken up but had automatically turned on to his side and continued to sleep peacefully. She doubted that Polonius would respond so obligingly.

Settling a silk shawl round her shoulders, Maudie picked up the Walkman which Posy had bought for her and fitted the earphones on her head, thinking about the conversation she'd had earlier with Mr Cruikshank.

'No luck yet, Lady Todhunter, but it's early days and the market's always rather dead during the month before Christmas. Lots of particulars are being sent off and I must say the photograph is really good, don't you think? By the way, one of our clients who was rather keen went back for another look, just from the outside, of course. I don't let the keys go. Anyway, he got rather lost and it was quite late when he found the house again. He says there was smoke coming from the chimney. That's a bit odd, isn't it?'

'Oh, I don't think so.' She'd tried not to feel worried. 'Rob lights the fire in the sitting room sometimes to keep the house warmed. He'd probably left it in. It would be quite safe in that big grate.'

'As long as you're happy about it. Just thought I'd mention it.'

'Did the client make his presence known?'

Ned Cruikshank had laughed rather self-consciously. 'To tell you the truth, he said it was so eerie up there in the dark that he didn't want to get out of the car. It *is* a bit isolated, isn't it?'

'Just a bit,' she'd answered. 'I can't say I blame him but we can assume, I imagine, that he won't be buying the house.'

Now, as she listened to the World Service, her uneasiness increased. She could imagine Moorgate, standing dark and empty at the edge of empty rolling moorland, and remembered Rob's question about ghosts.

'Rubbish!' she exclaimed aloud. 'Utter rubbish!' But she was oddly glad of Polonius, snoring loudly in the kitchen.

Chapter Nine

Selina pushed her coffee mug aside and laid the newspaper flat on the kitchen table. Patrick had just left for school and she sat for a while staring sightlessly at the headlines, elbows on the table, chin in hands. She'd forgotten how big a part anger played when it came to jealousy; forgotten the overwhelming, obsessive need to possess. So it had been when Maudie arrived on the scene more than thirty years ago. She could remember quite clearly that, in replacing their mother, it had seemed that her father was rejecting her, Selina—and Patricia—too. That he could bring this stranger into their home, allow her to use their mother's things, and not be able to see it as a betrayal had been utterly beyond belief. Patricia had been less affected by it. She'd been too preoccupied with boyfriends and parties to enter into her sister's feelings but she'd been shamed into a certain amount of rebellion. Even now Selina's lip curled as she thought about Patricia's feebleness, her readiness to give in and accept the stranger within the walls.

'Daddy's still quite young,' she'd said defensively. 'He's very attractive too. All my girlfriends say how dishy he is. You just have to face facts.'

What a shock it had been to see him in that light; the light of a lover. How cruel of Patricia to force her younger sister to see her father as someone who was capable of wanting a relationship outside his family. With their mother gone, it should have been enough to devote himself to his daughters—his daughters and his friends. Goodness knows, he'd had enough friends! Selina stirred restlessly. She'd often resented the great army of people who moved through the house, requiring attention, distracting her parents from her own needs.

'You mustn't be selfish, dear. Your father is a popular man who likes his friends about him.' How often darling Mummy had soothed and comforted. She was never too busy to have time for her children; with Mummy, she and Patricia had always come first. How safe Mummy had been; how constant. Her dying had been a betrayal in itself.

'How could you die,' Selina had demanded, weeping bitterly, night after night, 'when you knew how much I needed you?'

Nobody had warned her about death and its terrible, unimaginable finality. How many mornings she'd woken, almost weak with joy and relief, thinking that the whole thing was a terrible dream, only to have to live through the pain of it all over again. Yet nobody seemed to understand or care.

'Of course they care,' Daphne had once said, attempting to comfort her. 'The trouble is that Patricia and your father are attempting to cope with it too, you see, and so they are unable to help you as much as you feel they should. It's hard, very hard, Selina, but you must be as brave as you can. I'm always here if you need me.'

Oh, she'd been trying to help. Selina shrugged, remembering, but she hadn't wanted Daphne's help. Daphne was kind enough and Mummy's best friend too, but it was Daddy that she'd needed then. He'd been shocked and desolate, true enough, but not for long. Barely nine months later Maudie had been with him when he'd arrived at Granny's one afternoon. Granny had been polite but cool, Daddy had been doing that bluff, hearty sort of act, which was an attempt to cover his embarrassment, and Patricia had been avidly curious about Maudie.

'You have to admit,' she'd said afterwards, 'that she's rather attractive. Quite sexy in a kind of casually indifferent sort of way. Lovely long legs.'

Selina could recall that she'd stared at her, baffled, frightened. 'What do you mean?'

Patricia had rolled her eyes. 'Grow up, can't you? He's going to marry her. He's in love with her. You could see it a mile off.'

Now, Selina balled her hands into fists. How well that expression suited Patrick and Mary. 'He's in love with her. You could see it a mile off.' Her father's expression when he had looked at Maudie, the lingering hand clasp and the reluctant parting of flesh had been repeated that night of the party; oh, the signs were clear enough. Clear and appallingly familiar. Familiar as the upsurge of rage; the obsessive need to cling and hold; the crushing humiliation of a man's disloyalty.

'He doesn't love you less, Selina,' Daphne had insisted. 'Love is not a finite commodity. You did not love your father less because you loved your mother or Patricia. Your father doesn't love you less because he loves Maudie. Be generous, my dear.'

It was a concept which had remained foreign to her. Even with her own children she'd needed to be first. Patrick was their father, the provider and protector, but it was to her they brought their triumphs and disasters. *She* must be first in their affections. The boys had always complied quite readily—but Posy's disloyalty had enraged her. Her boys had always responded quickly when she pointed out how hurtful it was when their girlfriends attempted to displace her but Posy had remained unmoved. Even Selina's own friends couldn't understand why she'd felt so betrayed; couldn't see how destructive it was to one's self-esteem to discover that someone else was preferred; or how humiliating to imagine the victor's private triumph. And that it should be Maudie of all people had been an especially bitter pill.

Yet even the enormity of Posy's defection paled beside Patrick's. Mary's image rose in Selina's mind and she felt a suffocating, impotent fury. How the wretched woman must be laughing, enjoying the knowledge that it was *she* whom Patrick had chosen, that for her he had rejected and betrayed his wife. Selina willed down her rage, subduing it, knowing that it must not be allowed to cloud her judgement, aware that subtlety was more effective than cheap gibes or a show of contempt. Her wars against her father and against Posy had not succeeded but this time she would win. As yet nothing had been said. Patrick had gained control of his emotions and was playing it very calmly and carefully. He'd even mentioned a weekend away in Oxford, something to do with school, he'd said. Later he'd talked about it in detail, describing some seminar and lectures, but she was not deceived. He hadn't looked at her, and his guilt was almost tangible, but she hadn't dared speak. She'd hardly been able to contain herself at the thought of them together. Hot, spiteful, beastly words had filled her mouth, acid as bile, and hatred for Mary had been so strong that she'd felt almost frightened.

'I hate her,' she said aloud to the quiet kitchen. It was some kind of relief to say the words. 'The little cow is going to be truly sorry.'

She knew that Patrick was equally to blame but he could be dealt with later. Suddenly Selina remembered a line from some film or play she'd once seen. The wife had said sweetly to her husband, 'Don't torture yourself, darling. That's *my* job.' She laughed suddenly, good humour almost restored. Somehow she found the thought a comforting one.

'She knows,' said Mary. 'Of course I realise that. But if you deny it what can she do?'

'God knows.' Patrick spoke quietly, not wanting to wake Stuart. 'But at least we'll get our weekend.'

'It's so risky.' Her small face was drawn and tired. 'Honestly, Pat, I'm a bit worried to tell you the truth. I'm not sure we should take the risk.'

'It'll be OK,' he insisted. He couldn't bear to forgo the weekend. He'd lived on the expectation of it for weeks; it was almost the only thing sustaining him. 'Why are you worried now? Nothing's changed.'

'Oh, yes it has. I've met her now.' Mary shook her head. 'She's a formidable lady, Pat. She doesn't look like she gives in easily and I've a lot to lose.'

'Please, darling,' he said urgently. 'Please don't give up. We want to be together, don't we? Properly, I mean. Not just occasional evenings and a weekend here and there. I want to look after you both. I need you.'

'I know.' She shifted a little, turning away from him as much as the small sofa would allow. 'It's just that it seems so much more difficult than I first thought.'

'You're tired,' he said tenderly. 'You look frazzled to death. Leave it all to me. It's just that I don't want you hurt on the way through, so I have to be careful.'

'I know.' She hunched her shoulders, attempting to withdraw her hand, which he continued to hold tightly. 'Only . . . Well, I'm not sure I've been thinking straight, Pat. It's really good, you being around and . . . well, having a man in my life again. It's almost like being on holiday. Something different and fun. But now I've met Selina it's become real.'

'I know,' he said eagerly. 'I know just what you mean. I felt exactly the same after the party. But that doesn't mean we have to give up on it, Mary. It might mean a bit of a fight but isn't it worth it?'

'I've done fighting,' she said flatly. 'Been there, seen the film, bought the T-shirt. I'm tired of fighting.'

He stared at her, hurt and frightened. She looked away from him. His expression made her feel guilty and she could almost feel the weight of his love settling lightly but irrevocably over her shoulders. She was very fond of him, and their brief moments of love, as well as the relief and comfort of physical passion, had been a tremendous boost during a drab, exhausting period in her life—but things were changing. She was in control again, working, earning money, independent . . .

Mary thought: Do I really want an insecure middle-aged man with family problems rotting up my life for me?

The thought made her feel ashamed. Patrick had been very kind to her and she'd been too grateful, too ready to try to repay his kindness. She'd believed him to be a man who'd been neglected by his wife and was looking for a little comfort. She'd gone along with him, dreaming their little dream, but not taking it too seriously and imagining that he was doing the same. The expression on his face showed her that she was wrong.

'Look,' she said gently. 'Your wife looked like a lady who has no intention of being left. She's not going to lie down quietly so that we can walk over her, off into the sunset. I can't afford any mess or muddle, Pat, you know that. Stuart has to come first. He's vulnerable and weak. He's settling down really well at school and I think that it's because he's feeling secure for the first time since the accident. No one's going to take that away from him, Pat. No one.'

'I know,' he said wretchedly. 'Of course I know that. But she doesn't really want me. I'm sure of that. If I make sure she's well provided for—'

Mary laughed. 'You're kidding,' she said. 'You know your wife better than I do but I simply wouldn't count on that, I really wouldn't.'

His look of despair made her feel guilty and ashamed. He'd been so sweet, so generous.

'Look,' she said, giving in, 'of course, we'll have our weekend. We've got it all planned now, so why not? We'll talk everything through then but please leave things just as they are until afterwards. Don't rock any boats or we might find everything ruined. Promise?'

He promised. Of course he did. She knew just how important the weekend was to him. After he'd gone she went in the small bedroom to look at Stuart. She kissed him lightly, moved by a fierce protective love for him. Nothing must hurt him further; nothing and no one.

Walking home, Patrick tried to pin down his ideas. He must work through this sensibly, positively, but he was aware of the dangers. He could not protect Mary and Stuart, although he wanted to think that he could. If Selina chose to spill the beans to the school governors it was likely that he or Mary—or both—could suffer. It was possible that nobody would give a damn but he couldn't take the chance. So how could he work through it? If only he had enough money to set Mary up in her own place, where he could join her when the dust settled, then at least she would have a certain security. It would be unforgivable to damage her— yet he needed her; needed her desperately. Life would be intolerable without the thought of her in the background. Her little flat, plain and poor though it was, had become a haven for him. On these evenings, when Selina was at her bridge club and imagined him to be having supper at the pub, he and Mary were always together. He'd buy a takeaway and a bottle of wine which they'd share at the small rickety table and afterwards they'd make love. Oh, how long the summer holidays had seemed; how interminable. No school and the bridge club closed for six weeks had cut their opportunities considerably. It was the memory of those endless weeks which had made him determined to force things to a conclusion. Yet, this evening, he'd felt a drawing back on Mary's part; a reluctance.

He pushed the thought away from him. After all, it was perfectly reasonable that she should feel nervous. That meeting with Selina had put the whole thing on a different footing and it was unreasonable to hope that Mary would be unmoved by it. She had so much to lose that it was only natural that she should have moments of panic. Their lovemaking had been as good as ever, the weekend away shimmered temptingly ahead, and he felt refreshed and confident again. Somehow he *must* make it work. As he opened the gate and felt for his key, he glanced up at the smart little terraced house. Simple though it was it was a great deal better than most of his colleagues could afford. This was thanks to Hector's generosity, of course, and Patrick knew that it was incumbent upon him to make certain that Selina did not suffer financially either. He must be fair to them both, but how was it to be done?

A quick glance round showed him that Selina was not yet home. Relieved, Patrick hung up his coat and hurried up the stairs. With luck he might be in bed and feigning sleep before she arrived back.

Chapter Ten

Polonius sat on the veranda watching Maudie rake the leaves from the lawn. Each time she turned to look at him he sat up, his ears pricked, hopeful that she might allow him to join her—but Maudie refused to be moved by his eager expectancy. The long sheltered lawn with its high, thick hedges was approached only from the French windows of the bungalow and it had a secret, magical quality, rather like the gardens described in fairy tales. Beneath the hedge the first tiny snowdrops would appear, piercing the frozen earth, their pale, delicate heads drooping on green stems. These 'fair maids of February' were often to be found just after Christmas in this mild climate and Maudie always felt a glow of joy when she saw them gleaming bravely on a dull, cold winter morning. As spring approached primroses could be seen amongst the wet grass, growing with clumps of sweet smelling violets, and Maudie would wander contentedly along the winding paths, greeting these long familiar friends, waiting for the first showing of the daffodils' bright trumpets and the dainty lady's smock. She had no intention of allowing Polonius's huge paws to crush these fragile plants and, whilst he was allowed to roam freely around the back of the house and in the woods, here, in this little sanctuary, he was confined.

Maudie leaned the rake against the wooden seat and looked down into the still, quiet water of the pond. This was the natural pond where frogs and toads returned each year to breed so that, later, the water would be seething with wriggling tadpoles. In summer, around its edge, yellow stonecrop would flower amongst the slates and campanula would tumble, nodding at its trembling image in the cloud-reflecting water. The white blossoms of the weeping cherry would float and drift amongst the weed whilst above them dragonflies would hover with shimmering wings. Even now, on this chill, dank November morning, a pink primula blossomed bravely in its terracotta pot and the leaves of the azalea were greeny-bronze.

In the lower pond Maudie could see the hint of gold and the flick of a tail in the shadowy depths. There were goldfish here although it was difficult to see them. In this boggy corner, hidden from the sun except at the height of summer, the tall yellow flag *Iris pseudacorus* and handsome bulrushes made their home alongside the pretty *Butomus umbellatus*, with its rose-pink blossoms, and the gay yellow marsh marigold. Between tall stems and lush wet grasses, below the spongy leaves of the water dock, tiny froglets made their slow progress away from the safety of their pond, protected from the greedy eyes of predators. Here great toads squatted in magisterial comfort, watching for slugs, blinking lazily at the small red damselflies which flitted restlessly around them.

Maudie straightened up. Those warm, languorous days were yet far ahead; first came Christmas. As she trod the path back to the veranda she allowed herself a moment of sheer, childish thrill. Another card from Posy had arrived this morning.

'How would you feel about me spending Christmas with you,' she'd scrawled, the words wedged between all her news.

It was impossible, of course. Coming on top of the news about Moorgate it would be the final straw for poor Selina, yet how to refuse? How could she bring herself to resist such a delightful treat? Pausing to pat Polonius, who had watched her approach with great eagerness, she stepped over the low chain which was slung between the supporting posts and kicked off her gumboots. Presently she would go into Bovey Tracey to do some shopping but first a cup of coffee would not go amiss. As she put water in the percolator and spooned coffee into the filter she was remembering Christmases with Hector. For him it was a time of parties, theatres, dinners, and he was never happier than to be dressing for some formal event; wandering between the bedroom and his dressing room, white shirt-tails dangling, his legs long and elegant in knee-length black socks, bending so that he might peer into her looking-glass whilst he tied his bow tie. His face would appear beside her own, frowning in concentration, and she would pause in the application of her make-up to look at him.

'Let's not go,' she'd say suddenly. 'Let's stay here and make love'—and he'd hesitate, his hands stilled, gazing at her in surprise, shocked but delighted at such a notion.

'Honestly, darling.' He'd laugh, stooping to caress her. 'Don't think I'm not tempted but we've accepted now. Can't let people down,' but he was pleased, all the same: amused and flattered to be desired so unaffectedly.

Waiting for the light on the percolator to show that the coffee was ready, Maudie chuckled to herself. It was clear that Hilda had never been so natural with him. She would have been obliging in intimate matters, but she would never have taken the lead, and Hector found this new approach rather fun. In other respects he had been somewhat less pleased by Maudie's self-confidence; less able to be teased.

'You're hectoring,' she'd say, when he came striding into the bathroom, voicing his opinions on this or that political situation.

'I thought you might be interested in my point of view,' he'd answer rather huffily, stopping short in his peroration, irritated by the pun on his name . . .

'I *am* interested,' she'd answer calmly, soaping herself, 'but don't *teach* it to me. Let's have a discussion about it, not a lecture.'

He'd go away, hurt, but gradually he'd realised that she was capable of holding her own in any debate he might choose and began to enjoy the stimulation of an exchange of views.

'Poor old Hector,' Daphne had said one day, a year or so after Maudie and Hector had married. 'You're a bit of a shock for him. Hilda had all the mental stubbornness of the rather stupid person, you know. Her beliefs were formed early by other people and she stuck to them. Fortunately, most of them were formed by Hector so there were very few dissensions.'

Maudie had thought of Daphne and her remarks later that same day when Hector began to read aloud to her from one of the articles in the paper. After a minute or two she'd interrupted him.

'I'm reading, Hector,' she'd said, holding up her book.

He'd stared at her. 'I beg your pardon. It's just that this is a subject on which you hold quite strong views.'

'I know,' she'd answered. 'I read it this morning. I'm quite capable of assimilating facts from a newspaper article, you know. I don't have to be read to as though I were a child. I thought he put it very well, actually.'

She'd continued with her book and Hector had shaken out the pages crossly. No doubt Hilda would have sat sewing or knitting, listening meekly, ready to be instructed. 'Yes, darling,' she'd have said. 'Oh, really? Oh, yes, I quite agree,' and Maudie had suddenly wanted to burst out laughing, but instead she'd got up and, pausing briefly to touch his shoulder, had gone to pour him a drink. When she'd brought it to him he'd taken the glass but held on to her hand and kissed it. He was never one to bear a grudge.

'Oh, Hector,' she sighed, now, switching off the percolator and pouring strong black coffee. 'I'd give anything to have you back. I'd even let you read the newspaper to me.'

Polonius suddenly thrust a cold nose into her hand and she started, spilling some coffee, cursing under her breath. 'Wretched animal. No, we are not going for a walk. Not until later. I have to go shopping. I might take you with me, although you don't deserve to go. Not after yesterday.'

Polonius flattened his ears, exuding a winning air of kindly benevolence, but Maudie was unimpressed. He was still partially in disgrace after an incident which was affording her a certain amount of amusement. They'd been returning from their walk, rounding the curve in the lane, when they'd observed the car parked beyond the entrance to the drive, beside the little bridge. A couple were climbing out, accompanied by a Jack Russell who immediately raced towards them barking hysterically.

Polonius had stopped short, ears pricked, gazing at this intruder in amazement, and Maudie had clasped his collar firmly.

'Don't worry,' called the owner, making no attempt to restrain his dog. 'He won't hurt you if you stand quite still.'

'Cheeky bugger,' muttered Maudie, releasing her grip. 'Go on, Polonius. Lunch!'

Polonius had needed no further encouragement. With a deep, baying bark, he'd set off like a bullet from a gun. The terrier had paused, given one last defiant yap and scuttled back to his owners who were now proceeding less confidently.

'He won't hurt you if you stand quite still,' shouted Maudie, enjoying the spectacle of the terrier with his tail between his legs. 'Polonius! That's enough now. Here boy! Here! *Polonius!*'

Polonius had been quite deaf to entreaty, however, and, having dealt with the intruder, was now determined to see the whole party off his territory. The couple had hesitated for a moment and then made a hasty dash for the car, scrambling in, slamming doors just as Polonius had arrived beside it, still barking. They'd driven away and Polonius had returned, tail wagging, evidently pleased with himself.

'You're supposed to come when I call you,' she'd scolded—but he'd merely shaken himself victoriously and trotted ahead of her, up the drive, hoping for a reward.

'I might take you with me,' she said now. 'But you'll have to be patient. I have quite a lot of shopping to do and you'll have to wait in the car.'

Whilst she sat at the table in the living room, making her list, her glance returned occasionally to Posy's card. Was it really possible that she might come to stay for Christmas? Maudie shook her head. It was best not to be too hopeful.

I shall be going home this weekend to see the Ageds and collect some stuff, *she'd written*. I'll tell them that I'd like to stay with you over Christmas and I'm sure they won't mind. The boys will be around and I'll be there for some of the hols, anyway. Fingers crossed, babe! Wouldn't it be fun? Just you, me and Polonius. I do miss him but I'm so pleased he's with you. How is he?

Maudie looked at the great hound stretched before the fire, sleeping peacefully now, and felt oddly contented. She took a quick gulp of coffee and returned to her list.

Posy folded some jeans and a large black sweater and put them into her faded, battered holdall along with some books. It was important to her that her room in Hyde Abbey Road looked as Posy-ish as she could make it. They were not allowed to put up shelves or hammer nails into the wall but fortunately some previous tenant had been blissfully ignorant of—or utterly indifferent to—this tiresome rule and her own room had plenty of picture hooks. She'd made a point of showing these to the landlord, lest she was held responsible for them at a later date, and he'd agreed that they might be left *in situ*. Slowly, she'd been moving her few belongings to Winchester and now her bedroom here in London had a rather desolate air.

She sat on the edge of her bed and looked round the small room. It was odd that she felt more comfortable at the house in Hyde Abbey Road;

more relaxed with Jude and Jo and the others than with her family. Posy struggled with her guilt. After all, surely it was more natural to want to be with friends of her own age than with two middle-aged people, especially now that the boys were rarely at home and she wasn't allowed to keep Polonius? She pushed both hands through her thick black hair, straining it back from her face. It was a nervous gesture she'd had from childhood and Jo and Jude teased her about it.

'Posy's stressed out,' they'd warn each other. 'Watch it. Come on, Posy. Chill!'

She'd tried to control it but each time a real anxiety presented itself she'd find herself dragging her hands through her hair, pulling it until it hurt, as if this might in some way distract her or calm her. This time it was the thought of Polonius, which had automatically associated itself to Maudie and Christmas, that had triggered it. Being nonchalant about spending Christmas with her step-grandmother was one thing; actually broaching it with her mother was another. Posy drew up her legs and sat cross-legged, frowning. Mum was being a bit peculiar; still set on buying Moorgate but behaving like she was trying to needle Dad with it, and Dad wasn't responding. He wasn't doing his placating 'of course you must have it if you want it, love' stuff which he did when he wanted some peace, but he wasn't actually arguing about it either. It was like he was marking time; waiting for something. He was absent-minded, preoccupied, although he'd been like that for a while now, even before she'd gone back to Winchester, and Mum was kind of watchful but as if she knew a secret and was hugging it to herself. Perhaps she had some money tucked away somewhere and intended to buy Moorgate whether Dad wanted her to or not. Anyway, she'd done the usual anti-Maudie bit and it had been difficult to just say straight out, 'Oh, by the way, I thought I'd spend Christmas with her.'

Posy tugged at her hair, climbed off the bed and went downstairs. Patrick was sitting at the kitchen table, reading. He glanced up at her, smiling, but he looked old and tired and she felt another pang of guilt.

She thought: I won't feel guilty about him. I simply won't. Maudie's old too, and all alone.

'I had an idea about Christmas,' she said, sitting opposite, trying not to notice his strained expression and restless hands. 'I wondered about spending a few days with Maudie. The boys will be with you and she's all on her own. And I have to think about Polonius . . .'

Her voice trailed off and she looked away from him, waiting for reproaches. She knew that he loved her and that he would miss her but she tried to harden her heart, ready to argue her corner.

'I don't see why you shouldn't,' he said. 'I guessed with Polonius down with Maudie you'd be more inclined to go there than come here.'

'Oh, don't say it like that,' she cried, compassion making her sound cross, 'as if I love Polonius more than you. You know I don't. It's just unfair to load him on to Maudie and leave it at that. Mum said he could come home for holidays but now she's changed her mind. I'll be here for some of the time.'

He raised his hands pacifically. 'Look,' he said gently, 'I'm not arguing. We'll miss you—of course we will—but you'll be around for a week or two, I expect. I think it's a nice idea. There's no point in inviting Maudie up here, after all, and she'll be delighted. It's good of her to have Polonius.'

She watched him suspiciously, trying to detect signs of martyrdom, but he seemed genuinely undisturbed and she felt a wholly unreasonable stab of hurt pride.

'What d'you think Mum will say?' she asked.

He shrugged. 'Does it matter? If you've made up your mind, stick to it. That's my advice.'

She stared at him curiously, anxiously. This indifference was strangely out of character and she wondered if the Moorgate business were seriously upsetting him.

'This Moorgate thing,' she said impulsively. 'It's just a bee in Mum's bonnet. She can't really be contemplating going to Cornwall to live. She'd die without a tube round the corner and Peter Jones and stuff. Don't let it get to you.'

He smiled at her, then, with real warmth, as though he were truly seeing her; really thinking about her. 'I won't,' he said. 'Stick to your guns about Christmas, mind. I'm going down to the pub for a pint. See you later.'

He went out and she sat still, puzzled. Sometimes he'd suggest she might go to the pub with him but it was clear, this evening, that he had no desire for her company. Presently Selina came into the kitchen. She raised her eyebrows when she saw Posy sitting there alone.

'Where's your father?' she asked. 'He was supposed to be getting the supper this evening.'

Posy felt a familiar sense of partisanship manifesting itself. 'He's gone to the pub,' she said casually. 'He looks a bit stressed out, I think. Worrying about something. Why don't you give him a break about this Moorgate stuff? You don't really want to live on the edge of Bodmin Moor, do you?'

Selina looked at her coolly. 'I don't think it's any of your business. You have your own life to lead now and I suspect we shan't be seeing too much of you in the future. After all, you've always made it very clear where your loyalties lie.'

They stared at each other, all the old antagonisms rising to the surface, and Posy recklessly seized her chance.

'I suppose you're right. Actually I've decided to spend Christmas with Maudie. Not the whole holiday, but a few days. Since she's kind enough to have Polonius . . .'

Selina gave a short laugh. 'Kind! She saw her opportunity and grabbed it with both hands. Typical bloody Maudie. She realised that by having that wretched dog your always indifferent kind of loyalty to us would be strained further and might snap altogether.'

Accusations of this kind had been commonplace all through Posy's life but she defended herself—and Maudie—as best she could.

'I don't think she thought about it like that at all. She just knew how miserable I was at the thought of him being given away. You didn't care. You said he could come back for holidays but you've gone back on your word, as usual. And it was I who suggested going for Christmas, not Maudie. Dad seems quite happy about it.'

Selina, enraged as always by the thought of Maudie gaining an advantage, imagining her private triumph, lost her patience. 'I'm sure he does. But then he's too wrapped up in the little tart he's having an affair with to care about any of us.' She saw shock replace the indignation on her daughter's face, saw the blank fear in her eyes and knew a brief moment of remorse. It was quickly smothered by a surge of self-righteousness. Hadn't *she* had to cope with just such a shock concerning her own father and Maudie when she was much younger than Posy was? And now Patrick, who knew how she'd been betrayed and hurt, was just as faithless. 'Perhaps I shouldn't have told you,' she said, rather ashamed by Posy's dazed expression though unwilling to acknowledge it, 'but you're quite old enough to deal with it. God knows, I have to! He spends every minute he can with her but he hasn't got the guts to admit it yet.'

'No.' Posy shook her head. 'I don't believe it. Not Dad. He just isn't like that.'

'Like what?' Selina's lips curled into her familiar inimical sneer. 'Oh, this isn't some passionate sex thing with a dolly-bird type. No, she's a fat, boring little nonentity with a crippled child. He sees himself as a knight in shining armour, rescuing her from her drab existence. It's a role he enjoys. God, he is so pathetic.'

'If he hasn't admitted it how do you know?'

'Because I *do* know,' Selina answered quietly. 'I've seen them together. You can take my word for it. Come on, Posy. You've seen the change in him. Admit it. You were saying as much just now.'

'So what will you do?' Posy felt oddly breathless.

Selina shrugged, eyes narrowed thoughtfully. 'I shall bide my time. I'm getting the house valued and I'm preparing to buy Moorgate. Not as a second home. Oh, no. She's not going to have him, I promise you that. If we have to live in Cornwall, then that's what we'll do. He'll have to make a move soon but, meanwhile, I wait.' She frowned and glanced at the kitchen clock. 'Talking of waiting, I suppose I'll have to get on with the supper myself.'

'I don't want anything to eat,' said Posy. 'I'm not hungry.'

She went out, upstairs to her bedroom. Sitting on the bed, driving her hands through her hair, she stared about her. Dull and uninteresting though the bedroom had become, she now realised how important it was to her to have this place of security; the comforting knowledge that home and her parents—especially her father—were there in the background, waiting should she need them. It was a shock to think of him in any other role than as husband and father; impossible to see him simply as a man, attracted to a woman other than her mother. She felt childishly angry that this new-found love was more important to him than the company of his own daughter. It was because of this unknown woman that he was preoccupied and indifferent, quite ready to allow her, Posy, to go off to Maudie for Christmas, no longer requiring her company down at the pub. Perhaps he had lied to her; perhaps he hadn't been going to the pub at all but was with the woman now. She simply could not think about them; her mind steadfastly refused to furnish her with new disturbing images of him and his mistress. How could she possibly face him on his return? Posy rolled over on to her side and drew up her knees, wrapping her arms about them, shivering. Presently she began to cry.

Chapter Eleven

'Where's Posy?' Patrick blinked rather blearily around the kitchen. 'She's not upstairs. Is she OK?'

'So very much OK that she's gone back to Winchester,' said Selina brightly. 'She didn't want to hang about, she said.'

'Gone?' Patrick looked at her disbelievingly. 'But it's barely eleven o'clock.'

Selina raised her eyebrows. 'So?'

'But I've hardly seen her,' he mumbled. Selina's shiny brittleness penetrated his heavy-headed stupor and he felt the chill of caution trickling down his spine. 'I thought we might go for a walk or something.'

He turned his back on her, switching on the kettle, suddenly alert. He'd got back later than he'd intended, slipping into the spare bedroom so as not to disturb Selina, but he'd been unable to sleep. There had been no answer when he'd telephoned Mary from the pub. Just her voice on the machine, asking callers to leave their names and numbers. He'd told her that he would almost certainly telephone at about this time so he'd assumed that she was dealing with Stuart and couldn't get to the phone. Presently he'd tried again but there was still no reply. Since she rarely went out in the evening—and he liked to think that she told him her plans— he'd gone back to the bar to finish his pint, anxious and rather puzzled. After a while he'd begun to work himself into a state of serious worry, imagining various scenarios in which Mary was unable to reach the telephone; that she'd fallen or been taken ill. After another fruitless call he determined to walk to the flat to make sure that all was well. As he hurried through the streets, he convinced himself that it was perfectly reasonable to check things out; that he had every right to be worried about her. Yet a tiny worming fear gnawed in his guts. Since the meeting with Selina some undefinable change had taken place in his relationship with Mary. After that first outburst was over she'd been just as loving, still looking forward to their weekend away, yet there was something . . .

When he'd arrived at the house the front door was locked as usual but he could see a light in her sitting-room window although the curtains were closed. He rang her bell several times but there was no reply and he'd stood, undecided, wondering what he should do. The landlord lived across the hall but Patrick was unwilling to rouse him by ringing his bell and asking him to check on Mary. It was quite possible, after all, that she'd pushed Stuart round to visit her parents, leaving her light on as a precaution in case they were late back, and he certainly didn't want to cause any trouble or make himself conspicuous.

Frustrated, still worried, he'd walked back to the pub and had another pint, trying to console himself. After all, since Mary knew that they were restricted to seeing each other on Selina's bridge evenings, there was no reason at all why she should stay in on a Saturday night . . . except that he nearly always managed to call her on a Saturday night one way or another. She always said how wonderful it was to hear him, that he'd cheered her up, and the thought of her sitting in her little room waiting for his call, Stuart asleep across the passage, gave him a warm, possessive glow. His disappointment was out of all proportion and he'd ordered a large Scotch in an attempt to cheer himself up. At last, after one final unrewarding telephone call, he'd set off home. The house had been in darkness and he'd gone quietly upstairs to the spare room—but not to sleep. He'd lain awake, worrying and miserable, until eventually he'd managed to persuade himself that she'd gone to see her parents, that there had been some kind of emergency, which had kept her there, and, promising himself that he'd speak to her first thing in the morning, he'd fallen at last into a troubled doze.

He'd woken late, feeling ghastly, longing for hot tea. Selina had left her bedroom door wide open but Posy's door was closed and he'd wondered if she were still asleep or whether she too might appreciate a cup of tea. There had been no answer to his knock and, opening the door a crack, he'd seen that her bed was empty. He hadn't noticed that her belongings were gone and Selina's news had come as a shock. Now, as he made his tea, some shadowy premonition, some shred of self-preservation kept him silent.

'The news of your affair with Mary upset her.' Selina sounded perfectly friendly, almost cosy, as if they were gossiping about friends. 'Well, that's understandable. I felt exactly the same when Daddy brought Maudie home. But you know all about that, don't you? You were so upset when I told you. Do you remember, Patrick? What a perfect *preux chevalier* you were. You considered it quite shocking that I'd had to come to terms with such things. You said some rather cutting things about Daddy at the time, if I recall. A dirty old man was one of them, wasn't it? But then, you were very young, weren't you, and Daddy seemed old to you? I suppose he was about your age now at that time. Fifty-ish. Odd, isn't it, how the young consider that anyone over forty is past it, and the thought of their parents having sex is bad enough, but to find out that your father is having a fling with another woman is terrible. I found it almost impossible to come to terms with, as you know. It's so utterly sordid. So tacky. You feel sick and you don't want to be near him or see him. All your respect vanishes. That's how Posy feels about you, of course.'

Patrick stood quite still, keeping his back to her, his hands trembling. He felt as if he were shrivelling inside as he imagined his daughter's clear-eyed, ruthless gaze. How cruel the young could be; how devastatingly cruel. Just so had he reacted when the young, tremulous Selina had poured out her pain; how self-righteous he'd been, how loudly disgusted by the needs of an old man. Oh, yes! Safe in his own youth and virility he'd been the first to condemn Hector's need for another, younger wife; very ready to enter into Selina's feelings, to sympathise with her.

'At least,' Selina was saying conversationally, 'Daddy was a widower. At least he wasn't an adulterous bastard.'

He took his hands away from the mug and pushed them deep into his pockets.

'Why did you tell her?' he asked, turning to face her. 'Why did you tell Posy before you even spoke to me about . . . your suspicions.'

She laughed contemptuously. 'Suspicions. You're not denying it, I notice.' She waited, interrogatively, but when he did not answer she shrugged. 'Posy noticed that something was wrong with you. So I told her what it was.'

He swallowed in a dry throat and his head rocked with pain. 'Since you'd suffered as much as you did in similar circumstances, I suppose it didn't occur to you to protect her from it?'

She raised her eyebrows, delighted at such an opportunity. 'My dear Patrick, don't accuse *me*! It's your job, as her father, to protect Posy. Don't expect to behave like a selfish, disgusting prat and then blame *me* if your daughter despises you. I notice that you're not particularly concerned with how *I* feel about it.'

He was suddenly, blindingly angry. 'Why should I be? You don't care about anything else that concerns me. You didn't give a damn until this happened. You still don't. Not really. You're a dog-in-the-manger, Selina. You don't really want me, except to pay the bills, but you're damned if you'll let go. Why?' He laughed hopelessly, mirthlessly. 'Why keep up this pretence?'

'Because I choose to,' she said. 'You're mine, Patrick, and I intend that we shall stay together. Make up your mind to it. And you can tell your little tart that if she doesn't lay off I shall write to the school governors. Don't forget that I'm particularly friendly with Susan Partington. She doesn't like adulterers either. Not since Paul went off with his secretary. You just tell dear Mary that. When you've done it we'll discuss selling this house and buying Moorgate.' She stood up but, at the door, she paused, looking him over. 'You haven't forgotten that we're lunching with Jane and Derek, have you?' she asked sweetly—and went away upstairs.

Maudie placed a log on the fire, closed the door and settled again in her chair, adjusting her spectacles, picking up her knitting. How amused Hector would have been to see her busy with her new hobby!

'I must say,' he'd admitted, in one of his rare bursts of criticism, 'that it's rather nice to be able to read without the accompaniment of clacking needles. Of course, Hilda knitted the most beautiful garments . . .'

Of course. Maudie grimaced, pushing the stitches along the thick wooden needles, stroking the nubbly hand-dyed wool appreciatively.

'Was there anything,' she'd asked despairingly of Daphne, 'that dear Hilda didn't do to perfection?'

Daphne had smiled at her. 'You know very well that there's a whole side to Hector that Hilda never touched. She never even guessed that it was there. Be content, Maudie. Leave the stuffy, serious, responsible part of him to Hilda. Don't regret it or yearn for it. You don't want it. That's not the Hector that you know and love. Don't hanker, my dear, let it go. Poor Hilda barely scratched the surface. Don't begrudge her whatever it was she had.'

How wise Daphne had been through all those early years; what a comfort. Her irrepressible sense of humour had carried them all through stormy patches; soothing Maudie's irritation, bolstering her in moments of inadequacy.

'She looks so damned smug,' she'd raged on one occasion, when Selina had insisted on turning her bedroom into a kind of shrine, and images of Hilda through the ages had smirked and simpered from every available flat surface. 'I wouldn't mind only it makes Hector feel so guilty. I don't mind her being dotted about the place, for heaven's sake. How could I? But he's brought out that Dorothy Wilding one again and stuck it on the piano.'

'Oh, my dear, no! Not that portrait with her gazing mistily over her shoulder like something rather ghastly out of a Barrie play?'

'Just so,' said Maudie grimly.

'It was her favourite,' mused Daphne, 'and one could see why. Clever old Dorothy Wilding managed to reduce that rather masterful chin and very subtly gave her eyebrows and eyelashes so that she really looked rather pretty . . . in a sickly kind of way.'

They'd sat together, rocking with laughter, until Hector had come in for tea and asked them what the joke was. His question had reduced Maudie to a state of nervous hysteria but Daphne had pulled herself together and reported some childishly amusing remark, attributed to Emily, which had convinced Hector though he'd clearly been puzzled they'd found it quite so funny.

The telephone bell, breaking into Maudie's thoughts, startled her and she put her knitting aside and reached for the receiver.

'Hello, Maudie. It's me.' Posy's voice sounded rather flat, as though she were exhausted. 'How are you?'

'I'm fine, my darling. Are you OK? You sound tired.'

'I am a bit. I've just got back from London.'

'Oh dear. Were things a bit difficult?' Maudie was reluctant to pry or encourage disloyalty but she was alerted by Posy's lassitude. 'Is Moorgate being a real problem?'

'Well, sort of. It was all a bit strained and stuff. Look, the good thing is that I can come for Christmas. They don't mind. Well, not really. Mum did her usual bit about my lack of loyalty but what's new?'

'Oh, darling, I'm so sorry.' Maudie cast about for words, feeling hopelessly inadequate. 'It would be simply wonderful if you could come. I should love it, but if it's going to make it unpleasant at home—'

'No. No, it won't.' She sounded defiant now. 'Anyway, who cares? It's all arranged. I'll go home first so as to leave them my presents and then come down to you the day before Christmas Eve. How's that?'

'It is simply perfect,' answered Maudie warmly. No point in questioning the child now, she realised that, but some instinct told her that it was important to make Posy feel especially loved. 'It's going to be such fun. I can't tell you when I last felt so excited. I shall tell Polonius.'

There was a small, rather watery chuckle at the other end of the line. 'Give him a hug for me. Is he OK?'

'He certainly is. He's still enjoying terrorising the local population and making his presence felt generally.'

Maudie recounted the incident with the Jack Russell and was rewarded by a stronger chuckle and a more cheerful note in Posy's voice when she said goodbye. As she replaced the receiver and picked up her knitting, Maudie suddenly realised that Posy had not once called her 'babe'.

'Something's wrong,' she told Polonius, who thumped his tail sleepily once or twice but was disinclined to any greater response. 'She's probably had a row with Selina over Moorgate. Damn and blast. If only I didn't have to sell . . .'

Posy went back into her room and closed the door. She'd been at Hyde Abbey Road for some hours but she'd found it very difficult to speak even to Maudie. To her relief, Jude and Jo were out and she was able to be alone, attempting to sort out her emotions. Last evening, she'd heard her father come back quite late—her mother was already in bed—and go into the spare room. This behaviour was extraordinary in itself and lent credence to her mother's accusations but, to begin with, Posy had wanted to give him the benefit of the doubt; to let him deny or explain it.

'You'll see,' her mother had said, almost cheerfully. 'He'll come back late, much later than he used to when he went to the pub for a quick pint. That's why he didn't want you along. He'll telephone her from the pub or make a quick dash round to see her. Then he'll come back, hoping I'm already in bed, and he'll use the spare bedroom. He never used to behave like that, did he?'

Posy hadn't wanted to believe her. She'd tried to explain it away by attributing it to her mother's natural possessiveness and ready jealousy but she'd been infected by her father's preoccupation, by his indifference, and she couldn't quite convince herself. Whilst her mother was watching television, she'd slipped out, hurrying round the corner to the pub.

'He's not here,' the barman told her. 'He's been telephoning someone and he got a bit restless and suddenly dashed off. He'll probably be back in a minute. Give him a message, shall I?'

'No, don't do that.' She'd been horrified at the thought. Would he think she'd been spying on him? 'Thanks, anyway. It really doesn't matter.'

It was only later that she saw how fear and guilt could corrupt. Why shouldn't she wander down to the pub to meet her father and have a drink with him? She'd done it before. Now, because she feared her mother's words were true, she could no longer approach her father in innocence. She had been made party to this web of deceit and she was unable to behave naturally. When she'd realised this—lying in bed listening to him creeping up the stairs, going into the spare bedroom—she knew that she simply couldn't face him in the morning. She feared that her own knowledge, his guilt and her mother's jealousy might combust in a scalding broth of fury and she shrank at the thought of it.

Now, as she sat cross-legged on her bed, she felt comforted by her conversation with Maudie. Nothing had changed at The Hermitage. Maudie was there with Polonius, waiting for her, and she could go for Christmas with a clear conscience. No matter how hard she tried to concentrate on this, however, other thoughts intruded. She couldn't believe how much it hurt to know that this unknown woman was more important to her father than she was; that she had been replaced in his affections so easily; that it was more important to him to be with this woman than with his own daughter. She'd genuinely believed that he would be terribly hurt when she'd said that she wouldn't be at home for Christmas—and he simply hadn't cared. He'd been kind, understanding and utterly indifferent.

Posy felt her lips trembling uncontrollably and dragged her hands fiercely through her hair.

'Don't be a wet!' she told herself. 'For heaven's sake! You're not a little kid. You're nearly twenty-two. Grow up and face facts.'

The bang on the door startled her so much that she cried out and Jude opened the door and put his head inside the room.

'Are you OK?' he asked. 'I've just got back. How about some coffee?'

'Yeah. Great!' she answered casually, pretending to be rooting for something in her grip. 'I'll be right there.'

He disappeared and she stood up, drawing a deep breath, controlling herself. Nobody must know yet, not even Jude and Jo, not until she'd got used to the idea. She stared at herself critically in the looking-glass, half imagining that her new knowledge must show in her face, pulled her hair forward over her eyes and went out to find Jude.

Chapter Twelve

'I must say I do love this old place.' Ned Cruikshank cast his Filofax and mobile telephone on to the working surface and smiled blindingly at Rob. 'If I had the money I'd buy it myself.'

'Would you though?' murmured Rob, making coffee. He glanced at Ned's shiny black loafers. 'Not a bit off the beaten track for you?'

Ned wrinkled his nose dismissively. 'Doesn't matter these days, does it? You can be on the A30 in minutes. Although I must say that socially it's a bit dead. OK if you were married and had plenty of local friends.'

'I have to say that you look as if the streets of London were more your natural habitat. However,' Rob said, passing him a mug of black coffee, 'first impressions aren't always reliable.'

'Oh, I'm a great countryman,' Ned assured him earnestly. 'Absolutely. I ride most weekends, if I can.'

'Ah, well.' Rob put the lids on the coffee and sugar jars. 'Still, you'd rattle about here on your own. Or am I making another assumption? You're not married or—'

'Good grief, no!' Ned willingly helped him out of his difficulty. 'But I wouldn't mind. I've nothing against it, if you see what I mean. Rather fun, I should think. Actually . . .'

The ringing of his mobile telephone put an end to a promise of confidence and Rob turned to look out of the window, pretending that he couldn't hear the one-sided conversation which was clearly a personal one. It was a clear, bright day; huge, feathery clouds drifting slowly, bumping gently, merging, re-forming. Sheep grazed on the moor below the house watched by a crow perched in the twisted, black, weather-shaped branches of an old thorn tree, which leaned out of the dry-stone wall. The slate roofs of the small village, huddled in the valley, gleamed grey in the wintry sunshine and, far away on the hill, a tractor was ploughing, churning over clods of heavy earth, a flock of seagulls screaming in its wake.

'Terrific view, isn't it?' Ned's voice behind his shoulder made him jump. 'Gets 'em every time. Not that we've had too many people round yet. It's not a good time of the year for these isolated properties. I was really pleased that we had the sunshine this morning. Do you think they really liked it?'

Rob looked noncommittal. 'Difficult to say. Some people think that they have to enthuse, don't they? I think the thought of having to ferry the kids everywhere didn't fill them with delight.'

Ned looked as put out as his round face and naturally cheerful expression would allow.

'You didn't have to lay it quite so firmly on the line,' he said. 'They were pretty keen, I thought, until then.'

'Sorry.' Rob shrugged. 'But they did ask about public transport. I don't think townspeople realise that out here you're not going to have a bus passing the gate every twenty minutes. They must have seen that it was going to be much too isolated for two teenage kids who have spent all their lives in a city. No point in stringing them along and then having the sale fall through at the last minute, is it? You might miss a genuine buyer.'

'You've got a point.' Ned brightened a little. 'I'm glad that Lady Todhunter lets you keep the range alight. Makes all the difference, doesn't it? The house feels warm and friendly. Don't you mind having to caretake, now that the work's finished?'

'Not particularly. I don't live far away and she'd soon get damp if she wasn't aired and heated. Pointless doing all that work and seeing it ruined through the winter.'

'Funny about those keys, wasn't it? I wondered whether one of your lads might have taken them. But I couldn't really see why anyone should.'

Rob frowned, remembering certain proofs of habitation. 'No reason at all,' he said firmly. 'Anyway, it's dealt with now. Have you got anyone else viewing before Christmas?'

Ned shook his head. 'Everything's dead as mutton at the moment and the office shuts tomorrow for a week. So.' He rinsed his mug at the sink and beamed at Rob. 'Good to see you again. Gave me a bit of a surprise to find you here but it was just as well since I managed to get held up. At least they weren't hanging about in the cold.'

'Oh, I keep an eye on the old girl but I don't have a routine. Best to be . . . unexpected.'

Ned looked puzzled. 'Unexpected?'

'Well, it's a lonely spot. Easy for someone to break in. If anyone were watching the place, for instance, it would keep them on their toes, if you see what I mean?'

'Mmm.' Ned glanced around almost nervously. 'Sounds a bit creepy, if you ask me. Perhaps it *is* a bit off the beaten track.' He hesitated for a moment and then laughed, picking up his Filofax, putting his mobile telephone into his pocket. 'But don't go saying that to the clients.'

'Of course not. But I shall tell the truth about transport and the weather, if they ask.'

'Fair enough. Well, I'll be off. Season's greetings and so on. See you in the new year.'

'Indeed. And the same to you.'

Rob strolled out, round the side of the house and into the yard, watching Ned climb into his car and shoot off down the lane with a fanfare farewell on the horn. He raised his hand, smiling. He'd become quite fond of Ned. The sound of the engine died away, the car disappearing amongst the trees, and he looked about him. The yard was tidy now; the stable repaired, the barn creosoted, all rubbish cleared away. He passed through the small gate which led to the front of the house, noting the first new green spears thrusting through the soil of the flower borders under the wall, appreciating the yellow stars on the jasmine which climbed over the porch. Crossing in front of the windows, he stepped on to the lawn which was divided from the moorland by its high escallonia hedge. He remembered the remains of a swing he'd found, rotting and broken, beneath its shelter and, for a moment, he'd imagined Moorgate as it had once been a hundred years before, with chickens running in the yard, children playing on the swing and the men coming in tired and hungry from the fields. He turned, half expecting to see the farmer's wife watching him from the porch, her hands folded under her apron—but no one was waiting by the door and the yard was empty. Laughing aloud at his foolish fancies, giving one last glance round, he went back inside.

———

Mary, shivering on playground duty, saw Patrick come out of the door and look about him. She felt a newly familiar sense of compassion and pity for him; compassion and pity—and guilt because she no longer really loved him. The little fragile flower of tenderness and pleasure had faded in the unkind atmosphere of other harsher emotions. Survival was instinctive and she could not allow herself to waver. As he approached she automatically hardened her heart against his look of eagerness, instinctively checking that nobody else observed his transparent pleasure.

'I missed you on Saturday,' he said at once. 'Are you OK? I've been so worried.'

Odd how the charm of his caring for her should have deteriorated into an irksome irritation.

'We're fine,' she said, looking away from him, smiling brightly at the children milling about them. 'Nothing to worry about. I had to go and see Mum and Dad but we're all fine.'

'I need to see you. I've had a showdown with Selina. I simply must talk to you.'

Her heart was weighty with foreboding, making her angry with him. Why couldn't he simply accept that whatever had been between them was all over? Their little moment was finished, past, and she wanted him to let go, to relinquish his hold. She knew that he would not; that he would cling to her, possibly dragging them all down. Self-preservation stiffened her resolve, warning her against giving in to his need, or comforting him. Yet she wanted to be kind; to let him down lightly.

'Please, Mary.' He stood with his back to the playground, his face miserable, and she wanted to scream at him to go away, to stop taking risks with her life, yet compassion wrung her heart and she knew that she could not be cruel to him.

'Isn't it bridge night?'

'Yes, it is.' He watched her hopefully. 'But I wanted to be sure you'd be in. Can I come round?'

'Of course.' How weak she was; how foolish to give way so quickly, but he was right. They needed to talk. 'Yes, come round as usual.' She gave him a swift smile. 'Better go now.'

'Yes. Yes, of course.' His relief was almost tangible and she felt a surge of the old affection for him. 'See you later, then.'

'I'll be there.'

She turned away from him, wishing that she could comfort him, reassure him, knowing that she couldn't.

'Are you going out tonight?' Selina was in the doorway, bright-eyed, inquisitive. 'Or have you work to do?'

He thought: It's almost as if she's enjoying all this. But how can she be?

'I'll probably go round to the pub,' he said casually. 'I'll see how I feel.'

'Only'—she was smiling at him—'I'm wondering whether I'll go to bridge tonight.'

He was unable to hide his shocked reaction although he did his best to cover his lapse. 'Aren't you feeling well?'

'I'm a bit low, to tell you the truth. Well, who wouldn't be under the circumstances?'

He remained silent, praying for release, whilst she watched him. 'Perhaps,' he mumbled, after a moment, 'it would do you good to get out.'

She laughed, a loud, harsh laugh, and he winced away from her. 'Have you anything to tell me?'

'No,' he answered, confused. 'No . . . What do you mean?'

'Oh, I think you know very well what I mean.' She seemed amused at his discomfiture. 'Another thing. That weekend away in Oxford. I think I'll come with you.'

This time it was quite impossible to hide his dismay. 'It's out of the question,' he said. 'It's . . . Everything is arranged.'

'Oh, surely not,' Selina said gently. 'I'm sure we can change your single room for a double. Or is there some faint chance that you've already booked a double? Anyway, I've decided that it would do us good to get away for a weekend. I know you'll be busy but I'm sure we'll manage to have some time together. Oh, and Susan Partington's coming to lunch on Wednesday. She and I haven't had a good gossip for ages. I just thought you'd like to know that. Well.' She stretched, breathing deeply with satisfaction. 'So that's that, then. Do you know, I'm feeling much better. I think I'll go to bridge, after all. It will give you the chance to get things sorted, won't it? See you later.'

Patrick put his head in his hands. It seemed that Selina held all the cards. His only hope was that Mary might be prepared to trust him; to love him enough to take a chance for him. As long as he could look after her, and there was no question of Stuart being put at risk, surely they might scrape through? He could work for all three of them, support them, if only Mary would let him.

He heard Selina call goodbye, heard the front door slam. He waited for a few moments, listening, before he stood up and went downstairs. Taking his coat, he stepped out into the wet evening, walking briskly, his head bent against the drizzle.

'No.' Mary shook her head. 'Absolutely not, Pat. I just can't.'

He stared at her, desperately, trembling with frustration. They'd made love almost immediately after he'd arrived. She'd seen the expression on his face and had simply opened her arms to him. He'd seized her, kissing her hungrily, and she'd responded to his need. Afterwards she'd made them coffee and, encouraged by her readiness and her warmth, he'd poured out his ideas, his plans for the three of them, feeling confident that she would understand and be sympathetic. He'd explained that, although Selina would probably keep the house, he could support the three of them; they would find somewhere else to live, near Stuart's school, and even if they both lost their jobs they would soon find new ones . . .

She'd begun to draw away from him, to free herself from his embrace. He'd talked on, urgently, persuadingly, trying to force her to share his optimism, but she'd become stiff and unresponsive.

'Please let's try,' he'd pleaded. 'We can't just give in to her, Mary. You can trust me to look after you both. I love you. I can't bear the thought of us parting. Just think how wonderful it would be, Mary. To be together properly without all this lying and subterfuge. Isn't it worth taking the risk?'

'No,' she'd said. 'Absolutely not, Pat. I just can't.'

Now there was a silence which neither seemed capable of breaking. Patrick sat staring bleakly ahead of him and she sipped distractedly at her coffee, miserable but unyielding.

'You don't really love me at all, do you?' he said at last.

There was no pleading in his voice, no self-pity; just a stating of bald fact. She looked at him unhappily, not wanting to hurt him, determined not to give way.

'I *do* love you, Pat,' she said quietly, 'but I suppose I don't love you enough to take such risks. You know how it is with me. It's been hell, trying to cope with Stuart, nowhere to live, no money, and I just can't do it again. Oh, I know you'd want to work for us and protect us but just suppose Selina really puts the boot in and we get suspended—what then? It might work out in the end but what happens meanwhile? Perhaps nothing would happen. Perhaps nobody gives a shit whether you and I are having an affair and we'd both keep our jobs. But we can't be certain, can we? We work at a Church of England primary school and your wife is great friends with the governors. Sorry, Pat.' She shook her head. 'The odds are stacked against us. I only hope we haven't blown it already.'

'Selina hasn't said anything yet.' He clasped his hands, staring down at them. 'She's giving me the chance to finish with you. We've got until Wednesday.'

'Wednesday?' She frowned at him, puzzled.

'She's invited Susan Partington to lunch on Wednesday.' He sounded very tired, almost indifferent. 'She's one of the governors. Her husband ran off with his secretary and she's very prejudiced about infidelity.'

Mary experienced a thrill of terror. Anger twisted inside her and she had to restrain herself from leaping to her feet, ordering him out of the flat. How could he sit beside her so calmly when exposure and disgrace loomed so close? How dared he risk her and Stuart when he knew what they'd already suffered? The thought of his selfishness nearly choked her but still she tried to control herself; to remember how he had helped her.

'Well then.' She cleared her throat, tried to steady her voice. 'It seems as if it's been decided for us, doesn't it? I can't really believe that you'd be prepared to put Stuart at risk, Pat. Even if *we* were prepared to take the chance, we can't leave him out of it. I'm sorry. I hate this, I really do, but we've got to finish it.'

'I suppose I knew it all along, really.' He glanced at her and she saw that there were tears in his eyes. 'Selina always wins, one way or the other. Probably because she has no inhibitions. She'd already guessed about the weekend.'

Mary shivered. 'How do you know?'

He smiled grimly. 'She told me that she wanted to come with me to Oxford.' He laughed, almost amused. 'I suppose I'll have to go now, won't I?' He hesitated, a last gleam of hope touching his face. 'Unless . . . ?'

'No,' she said quickly. 'No, Pat. We must simply forget our weekend. I had no idea that she was so . . . well, still in love with you, you see. I'd imagined, from what you said, that she didn't care.'

'Oh, she doesn't.' He stood up. 'Selina doesn't love me. She owns me and that's rather different. If she loved me it might all be more bearable.'

She wanted to go to him, to hold him tightly and banish the empty look from his eyes, but she willed herself to remain seated. It was kinder to make the blow swift.

'Thanks,' she said. 'I am really, truly grateful for . . . everything. It's been . . . good.'

'Yes.' He spoke on a deep breath, as if he were bringing a meeting to a conclusion, looking round him, checking that nothing was forgotten. 'Well, I'll be off then. See you in school.'

The door closed behind him. She sat, clutching her mug, tears trickling down her face, feeling mean and cheap. His dignity touched her as no pleading could have done and she was suddenly aware of all that she'd lost.

'You're a selfish cow,' she whispered. 'But what else could I have done? Shit!'

She got to her feet and went into Stuart's room, staring down at him, biting her lips, holding his hand in hers.

Chapter Thirteen

Maudie drove into the car park, switched off the engine and glanced round at Polonius. He was so large that it had been necessary to drop the back seat so as to give him enough room in the small Metro. She'd managed to find an expandable guard to wedge behind the front seats, to prevent him from panting down her neck, but he leaned on it so weightily that she was in continual fear lest it should collapse.

'You shall have a walk on the way home,' she promised, ignoring his pleading expression. 'You must wait patiently. You've got your bone and some water. Now be a good boy.'

He flattened his ears dejectedly as she wound down the back windows an inch or two, reached for her bag and then locked the door.

'Shan't be long,' she said encouragingly, feeling a traitor—she had every intention of having a cup of coffee in the Mill—and turned away, aware of his eyes fixed on her back. She knew that he'd rather be with her, even if it meant a longish wait in the car, than be left alone at home. After she'd finished shopping she'd drive up to Trendlebeare and give him a run. She wanted to see Max or Hugh at the Adventure Training School, to arrange some riding for Posy, and Polonius always enjoyed a good walk across the down.

Putting him out of her mind, Maudie tried to concentrate on her shopping. She loved Bovey, with the river running through the middle of the town and its busy, friendly atmosphere. The old moorland town had a sturdy, independent air and she felt an odd combination of privilege and contentment as she crossed the bridge, her list in her hand. She needed some cheese from Mann's, the delicatessen—some Sharpham would be rather pleasant—and a couple of lamb chops from David Pedrick. She must give David her order for Christmas now that she knew that Posy would definitely be with her. Perhaps goose as a change from turkey? Then, on to the bookshop, and a chat with Nick or Lindsey about an out-of-print book she hoped they might be able to trace for her.

It was nearly an hour later before she arrived back at the car. She'd met an old friend in the Mill and it had been very pleasant to sit by the window, watching the water racing by, gossiping with Jean as they drank their coffee. Refreshed by the coffee and the warmth of friendship, Maudie settled into the driving seat and headed out of the town towards Haytor. Trendlebeare Down was recovering from the fire which had burned across its slopes two years before but charred trees still stood, bleak and twisted memorials to the flames, whilst new pale, tufty grass grew amongst gorse and heather. She parked the car on the road below Black Hill and let Polonius out. He dashed away, bounding amongst the rocks, nose to ground, whilst she followed more slowly, looking away to the south towards Teignmouth, watching golden showers of sunshine slanting through the clouds, glinting on the grey waters of the estuary. Her thoughts drifted along at various levels: anxiety for Posy; the situation at Moorgate; Christmas; the beauty of the landscape . . .

Polonius's excited barking recalled her attention and she saw a horse and rider, picking their way down the hill. As they came closer she saw that it was Hugh Ankerton who, with Max Driver, ran the adventure school. She raised her hand to him, holding Polonius firmly with the other, and he came up to her waving cheerfully, controlling the horse who was dancing a little at the sight of Polonius.

'Hugh,' she said, 'how good to see you. I shall be along in a minute for a chat.'

'That's nice.' He smiled down at her. 'We haven't seen you for a bit. New friend?'

'He's Posy's.' Maudie stroked Polonius's head. 'She rescued him last summer. Her mother couldn't cope with him when Posy went back to college . . .'

'And you were selected from a host of applicants,' he finished for her, grinning. 'He's enormous.'

'He's *quite* good,' she said cautiously, whilst Polonius, tongue lolling vacuously, panted winningly. 'Don't be taken in by his expression of gentle charm. He's frightened the milkman into fits and made an attempt on the postman's life, as well as trying to supplement his dinner with any passing pets who happen to be out walking with their owners.'

'Poor old boy,' said Hugh, chuckling. 'She's just trying to blacken your character, isn't she?'

Polonius's ears dipped and his tail thumped. His wrinkled face bore the resigned expression of one who is constantly and unfairly maligned and Maudie shook her head.

'He lies in wait for unsuspecting visitors,' she said severely, 'and then rushes out at them, barking furiously. The man who delivers my logs had to be revived with brandy and he's no weakling, I assure you.'

'Well, why shouldn't he have some fun?' Hugh gathered up the reins. 'I'll tell Pippa to get some lunch on the go. What a pity Rowley's at school, he'd have loved him. What's his name?'

'Polonius. No, don't ask me. I have no idea. And I wouldn't dream of bothering Pippa with lunch.'

'It's not a problem.' Hugh was already cantering away, calling back over his shoulder, 'It'll only be soup or a sandwich. See you.'

Polonius watched him go regretfully. He knew an ally when he saw one.

'Don't worry,' said Maudie, reading his expression correctly. 'You'll be seeing him again in a minute. Hugh's an even bigger mug than I am, so you'll be on velvet as long as you don't try any tricks on Max or old Mutt.'

As they started back towards the car, Maudie was remembering her first visit to the school with Hector. How he'd loved riding out over the moor! The little group at Trendlebeare had made him very welcome: Max, Hugh and Pippa, not to mention the dog, Mutt. Slowly, Maudie had learned about them all through Hector's conversation. The adventure school had been Max's dream. Resigned from the Royal Marines, with a broken marriage behind him, he'd taken Hugh on to run the school with him. Apparently, Pippa had joined later, as cook, matron and general factotum. She had a small son, Rowley, and they too were the casualties of a broken marriage. By the time Maudie met them, Pippa and Max were married and Rowley was a cheerful six-year-old, prone to getting himself—and Mutt—into scrapes.

'It's a fascinating setup,' Hector had told her. 'Poor Pippa had a terrible time with her husband, it seems, and Hugh had some affair with a girl who killed herself. One of the stable blocks is dedicated to her.'

'They all seem jolly enough,' Maudie had answered, surprised. 'I didn't realise that Max wasn't Rowley's father.'

'He's very good with him, and with Hugh too. He's a good lad, is Max, and his old mum is a real tonic, I can tell you.'

Over the years she'd come to know them all very well, taking Posy—who loved to go riding with Hugh—to Trendlebeare whenever she came to visit and, although Maudie did not ride, she'd continued to keep the friendship alive. As she and Polonius approached the car, she was wondering about the dead girl and if she were the reason why Hugh had never married. He was such a nice man—and a very good-looking one. She found herself thinking about Posy again, but shook her head. Hugh must be in his mid-thirties; much too old for Posy. Anyway, they'd been riding together for years . . .

'No matchmaking,' she told herself sternly, opening the door to allow Polonius to jump in. 'No interfering. On the other hand . . .'

Polonius turned himself round and licked her face enthusiastically, causing her to jump back, hitting her head on the still open door. Cursing eloquently she slammed the door, wiping her face with her handkerchief, romantic notions quite forgotten.

Posy finished wrapping the last present and sat staring at the festive-looking pile. Confused and miserable she wound her arms about herself, bracing herself for the next encounter with her father. She hadn't imagined how difficult it would be to look at him. All easy familiarity had fled and she still feared that her knowledge might show in her face. She tried to convince herself that it wouldn't matter, now, if it did. She was aware that he knew she'd been told yet she had a horror of his being hurt by any expression which reflected the beastly muddle in her mind. At times she loathed him, imagining him with the other woman, betraying his family and being undignified.

Posy dropped her head on her knees. Oddly, this was really the worst thing—the thing about being undignified. Even when Mum was putting him down, being sarcastic, he'd stayed somehow outside it all. Oh, there had been times when she'd longed for him to stand up to Mum, to shout back, but, at the same time, it was his kind of dignified refusal to descend to that level which she'd grown to admire. They'd had lots of fun times on their own together, without Mum or the boys, and he'd always stood up for her when it came to Maudie. She'd never cared about him being quiet and dull, which is what Mum called him, because he'd always been there, solid and unchanging, and she'd liked that feeling. Now it was different. Now there was someone else that he cared about. Someone that he was being *silly* about. It was simply terrible; imagining him being silly. He was too old to be falling in love and behaving in that awful way. Like old people dancing to the Beatles, wearing terrible clothes and waving their hands over their heads, pretending that they were still like they'd been thirty years before. It made her feel hot and uncomfortable and ashamed for them. Jude always laughed at her when she was like this and told her that she was intolerant. Perhaps she was but, especially now, she couldn't seem to help herself. Ever since she'd been home she'd tried to avoid her father and she longed to be away, off to Devon and Maudie. What was even worse was that she could see that Mum was quite enjoying the situation, which was really bizarre.

Posy sat up straight, listening, as she heard footsteps coming slowly up the stairs. They paused on the landing and she willed them past her door, into his study. The light tap brought her to her feet, and by the time he'd opened the door she'd leaped from the bed and was standing by the window.

'Hi.' He smiled at her but his eyes were wary. 'I was wondering if you needed a lift to Paddington?'

'Oh.' It was almost a gasp of fright before she controlled herself. 'Well.' She stared about her, as though the walls and furniture might supply her with the answer. 'Won't that be a bit of a drag? I mean—I can manage . . .'

He gave a ghost of a chuckle. 'I don't doubt that for a moment but since I can't imagine you going away without enough luggage for a year or two I thought it might help a bit.'

'Well, thanks.' How could she refuse? It was Christmas and for the first time in her life they wouldn't be opening their presents together. Tears gathered behind her eyes and she hastily seized her battered travelling grip, swinging it on to the bed. 'I haven't done too badly this time, actually, but I've got to put some presents in yet. Have you seen what I've got for Polonius . . . ?'

'Posy.' His voice was quite gentle. 'I know that Mum's told you about Mary and I'm sorry. It must have been a terrible shock. I wish she'd left it to me. It's not quite how it might have sounded.'

She gaped at him, hot with distaste and a terrible pity, the rubber toy hanging from her hands.

'I don't want to talk about it.'

'Oh, Posy—'

'No.'

She was a small girl again, feet planted firmly, head lowered, eyes narrowed warningly. Patrick's heart contracted with love. So had he seen her on countless occasions in the past; protecting a beloved possession from her brothers' teasing; defending herself against Selina's gibes about Maudie. The ridiculous toy, clutched in her hands, made the scene more poignant. He longed to hug her, to remove the pain, but, for the first time in their lives, it was he who was inflicting it.

'It doesn't change anything,' he said urgently. 'Try to understand that. *You* have new friends, now, new interests, new allegiances. We have to make ourselves big enough to contain them all. Nothing and nobody changes how I feel about you.'

'I don't want to talk about it.'

He sensed the panic behind the stubborn reiteration and took a deep breath.

'OK,' he said lightly. 'Fair enough. Don't worry. I won't start again in the car so you can have your lift quite safely. We ought to be away by half-past eleven to be on the safe side.'

She waited until the door closed behind him and then she began to pack, jamming things into the bag.

'It's not true, anyway,' she muttered, justifying herself. 'It *does* change things. He didn't care about me not being home for Christmas.'

She flung the toy in, on top of everything else, and sat down, wrenching her hands through her hair, reminding herself that the decision to stay with Maudie had been made before she'd known about his affair. How childish it was to announce that you'd be away and then be upset when nobody minded! For a brief moment she allowed herself to imagine the bleakness of his Christmas. She was quite certain that the boys would be told—if they hadn't been already—and she could already sense his feeling of isolation. Deliberately she hardened her heart. He shouldn't have started messing about, behaving as if he were twenty instead of fifty. She zipped up the grip and flung her long black coat—discovered in a charity shop in Winchester—on top of it. Gathering up the pile of presents she went downstairs to put them under the Christmas tree. The house was decorated, ready for the boys' arrival, but she was glad to be going to Maudie: to Maudie and Polonius.

Driving back from the station through the busy streets, Patrick wondered why he hadn't told Posy, why he hadn't just said it, despite her refusal to be involved in conversation.

'It's over.' He could have made it clear, even if she hadn't wanted to discuss it. 'It's finished.' At least the knowledge that the affair had come to an end might have comforted her. Yet he'd been unable to say the words and it was clear that Selina had not done so either. He'd rather hoped that Selina might have put Posy's mind at rest. After all, she'd told her in the first place. If Selina had held her tongue Posy would have known nothing about it. How shaming it had been, admitting that it was over, that Mary had been prepared to let him go rather than risk losing her job and her home. How amused Selina had been, milking the scene for every drop of humiliation, revelling in his discomfiture.

'So she's not going to put up a fight for you?' She'd pretended to sympathise. 'What a shame. And you were prepared to risk your little all for her. Poor old Patrick. So embarrassing to throw down the gauntlet and have people treading it into the mud without a backward glance, isn't it? At least I won't have to tell Susan that you're behaving like a teenager. Well, that's a relief, anyway. You're not much of a man, Patrick, but I still have some pride left. So what about our weekend in Oxford?'

'I'm not going to Oxford. I never was, as you well know, and I don't intend to change my mind at this late date.'

She'd shrugged. 'Oh, well. I can't say I'm disappointed. Dreary place, if you ask me. Anyway, we must save our pennies for Moorgate. Don't look so surprised. Had you forgotten about Moorgate? Oh dear. Well, I haven't. It's been such a comfort to me, whilst you've been off with your little tart, thinking about happier times. I'm still certain that we could buy it. I'm not so sure, now, that we want to live there permanently but I think it would be a great comfort to know it was there—if you know what I mean?'

He'd gone away, then, leaving her to her triumph—and to her fantasies. The thought of Mary was a constant ache in his heart and the realisation that Selina intended to pursue her romantic desire to possess Moorgate filled him with despair. He'd awaited Posy's arrival with trepidation and had seen immediately how it was to be. Selina was certainly right about Posy's reaction: she despised him. Yet he had not been able to say the words which might have healed the breach.

'It's over.' 'It's finished.'

It had been bad enough, seeing Mary at school, watching her with the children in the playground, working in the classroom. It was a hundred times worse knowing that he would not see her at all for three long weeks. To protect Mary he'd told Selina that the affair was over but at the bottom of his heart lay the hope that somehow the miracle might happen, that Mary might relent. Each time the post arrived or the telephone rang, each time he saw her, he hoped that his misery would be relieved. He imagined scenes in which she told him that she'd changed her mind, that she couldn't manage without him, that somehow they'd survive—and each time she told him that she loved him. As far as he was concerned it wasn't over. He needed her; he simply couldn't stop loving her at will.

As Patrick drove home he knew why he'd been unable to say the words to Posy: they simply wouldn't have been true.

Chapter Fourteen

Seated either side of the fire, Polonius stretched between them on the rug, Maudie and Posy seemed utterly absorbed in their separate occupations: Maudie knitting, Posy reading. They'd agreed that there was nothing worth watching on the television and Maudie had suggested that she might listen to the tape which Posy had bought her for Christmas. It was at least the fourth or fifth time she'd played it but she was so clearly delighted with the recording by Lionel Hampton that Posy was only too pleased to agree. Anyway, she was rather enjoying it, too. It was really good to be here with Maudie, listening to the jazz, her feet resting on Polonius's back. Although it was very quiet, and she missed her friends, she knew that it had been right to spend Christmas here. Maudie's pleasure in her company was very real although she was never extravagant with her emotions. Glancing covertly at her, Posy tried to analyse exactly what it was about Maudie which made her such a good companion. There she sat, glasses slipping down her nose, her short grey hair brushed back from her face, frowning as she counted her stitches. She was wearing a cherry-red, lambswool roll-neck jersey, under a padded moleskin waist-coat, and her long legs were encased in dark green cords. On her feet were the sheepskin-lined boot-socks which were also Posy's present.

The thing which had always drawn her to Maudie, Posy decided, was that she didn't fuss. There were no emotional confrontations, no hidden agendas. There was a detachment which gave you room to breathe—yet she was not indifferent. The point was that she didn't seek to possess you whilst offering her love. Several years ago, Posy had tried to explain this concept to her mother, without success.

'It's easy for Maudie,' had been the answer. 'She's not related to you. She's not your real grandmother. You wait until you have children of your own and then you'll understand.'

This continual inference that Posy was ungrateful, disloyal, an unnatural daughter, was wearing—and hurtful. She'd never been able to see why she couldn't be allowed to love both her mother and her grandmother; couldn't understand why there had to be a choice.

'Of course you can't,' her mother had retorted. 'You've never made the least effort to understand my feelings. You choose to ally yourself with someone who's made my life miserable and expect me to be delighted about it. How Maudie must be laughing!'

'She doesn't laugh,' the young Posy had protested. 'We don't talk about you at all.'

This assurance, apparently, had not been as comforting as she'd hoped and the difficulty remained unresolved. Her father was much more reasonable and had done as much as he could to ease the situation.

Posy dug her toes into Polonius's back in an attempt to relieve her feelings, remembering the telephone conversation with her father on Christmas Day. He'd been cheerful, thanking her for his present, asking after Maudie. She'd managed to talk to him almost as if nothing had happened—it was easier at a distance—and then the boys had taken their turn. Her mother, it seemed, was too busy with the lunch to come to the telephone but sent her love, and Posy had felt irritated and hurt that she couldn't be bothered to leave the turkey for five minutes to wish her a happy Christmas. The call had unsettled her, reminding her of past Christmases, making her feel guilty. Eventually, after several glasses of wine, she'd blurted it all out to Maudie and then burst into silly, pathetic weeping. Maudie's reaction had been so unexpected, however, that she'd been brought up short, sniffling into a tissue, wide-eyed with surprise.

'Good grief!' she'd said, bottle poised above her glass. 'You amaze me. Patrick, of all people. I'd never have believed he had the gumption.'

Despite her shock, another emotion had penetrated Posy's confusion. For a brief moment she'd seen the situation through Maudie's eyes; seen her father as a man, independent of his family. For those few seconds she'd been able to think of him, not as a father, not as a husband, but as a stranger, and a new emotion had stirred deep down inside her. She'd tried to hold on to it but it had eluded her; the moment had passed, but she'd been subtly changed by it. She'd realised that Maudie expected her to approach it as another adult might and she'd felt flattered but at the same time affronted. After all, it was her father they were discussing. Nevertheless Maudie's reaction had comforted her. It reflected Maudie herself: detached but human. Yet surely she couldn't approve? She'd almost immediately apologised.

'Sorry,' she'd said. 'You took me by surprise. It sounds so un-Patrick-like. Are you absolutely certain?'

Posy had answered that she was quite certain but that she didn't really want to talk about it. This wasn't quite true but she couldn't bear to discuss her feelings, even with Maudie, yet she'd felt rather deflated when Maudie had taken her at her word.

'I can understand that,' she'd said. 'It takes a bit of getting used to, I imagine. Just don't get things out of proportion.'

Easier said than done. It had seemed all wrong then, on Christmas Day, after eating the goose and opening the presents, to spoil the festive atmosphere. Now, she wished that she'd had the courage to talk it through, describe her feelings, but it was difficult to raise the subject again. How was it to be done?

'By the way, you know what I was saying about Dad having an affair . . . ?' Or, 'So you don't think that being unfaithful is all that bad, then?' No, she simply couldn't just mention it as casually as though she were asking what they would be eating for supper. Perhaps an opportunity might arise quite naturally and she'd be able to take advantage of it. Posy settled back in her chair and tried to concentrate on her book.

Apparently absorbed in her knitting, Maudie was aware of Posy's pre-occupation with things other than her book. She'd been furious with herself for her spontaneous reaction to Posy's disclosure, yet instinctively she'd held back from sympathising. She didn't quite know why—after all, it must have been a frightful shock for the poor child—nevertheless she'd resisted the urge to become affected by Posy's evident distaste. Maudie didn't approve of adultery but there were sometimes extenuating circumstances. She considered it either heroic or just plain stupid to remain married to Selina for thirty years and had a sneaking sympathy for Patrick's outburst. At the same time she was amazed by it. She'd respected Posy's request, and they hadn't discussed it since, but she'd given it a great deal of thought.

Rooting about for another ball of wool, she was remembering Hector's reaction to Patrick's request for Selina's hand. Naturally, he'd known about the younger man's attachment to Selina and her reciprocal affection but he'd been unhappy about agreeing to an engagement.

'Nice enough fellow,' he'd admitted privately to Maudie, 'but there doesn't seem much *to* him, if you see what I mean. Still, Selina seems very fond of him . . .'

Maudie had remained silent, resisting the urge to support Patrick's suit. The thought of a married Selina, a Selina who lived somewhere else, a Selina who would no longer be able to ruin the peace by moods and sulks, was too wonderful to contemplate. Guessing that enthusiasm on her part might make Hector suspicious she'd held her tongue. To Daphne, however, she'd been much more forthcoming.

'Oh, my dear,' she'd replied at once, 'I couldn't agree more. Much better all round if Hector gives his blessing cheerfully. Selina is quite determined to have her way so he might as well give in gracefully. Of course, Hilda would have had a fit.'

'Would she?' Maudie had been intrigued. 'But Patrick's so . . . so spotless. He's so utterly *nice*. Naturally, he's rather cool to me but that's because he's been brainwashed by Selina and regards me as the wicked stepmother. Even so, he can't help being very polite, which irritates Selina no end. She longs for him to be devastatingly rude to me but the poor boy simply cannot overcome his inherent niceness. From what you've told me about her I should have thought that Hilda would have loved him. His manners are so good.'

'She would have approved of his being a well-brought-up young man but it wouldn't have been quite enough. Where her daughters were concerned she was very fussy. "He doesn't quite suit." It was such a favourite expression of hers. She would have wanted a stronger character for Selina and she'd have probably been right. Once the first flush passes I fear that she'll walk all over him.'

'I must admit that you have a point.' Maudie had shrugged. 'Every time he takes his jacket off I expect to see the word "Welcome" printed on his chest. Still, there's nothing I can do about it. She certainly wouldn't listen to me. Hector must do what he thinks best.'

'What does he say about it?'

'Much what you've said Hilda would say. But he hates being cast in the role of unsympathetic father and Selina will soon win him over. I have to say that Patrick shows up very well when Hector's hectoring and doing the heavy father act. He stands up to him very bravely and looks quite zealous on occasions.'

Daphne had chuckled. 'Young Lochinvar has come out of the West. Yes, Patrick's exactly the sort who needs a cause, isn't he?'

Now, as Maudie attached the new ball of wool to her knitting an idea occurred to her.

'I do begin to wonder,' she said thoughtfully, 'whether your father's so-called affair isn't little more than helping some damsel in distress. However, we won't talk about it if you'd rather not . . .' She hesitated, fearing that she was speaking out of turn, but Posy looked up from her book almost eagerly so she decided to continue a little further. 'He's a very chivalrous man, you know, and a very kind one. It's possible that things might have got rather out of hand but perhaps we shouldn't be too hard on him. Your mother has many excellent qualities but she's probably a bit short on the kind of affection that your father needs. Poor old Patrick. It would be just his luck to be caught out in what is probably little more than an act of compassion.'

She paused again but this time Posy seemed very ready to talk. 'Mum did say that she wasn't a dolly bird, this . . . Mary.' It was still oddly difficult to use her name. 'She said she was a boring nonentity with a crippled child.'

Maudie swallowed down a sigh of relief. So her intuition was probably sound. 'Well then. It's just possible that they've got a bit tangled up emotionally. It can happen very easily, you know. Oh, I can well imagine that it horrifies you to think of your father as a man with ordinary needs but you must try to be adult about it, Posy. I'm not condoning it but a small allowance of compassion might not come amiss.'

'It's just,' Posy cast her book aside and drew up her knees, 'like, you know, it's not as if he's young or anything. It makes him look pathetic.'

'Lack of dignity in the old is so shocking to the young,' murmured Maudie. 'It's *their* prerogative to be shocking or outrageous or even simply sexy. We've all felt it. That's why your mother hates me, of course.'

Posy stared at her. 'Hates you?'

Maudie raised her eyebrows. 'Don't pretend that it comes as a surprise.'

'No, well, perhaps "hates" is a bit extreme but I just meant that I can't see the relevance.'

'Can't you? Well, think about it. Selina was nearly thirteen when her father married me. Her mother was not long dead and she was obliged to face several uncomfortable facts. First of all, she felt a sense of betrayal, which is probably exactly how you are feeling now. It was a shock to learn that Hector was not satisfied with being merely a father, that he needed other company and stimulation. Secondly, she had to confront his sexuality. He was a little younger than Patrick, not much, but as far as Selina was concerned he was old. To have to think about him like that in conjunction with me was appalling for her. Naturally, she didn't want to have to blame him so I became the scapegoat. I didn't mind to begin with because I thought she'd grow out of it but she never did. She waged a continuous, exhausting war and I became thoroughly tired of it. Poor Hector was caught in the crossfire.'

'I'd never seen it like that,' said Posy slowly. 'It was like she had an obsession about you and I could never see why.'

'Well, now you can understand it. Supposing Patrick brought—what did you call her, Mary, was it?—Mary then. Suppose he brought her home. How would you feel?'

'But Mum's not dead,' protested Posy. 'Grandfather wasn't committing adultery.'

'That's what I kept saying,' sighed Maudie. 'But it made no difference to Selina. The difficulty was that she felt I had supplanted her, as well as her mother. She was jealous. She didn't feel her father could love all of us and she was afraid.' She looked at Posy's downcast face. 'Sound familiar?'

'I do feel like that, I suppose,' she admitted at last. 'I feel hurt. As if he's risking his family for this woman which means he must love her more than he does us.'

Maudie was silent for a moment, feeling herself on delicate ground. She had already risked a great deal. She had no wish to lose Posy's love or respect but nor did she wish to watch the child suffer.

'Try to see it his way, just for a moment,' she said gently. 'Patrick adores you, you know he does, but you're grown up now. You've very nearly left home, you're making new friends and soon you'll be gone. The boys have already flown the nest. Without wishing to condemn your mother I think you'd agree that she's not a very comfortable person to live with. This Mary probably makes him laugh, makes him feel good. He's probably been able to help her in some way and he feels valued, important. Selina isn't too bothered about making people feel special. The danger is to think that he's weak in needing any kind of affection outside his home. Well, perhaps that is so, but we have to remember that he's human. It's fine being lofty and high-minded, condemning people who need affection, kindness, attention, especially if the high-minded one is surrounded by friends and his life is interesting and fun. It's easy to judge someone who isn't coping, who is lonely, ignored, taken for granted, and who is suddenly offered love. It's possible, you know, to feel invisible. I suspect that your father has probably been feeling invisible for quite a while and it's a pretty heady experience to be noticed, admired even. You may think that Patrick's well past his sell-by date but I promise you he's still an attractive man. And he's a very kind one. I'm not condoning adultery, Posy, but let's not be too harsh on him. Selina will sort it out, I have no doubt of that. As to his loving Mary more than he loves you, I think you'll find that Patrick is capable of a great deal of love. It isn't on ration, you know.'

'I know,' Posy mumbled, 'but it's like I don't know him any more. He's become a stranger.'

'It's always difficult seeing people we know really well in a different light,' mused Maudie. 'It's like seeing a social acquaintance at her office or a workmate in the bosom of his family. We have all these complex sides and we respond to each one differently. This is what makes growing up so painful. We have to learn to adapt, to be generous. I'm afraid I haven't been generous with Selina. I tried for a while but when she refused to make any effort to meet me halfway I gave up on it. Between us we made Hector's life hell. It's more difficult for you because you stand between Selina and Patrick. If you can walk a fine line between them it will be a very adult thing to do. You're older than Selina was when I married her father so there's a very good chance that, once you've recovered from the shock, you'll be able to deal with it.'

'I don't *want* to take sides,' cried Posy, dragging back her hair, 'but it's not that simple. I can understand that Mum's asked for it, in a way, but I can't just say, "Oh, great, Dad. Cool. I think it's fab." I know what you're saying sounds right but I can't just go along with it.'

'I'm not suggesting that it's simple or that you go along with it. I'm simply asking that you don't condemn and reject him out of hand. You might say that by not condemning it you are, in fact, tacitly approving it, but that is very black and white. There are so many shades of grey. Try to detach yourself emotionally. Try to see that it needn't be your problem, that it needn't affect you. Remain affectionate and friendly to them both.'

Posy shook her head. 'It's impossible,' she said wretchedly. 'It's this feeling that I don't know Dad any more. I can understand about the invisible bit. He was just there, in the background. But he made me feel safe and now I can't feel that any longer. I can't just pretend nothing has happened, Maudie. I can't!'

'Of course not,' agreed Maudie. 'That would be too much to ask after such a shock. I was just suggesting that you might try to think about your father less harshly. Sorry, Posy. I shouldn't interfere. Talking about things isn't always helpful. I just suddenly remembered when I first met Patrick. Selina was about your age and your grandfather was concerned that Patrick might not be tough enough to look after her.'

'What was he like when he was young?' Posy was interested, despite her own unhappiness.

'He was a nice-looking young man with very good manners. We all liked him. He overcame your grandfather's anxieties by sheer will and determination. You see, he felt that he was rescuing your mother from her wicked stepmother and her unfeeling father and he was absolutely determined that he would win her. That's what I meant about him being chivalrous. Patrick has that streak in him and this young woman has probably given him a cause to fight for again. Perhaps it is to do with her crippled child, or he might have found her some work or accommodation, and she's been grateful. Gratitude can be so dangerous if the recipient is a bit lonely.'

'You make him sound really sad,' said Posy irritably. 'I don't want to think about him like that.'

'That's because you don't want to think about him as a person in his own right. You want to think about him as some nice, solid, dependable shadowy figure who is always there when you need him but can be put on hold when you don't. That's very nice for you but where does it leave Patrick?'

'He's my *father*,' cried Posy. 'That's what being a parent is all about. I'd want to be there for *my* children.'

'Of course you would,' said Maudie remorsefully. 'That's always been my problem, you see. I've never been a parent so I see it from the other side. It seems to me that being a parent can preclude you from being any-thing else—which is a bit unfortunate. Or perhaps it's simply that, not being a parent, I can't fully enter into that particular obsession which often goes with it. Either way I shouldn't have interfered. Shall I make a pot of tea? And perhaps a piece of Christmas cake?'

In the kitchen she stood watching the kettle, cursing quietly to herself. It was too much to expect the child to be able to take such a detached view: too much and probably quite wrong. Maudie smiled wryly. After all, disliking Selina as she did, it was hardly likely that her own point of view would be totally unbiased and she'd had no business to attempt to exonerate Patrick. The kettle boiled and she began to make tea.

Staring at the fire, Posy was brooding. It was odd to imagine her mother feeling about Maudie as she, Posy, was now thinking about Mary; odd and unsettling. Upsetting, too, to believe that her father had needed to look outside the family circle for affection. The tape finished playing and clicked into silence; Polonius yawned, stretched mightily and sat up. When Maudie came in with the tray Posy was putting logs on the fire, teasing Polonius with his new toy. She smiled rather shyly at Maudie and hurried to clear a space on the table for the tray. As she put some books away, the envelope from the Scotch House was dislodged from between the pages and the woollen squares drifted to the floor. Posy bent to gather them up.

'Aha,' she said, attempting her usual manner. 'Goodies from the Scotch House, I see. Are you ordering a new skirt?'

'I'm thinking of it,' answered Maudie cheerfully, grateful for a complete change of subject, remembering that it must be at least six weeks since the samples had arrived, along with Posy's card begging her to give Polonius a home, and the letter from Ned Cruikshank about Moorgate. 'Do you know I'd quite forgotten about them. They came ages ago. Let's have a look at them and you can give me some advice.'

Part Two

Chapter Fifteen

Passing through the hall of the narrow terraced Georgian house in Jericho, Melissa bent to pick up the envelopes which lay scattered on the doormat. She wore an ankle-length bouclé wool cardigan, over narrow jeans and a long tunic, and her feet were tucked into soft leather bootees. The effect was medieval, an image accentuated by the short, curly, fox-red hair, bound back from her thin, pointed face with a plaited silk scarf. She passed down the hall into the kitchen where her brother and his small son, Luke, were eating breakfast.

'Bank statement,' she said, flourishing the letters in front of his eyes. 'House details. And someone telling you that you've won six hundred thousand pounds.'

Mike Clayton continued to spoon the soggy, milky mess into Luke's mouth, clearly unmoved by the treats in store for him, and Melissa sat down at the end of the table, poured herself some orange juice from the jug and twiddled her fingers at her nephew. He beamed gummily at her, crowing loudly, so that the cereal ran down his chin. Patiently Mike spooned it back into Luke's mouth and took a quick swallow from his own mug of black coffee.

'You might as well open it,' he said indifferently. 'You can tell me how much more I have to order before I can really win anything and then only if I send back the winning number. I refuse to buy anything I don't want and if it says "If not ordering see the rules on the back of the page" you can bin it. I'm convinced that they don't bother to look at anything that isn't in the official envelope.'

'I fear that you're right.' Melissa was busy opening the bulky communication with the butter knife. 'Ah, here we have it. "Your name was among more than one million names scanned and identified by our IBM computer," blah, blah, blah. Oh, this is it. "If you are not ordering this time do not use the pre-paid envelope and see the rules on the back of the official letter." '

'Chuck it,' advised Mike. 'I refuse to be blackmailed.' He held a feeder to Luke's mouth, tilting it gently as Luke gulped back his milk. 'I have a feeling that we're not the get-rich-quick kind.'

'You're not doing too badly,' said Melissa, pushing the sheets of offers and bargains back into the envelope. 'The book's doing well and you've got some good ideas for the new one. Just think yourself lucky that you managed the transition from playwright to novelist so painlessly.'

There was an uneasy silence, broken only by the sound of Luke's gulping. Melissa reached for the house details, aware of her tactlessness, whilst Mike, frowning thoughtfully, watched Luke. He'd met Luke's mother during the staging of his second play and, passionately in love with her, had re-written her part with loving, brilliant fervour. She'd received such rave notices once it moved to the West End that hundreds of offers for work had rolled in and, eventually, even Hollywood had taken an interest in her. It continued to be a bitter reminder to Mike that, had he been a little less clever, a little less besotted, his wife might still be here with him, looking after her child, instead of abandoning them both for a glittering career in America. He'd attempted a novel whilst looking after Luke, when Camilla had first begun filming in the States, and was delighted and surprised by its reception from one of the major publishing houses. At the same time that he'd learned that Camilla would not be coming back, he'd been offered a two-book contract and was relieved that the very respectable advance enabled him to concentrate on his second novel. He was glad to be done with the stage, and the permanent reminders of Camilla, but he had by no means recovered from his wife's defection.

Mike wiped the milky bubbles from Luke's chin and glanced at his sister. She was absorbed with whatever it was she was reading and when she looked up at him her face wore a rapt expression.

'Oh, Mike,' she said. 'This house. It sounds simply perfect. We must buy it. You want to be in the country so as to be able to write in peace and quiet, don't you? Well, this is it. Just look at the photographs.'

He reached for them, studying the picture of the old farmhouse, sturdy and strong; looking at the pictures of the sitting room and study with their beamed ceilings and huge, open fireplaces.

'But it's on the edge of Bodmin Moor,' he said, surprised, reading the details. 'Why on earth have they sent me something so far afield?'

'They've got a branch in Truro,' said Melissa. 'And what's wrong with Cornwall? The country is the country.'

'Well, not quite.' Mike began to read the rest of the details. 'It's a hell of a long way from London for a start.'

'Oh, London.' Melissa made a face. 'Does that matter so much any more? Writing novels isn't quite the same as writing plays, is it? You can write novels anywhere. And think how wonderful for Luke.'

He looked at her, hating to pour cold water on her excitement, longing to be able to give her some happiness.

'Perhaps we'll go down and look at it,' he said cautiously. 'A bit later on in the spring. Make a little holiday of it . . .'

Melissa had taken the details from him and was studying the photograph again; her face was dreamy and her green eyes were cloudy with visions.

'Isn't it odd?' she said. 'I feel as if I know this place. Isn't that strange? Oh, Mike, I feel I want to see it. I've been thinking of going away for a little while, haven't I? Just a few days or, perhaps, a week. I think I'll go to Cornwall.'

'Look,' he said anxiously. 'It's a long way to drive, Lissy. Don't be silly about this. We'll all go if you really want to.'

'No,' she said quickly. 'No, Mike, honestly. It would be crazy to cart Luke down to Cornwall in February, I quite see that. Only . . . only I just feel I must do this. Please.'

He looked away from her, longing to agree, racked with worry.

'I'm OK at the moment,' she said gently. 'Robin said it could be six months, didn't he? Well then. A week or two out of six months. It would be such heaven, Mike.'

He swallowed hard, not wanting to be selfish, sensing her need. Well, it was her life, what was left of it, and they couldn't spend every minute of it together.

'If you're sensible,' he said. 'And don't overdo things.'

'I won't,' she said joyfully. 'How wonderful to have something to plan. A point for going on a jolly. We'll find somewhere for me to stay and I'll go and look at . . .' she peered down at the particulars ' . . . at Moorgate. What a fantastic name. The gate to the moor.' She smiled at him. 'Don't worry, Mike. I'll be very good. I promise.'

Walking in the woods with Polonius, Maudie was thinking about Daphne. Ever since Christmas life had seemed rather dull and she found herself possessed by a poignant longing for the past. No matter how firmly she told herself that this was foolish, the feeling persisted. She wondered if it were the decision to sell Moorgate which had triggered these unsettled sensations: coming to terms with Hector's death; brooding over their life together, remembering the resentments and irritations caused by Selina's rejection. More recently there was the news of Patrick's infidelity and Posy's reaction to it. It was irrational to feel sympathy for Posy when, in the past, she'd expected Selina to cope bravely and positively with a similar situation.

'Perhaps I was too hard on her,' she murmured, pausing to watch a tiny goldcrest flitting restlessly amongst the branches of a small conifer, listening to his high-pitched, squeaky twittering song as he clung upside down, searching for insects. The sound of the roaring tumbling water was a disturbing, almost menacing presence, echoing through the quiet, windless woods. After a week of heavy rain the river raced between its banks, setting the overhanging branches to a restless dancing sway, drowning the reeds, swirling into crevices and tugging at strong, woody roots. A small party of mallards had taken refuge in a sandy pool, protected from the rushing, foaming torrent by a great tree trunk which had stuck fast, forming a calm oasis. A few of the ducks paddled, quacking foolishly, dabbling cheerfully, whilst others, perched on the log itself, roosted quietly, beaks tucked beneath folded wings. The sun, a pale lemon disc, leaked into a grey canopy of unbroken cloud, high above the bare, twiggy branches of the great trees which reached towards it.

Polonius appeared, crashing out of the undergrowth in pursuit of a squirrel, his high, ecstatic barks splintering the silence, dead leaves and earth churning beneath his paws. The squirrel raced for safety, darting up the smooth grey bole of a towering beech, turning to chatter insults at the animal now far below him. Polonius hurled himself impotently skywards whilst a woodpigeon, disturbed by the unexpected advent of the squirrel, clappered noisily away.

'Forget it,' advised Maudie. 'We all have our limitations and you might as well face facts. You'll never be able to fly. Come on.'

Polonius grumbled discontentedly but followed her away from the tree and presently picked up another scent. Maudie strolled after him, her hands thrust into the pockets of her warm padded jacket, her thoughts with Daphne. They'd spoken at Christmas, as usual, but, once Posy had gone, Maudie had telephoned Daphne again to tell her about Patrick.

'I simply cannot believe it,' Daphne had said firmly. 'Not Patrick. Selina will simply marmalise him.'

Maudie had laughed, really laughed, for the first time in several days.

'I said more or less the same thing,' she'd said, 'only out loud to Posy.'

'Ah.' Daphne had understood at once. 'That wasn't terribly tactful, love, was it?'

'I know,' Maudie had cried remorsefully. 'I could have bitten my tongue out but I simply couldn't help myself. It's been a bit grim, Daffers. Posy is seriously upset.'

'Mmm.' Daphne had been thinking it through and Maudie had felt the usual relief at sharing with this old friend who'd supported her through so many unhappy moments.

'It came to me,' she'd told her, 'that Posy is feeling about this woman, Mary, exactly as Selina felt about me all those years ago. I expected Selina to behave reasonably but now I'm wondering if I was very harsh with her.'

'But Hector was a widower.' Daphne had sounded surprised. 'Not quite the same, is it?'

'Well, no, but Posy seems to be reacting just like Selina did. She feels betrayed, as if her father is putting the family at risk for love of this Mary.'

'I can understand that,' Daphne had said thoughtfully. 'And, of course, he is. Hector would never have done that. He couldn't have known that Selina would react so violently and he always did his best to reassure her. Often at your expense, Maudie, I know, but that's because he expected you to understand.'

'I know.' Maudie had felt miserable again. 'But I didn't. Not always. I felt insecure, too. Poor Hector. If only I could get rid of these wretched doubts and resentments. It's selling Moorgate that has brought all this on.

I wish I could manage without selling it but I can't. And I wish I knew what happened to Hector's investments. It's like a wretched worm, gnawing at my peace of mind.'

There was a moment of silence before Daphne spoke again.

'Oh, Maudie,' she'd said sadly, 'I hate you to be like this. Look, I'm hoping to come over later on this year and then we'll have a proper talk. It's so frustrating trying to communicate properly at this distance.'

'Are you really? How amazing.' Maudie had been swamped with delight. 'Do you know I was thinking of flying out to see you all, once Moorgate was sold. It was going to be my treat. It occurred to me that although you've been over several times I'd never been to visit you. Of course, Hector wasn't up to it . . .'

'Well, now you can save your money,' Daphne had said, 'and get ready for us to have a good time together. I'll talk to Emily and make some plans. As for poor Posy, we'll simply have to hope that the affair blows over. Selina will never let him go.'

'That's what I thought. But I have to say it's made me do a bit of rethinking.'

'Well, don't let it get out of proportion,' Daphne had warned. 'And Maudie, never forget how much Hector loved you.'

'I know he did,' Maudie had answered wretchedly. 'Of course I do. It was just that he was so different at the end. And then there's the thing about his investments . . .'

'Put it right out of your mind for the moment. Concentrate on all those wonderful times you had with him. I knew Hector for most of his adult life and I never saw him as happy as he was with you. Believe it, Maudie, hold on to it. Don't let it be ruined. Hector wasn't himself at the end, you know that. You know what Alzheimer's does to people. As for the money, perhaps you just misunderstood what he actually showed you. Portfolios are very muddly things if you haven't the head for it and you've always admitted that you were never too interested. Think about the good times and make some plans for my visit. I long to see Polonius . . .'

Turning for home, shouting for Polonius, Maudie realised that she was hungry; hungry and much more cheerful. Posy, back at college, had telephoned to ask if she could come down for the weekend and had muttered, in passing, that things were a bit better at home—much to Maudie's relief—and there was Daphne's visit to look forward to. All she needed now was a buyer for Moorgate.

Enjoying a well-earned rest from shopping, relaxing in Peter Jones's coffee shop, Selina, too, was thinking about Moorgate. The bank had refused to agree to lend the balance required for the deposit and she was trying to bolster up the courage to speak to Maudie so as to ask her to give her special terms. She'd spent several days trying to overcome her reluctance. It wasn't simply that she knew Maudie utterly disapproved of her attempting to buy Moorgate; she also knew that Posy had told her grandmother about Patrick. She'd asked Posy outright and Posy had answered just as bluntly.

'Why shouldn't I?' she'd demanded. 'I was very upset about it. Why shouldn't I tell her?'

'Oh, don't imagine that I expect loyalty from you,' Selina had snapped. 'Naturally you'd go round washing our dirty linen in public.'

'I haven't told anyone else,' Posy had said, stung by her mother's accusation. 'You shouldn't have told me if you'd wanted it to be a secret. It isn't anyone's business but yours and Dad's, anyway. I wish you hadn't told me.'

'I expect you do.' Selina had shrugged. 'Anyway, it's all over. Your father has come to his senses.'

Posy's expression of overwhelming relief, the visible relaxing of her whole body, had almost shocked Selina. Assailed by an unfamiliar sense of guilt, she'd tried to make it up to Posy during the last week of her holiday and she'd been met, to her surprise, by a readiness to meet her halfway. Patrick, who seemed to be in a state of numbed indifference, was pleasantly polite to both of them and a kind of truce had descended upon the household. Only the question of Moorgate remained a subject of dissension.

Selina sipped her caffè latte thoughtfully. Now that Patrick had returned to the fold, she'd decided that to bury themselves in a remote farmhouse in Cornwall would be foolish. Nevertheless, she couldn't let Moorgate go. The idea of possession obsessed her. The old farmhouse should remain in the family and, somehow, she simply must find a way to achieve her desire. Meanwhile, at any moment, some other person might make an offer on it. There was really no time to waste. She'd rather counted on exploiting Patrick's sense of guilt—a ploy which had worked excellently in the past—but there was something about Patrick which made him oddly unapproachable at present. He refused to respond to emotional blackmail and, for the first time in their married life together, she felt slightly wary of him. Her cunningly phrased suggestions that the purchase of Moorgate would be an excellent expiation for his sins fell on stony ground and his cool, puzzled response made her nervous. At the same time, her determination to own Moorgate grew stronger. It was part of her history, full of happy memories; she owed it to her mother to preserve it if she could. Perhaps, after all, an approach to Maudie, subtle and well prepared, was worth a try.

Chapter Sixteen

Melissa drove carefully, watching for the turning off the A38. Mike had written the instructions on an A4 pad which lay on the passenger seat, and to which she referred from time to time, but she knew the road very well. She was aware, however, that he would feel happier knowing that the directions were at hand and the small VW Polo contained every possible aid in case of emergency.

'It's only February,' he'd said, packing rugs, gumboots and even a small spade into the hatchback. A hamper was already on the back seat, containing two flasks full of boiling water and the means to make tea or coffee, as well as biscuits and some chocolate. 'It's quite possible you might get some bad weather. You've got your mobile, haven't you? And the RAC membership card?'

She'd reassured him, feeling touched, hating to leave him and Luke, but driven by an inner need. They'd waved her off, standing on the pavement, and she'd suppressed the urge to stop the car and run back to them. They were all she had, and she loved them both so much—why waste precious time on a mad dash to the West Country?

'Because I must,' she'd told herself desperately, weaving her way out of Oxford. 'I need to feel normal. I want to pretend that I'm like anyone else and I can't do that with darling Mike. However hard he tries, it's there at the back of his eyes. I want to be looked at by people who don't know.'

Gradually the panic and guilt receded; slowly she thought herself into her other persona: the Melissa who had all her life before her; who was healthy and free and looking for adventure. She'd taught herself to do this as a means of escape from despair. Sometimes it was a slow, painful effort, wrestling with her willpower in an attempt to beat down fear, but it was easier when there was something on which to concentrate. She glanced at the details of the farmhouse, also lying on the front seat, and excitement bubbled quietly inside her. Presently she began to enjoy herself. The day was bright and sunny, full of hope, promising miracles, and she sang to herself as the miles sped away beneath the wheels. She'd promised not to attempt the journey in one day and had decided to break the trip just before she turned off the A38 on to Dartmoor.

'You could carry on into Cornwall on the A38,' Mike had told her. 'You could shoot off at Liskeard. Much quicker.'

'It's boring,' she'd shrugged, wrinkling her nose, 'dragging through Plymouth when I could be driving over Dartmoor. You know how much I love moorland, Mike. I can go across to Tavistock and then Launceston. Much nicer.'

He'd agreed—but with the proviso that she had a night's sleep before crossing the moor. She'd laughed at him.

'Anyone would think it was the Kalahari,' she'd said teasingly. 'But OK. It'll be nice to take my time.'

He'd made certain that she'd booked a room at The Dolphin in Bovey Tracey and together they'd traced the route across the moor to Tavistock and on to Launceston. She'd reserved a room for two nights in Padstow but she refused to do more than that.

'I want to be free to move about,' she'd insisted. 'It's an adventure, Mike, not a package tour.'

He'd agreed, understanding, and she'd promised to keep in touch daily. So she would, it was only fair and, anyway, she'd want to know that he and Luke were OK too, but slowly she was beginning to experience the sense of freedom that had become so elusive. By lunchtime, driving into Sherborne to find somewhere to eat, she'd very nearly completed the transition. She could think about her brother and his child calmly, without guilt, and was managing to hold at bay the tiny demon of fear that lived permanently now in her mind and in her heart.

As she ate a large piece of locally made applecake and sipped her coffee, she looked at the house particulars. She'd brought them with her almost as a talisman, slipping them into her leather shoulder bag which always contained a battered leather-covered copy of *The Golden Treasury*, some chocolate, her purse, mobile and other necessities. The farmhouse, after all, was the reason for her journey. She was travelling to the West Country to look at houses for her brother who was a writer. If anyone asked she'd tell them that she was a lawyer working in one of the City law firms, living in a flat in Dulwich. Well, so she had been until a year ago. Apparently concentrating on the description of the large kitchen, Melissa was well aware of the attention she was receiving from a young man at a corner table. She felt a surge of gratitude, blessing him silently for his admiration which bestowed a kind of strength upon her. There was no sympathy or compassion in his eyes, just a simple, natural interest shown by a man for an attractive woman.

Melissa put her hands to the scarf wound around her hair which had grown back well, once she'd refused any more chemo. She mourned the long thick, rippling bronze mane but she was grateful that, though still very short, her hair curled into pretty, springing tendrils. 'I've had enough,' she'd said to her GP. 'I know it's inoperable and I know I may not have much longer. I'm going to enjoy what's left to me,' and he'd agreed with her, defending her from the specialist and the other doctors, agreeing that she had the right to take her life back to herself. It had been a relief when Mike had needed help just then, so that she could move to Oxford, free of that terrible, suffocating sympathy. Some of her friends had been unable to believe that she was 'giving up' and talked severely about denial; others attempted to persuade her to try homoeopathic treatment; yet others saw her as a statistic or as an insurance—because *she* had been struck down *they* had been passed over—and were almost grateful. What she really missed was the ordinary, cheerful rough and tumble of daily life. The terrible privileges of the sick were weighty, paralysing, and she was determined to throw them off.

She finished her applecake, drew her thick, woollen ruana more closely about her—it was tiresome that she felt the cold so keenly—and slid the sheets of paper back into her bag. On her way out she smiled at the young man, rejoicing in the answering flash in his eyes, but was gone before he could react. Back in the car she breathed deeply, feeling stronger and more confident as she headed towards the A30. She loved being in the car, a small, private world in which she could talk to herself, sing, scream, even, if she felt like it; in the car she was on equal terms with her fellow man.

Yet later, as she drove off the A38, following the signs for Bovey

Tracey, she acknowledged the fact that she was weary. The day had been a busy one and she would be glad to rest. She would telephone Mike so that he knew she'd arrived safely, then a soak in a hot bath and a sleep before dinner would refresh her. Tomorrow morning, she promised herself as she parked the car, she would allow herself an hour or so to potter in the town before setting off on the second half of her journey.

The next day was Saturday and the town was busy. Melissa strolled along Station Road and crossed the bridge, pausing to watch the river flowing beneath it, past the now defunct wheel on the Mill. The lovely old stone building housed a craft shop, as well as an exhibition gallery and café, and she'd decided to have some coffee there before she set off to Tavistock. As she mingled with the locals she was aware of a delicious sense of anonymity; a release from responsibility. It was a holiday feeling, and a few early daffodils growing beside a cottage wall promised that spring was at hand, despite the icy breath of wind on her cheek. Beyond the trees and the huddle of roofs, the high shoulder of the moor made an impressive backdrop; serene and lofty, its stony peaks touched by sunlight, it lent a protective presence to the bustle and activity of the small town.

Melissa browsed for a while in Cottage Books, bought some chocolate for the journey at Mann's delicatessen and retraced her steps to the Mill. Despite the sunshine it was not warm enough to sit at one of the tables in the courtyard and, glancing in curiously through the windows which showed tantalising glimpses of the craft shop and the current exhibition, she headed for the café doors, suddenly needing to be inside in the warm. Choosing from the delicious array of cakes, asking for some coffee, took several minutes and by the time she looked about her she saw that all the tables were occupied. She hesitated, dismayed, balancing the tray in her hands, until she saw that only one person was sitting at the table by the window. She threaded her way between the morning shoppers and paused hopefully. The girl was young, twenty-ish, and rather striking. Her narrow eyes, honey brown beneath the heavy fall of shiny dark hair, were bright and interested, and she gestured readily as Melissa asked if she might share with her.

'Of course,' she answered. 'It's rather busy this morning. Everyone's coming in to get warm.'

'The sun deceived me,' said Melissa cheerfully, putting her plate and her coffee on the table. 'I didn't realise how cold it was. Oh! How lovely the river is.'

Below the window the water raced by, silvery bright, glinting and dazzling. On the bank opposite, trees leaned over the river and a grey wagtail scurried and bobbed amongst their roots. A bluetit clung to the nut container which hung from one of the branches, eating busily, whilst a rival contender watched from a neighbouring twig.

'I've written down the bluetits and the wagtail,' said the girl. 'I always hope I shall see something really bizarre but I never have.'

Melissa looked puzzled and the girl pushed a diary towards her. Under each day's heading, sightings were noted down by visitors and she saw, now, that a pair of binoculars stood on the window sill along with several reference books.

'What a nice idea,' she said. 'I hope I see something. Only I'm not very good about birds. I know a robin when I see one but I wouldn't have a clue about wagtails.'

'There are other things too. Water voles and mice. Of course, some people like to be funny. Someone's written "the *Titanic*, sinking" and "Free Willy" and things like that, but there's a really nice one here. "My darling wife, Anne, on our thirty-fifth wedding anniversary who, after thirty-five years and five kids, is still the best bird around for me." Isn't that lovely? Fancy having that written about you after all that time. Wouldn't it be brilliant?'

Looking into the younger girl's glowing face, Melissa felt a sudden, devastating, overwhelming sensation of loss. There could be no such epitaph for her. No one would ever write of her in those terms; there would not be the length of years to build so strong a bond. She broke the piece of sponge apart with her fork, pretending to be speechless at such charming devotion, trying to smile. The girl was leafing through the diary and, watching her, Melissa was aware of an odd feeling of . . . of what? She frowned, trying to define it, swallowing some coffee in the hope of easing the constriction in her throat. The girl smiled across at her and Melissa felt absurdly touched, as if she had been offered something vital, included within a tight-knit circle of affection and kinship, and her sense of loss was diffused in the warmth of the girl's smile.

'You might see a dipper if you were really lucky. Or a kingfisher.'

'That would be wonderful.' Melissa began to eat her cake. 'Are you a local?'

'Sort of.' She sounded defensive. 'My grandmother lives here so I've been coming to Bovey all my life nearly. My parents live in London but I'm doing a theatre studies course at King Alfred's in Winchester.'

'What fun.' Melissa had regained her composure and now studied her companion afresh. 'Are you going to be an actress?'

The dark girl shrugged. 'I don't know really. I wish I did. It's awful not knowing what you want to do. People expect you to have a vocation from the age of ten, these days, and you feel a bit of a failure if you don't.'

Melissa chuckled mischievously. 'Perhaps you want five children and a husband that writes nice things about you when you're sixty.'

'That's the trouble. I probably would but it wouldn't do my street cred any good to admit it to my mates.'

'Have you anyone particular in mind?'

'No, not really. Well, there's someone I go riding with but he's much older. He's nice, though. He was in love with someone but in the end it didn't work out and he's never found anyone else. I've always had a thing about Hugh from when I was a little girl but it's not really serious. I can talk to him, though. He really listens, if you know what I mean. Not just surface stuff, but properly.'

She sighed, propping her elbows on the table, chin in hands, and Melissa felt another wave of what she could only describe as an intense familiarity; a deep sense of comradeship. Before she could speak, however, the girl straightened, her eyes fixed on something beyond the window.

'Look,' she said. 'There's the nuthatch. Isn't he brilliant? I love the way he really goes for the nuts, as if he has to kill each one before he can eat it.'

'And upside down to boot,' agreed Melissa. 'He's very handsome, isn't he? Shall we put him in the diary?'

'You can have him,' the girl said generously, pushing the book across the table. 'Go on. Are you staying in Bovey?'

'Just overnight.' Melissa was busy writing. 'I'm on my way to Cornwall. House-hunting.'

'Oh, really?' She sounded interested but before she could pursue it, someone called 'Posy' and she turned. 'It's my grandmother,' she said. 'I have to go. I hope you enjoy Cornwall. 'Bye.'

'It's been so nice to meet you . . . Posy.' Melissa watched as the girl collected her belongings and, with a farewell smile, made her way between the tables. She saw her greet the tall, elderly lady and, when they'd disap-

peared, Melissa turned back to the scene outside the window feeling foolishly bereft.

'Posy,' she murmured. It was an unusual name and she decided that she
rather liked it, that it had suited the dark girl who had been so friendly.
Her spirit was brushed again with a sense of loss; a tiny ache was located in
her heart. Posy's warm vitality and youth had underlined her own sense of
frailty and as she finished her cake, her eyes still on the nuthatch, Keats's
well-loved words drifted in her thoughts. This poem, his 'Ode to a
Nightingale', had comforted her during those earlier, terrible months and
now, today, they haunted her again; pointing a bitter-sweet contrast,
between herself and Posy. ' 'Tis not through envy of thy happy lot, But
being too happy in thine happiness, That thou, light-wingèd Dryad of the
trees . . . Singest of summer in full-throated ease . . . Tasting of Flora and
the country-green, Dance, and Provençal song, and sunburnt mirth! O for
a beaker full of the warm South! . . . That I might drink, and leave the
world unseen, And with thee fade away into the forest dim . . . Away!
away! for I will fly to thee . . . on the viewless wings of Poesy . . . Now
more than ever seems it rich to die, To cease upon the midnight with no
pain, While thou art pouring forth thy soul abroad In such an ecstasy! . . .
Thou wast not born for death, immortal Bird! . . .'

Odd that the girl's bright, young, eager face should make her own dark,
cruel, secret terror easier to bear; an assurance that, in some future
unknown world, they might be together.

Melissa thrust aside such fanciful imaginings and brought her energy
and mind to bear on the journey ahead. It was a wonderful day for a drive
over the moor and, with luck, she'd be in Padstow by teatime. She picked
up the diary again, her spirits rising, and wrote beneath her earlier entry:
'Met a great chick called Posy.' Perhaps she'd see it and it would make her
smile, next time she came in for coffee. It wouldn't make up for the
thirty-five years of marriage and five kids but it was better than nothing.
She hesitated for a moment, the pencil still in her hand, and quickly, lest
she should change her mind, wrote a few more words. 'Thou wast not
born for death, immortal Bird!' Gathering up her bag, shrugging herself
into her ruana, she hurried out into the cold spring sunshine.

Chapter Seventeen

'I'll drop you at Trendlebeare,' said Maudie, clearing away the breakfast things on Sunday morning, 'and take Polonius for a walk while you're riding. You mustn't be too long or you'll miss your train.'

'Just an hour,' said Posy. 'I warned Hugh that it would be a short one. Are you sure you'll be OK?'

'Quite OK. I shall have some coffee at the Roundhouse. Don't worry about us.'

'I feel a bit guilty about you missing church.'

'Posy,' said Maudie warningly, 'I thought we'd agreed about the G-word. No more guilt. I shall go to Evening Prayer when you're safely on your way to Winchester. Now just get a move on and stop fussing.'

Posy grinned and disappeared in the direction of her bedroom. Maudie gave a sigh of relief and carried the tray into the kitchen, followed closely by Polonius.

'You know you don't get leftover toast,' she murmured. 'The birds need it more than you do. Oh, well, perhaps a crust . . .'

Polonius crunched happily, licked his chops and looked hopeful.

'No more,' she said firmly. 'That's it.'

She began to wash up and he pottered off into the hall where he lay down, waiting for Posy to appear. Twenty minutes later all three of them were in the car. As she drove up the hill past Forder, Maudie was pleased that Posy would have the opportunity to confide in Hugh if she needed to talk about the situation at home. Since Christmas there had been a tacitly agreed avoidance of the subject and, apart from the hint that things were much better now, Maudie had no idea what might be happening between Patrick and Selina—although Posy had warned her that Selina's heart was still set on having Moorgate. She knew, however, that, since she'd been quite small, Posy had found it easy to unburden herself to Hugh. Maudie could understand that; there was something comfortable and reassuring about Hugh, underpinned with an unusual wisdom which made him a natural confidant. He was also good-looking and rather sexy which, in Maudie's book, was a delightful bonus.

'Don't you find it extraordinary,' she said, following this train of thought, 'that that girlfriend of Hugh's gave him the push?'

'Yes,' said Posy after a moment, somewhat startled by this unexpected question. 'Well, I do, actually. You know about the girl who died? And he thought it was all his fault and he couldn't get over it? Well, Lucinda—that's his girlfriend—got fed up with it and took a job abroad.'

'I know about that,' assented Maudie, slowing down as the car approached Shewte Cross, 'but Pippa told me that she came back. The trouble was that she simply couldn't face the thought of living in the middle of Dartmoor running an adventure school so she went off again.'

'It's really sad.' Posy looked quite distressed. 'He couldn't bear to give it all up, you see, but having to go through her leaving him all over again really screwed him up. It was like losing her twice.'

'I suspect that it became a test. Each wanting the other to give in and admit that love was greater but neither of them could.' Maudie sighed. 'Well, all I can say is that it's a terrible waste of a rather delicious man.'

Posy chuckled and then fell silent, frowning. It always confused her that, whilst she found it rather funny when Maudie spoke like that about men, she simply hated it when her mother did the same. It embarrassed her horribly and she felt hot and cross. Maudie, sensing a change in the atmosphere, searched for a different subject.

'Isn't it amazing,' she asked randomly, 'how quickly nature recovers from disaster? You'd hardly know the moor was burned so badly just a few years ago here, would you? It's probably done it the world of good, actually. What a simply glorious morning. I hope Polonius is feeling energetic.'

'Polonius always feels energetic,' said Posy, good-humour restored. 'You'll tire before he does.'

Squashed in the back, Polonius whined briefly, longing for freedom.

'Nearly there,' said Maudie, as the car swung right over Haytor Down. 'I shan't come in, Posy. I know Pippa's got a houseful this weekend ready for half term. I'll be back in an hour. Give them all my love and enjoy yourself.'

Posy stood for a moment in the road, waving after them, before setting off down the track. At the gate she paused. In the yard a minibus had been stacked with canoes and she could see Max's tall, lean form, firm as a rock, about which swirled an excited jumble of small boys. Rowley's blond head bobbed amongst them, organising them into the bus, whilst Pippa loaded a box containing packed lunches into the boot.

Posy thought: What fun it is. How wonderful to live here, out on the moor, instead of being stuck in the City doing some boring nine-to-five stuff in an office.

Hugh was coming towards her, leading two horses, and she went to meet him.

'Wonderful day,' he said. 'Let's get going while we can. Max is muttering about leaving all the real work to him and accusing me of sneaking off and so on.'

Posy hesitated, one foot in the stirrup. 'Are you sure it's OK?'

'Of course it is.' Hugh grinned heartlessly as he swung himself into the saddle. 'He's always like this with a new intake. After all, he's got Rowley. He just likes to make a point. Max never changes.'

They walked the horses up the drive and crossed the road. Once on the slopes of Black Down they broke into a canter. The cold blue air seemed to fizz like wine as the moor unfolded at their feet, stretching into an infinite distance, hill upon hill. As they trotted beside the Becka Brook Hugh reined in and brought his mount alongside Posy's.

'You're looking good,' he said, studying her. 'Better than last time.'

She smiled at him gratefully. 'I *am* better. Things are . . . easier. You were right, Hugh. Apparently Dad's . . . thing seems to have finished. Perhaps it wasn't as bad as I thought it was, after all. He's still very subdued and stuff but Mum's absolutely sure that it's over.'

'Things get out of proportion.' Hugh leaned forward to pat his horse's neck and the warm flesh twitched appreciatively at his touch. 'Everyone gets a bit heated and emotions can spiral out of control.'

Posy grimaced. 'Mine certainly did,' she admitted. 'But it was really clever of you to know that it might be something quite different from an affair.'

'Not really.' He shrugged. 'It happened to my parents once. Actually it was my fault, really. It was when I was still in a state over Charlotte and my parents were getting a bit desperate. Dad decided to approach Charlotte's mother about it without telling Mum and she got the idea that he was having an affair with her. It got really out of hand and Mum was convinced that Dad was being unfaithful. Luckily it was sorted out before any real harm was done. It just occurred to me, when you told me about your father, that it might be something similar.'

'Well, he was certainly helping Mary,' said Posy cautiously. 'I still don't know if it was any more than that but Mum seems OK now.' She hesitated, gazing out towards Hound Tor. 'Dad's not his usual self, though. He's very quiet. Sort of abstracted.'

'He's probably had a bit of a fright,' said Hugh reassuringly. 'He might have got quite fond of this other woman and then realised that it was getting out of control. Could be anything. Don't start imagining things.'

She smiled at him, stretching a hand to him. 'I won't. Honestly. Thanks, Hugh.'

He held her hand for a moment and then let it go. 'Mind you don't. Come on, let's make for Honeybag Tor, shall we?'

Single file they guided their horses down the bank, splashing through the brook, and set out together, beneath Greator Rocks, cantering over Houndtor Down in the bright sunshine.

In the end, Melissa came upon the house quite by chance. She'd lost her way in the winding Cornish lanes, driving slowly, peering at fingerposts which bore unlikely—and occasionally oddly religious—names, wanting to get a feel of the place before contacting the agents next morning. There were no precise instructions on the details—'Clearly they don't want people nosing round,' Mike had said—but between them they'd drawn a circle on the map, noting the given distances from the A39, from the coast at Tintagel and from Launceston.

'Its name shows that it's at the edge of the moor,' she'd said, as they'd pored together over the map, 'so it's got to be within this small area. It should be obvious.'

It might have looked obvious on the tourist map but here, in the twisty, secret, unmarked lanes it could just as easily have been a maze. Nevertheless, she was enchanted. There were primroses growing, luminously pale, on the steep banks beneath the trembling catkins, and violets clung, sweet-scented, amongst woody roots. She drove slowly through a small hamlet, granite cottages huddling about a grassy triangle with a stone cross set in it, and plunged once more into a deep, narrow lane which curved sharply left, uphill, and opened suddenly upon a grove of trees to the right. To the left was the house. It was set back a little from the lane, settled well in, comfortable, solid; an old farmhouse washed a deep, warm cream with—surprisingly—dark red painted window frames and gutters. It should have looked odd but to Melissa's fascinated gaze it looked wonderful. The 'For Sale' board leaned a little drunkenly against the low stone wall.

She edged the car in close to the wall and switched off the engine. Silence. Presently she became aware of the cawing of rooks and, further off, the plaintive bleating of lambs. She stepped out of the Polo and stood in the sunshine, looking across the roof of the car at the house. It wasn't particularly large or architecturally beautiful, just a stone and slate farm-house, but she felt, quite simply, that it was hers. The front garden was tiny, but crocus and daffodil were growing in the narrow beds beneath the windows and jasmine climbed the porch. There was a small gate in the wall, which closed the garden off from the yard to the left, and the flagged path led across to the lawn which spread away to the right of the house, encircled by tall shrubs. The outbuildings had been restored and the yard was empty.

Melissa closed the car door quietly and strolled to the wrought-iron gate. 'Moorgate'—the legend was painted in black on a small wooden board attached to the gate. Moorgate. The gate to the moor. She glanced up the lane, which curved to the right and wound out of sight. There was no reason to believe that the moor was not just around the curve. She laid her hand upon the gate, pushing it gently, and passed into the garden. It was a matter of a few steps to the front door but she chose, first, to walk upon the springy turf of the lawn and to look more closely at the tall, flowering shrubs. Here, hidden from the lane by azalea, weigela and lilac, out of the wind's touch, it was warm, and she moved slowly, looking up at the shrubs, noting the buds already formed. After a while she returned to the path and stood looking at the house. Her whole instinct told her that it was empty but, simply to prove that it was so, she rang the bell. No one came hurrying to answer it. Gently, very gently, she turned the door handle but the solid oak door remained firmly closed. Cupping her hands about her eyes she looked through the windows, into the rooms on either side of the porch. They were similar: large, heavily beamed, with great granite fireplaces and shelved recesses. Both were full of sunlight, newly painted and quite empty of furniture.

She wandered back along the path, round the corner of the house and stopped short with a tiny cry of amazement. The moor, stretching as far as the eye could see, flowed like some great ocean up to the very house. The path finished in a cleared turfed square, enclosed by a ring fence, and beyond it she could see the lambs with their mothers and, beyond again, ponies grazing. Outcrops of granite burst haphazard from the peaty earth and she could hear the sound of water singing in some nearby coomb which was hidden by the folded brown cheek of the moor. The ponies, disturbed by something she could not see, skittered together, prancing and whinnying, so that the sheep raised their heads, crying to their lambs who raced on springy legs to press against reassuringly warm, rough, woolly flanks. Here on the north side, out of the sun, the air was icy and, pulling her ruana more closely round her, Melissa turned her back on the moor and gazed up at the house. A huge glassed porch enclosed the back door and once again she went to peer in at the windows. On either side of the porch, the windows let in to the same room: a huge kitchen with a range. There was a door at either end and one opposite the window which almost certainly led into the hall. Standing on tiptoe she could see the sink unit directly below the window and imagined herself standing there, washing up, preparing vegetables, gazing out at the moor.

Once again Melissa stepped back, staring up at the windows on the first floor. There were five bedrooms altogether—and what views the rooms on this north side of the house must have! Whoever lived here, however, must choose to wake to the morning sun or to breathtaking views; must decide between moonlight or the shadowy moorland. She crossed the turf behind the house and entered the yard. Logs were piled in the corner of an open-fronted barn next to a loosebox and a washing line was strung between two sturdy poles. Leaning for a moment on the five-bar gate, she watched the rooks. Noisy, acrimonious, but sociable, they congregated in the tall trees across the lane; the beginnings of bulky, twiggy nests conspicuous amongst the bare branches.

Melissa thought: How wonderful to live in a place where the only sounds you can hear from your front gate are made by rooks and lambs.

She let herself out, closing the gate carefully behind her, climbed into the car and drove slowly up the lane.

Chapter Eighteen

Later that same day, arriving home from Newton Abbot, having seen Posy off on the train, Maudie was just in time to snatch up the telephone receiver.

'Yes?' she said, in her usual faintly peremptory manner. 'Hello?'

Selina sounded slightly breathless. Maudie's telephone manner always irritated her but this evening she could not allow herself the luxury of irritation.

'Oh, Maudie,' she said brightly. 'How are you? Is Posy with you?'

At the other end of the line Maudie smiled evilly to herself. It was a good ploy but she knew a trick worth two of that.

'Long gone, I'm afraid, Selina,' she said cheerfully. 'So sorry you've missed her. You'll catch her later on this evening, I expect.'

The finality in her voice, the implication that she was about to replace the receiver, hurried Selina into speech.

'Oh, right. OK. I'll do that. But how are you, Maudie? Have you had a nice weekend together?'

'Very nice. It's such a treat to have Posy to stay.'

Even if it means having to put up with Polonius. The sour words rose to Selina's lips but she bit them back.

'It was good of you to take Polonius.' She couldn't resist a tiny, tiny dig; a hint that she knew exactly why Maudie had given a home to the wretched animal.

'It was a ruse on my part.' Maudie had no intention of letting the insinuation go unremarked. 'He's my bribe. But you suspected that, didn't you?'

Selina gritted her teeth together. 'Nonsense.' She laughed lightly. 'You've never needed bribes where Posy's concerned. She's always adored you.'

'Extraordinary, isn't it?' Maudie invited Selina's bafflement. 'And in the face of such determined opposition, too. Anyway, never mind all that. What can I do for you, Selina?'

Selina, who had hoped to work round to Moorgate by degrees, having invoked Hector's memory and passed on to happy holidays and family loyalty, glared at the telephone receiver.

'I was thinking about Moorgate.' She abandoned any hope of subtlety and went straight to the point. 'I'm really serious about buying it, Maudie. I'm hoping you'll be prepared to talk terms with me.'

'Are you selling the London house?'

Selina frowned at such a blunt question. 'No,' she said. 'I . . . We did think about it but decided against it. No, we want to keep Moorgate as a holiday home. As it was for us when we were children.'

'But it wasn't, Selina. Not as we think of holiday homes now. When your mother was alive the tenants were prepared to let you use it for a few weeks each summer and later on there was a gap between long-term tenants. Moorgate has never been a holiday home. You know very well that if it's not lived in it will be damp and uninhabitable in a matter of months. Anyway, forgive me for being impertinent, but how on earth could Patrick afford to buy it and run it on his salary?'

'It would be difficult,' said Selina stiffly, 'we realise that, but we think it's worth the sacrifice.'

'Whose sacrifice? His or yours? What sacrifice will you be making, Selina?'

'I really don't see that it's any of your business. I'm simply asking if you will take it off the market while we get our act together. I don't think that it's too unreasonable given that really you have no right to it at all.'

'Oh, not that again, please,' said Maudie wearily. 'The answer is no. If you haven't been able to sort yourselves out since last November I can't see why you should now. And I have no intention of allowing you to drive yourselves into the ground with such a burden round your necks. Your father would never have approved of it. If you want to sell up and live on the edge of Bodmin Moor that's one thing and I can't stop you. If you do, then you shall have every opportunity to buy Moorgate. Otherwise you'd be committing financial suicide and you know it. Or if you won't accept it, Selina, I'm sure Patrick knows it.'

'So you won't help us?'

Maudie sighed. 'I thought that that's exactly what I was doing. Very well. I'd like to speak to Patrick.'

'Why?'

'Because Patrick's the breadwinner. I want to hear how he plans to finance this operation. I want to see figures before I consider it. Is he there?'

'No,' she answered sulkily. 'Anyway, I speak for Patrick.'

'Oh, I know you do,' said Maudie. 'But just this once I want to hear him say it and I want to see how he plans to achieve it. Your father would have needed to be certain before he was a party to this, Selina, as well you know. So ask Patrick to call me when he gets in, will you?'

She winced as Selina slammed the receiver on to its rest and replaced her own rather thoughtfully.

'I behaved badly,' she told Polonius remorsefully. 'I intended to be much nicer to Selina but she always rubs me up the wrong way.'

As she hung up her jacket, filled the kettle with water and opened the stove, she remembered her good intentions. Posy's feelings about Patrick had opened her eyes to the way the young Selina might have felt and she couldn't quite shrug off her feelings of guilt, despite Daphne's words of comfort. Whether Hector was a widower or not, Selina had probably found the whole idea of his relationship with Maudie quite repugnant and it was specious to be sympathetic to Posy's reaction without giving some retrospective thought to Selina.

'Oh, guilt! Guilt!' she cried angrily, thrusting logs into the glowing embers. 'How tiresome it is to feel responsible for people.'

Polonius watched her anxiously. He'd grown used to a peaceful tenor to his life and Maudie's sudden burst of frustration reminded him of earlier, unhappier days. Sensing his anxiety, she paused to pull his ears.

'I'm a selfish old woman,' she told him. 'I like to have my own way. Well, who doesn't? But I was going to be nicer. I was going to be friendly to Selina. To try to make up for being thoughtless all those years ago. But now I see that it was doomed to failure and I feel mortified by my lack of will.'

Polonius thumped his tail obligingly, relieved that the storm was passing and that he was not the cause of it. Maudie shut the stove doors and he lay down in his usual position on the rug. She stared down at him, still feeling dissatisfied with herself.

'Honestly,' she muttered, 'my good intentions didn't last five minutes. The trouble is that Selina and I are simply incompatible. We all knew that on day one. How she disliked me!'

As she went back to the kitchen to make some tea she recalled a scene some twenty years before when Hector had been told that he was to receive a knighthood. He'd attempted—unsuccessfully—to hide his delight by joking about it, explaining the system.

'It's easy enough to remember,' he'd said. 'CMG stands for Call Me God. KCMG is Kindly Call Me God. And GCMG is God Calls Me God.'

Selina had been beside herself with pride and she'd made sure that everybody she met knew about it: 'That was just before Daddy was K'd . . .' 'Oh, well when Daddy was K'd . . .' Somehow she'd managed to drag it into even the most unlikely conversation but to Maudie she'd been unable to contain her resentment.

'You don't deserve it,' she'd said furiously. 'It's Mummy who should be Lady Todhunter, not you. It isn't fair.'

'My dear child, I couldn't agree with you more,' Maudie had answered. 'I promise you I find it utterly embarrassing to be called Lady Todhunter. The whole thing is quite ludicrous.'

It had infuriated Selina even more to learn that Maudie wasn't over-whelmed by such honour and her rage had become quite coruscating in its vehemence. Once more Hector had been obliged to intervene and Daphne had privately taken Selina aside and pointed out that her sulks were spoiling her father's pleasure in his achievement.

'Although I have to say,' she'd said later to Maudie, 'that you are being quite unnatural about this. We'd all give our eyeteeth to be Lady What-ever and you're behaving as if it's simply rather tiresome.'

'It just seems so utterly unreal' was all Maudie had answered, though she'd tried to be thrilled for Hector's sake.

Maudie carried her tea into the living room and sat down at the table, still remembering. Her attempt had never really come off and she knew that Hector had been well aware of the sardonic gleam in her eye when people 'sirred' him.

She thought: I made him uncomfortable and he was never really able to luxuriate in his glory when I was around. Poor old Hector. What a cow I am!

Yet she knew that she was right about Moorgate. It would be disastrous for Selina to buy it and she could only hope that Patrick was not submitting to emotional blackmail and would stand firm. Maudie picked up the envelope from the Scotch House, tipped the pieces of tartan cloth on to the table and shuffled them absently. She needed a buyer; someone who would make an offer and put a stop to Selina's nonsense.

'Who was it?'

Selina whirled round on her chair, caught in the act, already mentally inventing a reason for slamming down the receiver.

'It was . . . I was just . . .'

'It was Maudie, wasn't it?'

She watched Patrick warily. He seemed to have passed beyond her reach and even now was regarding her with a polite indifference which was oddly unnerving. For the first time in their married life he was untouched by her anger, her scorn or her wheedling. Now, of all times, when he should be desperate to make reparation, he was unmoved.

'Yes, it was Maudie,' she said quickly. 'I was talking to her about Moorgate.'

'Oh, Moorgate. You never give up, do you, Selina?'

His amused, casual reaction increased her anxiety. 'I still feel we could buy it if we made an effort. Especially now . . .' Her voice died under his puzzled scrutiny.

'Especially now? I think not. If you want to sell this house and move to Cornwall that's fine. As far as I'm concerned this house is yours and you can do what you like with it. You could sell it, buy Moorgate and have a bit over and then it's up to you.' He shrugged. 'As for me. Well, I think I've had enough.'

'Enough? Enough of what?' Fear made her shrill. 'What do you mean?'

'I've had enough of you. Of married life. Of being dull old Patrick Stone. I'm going to pack it in. Go off somewhere. Live a bit before it's too late.'

'I hope you don't mind if I say that you sound like a corny character in some third-rate melodrama.'

If she'd hoped to sting him into a defensive stance she was disappointed. He laughed.

'I don't mind what you say. I'm past caring what anyone says. I just thought you should know where you stand regarding Moorgate. Count me out.'

'Don't be such a fool—'

'Oh, but I *am* a fool, Selina,' he cut in quickly. 'Nobody should know that better than you do. I'm going down to the pub. I'll get something to eat there so don't wait up.'

She heard the front door close but she seemed unable to rise from her chair. Of course, it was ridiculous and he didn't mean a word of it, she told herself. He was trying to make himself interesting, hoping to distract her from his unfaithfulness. Nevertheless, a tiny, panicky voice was asking what she would do if he were serious; how she'd cope if he'd really had enough? She had no answer, however, and presently she got up and went into the kitchen to pour herself a drink.

In the pub, Patrick ordered a pint and stood waiting, staring reflectively at nothing in particular. Ever since Christmas an odd kind of lassitude had been growing in him; an apathetic indifference. Even the pain of seeing Mary at school had lost its keen edge of misery and lately he'd felt merely sad. It was worrying—or it would be if only he could make that much mental effort—because it was rather unpleasant, this lack of emotion. At least his desperation had carried with it the comfort of feeling alive; these days he simply felt detached.

He paid for his pint, remembering other evenings; marking time until he could go out to the telephone and speak to Mary. How vivid life had seemed then, how charged with excitement. She'd made him feel necessary; given a purpose to his existence. Now there was nothing. Nobody needed him and he was important to nobody.

Patrick swallowed some beer. Well, at least there was a freedom in that; an opportunity to begin something new. The important thing was not to feel sorry for himself.

'The world is my oyster,' he announced suddenly—and caught the surprised glance of the young barman. He took another draught, suppressing a rising desire to laugh, and almost choked. As he set his glass down on the bar, still trying to control the urge to giggle foolishly, he wondered whether he might be having a nervous breakdown.

Travelling back to Winchester, Posy was thinking about Hugh. She'd had a massive crush on him when she was fourteen, which even now embarrassed her when she remembered it. Fortunately, Hugh had handled it with such tremendous tact that she still wasn't quite certain whether he'd really been aware of it. She reminded herself that she'd been so sensitive about it, so anxious lest she made a fool of herself, that it was perfectly reasonable to believe that Hugh had noticed nothing. Being at school in London, only able to visit Devon occasionally, the infatuation had soon dwindled for lack of sustenance but she'd retained an affection for him. Perhaps it was the romantic setting which kept him at the forefront of her mind, especially now with all the upheaval going on at home. To live in the country with dogs and horses had always seemed like heaven and, just lately, she'd felt that she and Hugh were growing closer. He always seemed so pleased to see her, to really care about her, and he'd been so sweet when she'd poured out her fears about her father. Knowing that Hugh was very reserved when it came to personal matters, she was secretly very proud that he'd told her about his guilt over Charlotte's death as well as describing the way he'd felt about Lucinda. It had strengthened the bond of friendship between them, enabling her to confide in him.

It was already dark outside and Posy stared thoughtfully at her reflection in the window. Of course, it was silly, really, to imagine anything romantic happening between them. After all, he was nearly fifteen years older than she was. To him, she must still seem like a kid. For some reason Posy found herself thinking of the girl she'd met at the Mill on Saturday morning. How marvellous to look like that; to have those wonderful cheekbones and green eyes, and that clever way of twisting her scarf round her head. She'd had such style, such confidence. Of course, she was probably twenty-six or seven, had some brilliant career in the City and a host of admirers. Posy sighed enviously, dragged her book from her holdall and settled down to read.

Chapter Nineteen

The agent was already waiting for Melissa. His hatchback was in the yard and he was standing by the gate in the cold, bright sunshine. He raised a hand to her, swung wide the gate so that she could drive in, and then hurried round to open her door for her. She smiled at him as she climbed out, noting the fresh, newly scrubbed complexion and floppy fair hair. He wore a Barbour over his dark suit and his silk tie was adorned with dancing polar bears.

'Mr Cruikshank.' She shook his hand as he beamed at her. 'What a fantastic morning.'

'It's simply perfect, Mrs . . . er, Miss Clayton.'

He hesitated questioningly but she made no attempt to clarify the matter, leading the way through the smaller gate into the front garden whilst he followed, fumbling with the keys. She waited impatiently as he fitted the key into the lock, opened the door and stood back for her to enter.

'I'm not too good at the official bit,' he told her. 'It always seems a case of stating the obvious, so I tend to let the client decide which room he's looking at, if you see what I mean.' He glanced at some papers he held. 'You've brought the details with you?'

'Oh, yes.' She was looking down the hall, noting how the stairs were placed. 'I do agree with you, actually. It's so irritating to be told what a kitchen is. Or a bathroom.'

He looked pleased, flattered that she agreed with him so readily. 'Well

then. I'll simply say that the whole place has just been thoroughly renovated. No expense has been spared. New wiring and plumbing . . .'

She went before him into the sitting room, pulling the scarf from her
hair, and stood rapt with delight, imagining a huge log fire burning in the
massive granite fireplace.

'Impressive, isn't it?' he remarked, but when she didn't answer he mis-
took her silence and began to speak about gas fires. 'They can look quite
real, you know, and they're frightfully efficient. Removes the back-breaking
bit and cuts down mess . . .'

She glanced at him absently and, with a last look about the room,
crossed the hall to the study. He followed her, watching as she wandered
about. She touched the wood-burning stove and snatched her hand away
quickly, frowning.

' . . . quite sensible to install a woodburner,' he was saying now. 'More
economical. Perhaps that would be a good idea for the sitting room . . .'

'Is this the way to the kitchen?' Melissa asked, striding down the hall,
flinging open a door. 'Ooooh . . .'

Mr Cruikshank stood at her shoulder. 'Breathtaking, isn't it? Imagine
looking out at that every morning.'

Melissa felt obliged to contribute something; to reassure him. 'It's
utterly wonderful,' she said sincerely—and he gave a sigh of relief.

'The stove is fantastic,' he said, happy now that he'd had a positive reaction. 'It heats the water too, and supplies a heated towel rail in the bathroom and a radiator in the master bedroom. Lady Todhunter very sensibly
keeps it alight so as to keep the house aired.'

'It feels very warm.' She glanced round the huge kitchen. 'It's north-
facing, isn't it?'

'Wonderfully cool in summer,' he said quickly. 'This slate floor is a
masterpiece. Now, at this end there's the old dairy which has been con-
verted to a larder and utility room. The other side, over here, is the office
and a loo and a storeroom. Plenty of space. Did you say you had a family,
um, Mrs Clayton?'

'Oh, yes. I have a family,' she answered airily, looking into the office.
'May I see upstairs?'

'Of course,' he said quickly. 'Back into the hall. Lovely old original oak
staircase.'

She ran up lightly before him. The staircase turned to the right and opened into a passage with a room on each side. On she went; up two steps, round a corner, down three steps. She stopped, enchanted. There was a wide landing and a big window with a deep seat, where one could sit and stare out at the moor.

' . . . five bedrooms,' he was saying as he caught her up. 'One's very small but the biggest room has windows both east and south. Here we are . . .'

'No *en suite* bathroom?' she asked idly, teasingly, as she followed him into the large, sunny room.

'Rob Abbot stuck his heels in.' He sounded almost vexed. 'And Lady Todhunter agreed with him. She said it was a farmhouse not a hotel.'

'I couldn't agree more,' said Melissa, strolling over to the window and staring down into the lane. 'But there are two bathrooms?'

'Oh yes,' he replied quickly. 'One's tiny but it's there.'

The rooks were still busy in their tree, their raucous cries ringing in the peaceful, icy air. She leaned her forehead against the pane of glass, aware of a deep happiness.

'I love it,' she said dreamily. 'I absolutely love it.'

A short silence.

'Well.' Mr Cruikshank sounded confused. 'Well, then. Miss . . . er, Mrs—'

'I'd like another look,' she said, turning swiftly round. 'Alone. I need to be quite alone.'

His startled expression made her want to laugh. 'Of course. I quite understand. I'll be downstairs. Take all the time you need.'

He went away, across the landing, along the passage, down the stairs. When she could no longer hear him she gasped, a huge, deep breath, and whirled lightly on her toes. Sunshine splashed on the warm cream wall and flowed down on to the bare varnished boards. Quickly she went from room to room, learning them, imagining them furnished and lived in, and when she could delay no longer she went downstairs. She saw the front door close tactfully behind the agent and paused in the hall before going once more into the sitting room and study, and finally the kitchen.

Presently she went to find him. He was on the lawn, examining the shrubs, but turned as she approached, watching her eagerly.

'It's . . . perfect,' she said.

He smiled blindingly at her. 'I have to say I agree with you. If I had the money I'd buy it myself.'

'Would you?' She smiled back at him. 'You don't look like a country-man, Mr Cruikshank.'

'That's what Rob Abbot said.' He was too shy to insist that she should call him Ned. 'I *do* love the country but actually I'm transferring to the London branch. Should be fun . . .'

'Rob Abbot?' She was frowning, not really paying attention. 'You mentioned him before. Who is he?'

'He's the chap who did all the work on the place. Lady Todhunter had terrific faith in him but he likes his own way, does Rob. He's a great guy, though. We've become good chums since the key business.'

'Key business?'

Standing in the shelter of the tall shrubs, warm in the sunshine, he told her about the mystery of the keys, the locked rooms, the fear of a squatter.

'How strange,' she murmured. 'How very strange.'

'All done with now, though,' he said quickly, fearing that he might have given her a distaste for the house. 'It all came to nothing. It's a wonderful position, isn't it? So peaceful.'

'Mmm.' She turned away from him, biting her lip.

'Well.' He didn't want to sound too eager. 'Seen enough inside? Want to have a look at the outbuildings?'

'What I'd really like,' she said persuasively, 'is to spend some time getting to know the place. I live a long way away, Mr Cruikshank, and I can't simply pop up and down. Do you think I could have the key, just for a couple of days?'

He looked dismayed. 'I don't think I could do that. Company policy . . .'

'After all, the place is empty, isn't it? It's not as if I'm going to make off with the furniture.'

'We're simply not allowed, you see . . .'

'It's a lot of money . . .'

Another pause.

'I could come again, any time you like,' he said unhappily. 'I'm honestly not being difficult.'

'It's not quite that simple,' she said wistfully. 'You see, if I could have the key I shouldn't bother to go and see all the other houses I have lined up. I'm certain I should just settle for this one. On the other hand . . .'

She shrugged and he stared at her desperately.

'It's more than my job's worth.'

'But didn't you say that you were transferring to London?'

He looked alarmed. 'Same company . . .'

'But a long way off. When are you leaving?'

'Well, this weekend, actually.' He brightened. 'Listen. Rob Abbot has a set of keys. He sometimes shows clients round only I couldn't catch him this morning. Supposing I arrange with him—'

'What a good idea,' she interrupted swiftly. 'You can say that Mr Abbot has mislaid his keys and you've left yours with him so that he can show people round. Meanwhile I'll take my time, measure a few things, and then leave the keys with Mr Abbot. Brilliant! How clever you are, Mr Cruikshank.'

'Well.' He hesitated, his intention having been quite different but somehow finding it impossible to say so. She was certainly very keen and, after all, it wasn't a bad story and he'd be gone by the weekend. 'I suppose so. But you mustn't drop me in it at the office.'

'As if I would.' Her smile was brilliant. 'Now, how can I contact Mr Abbot? I promise I shan't keep the keys a moment longer than I need.'

She accompanied him into the yard, promising to be in touch very soon, and went out into the lane to wave him off, shutting the gate behind her, the keys held tightly in her hand. When the noise of the engine had died away, and the only sounds she could hear were the rooks' strident conversation and the high, thin cries of the lambs, she turned very slowly and looked up at the house.

Rob Abbot locked the door of his mobile home, which was parked in the corner of the farmer's field, climbed the stile and set out over the moor. The house stood above him washed warm by the evening sun, the grove of trees creating a dark backdrop. It was becoming more difficult, with spring drawing on, to make his entrances and exits unseen but he'd dropped a few hints that he was caretaking the place and hoped that this was enough to satisfy any inquisitive eyes. He knew that he was obsessed but he simply couldn't help himself; from the earliest days the house had charmed him. He remembered standing in the damp empty rooms, seeing all the character and beauty beneath sagging wallpaper and peeling paint;

envisaging the grain and sheen of oak beneath scratched paint and dull varnish. The vision had remained before him as he'd worked, as each room had responded to his loving care. After a while he'd been unable to bear to leave the house. It had been impossible to imagine anyone else living there. He'd needed to return, once he'd dropped the men off, so as to be alone in the house, to feel the peace settling on it again after the hammering and sawing and general busyness of the day. He'd park the pick-up by his caravan and, packing up a few necessities, he'd slip away, over the stile and across the moor in the shadow of the thorn, letting himself in by the side door.

Pausing in his climb, staring up at the windows which reflected the blazing fire of the sunset, he laughed as he recalled how he'd fought a rearguard action with Lady Todhunter and the wretched Ned Cruikshank. Ned was easy meat, of course, but Lady Todhunter was quite a different kettle of fish. He could still remember the shock he'd had that morning when he'd come round the corner of the house and found her standing in the yard. Rob blew out his lips, remembering his fear that she might guess what was going on. He'd suggested she should move her car into the yard, so as to give him time to dash back into the house and hide all obvious signs of occupation, but at every step his heart had been in his mouth.

'It doesn't feel as cold as I'd expected,' she'd said, drinking her tea, 'and what's that smell. Bacon?'

He'd had to think on his feet with that one and he'd come out with a feeble suggestion of ghosts. It had distracted her—but only momentarily—and he was ready for her when they got to the sitting room and she'd asked if he'd been lighting fires. Nevertheless, it had been a very nasty moment. Once she'd agreed that he should keep an eye on the place, light up the Esse, make certain that the place was warm, it had made life much easier, giving him an excuse for being around at odd moments—but he'd lost his secret, private quarters. The office, with the loo and storeroom, had made a perfect base within the house. He'd been able to keep his bits of furniture, a cache of food, some blankets, well out of the sight of prying eyes. How his heart had pumped when she'd suggested breaking the door down while she watched. The idea of squatters had been a brilliant one; it had bought him the time he needed but that was all. At least he'd been given the opportunity to carry on working on the office, of staying in the house, but with Ned Cruikshank rolling up with potential buyers his peace of mind was shattered. Fortunately, nobody as yet had asked to see what was inside the locked cupboard under the stairs.

Striding over the sheep-nibbled turf, Rob smiled to himself as he thought of how eagerly Ned had accepted him as a caretaker, as someone responsible enough to show clients round. The fact that Lady Todhunter trusted him was enough for Ned, always glad to be saved the long drive from Truro, and how easy it had been to drop a word, here and there, to put those clients off and frighten them away. For how much longer, he wondered, could he hold out before someone made an offer and pipped him to the post. His fists, driven into his pockets, tensed with frustration. He'd almost exhausted his list of cash-raising possibilities and time was running out. Oh, it was easy to deter potential buyers with horror stories of the climate when the rain was lashing down, or you couldn't see ten feet beyond the window because of rolling mist, but with the summer ahead it would be much more difficult.

Glancing up, as he neared the house, he frowned, narrowing his eyes. He thought he saw someone standing at the kitchen window, staring out over the moor. Instinctively he drew back into the shadow of the thorn, watching. The sun was settling lower now and the dark window seemed to frame a pale, insubstantial form; a woman looking out. He'd imagined it before, and his stories of ghosts weren't quite without foundation, but his ghosts were simply the kindly echoes of those who had gone before and he did not fear them. He mocked at himself—he was letting the house get to him, he knew that—and when he looked again there was nothing there. He covered the last few yards swiftly, swung himself over the ring fence, checked that Ned Cruikshank's car was not in the yard and finally let himself in through the back door.

The kitchen felt warm and welcoming and he breathed more easily, relaxing as usual now that he was home. He took the frozen dinner from his backpack, peeled off the lid and put the silver foil dish into the oven of the Esse. Next he stood a carton of milk on the draining board and pushed the kettle on to the hotplate. A china mug stood upside down on the draining board and he placed it the right way up and took a tea caddy and a bag of sugar from the cupboard under the sink. He laid the backpack on the floor, first removing his mobile telephone, and then stood for a moment, looking at the mobile and frowning. Laying it beside the mug he went out into the hall, taking a key ring from his pocket as he went. At the foot of the stairs he hesitated, trying to identify the faint, elusive scent which lingered, drifting in the cooler air of the hall. Shaking his head, wondering if Ned had been round earlier with a client, Rob unlocked the small padlock and opened the cupboard door. First he brought out a gate-leg table, then a rickety, cane-seated chair, and finally two large beanbags. He took the table and chair into the kitchen, set them up beside the Esse and then went back through the hall and into the sitting room. Here he picked up a long, heavy, cast-iron poker, pushed together the remains of burned wood and hot ashes and then carefully placed other logs on top. From the pile of wood, stacked at one side of the inglenook, he drew out a pair of bellows and began to blow new life into the ashes. Presently, when he was satisfied that the fire was well alight, he went out into the hall, returning with the beanbags which he put together before the fire.

As he straightened up he paused, listening intently. Was that a footfall in the big front bedroom overhead? He glanced at his watch, shrugging off his jitters, and then out at the twilight, wondering whether to fasten the shutters. Unwilling to close out the quiet, gold-flushed evening, he went back to the kitchen and made himself a mug of tea. Stirring in the sugar, he stood looking out over the flowing, rippling moorland, enjoying the last of the sunset, listening to the blackbird who was singing in the garden. He sipped the hot sweet tea with pleasure, filled with a poignant sense of undefined longing which these very early spring evenings often induced, aware of the house breathing around him, echoing with former lives and other passions. With a sigh, he set down the mug and went back to build up the fire.

The girl was standing by the inglenook, staring down at the beanbags. He checked just inside the door, with a barely concealed gasp, his heart hammering against his ribs, and she turned to look at him. She was quite beautiful; slender, with a sweet, bright face and an enchanting air of eager vulnerability.

'Hello,' she said. 'You must be Rob Abbot.'

Chapter Twenty

Afterwards he could never remember exactly what happened next. He was plunged into madness, into magic, into love.

He stared at her, as if she were a ghost—'I thought you were,' he admitted later—and she began to chuckle, going towards him across the bare clean boards, her hand outstretched.

'I'm sorry,' she said repentantly. 'I tricked Mr Cruikshank into letting me keep the keys. I simply couldn't bear to leave Moorgate, you see. My name's Melissa.'

He cursed then, but laughing at himself, reaching for her hand, feeling an absurd desire to raise it to his lips.

'I knew that wretched boy would bring me down,' he said ruefully. Yet he smiled at her, not feeling in the least at risk. 'I realised earlier that my mobile has been switched off all day. You've caught me red-handed.'

She seemed to be in no hurry to reclaim her hand. 'I guessed,' she said—and her eyes twinkled mischievously. 'He told me about the missing keys and all the other things and I just knew what had happened. You see, I would have done exactly the same myself. Well, I have, haven't I? I've tricked him into letting me have the keys so that I could be here alone, pretending that Moorgate was mine.'

'After only one viewing?'

'Oh, yes. That's all it needed. What about you?'

'Not much longer, I must admit. Once Lady Todhunter had gone, that very first time, and I was able to be alone, the magic began to work. I just felt I belonged here.'

'That's it,' she agreed eagerly. 'Oh, I was very taken with the photograph but as soon as I saw the house I felt like that. As if I belonged.'

'Well.' He raised his eyebrows, teasingly. 'In that case, we have a problem, don't we?'

'Do we?' she asked provocatively—and he burst out laughing, in love, crazy, utterly happy.

'And I've only enough supper for one,' he said. 'Never mind. We'll share.'

'I happen to have a delicious home-made steak and kidney pie in the hamper in my car,' she said demurely. 'As well as some fruit and chocolate and a rather good bottle of Chablis.'

He stared at her. 'You really meant to spend the evening here?'

She shrugged. 'I meant to stay as long as I could. So I came prepared. I saw that the stove was working and when I touched that woodburner in the study it was hot, so I thought I'd manage quite well.'

He stared down at her, serious now. 'You didn't think you'd be frightened? Not all on your own out here on the moor?'

'I didn't expect to be alone,' she said candidly.

He took a deep breath. 'I could be a madman,' he told her, almost crossly. 'A psychopath.'

'But you're not, are you?' She smiled at him. 'You just love Moorgate. So do I. For a moment in time we could enjoy the house together.'

'Melissa.' It was as if he were tasting her name, experimenting with it— then he frowned. 'But where on earth is your car?'

She laughed. 'It's hidden up a little track a hundred yards down the lane, just before you get to the trees. I was going to unload it when it was dark, just in case anyone saw me.'

'How very intrepid you are,' he said admiringly. 'Are you afraid of nothing?'

She turned away towards the fire, lest he should see the involuntary flicker of sadness. 'I'm afraid of being cold,' she said lightly. 'I do so feel the cold, which is why I was so pleased to see the Esse and the fires.' She touched the beanbag gently with the toe of her leather boot. 'I never thought about beanbags. What a clever idea. You sleep on them beside the fire?'

'Yes,' he said quickly, too quickly, visited suddenly by an intimate image.

There was a silence.

'I have some rugs,' she said at last. 'Nice warm rugs. Perhaps I could trade one of my rugs for one of your beanbags?'

'We'll manage somehow,' he said, glad to be free of the awkwardness. 'We'll pile the fire high with logs and tell each other ghost stories until we fall asleep. How does that sound?'

'It sounds perfect.'

He thought he saw the glint of tears in her eyes but decided it was simply the firelight.

'Shall we get the car unpacked, then?' he asked. 'Then we can really settle in. Close the shutters and batten down the hatches.'

'I have a picnic chair and a table,' she offered, 'and some knives and forks and things.'

'We'll go and forage,' he said cheerfully. 'The chair will be useful. I've only got one. Let's go before it gets too dark.'

She followed him out through the hall, into the kitchen. Outside the back door they paused. The night was cold and clear, stars twinkled frostily and a thin sickle moon was caught in a delicate net of black, bare branches. Their breath smoked in the icy air and he felt her shiver beside him.

'Come on,' he said. 'It's going to be cold tonight. Thank heavens we've got plenty of logs. Whatever happens, at least we won't freeze.'

Much later, giving Polonius his last outs, Maudie huddled into her shawl and stamped her feet.

'Hurry up,' she said. 'Just get on with it, will you. I'm freezing.'

Polonius ignored her, scenting rabbit and possibly fox. As she waited for him, she watched the frost-rimed grass sparkling, ghostly white, and listened to the creaking of the trees and the stealthy rustling of the birds roosting in the hedge. An owl called, down in the woods, answered by another closer at hand, and Maudie was suddenly aware of the presence of the trees, tall and dark beyond the gate, massed and silent, waiting and watching.

'Don't be fanciful,' she said, ridiculing a foolish trickle of fear. Polonius thrust a cold wet nose into her hand and she jumped violently and swore loudly. Back inside, she made up the woodburner and boiled the kettle so as to fill a hot-water bottle.

'Snow is forecast,' she told Polonius, who was enjoying his bedtime biscuit. 'But I think it's too clear to snow. Still, I'm glad Posy is safe in Winchester.'

Polonius wagged his tail obligingly, snuffling about for any missed crumbs, waiting whilst she filled the bottle and went away to put it in her bed. As she settled Polonius for the night, built up the stove and prepared herself for bed, Maudie was brooding on Selina. It was odd that now she was in a position to call the tune, she was getting very little pleasure from it. Thus far their battles had been pretty evenly matched—and there had been Hector in the role of referee—but, for the first time, she was holding all the cards.

'He who pays the piper calls the tune,' she murmured. 'Moorgate is mine, whatever Selina likes to say about it, and I shall do what I like with it. It would be madness to encourage her to buy it.'

For once, however, there was none of the sense of triumph she'd experienced in the tiny, bitter fights when she'd managed to score a point or two. Now there was a sense of—Maudie frowned, trying to identify this new sensation. It was a kind of dissatisfaction, edged about with irritation and guilt. She climbed into bed, pulling her silk shawl about her shoulders, cross with herself. Why couldn't she simply sell Moorgate and have done? Why not enjoy herself, thinking of the repairs that could be made and the car she might buy? Most of the money would be invested, anyway, against future emergencies but chiefly—she hoped—for Posy. Naturally, if Selina were to have a severe financial problem then she would help her but Hector had been generous to his daughters and such help shouldn't be necessary. As usual, when she arrived at this point in her reflections the question of Hector's investments slid unbidden into Maudie's mind. What could have happened to such a large sum of money?

Resolutely she pushed the thought away, concentrating instead on the plans for Daphne's visit later in the year. Excitement pulsed in her heart; what fun they'd have together. Selecting a tape from the pile in her bedside drawer—Schubert's *Winterreise* cycle—putting on her earphones, Maudie prepared herself for sleep.

In the kitchen at Moorgate, Rob and Melissa were sharing their supper. Sitting at the table, they discussed how the kitchen should be furnished. Melissa had the caned chair—the deckchair was too low and even with a rug folded on the seat, Rob had to reach a little to manage his pie—and they'd placed the table as near to the Esse as they could.

'It would make such a difference to have rugs on the floor,' Melissa said, watching as Rob dealt with the wine, 'and curtains, of course. Much more cosy. I'd have a really big kitchen table and a huge dresser.'

'I've often wondered whether it would be possible to find a dresser large enough.' Rob poured the wine into the glasses from the hamper. 'I think that it might have to be a built-in one, along the whole of the back wall.'

'Yes.' Melissa didn't sound too sure about it. 'But then it would look new, wouldn't it? Bright and shiny and rather horrid.'

'Not necessarily.' Rob settled himself on his folded rug. 'It could be made from old, reclaimed wood. Then it would look old but it could be made the right size for the room. Same thing with the table.'

'That would be terrific.' Her eyes shone as she looked at him and then glanced at the wall, imagining it. 'Oh, I can just see it. With lots of lovely bits of china on it. Not matching, you know, and Grandmama's old Victorian tat, but really treasured pieces that all seem to go together because they've been specially saved or bought. Because they're loved and because you simply couldn't live without having them. Do you know what I mean?'

'I'm beginning to think I do,' he said—and raised his glass to her.

She blushed fierily, colour washing beneath the fine pale skin, and she lifted her own glass to hide her confusion.

'It's the only way,' she said, ignoring the meaning behind his words, 'to make old and new live happily together. The trouble is with a dresser that size, the shelves would be practically empty for ages until the pieces built up over the years.'

'Sounds OK to me,' said Rob comfortably, attacking his pie. 'It would be a lifetime's work.'

He looked at her, surprised at the sudden silence. She was frowning down at her plate, lips pressed tightly together; almost, he thought for a mad moment, as though she were trying not to cry. This was so foolish he rejected it even as he thought it, deciding, instead, that his remark must have been too near the mark again. Of course, it was madness to feel so immediately happy with her, so content; that it was absolutely right that they should be planning how to furnish the kitchen and contemplating a lifetime together. Even if she felt the same it was unfair to put her in a position where she was obliged to admit it. He must give her space, allow her some dignity and pride. As for himself, he had no need of either; he was floating on a cushion of wellbeing and happiness.

'I'll show you the ford, tomorrow,' he said. 'There's a lovely old clapper bridge for wheeled traffic but we'll splash through the water properly. I hope you've brought some wellies with you?'

'Oh yes.' She seemed to have recovered herself. 'As you've seen I'm always well prepared. I would have been a first-rate girl guide if my mother would have let me join.'

'Why wouldn't she?'

Melissa put her elbows on the table, the glass cradled in her hands. 'My mother was a recluse,' she said. 'She couldn't possibly imagine anyone wishing to join anything. She made us feel inadequate if we asked to have friends to stay, if you know what I mean. It was odd, in her eyes, to need anyone.'

' "Us"?' he questioned gently. He had an overpowering need to know everything about her.

'I have a brother,' she said, after a moment. 'In the end, my father sent us both off to school together. It was the only way we could make friends properly or have any kind of social life. My mother died quite young, when I was fourteen. My father is still alive. He married again, a much younger woman, and had another family. He gave me and Mike twenty thousand pounds each and told us not to expect anything else from him. It was fair enough—very generous, in fact—but we've drifted a bit. His second wife isn't that keen on us. She feels she has to protect her own children, I expect.'

'You and your brother are close?'

'Oh yes.' Melissa smiled warmly. 'Very close. He's a dear. He has a small boy called Luke. And you?' She raised her eyebrows enquiringly. 'Tell me about you. Apart from loving Moorgate, I mean.'

'Oh, I come from quite a big family.' He leaned back in the little chair, which creaked warningly. 'All scattered about, though. We stay in touch at a distance. My mother is a Scot, a formidable woman who went to live with her sister in Inverness when they were both widowed. We're all very fond of one another but none of us is very close. Moorgate has been the only great passion of my life.'

They looked at one another a long heart-stopping moment. The words 'until now' drifted unspoken in the air and, quite involuntarily, Rob stretched out a hand to her across the table. After a moment, she laid her own hand in his and he held it tightly for a few brief seconds.

'You're cold,' he said sharply, coming to his senses.

' "My tiny hand is frozen",' she sang, laughing at him. 'I told you, I'm always cold.'

'It's a bitter night,' he said worriedly. 'Let's make some coffee and take it in by the fire. I piled the logs halfway up the chimney. It should be roasting in there. If only we had comfortable chairs . . .'

'Big, squashy armchairs,' she said dreamily, watching him push the kettle on to the hotplate. 'And a sofa, don't you think?'

'Oh, definitely. Perhaps two, facing each other, either side of the fire-place?'

She wrinkled her nose, shaking her head. 'Too formal. It's not a Regency drawing room, is it? What have you done with the chocolate?'

'Still in the hamper.' He peered inside. 'Goodness. That's quite a selection.'

'I love chocolate,' she told him. 'The only great passion of my life, until,' she hesitated, smiling to herself, 'until Moorgate.'

'Take the chocolate,' he said, wrapping her ruana about her, 'and go and get warm. I'll bring the coffee.' He held the soft wool together under her chin and then kissed her lightly on the forehead. 'Go on. I shan't be long.'

She sat on the beanbag, her knees drawn up to her chin, staring into the flames, the chocolate forgotten, wondering if they were both quite mad.

She thought: What would Mike think if he knew what I was doing?

He would be desperate with anxiety, of course. 'Are you crazy?' he'd shout. 'He sounds an absolute nutter. Get out as quick as you can.'

Melissa hugged her knees. It would be useless answering that Rob was so terribly sane that someone called Lady Todhunter trusted him with her house, that Mr Cruikshank liked him. Mike would be able to list at least a dozen personable, delightful homicidal maniacs—and he'd be right, of course. Yet she was not afraid. Perhaps it was because she had so little to lose; perhaps it was because her instinct told her that there was no need of fear. When he'd raised his glass to her she'd been filled with a wild elation; when he talked as though he'd already calmly accepted that they would share a lifetime together she'd wanted to weep. How right it had sounded, how natural, but how differently he would behave if she were to tell him that her lifetime was at best six months long.

It was such relief, such an absolute joy to act as if she were fit, ordinary, unhampered by such terrible knowledge. All the careless freedom of her young life had been done away with, nothing now could be taken for granted, but with Rob she could, for a short while, step out of time.

'Here we are.' The door had opened behind her and Rob was smiling down at her. 'Coffee. What we need is a tray. I'll have to go back for milk and sugar. I forgot to ask how you have your coffee.'

'I'm afraid I like milk and sugar,' she said apologetically. 'Shall I come and help carry?'

'Certainly not. Stay by the fire and keep warm.'

He went away again and she sat smiling to herself, liking his protectiveness, feeling ludicrously safe, terribly happy.

'Now.' He was back again, carrying the hamper. 'What a very useful thing this is. Every mod con as dear Ned would say.'

'I like him.' She defended Ned. 'He's sweet.'

'I agree.' Rob sat down beside her and began to take spoons from the hamper. He balanced the milk carton on the great granite slabs and put the bag of sugar beside it. 'I owe him a great debt of gratitude.'

She watched him covertly, liking the way his thick brown hair curled at the back of his neck, noting his deft hands, the long, strong back. He turned suddenly, meeting her eyes, and once again she felt herself blushing. He looked away quickly, fiddling with a spoon, and suddenly it was desperately important to let him know something of what she felt. Up until now he'd made the first tentative moves but instinct told her that he would go no further until she gave him some indication of her own feelings.

'This is so nice,' she said warmly. 'The fire and the coffee and—everything. It's as if I've stepped into a fairytale. It's all so magical.'

It was his turn to feel a little shy. 'It's the same for me,' he mumbled, pouring milk from the carton. 'Crazy, isn't it?'

His sudden loss of confidence had the effect of lifting her spirits. 'Let's be crazy together,' she suggested, liking him for his shyness. 'Tell me about the house. What it was like when you first saw it, and Lady Todhunter and everything.'

'Everything is a tall order,' he said, settling down beside her, lounging easily. 'But I'll try. OK. Are you sitting comfortably? Then I'll begin.'

Chapter Twenty-one

'That was your Aunt Melissa,' said Mike, putting down the telephone receiver and ruffling Luke's hair as he sat in his highchair. 'She's spent a comfortable night somewhere on the moor and is about to have her breakfast. Now we'll have ours, shall we?'

As he moved about, preparing Ready Brek for Luke, putting slices of wholemeal bread into the toaster, he was conscious of a relief from his anxiety. It was so difficult, keeping his fears from Melissa, trying as hard as he could to live as if she were not under a sentence of death. For short periods they managed it but it was impossible to maintain the pretence for long. To begin with she had been angry, bitter with resentment, railing against such a cruel fate, but gradually her rage had subsided and a quieter resignation had taken its place; resignation punctuated by periods of depression. Yet, once she had decided to let nature take its course, her natural resilience and optimism had reappeared along with a determination to enjoy wholeheartedly whatever time was left to her. He guessed that, paradoxically, although she needed him so much he was the one person from whom she could not hide her true feelings. This brief respite, this opportunity to be normal, was so necessary for her emotionally and spiritually; what toll it might take physically simply had to be accepted. Mike put the marmalade on the table, picked up Luke's toy car and rescued the milk in the saucepan on the electric ring. So far, with Melissa's help he'd managed without a nanny.

'Women bring up their children without a nanny,' he argued, when friends expressed astonishment at his coping on his own with Luke. 'Why shouldn't I? After all, I work at home.'

It was lucky that he liked to work late, writing in the evening when Luke was asleep in bed, but it was good to have Melissa around; good to have someone else to talk to, joke with, to discuss the work in progress over endless cups of coffee. He hadn't been able to talk to Camilla about his work, not that she'd been particularly interested anyway, but Melissa was different. They'd shared so much. Perhaps this was due to those isolated years of childhood when, denied friends and any normal social life, they'd been thrown upon their own inventions. He'd made up stories and written plays in which they'd acted, sharing the roles between themselves. Odd, then, that both he and Melissa were gregarious people who enjoyed parties and had plenty of friends. He'd loved the years in the theatre—the Camilla years—but, since Luke, he'd settled down to a quieter life: intimate suppers with just a few friends around the kitchen table; a pint at the pub with the locals.

With Luke growing up, Mike had been aware of a growing need to move out into the country again. He could remember his own childhood, the freedom and the space, and he wanted it for Luke. There was so much fear in the world, so much perceived danger, and he wanted Luke to develop with a balanced, happy view of people and the universe. He could remember a past when you could exchange greetings with passers-by, smile at children, embrace a friend and not fear that these natural expressions of a loving nature were misunderstood. Maybe it was already too late to hope for such a world for Luke—but he intended to try for it—although the edge of Bodmin Moor was perhaps a little extreme.

Melissa had sounded enthusiastic about Moorgate but the signal had kept breaking up and he hadn't been able to hear too much, apart from the happy lilt to her voice. It was evident that she was enjoying herself and that was all that mattered. He'd restrained himself from fussing, from reminding her not to get overtired. It didn't matter too much where she was—he could always contact her on her mobile—but it was necessary to know that she was safe and happy.

'It's good, Mike,' she'd said joyfully. 'It's really good. But oh! it's so *cold*.'

'You've picked the coldest week of the winter,' he'd told her. 'The weather's coming from Siberia. Be careful driving and keep warm.'

'I shall,' she'd said, 'don't worry. I'm having a lovely time. How are you? How's Luke?'

Amidst the crackling, her voice fading and suddenly returning, he hadn't been able to do more than give her their love and ask her to stay in touch. She needed to feel free, normal, untrammelled by fear. If she could achieve it for a week or two then it would be a wonderful miracle.

'Go for it, Lissy,' he murmured, sitting down at the table beside Luke. 'Here we are, old son. Breakfast at last.'

'Gah!' said Luke, drumming on his small table with his fists. 'Bah! Dadadada!'

'That's it,' said Mike. 'Me, Dad. You, Luke. This is breakfast. Open wide, please.'

'Hi, babe,' said Posy. 'I know it's an early one for me but I thought I'd just check you're OK down there. I understand that the West Country is freezing hard and pipes are bursting and cars crashing on black ice and goodness knows what.'

Maudie, delighted at being addressed as 'babe' again, felt her spirits soar.

'It's certainly cold,' she said, 'but everything's working properly, I'm glad to say. I saw the forecast yesterday, so Polonius and I went to Bovey to stock up, just in case. I shan't be taking the car out, so don't worry. How are you?'

'Great. Cold, though. This house is freezing. I went to bed in all my clothes . . .'

She chattered on cheerfully whilst Maudie felt as though some great weight was being lifted from her shoulders. When Posy finally rang off, Maudie returned to her breakfast.

'She's in splendid form,' she told Polonius. 'Such a relief. Now if only Selina would come to her senses we might all be able to return to normal.'

Before she could start on her toast the telephone rang again.

'Good morning, Lady Todhunter. It's Ned Cruikshank. Sorry to catch you so early but I wanted you to hear my news first hand. I'm being transferred to the London office at the end of the week.'

'Good heavens,' she said, startled. 'Well, I'm sorry to hear this, Ned. I shall miss you. I'm sure you're thrilled?'

'I am rather.' As usual he sounded slightly breathless and confiding. 'I shall be sorry in some ways, though.'

'Well, I hope I shall like your replacement and that whoever it is will be as enthusiastic about Moorgate as you've been.'

'Well, that's what I wanted to tell you.' He became even more confidential. 'I think I may have a buyer. A young woman. Very keen indeed. I hope to have good news for you by the end of the week.'

'But that's wonderful, Ned. I shall be very pleased to think that you brought it off and I hope you get a good commission.'

He laughed. 'So do I. Anyway, I wanted you to know the glad tidings but I'll ring you again before I leave. Just to bring you up to speed and to say goodbye.'

'That's very nice of you, Ned. I'll look forward to hearing from you. Is it very cold down there?'

'Freezing.' He made shivery noises. 'They say it's going to snow but it's a glorious morning. Must dash. Goodbye.'

Maudie replaced the receiver feeling quite shocked.

'Well,' she said to Polonius. 'What a morning we're having. I *do* hope he's right. It would solve so many problems.'

For the third time she sat down to her breakfast, watching the birds on the feeder, planning her day, more light-hearted than she had been for many weeks. A genuine buyer would let her off Selina's hook and she might be able to stop feeling guilty.

'The G-word,' she murmured, thinking of Posy. 'How it rules our lives. And I was going to enjoy myself so much, paying the piper and calling the tune. Oh, it's so *frustrating*.' Polonius cocked an eye at her and she nodded. 'Quite right. More important things to do. We'll have a walk out towards Lustleigh after breakfast. It's too good a morning to waste indoors.'

Breakfast at Moorgate was a rather patchy business; mainly coffee and fruit. Melissa woke to find Rob putting a mug of coffee beside her. She uncurled herself, shivering a little, glad to see the fire was newly made up.

'I didn't want to disturb you,' Rob said as he folded back the wooden shutters, 'but I didn't want you to be cold, either. It's quite warm in the bathroom if you feel you can brave it.'

He went away again, closing the door behind him, and she sat up, dazzled by the sunlight which poured into the room. She reached for the mug, cradling it in her hands, remembering. They'd sat together, talking for hours—or so it seemed—before they settled down to sleep. Somehow, the talking had eased them away from embarrassment and, when she'd come back downstairs from the bathroom, he'd made up a bed for her; her sleeping bag arranged on one of the beanbags with a rug tucked over it.

'In you get,' he'd said. 'I'm off for a quick sluice. Make yourself comfortable.' And she *had* been comfortable—and warm. She'd been aware of him during the night, moving quietly about, making up the fire, before settling down again, and she'd lain awake for a while, watching the shadows leaping and falling and listening to the hiss of the flames as they curled greedily round the wood. For once these wakeful periods were brief and full of anticipation and she'd slept well and felt unusually rested. She wriggled out of the sleeping bag and, mug in hand, rug trailing, went to the window. A rime of frost sparkled in the sunshine and the rooks were arguing in the tree across the lane. She sighed with deep satisfaction, excitement fizzing. Today he would show her the ford and they would walk on the hills and she would imagine—just for today—that they had a future together.

'Breakfast,' said Rob from the doorway, 'will be a little disappointing after the feast we conjured up last night. At least, I'm assuming that you haven't got a packet of porridge in the car or a boot-load of bacon and eggs?'

Melissa shook her head, laughing. 'I'm afraid not. I'm not a big breakfast eater, to tell you the truth, but this morning I'd kill for a plate of bacon and eggs. I wish you hadn't mentioned it. Oh, and some big field mushrooms and a sausage.'

'I know a café in Tintagel,' he said thoughtfully, 'which could answer most of those requirements. How about we try it? I could go out and shop and cook it on the Esse but it would be unfortunate if Ned Cruikshank turned up in the middle of it. Or Lady Todhunter.'

'Oh, heavens. Is that likely?' She looked alarmed. 'I must admit that having the keys has given me a false sense of security. I never imagined anyone else turning up. Do you really think Lady Todhunter might appear?'

'Unlikely but not altogether impossible. As caretaker I feel I can take certain liberties but I suppose we should keep within the limits of reality.'

Melissa made a face. 'How dull and unadventurous of you. Never mind. Tintagel it shall be.'

'We're OK early and late,' he said, 'but we must be careful during the day in case the wretched Ned takes it into his head to appear. Since you've got his keys it's most unlikely that he will, unless he telephones me first. I'll keep my mobile switched off.'

'Oh, no,' she said at once. 'Keep it switched on so that you can head him off. Or at least we'd be forewarned if he were determined to come down.'

They laughed together, like conspirators, and Rob looked about the room.

'I'll clear the stuff away under the stairs,' he said. 'Hide the evidence. Hurry away, wench, and get ready. I'm starving.'

She went upstairs, taking her coffee, smoothing the banister appreciatively, pausing to stare out of the landing window at the icy, rolling moorland where the lambs skipped erratically at their mothers' heels and a raven strutted, driving his beak into the frozen earth. The chilly spaces drove her into the warm bathroom and presently she was back downstairs in the kitchen, eating an apple whilst Rob tidied things into the hamper.

'What a useful man you are,' she commented, watching him. And a very attractive one, she might have added. He wore a thick fisherman's jersey and jeans, and his hair was clean and shiny, curling a little from his early morning shower. He glanced up at her but this time she did not blush or look away.

'Good morning, Rob,' she said. 'I can't tell you what fun I'm having.'

'We aim to please,' he said—and she went to him quite naturally and put her arms about him, hugging him. 'This is cheating,' he said, holding her tightly, his hands full of forks and plates, 'because you know I'm far too hungry to take advantage of you.'

She kissed him quickly and let him go. 'Let me do this,' she said. 'I know where everything lives. How far is Tintagel?'

'Not far,' he said, 'but we'll take your car, if you don't mind, and collect mine later.'

He'd already put away the table and chairs so that no sign of occupation was left and a few minutes later they went out, carrying the hamper and some rugs, to find the car.

'Gosh!' she said, gasping, waiting whilst he locked the back door. 'It's freezing.'

'The wind's from the north,' he told her. 'Come on. It'll be warmer in the sun.'

Inside the car it was like being in a fridge and her teeth chattered as she drove away down the lane, following his instructions until at last they came to Tintagel. They fed lavishly on eggs and bacon, with toast and more coffee, in the company of the café proprietor, who watched them meditatively. Content at last they sat back and looked at one another.

'I hope,' said Rob, trying to sound casual, 'that you aren't going to abandon me now that you are replete with victuals.'

'Certainly not.' She sounded shocked. 'You promised me the ford and a clapper bridge. You said that I could splash through the ford if I'd brought my wellies. I hope you are not intending to renege from your promise?'

He sighed happily. 'We shall splash together. I just wondered if . . . you had any other engagements.'

The diffidence in his voice moved her heart and she lightly touched his fist where it lay on the table.

'None,' she said. 'I'm a free agent. I spoke to my brother earlier on my mobile so my duty is done for the day.'

He turned his hand, holding hers, watching her curiously. 'Did you tell him where you were?'

She grinned. 'Not exactly. He knows that I'm staying on the moor and having a wonderful time. It's a pity, isn't it, that if you move about the signal breaks up a bit and it goes all crackly and you have to shout? Things like, "Sorry. Can't quite hear but I'm fine. Don't worry. I'll call you later." That sort of thing. I don't want him to worry but he might not *quite* understand.'

Rob began to laugh. He laughed himself into a choking fit and the proprietor, concerned, came and poured more coffee whilst Melissa watched sympathetically.

'No, he probably wouldn't *quite* understand,' he agreed at last. 'In his place I'd have had a fit and ordered you back to a hotel.'

'Exactly,' said Melissa comfortably, sipping the fresh hot coffee. 'You take my point.'

'You're in no danger from me,' he grumbled. 'Always was a fool with women.'

'I expect Jack the Ripper used to say the same thing,' she said cheerfully, 'but it's too late. I'm in love.'

He looked at her sharply, eyebrows raised.

'With Moorgate,' she said sweetly, challengingly, and he chuckled. 'Those keys aren't going back just yet.'

'In that case we'd better stock up for the day,' he suggested—and hesitated.

'Oh, at least,' she said at once. 'After all, tomorrow we could have a nice early breakfast, couldn't we? It's not that I don't like it here—the food's great—but I'd like to have breakfast at Moorgate.'

There was a short silence.

'In that case,' said Rob, finishing his coffee, 'we'd better do some shopping.'

Chapter Twenty-two

It was just after break, in the staff room, that Patrick noticed the advertisement. The paper had been folded back to the classified ads page and the headline caught his attention. 'Could you be a L'Arche assistant?' it asked. He'd heard of L'Arche; communities which looked after people with disabilities and learning difficulties. Perhaps it was Mary who had mentioned it. His eyes wandered over the column. 'There are no specific qualifications for being a L'Arche assistant, except being at least 18 years old . . . Others decide upon L'Arche as a career change. Many find the vocation fulfilling enough to stay for many years.' He remembered reading about Jean Vanier, a naval officer and then a professor of Moral Theosophy who gave up a promising career to help those who had been marginalised by society. He'd bought a little house and invited two such men into it—and so had started an incredible world-wide movement.

Patrick stood holding the paper, an idea forming at the back of his mind. The door opened behind him and Mary came in.

'Oh,' she said, taken aback, clearly expecting the room to be empty. 'Hello. I left my paper. Oh, yes. That's it. Were you reading it?'

Patrick looked at her, faintly saddened by her brittleness, still surprised by his own indifference. This odd depression, which numbed all feeling, was a strange business. He smiled at her quite easily, feeling in his jacket pocket for his pen and his diary.

'Mind if I jot down a number?' he asked, resting the diary on the table, flattening the paper. 'Won't take a moment. Just an advert that caught my eye.'

'Tear it out,' she said, almost impatiently, suddenly not caring about the paper, needing his attention.

'Thanks. I will. It's just this top corner. How's Stuart?'

'He's OK. Fine . . . well, you know.' She sounded flustered. 'He's making progress.'

'That's good. Splendid.'

Patrick might have been talking about a distant acquaintance, more occupied with what he was writing than with her or Stuart, and suddenly—and quite unreasonably—Mary felt affronted.

'You don't sound all that interested.'

He looked up at her in surprise, folding the piece of paper into his diary, and she bit her lip, annoyed with herself.

'I had the impression that you preferred me to keep my interest to myself.'

He wasn't huffy, she noticed, not martyred or hard done by, merely amused, and she felt her irritation grow. Had he shown the least flicker of hope, a renewal of his need of her, she'd have quickly put him back in his place. As it was she felt an unforgivable requirement to test her power, to experience the sense of being desired which his adoration had always supplied.

'I didn't realise you'd be able to switch off so easily.'

'Switch off?'

She shrugged. 'Forget us. Stop caring. Whatever.'

He frowned thoughtfully. 'Is that what I've done? Yes, I suppose it is.'

Contrarily, she'd always fancied him most when he'd drawn back a little, been less intense, and now she had a keen longing to turn back the clock. She knew she couldn't, knew the dangers still existed, that nothing had changed, but the knowledge of his love had been very sweet and there had been a strange little frisson in being at school with him once the affair was over. Just lately, however, he'd become withdrawn, aloof, and at some basic level she wanted to know that he still wanted her. His measured reply hurt her pride and, as he handed her the paper, she drew closer, looking up at him.

'I miss you,' she said. 'I really do. I wish things could be different.'

She looked for an answering response, for the flash of love in his eyes, but he simply smiled rather absently at her, as though she were merely a very good friend.

'Never mind,' he said, as if comforting her. 'Perhaps it was for the best.'

He went out, tucking his diary into his pocket, and she stood looking after him, angry and miserable, and, worst of all, humiliated.

Shopping in Tintagel, choosing supper, waiting in the car whilst Rob disappeared on a mission of his own, Melissa was wrapped in the delightful holiday anonymity that she'd first experienced in Bovey Tracey. She felt free, almost invisible. These nice local people, going about their business, barely spared her a second glance so used were they to visitors in their midst. No one looked at her with sympathy or avoided meeting her eyes because they couldn't bear to admit to their weighty, private knowledge. Sometimes, she knew, when friends burst out laughing at some joke or a television programme they suffered an immediate stab of guilt; that they should be able to laugh, knowing her situation, filled them with a kind of self-disgust.

'Please laugh,' she wanted to say. 'Please continue to live, to enjoy life,' but she knew that it would make the reaction worse. Either she ignored it or laughed too, but the responsibility was heavy. If she became tired or low in spirits, their response was far more exaggerated than if she'd been an ordinary, healthy person. In the end she was able to relax only when she was alone—or with Mike. Mike understood. It had been a relief to move from London to Oxford but, pretty soon, the rumours had spread, someone had seen her at the surgery, so that now, even in Oxford, she felt the pressure building again.

Perhaps that's why Moorgate had appealed so much; its isolation attracted her, promising peace. Now that she was here, however, now that she'd met Rob, she didn't want to think about practicalities. How could she imagine Mike and Luke moving into Moorgate now that she knew how much Rob loved it? To own Moorgate was his dream; he'd worked so hard on it, put so much of himself into it. For these few days she wanted to forget her real reason for coming; she simply wanted to postpone decisions, put aside reality, and lose herself in this small, magic world.

Rob was coming towards her, a bulky parcel under his arm and a carrier bag in his other hand, his expression a mixture of satisfaction and embarrass-ment. She was amused and puzzled but she did not question him.

'Right,' he said, settling himself beside her, the parcels stowed away behind them. 'Would you like to continue to drive us about or shall we get my old pick-up?'

Melissa instinctively felt that he didn't want to go back to his place and collect his own transport. She believed that he felt exactly as she did; that he wanted to be free of the real world for this short moment in time, to remain anonymous. Nobody here knew her or would recognise her car. They could be free; it was as if they didn't exist. Clearly he was a man who did not need to drive to establish his identity and he was a calm, relaxed passenger.

'I'm quite happy to drive,' she said. 'As long as you don't mind direct-ing me.'

'Oh, I'm good at that,' he said easily. 'I've always enjoyed telling people what to do. OK, then. We'll head for the wide open spaces, shall we?'

'I'd like to get up on to the moor,' she agreed, pulling away from the kerb, following his directions. 'I want to see Moorgate from somewhere else.'

'And so you shall,' he said. 'Do you have a hat as well as that scarf thing?'

She hesitated for a moment, foolishly sad that he would never see her with the thick long, bronze mass of hair that she'd had before the chemo, and he looked at her curiously.

'Yes,' she said quickly. 'Yes, I have a hat but you must promise not to laugh at it. Why do you ask?'

'It'll be seriously cold higher up,' he answered. 'The chill factor is sup-posed to be minus two. We may not be able to stick too much of it.'

She smiled at the 'we', suspecting that the cold hardly bothered him at all, liking him enormously.

'These lanes are so narrow,' she said—and gave a loud squeak as the car skidded on a patch of ice and then righted itself.

'The sun doesn't get to them at this time of the year,' he said, appar-ently unmoved. 'At least, not until the middle of the day. We'll cross the A39 in a minute. Not far now.'

The moor rose up ahead of them but she looked in vain for Moorgate.

'Don't worry,' he said, guessing her thoughts. 'You'll see her in a minute. Straight over here and then right. That's it. Now we're climbing. That's Rough Tor, see, away to the north there?'

Presently they came to the ford. The brown, peaty water flowed across the road and away under an old granite clapper bridge but Melissa drove through the stream and came to a rest just beyond it.

'Come on,' said Rob. 'We'll have a little stroll and I'll show you something.'

She dragged the sheepskin cap over her ears and climbed out. The wind was so sharp, so icy, it deprived her of her breath and she gasped, feeling the air freezing against her skin. Beyond the ford, ice had formed along the shallows beneath the bank and the grass crunched like glass under their feet. On the slopes below them a tractor was parked, whilst the farmer flung great forkfuls of feed for the sheep, and in the blue sparkling air a buzzard circled, crying insistently. Rob slipped an arm about Melissa's shoulder, turning her slightly, pointing.

'Look there,' he said.

They were looking at Moorgate from its north side. There it stood, comfortable, belonging, gazing out across the moor. It should have looked bleak, lonely, desolate, but it didn't. Melissa thought that it looked strong and welcoming and safe; safe as Rob's arm about her, holding her close. She looked up at him. He was staring at Moorgate, smiling a little, and she felt a sudden welling of desire, a tremendous need for him. He glanced down at her and his smile faded; his look intent.

His lips were burning cold but for once she was gloriously warm, the blood rushing in her ears and tingling to the tips of her fingers. After a long moment she drew back a little and he clasped her close, his cheek against hers.

'You do pick your moments,' he murmured in her ear—and she burst out laughing, glad to take refuge in simple, uncomplicated happiness.

'I love you both,' she said, meaning it. 'Doesn't Moorgate look wonderful? Just as if she grew out of the ground. I suppose you didn't think to bring some chocolate with you?'

'It just so happens,' he said, releasing her, digging into his pocket, 'that I did. So what do I get for being so clever?'

'You get half the chocolate,' she said promptly. 'Look at the lambs. How high they spring. I suppose you haven't got a flask of hot coffee slung about your person, too, have you?'

'No, I have not,' he said firmly. 'We'll have to go back to the car. I never knew a wench with such a passion for her vittles.'

'I need them,' she said simply, tucking her arm into his. 'What's that tor over there? Is it the one we saw earlier?'

'That's Rough Tor,' he told her as they stepped out briskly, 'and beyond that is Brown Willy, but we can't see it from here. There's lots to show you before we go . . . home.'

'Home.' She looked up at him, unable to conceal a wave of longing. 'Oh, if only it were.'

'Perhaps it could be,' he said tentatively. 'Perhaps there might be a way.'

She swallowed down her emotion, clutching his arm tightly. 'For today it is, anyway,' she said. 'And for tonight.'

She unlocked the car and climbed in whilst Rob lifted the hatch and opened the hamper. By the time he brought her the mug of steaming coffee she'd managed to control her despair, to will back the hope with which she dispelled her unexpected descents into terror. She smiled at him, taking comfort from his strong presence, accepting his love, knowing that she must try to live for the moment.

Selina stood in the hall, listening. Supper was finished and Patrick had disappeared up to his study, but the situation was not resolved. All day she'd been gradually building up the courage to confront him; to talk properly about this *impasse*. It was impossible to carry on in this miserable way, as if they were polite strangers who merely happened to share the same house. He was impervious to all the tactics she'd used so successfully in the past and she felt helpless and frustrated. She'd planned to discuss it immediately after supper—and had drunk several glasses of wine so as to bolster up her resolve—but Paul had telephoned at exactly the wrong moment. He'd been promoted and wanted to share the glad tidings with his parents but, by the time he'd finished telling her all the details, Patrick had cleared the table and vanished. He'd been particularly preoccupied, with a kind of suppressed excitement about him, and she was beginning to suspect that he'd revived his affair with Mary. Now, as she cautiously climbed the stairs, she could hear his voice: he was talking to someone on the telephone.

'That sounds fantastic,' he was saying. Then. 'If you could, I'd be terribly grateful.' Another pause. 'No, no. I quite understand. Yes, Brecon sounds wonderful.'

She thought: *Brecon?* Whatever is he talking about?

She heard the receiver go down and hesitated for a moment. The house seemed oppressively empty; silence flowed around her and she felt unbearably lonely. The thought of another sleepless night, alone in their bedroom, galvanised her into action. Reaching the landing, she tapped at the door and opened it. He was sitting hunched at the desk, staring down at it, deep in thought.

'Patrick,' she said, almost pleadingly, 'I need to talk to you.'

He raised his eyebrows in a friendly question but didn't speak.

'We can't go on like this, can we? I mean, hardly communicating, talking about the weather and you going off to the spare room every night. It's silly.'

'It's difficult to know how to handle it, isn't it?' he agreed, almost cheerfully. 'But it won't be for much longer, I hope.'

She was staring at him, frowning. 'What on earth do you mean?'

He looked surprised. 'Well, I've been trying to decide where I should go. What I might do. That sort of thing. But now I think I've found just what I've been looking for.'

'What the hell are you talking about?' Anxiety made her angry. 'If you think I'm impressed by this silly pretence you couldn't be more wrong. It's simply not interesting.'

'I don't think you've ever thought me interesting,' he answered. 'But at least I'm not pretending. I thought we'd agreed that whatever we had together has outlived itself. It was bound to happen once the children were gone. Looking back, I can see that there wasn't much to begin with. You used me to get away from Maudie and Hector, and the children were the glue which held us together. It's dried up now, peeled off, and we're back where we started. If your father hadn't injected slugs of cash from time to time we probably wouldn't have lasted this long. You've always wanted more than I could give you, Selina.'

'This is all utter nonsense. Just because I stood up for myself over the Mary thing—'

'Precisely.' He gave a short laugh. 'You stood up for yourself. You didn't fight for *me*.'

She frowned again, puzzled. 'What d'you mean? Of course it was for you.'

'No.' He shook his head firmly. 'No, it wasn't. You didn't fight to get me back because you love me. You did it because I am one of your possessions. Love was not involved, Selina.'

'You're wrong,' she said quickly. 'Look. This has just got completely out of hand—'

'That's quite true,' he agreed. 'It has got completely out of your hands, Selina. For once my life is in my own hands and I intend to live it my way. You're no longer calling the tune. You've dominated and controlled us all—well, except for Posy—for nearly thirty years and I've had enough.'

'Oh, I see.' She folded her arms under her breasts, her lip curling. 'And so just because I refuse to condone your sordid affair with some little tart you're running out on me. You're reneging on your marriage vows, betraying your children and abandoning your wife.'

'Yes.' He looked rather struck by this catalogue of misdeeds; almost proud. 'I suppose you could say exactly that. I hadn't quite seen it in those terms—'

'May I ask how you *had* seen it?'

He ignored the tone of heavy irony. 'I saw it as a relationship which was worn out, dried out and tasteless. The boys have never been too bothered about me and I've nearly managed to alienate Posy, who will soon be too busy with her own life to care either way. As for you, well, I've annoyed and irritated you for more than a quarter of a century. You've decided where we live, who our friends are, where we have our holidays and how our money is spent, and you're still not happy. You've humiliated me, hurt me and ignored me.' He paused for a moment. 'Have you noticed, Selina, how you never use the words "we" or "ours"? Only "I" and "mine"? Just a small point but a significant one. I accept that to leave a wife to fend for herself is a disgraceful thing to do but I intend to do it. This house is worth at least three hundred thousand pounds. You can downsize and have enough to invest for a reasonable living when you put it with the other pensions we have. You won't starve.'

'I'm beginning to wonder if you're ill. I think you've lost your senses.'

He shrugged. 'You would. But I'm fairly sane, I think. Just heady with the sensation of freedom.'

'And you think it will be that easy? That I'll let you stroll off into the sunset? I don't want to sell this house and downsize. I like it here. I'm not moving into some grotty little flat.'

'Suit yourself. Thanks to your father we don't have a mortgage and you've got some savings. Stay here and work. I know you never have but it's never too late to try something new.'

'You're mad.' She was quite serious. 'You're having some kind of breakdown.'

He laughed. 'It's funny you should say that. I had the same thought myself.' He looked at her sympathetically. 'Poor Selina. It's come as a shock, hasn't it? The worm turning and so forth. Don't worry, I shan't take anything that's yours.'

'Don't be so bloody offensive,' she shouted. 'You're crazy. Off your head. I shall speak to my lawyer in the morning.'

'*Our* lawyer,' he corrected her gently. 'Steve is my lawyer too, remember.'

She glared at him, furious but impotent. 'And have you told him that you're leaving me to go to Brecon? Got another little tart there, have you?'

She went out, slamming the door behind her, running down the stairs. Patrick sat quite still, staring reflectively at the door. Presently he picked up a piece of paper, studying it carefully.

Could you be a L'Arche assistant? Some people come from sixth form or college. Others decide upon L'Arche as a career change . . . Many find the vocation fulfilling enough to stay for many years . . . Assistants receive free board and lodging and a modest weekly income . . .

Chapter Twenty-three

Once again she was alone in the house. They'd returned as dusk was beginning to fall, after a day of exploration, and when Melissa was beginning to feel very tired.

'It feels warmer,' she'd said, as they unloaded the car. 'Or am I imagining it? I'll still be glad to get indoors, though.'

Rob had paused, his arms full of parcels, looking away to the north. Pillowy, downy clouds lay piled, layer upon layer, advancing slowly, and he'd begun to whistle thoughtfully under his breath as he followed her into the house. The kitchen was warm and, leaving Melissa to deal with the putting away of their supplies, he'd gone through to the sitting room. Earlier that morning he'd built up the fire with the biggest logs he could find and it was still burning, though very low. He'd dragged the remaining logs together, piled more dry ones on top and begun to ply the bellows. Soon the flames were leaping, the wood crackling, and he'd left it so as to check the wood-burning stove. Back in the kitchen he'd washed his hands at the sink, drying them on the towel he kept on the rail of the Esse.

'I've had a thought,' he'd said, quite casually. 'I might bring a few things up from my place. Just to make us more comfortable.'

She'd glanced at him, surprised, still feeling that he didn't particularly want her to step out of this charmed circle.

'I suppose you could take the car?' she'd suggested uncertainly. 'You're probably insured to drive other vehicles.'

'Oh, I shan't bother,' he'd answered quickly. 'I'll walk down and bring back the pick-up. Not a problem. See you later.'

He'd smiled at her across the spaces of the kitchen, uncertain how to take his leave of her, and then had gone out quickly. Standing at the window she'd watched him climb the rail fence and stride off across the moor, keeping in the shadow of the thorn.

After a while, she turned, leaning back against the sink, looking about her, alone again. It was at about this time yesterday that she'd watched him climbing up the same way, pausing occasionally to look up at the house. She'd moved back, lest he should see her, and then she'd heard him enter. Standing in the shadow of the stairs, peering from the landing, she'd watched him moving about, heard him preparing the house. She smiled as she remembered his shocked gasp when he saw her standing by the fire; could it really be only twenty-four hours ago? It was unusual to feel so at ease with someone so quickly; to be so comfortable. Yet underneath the camaraderie was an exciting undercurrent.

Melissa shivered a little, hugging her warm soft pashmina around her. She felt terribly tired. Passing through the hall into the sitting room, subsiding on to the beanbags which Rob had brought out again, Melissa felt a twinge of guilt. She knew that Mike would have thoroughly disapproved of such a long and active day, and she also knew that she should telephone him so as to reassure him that all was well. This weariness, however, the weighty, weary limbs and a faint nagging pain, kept her pinned to her soft bed.

'I'll do it in a minute,' she murmured, watching the flames, conscious of the pain. 'I'm having such fun. Mike won't begrudge me it.'

She lay, listening to the rooks settling for the night, as the light receded and the room grew dimmer. Her exhaustion and the pain were grim reminders of reality and, against her will, she felt the tears sliding down her cheeks. Never had she wanted so much to live, to be fit and normal, happy and uncaring and healthy. As she lay, huddled in the firelight, she imagined she could hear the life of the house going on around her.

'Huge comfortable sofas . . .' A man's voice, oddly familiar.

'Oh, yes, but not too smart. No fussing if the dogs climb on them.'

'Or the children?' He was smiling, she could hear it in his voice.

'Of course not.' The voice was indignant. 'It's their home, isn't it?'

'So what about this as my study, then?'

The voices faded a little and Melissa stirred. They'd crossed the hall and were standing inside the other room.

'It would make a wonderful playroom.' The voice was wistful, now. 'A really terrific living room for everyone. And it's so sunny.'

'Perhaps you'd like me to work in the loosebox?'

'The pony wouldn't like that.'

They laughed together, softly, intimately, and Melissa strained towards them, trying to see them, following them up the stairs.

'It's such a lovely room.' They were standing together at the window of the big bedroom. 'We'll have the bed facing the window so that we can see the trees.'

'This is the nursery.' How confident she sounded. 'Isn't it perfect? With the room next door, and the small bathroom, it makes it the children's quarters.'

'I must put up a swing on the lawn.'

'Under the escallonia hedge.'

They'd stopped to look out of the landing window and she heard the sound of a child's voice calling to them.

She tried to struggle up, to go to the child, but she was too tired, her limbs were too heavy. They were coming down, though, calling to the child, the man was swinging him up into his arms, murmuring endearments. Melissa relaxed, drifting, dreaming, until she could see them again. They were in the garden. The sun was hot and the girl, standing with her back to Melissa, wore a cotton sun hat.

'Be careful,' she called to the small boy on the swing. 'Be careful. Not too high.'

He was singing to himself, laughing as he swung, and the girl went to look into a pram which was standing in the shade of the escallonia hedge, rocking it with a proprietorial air which was absurdly touching. She turned suddenly, smiling at Melissa, who smiled back, recognising her, holding out her arms in welcome.

'It's you,' she murmured—and felt herself lifted, held tightly.

'You were dreaming,' Rob said. 'I was afraid of startling you.'

She clung to him, wrenched with a terrible sense of loss, quite unable to speak. He continued to kneel beside her on the floor, cradling her.

'Sorry,' she muttered at last. 'Really silly. Just a very vivid dream. I'm OK now.'

He released her, going to close the shutters against the dark, piling more wood on the fire.

'Do you feel up to coming to see what I've brought back with me?' he asked.

'I certainly do.' The dream was fading now and some of her weariness was receding with it. 'It sounds very mysterious.'

In the kitchen was a wooden armchair with comfortable cushions and another dining chair. Two electric heaters stood beside them. Melissa began to laugh.

'How very clever of you. But why only one armchair?'

Rob laughed with her. 'I only have one armchair. Everything else is built in. It's for you.'

'It's a nice big one,' she said thoughtfully. 'Perhaps we could share it? Or am I being forward?'

He grinned. 'Wait until you see what's upstairs.'

She climbed after him, some of her former weakness returning, but he was too tense to notice it. On the floor of the main bedroom, plump and welcoming, lay a pumped-up king-sized air bed and several pillows.

'Now who's being forward?' he asked. 'I bought it earlier in Tintagel at the camping shop.'

'Oh, Rob,' she said, 'what a brilliant idea. We should be warm enough on that, shouldn't we?'

He chuckled. 'That's the last of my worries. We'll bring up all the rugs and both the heaters.'

'And some chocolate,' she said, 'and several flasks of hot coffee.'

'Every mod con,' he agreed with relief. 'I thought you might slap my face and go off in a huff.'

'No you didn't,' she said comfortably, taking his arm. 'You knew very well that it was exactly the right thing to do.'

He grimaced. 'I wasn't quite that confident, but never mind. I'll bring the heaters up so as to get the room really warm, although I have to say that this radiator run off the Esse does pretty well. It's almost too hot to touch but we'll need it. I think it'll be another cold night.'

'Probably. Although I feel it's a bit warmer.'

'Mmm.' He followed her downstairs, grinning guiltily, secretly, to himself. 'I'm sure you're right. How's supper doing? I'm starving.'

Because Rob had taken the action needed to remove any further embarrassment, dinner was a straightforward relaxed affair and they were able to talk easily and naturally. Rob told her about his desperate bid to buy Moorgate, his race against time and how he was trying to raise the deposit.

'That's the real problem,' he said. 'I've got loads of work. I'm doing well, now. I can cope with the mortgage. But the deposit is something else. I'm terrified that some rich yuppie will come along and snap it up under my nose.'

'So how do you deter them?' she asked.

'Oh, it's easy. Most of them want to live in the country but they have an image of a nice, clean, sanitised world beyond their gate. Mud, cow-shit, no streetlights don't really appeal, and Moorgate still has the look of the farm about it. It isn't a rectory with a long drive and grounds all round it. Then again, there's the weather. Days of driving rain and fairly consistent southwesterly winds are a turn-off. It's bad luck if they turn up on a glorious day but it's not too difficult to convince them that that's the exception rather than the rule. If they have teenage children—as long as they aren't horse mad—it's no problem at all. They can see for themselves that there are no discos, swimming baths, recreation grounds, public transport and so on, and they have no intention of allowing their parents to be so selfish.'

'It sounds as if you don't have much to worry about, after all,' she said.

'Ah.' Rob shook his head. 'But then there are the people like us. People who want peace and quiet and don't mind a twenty-minute drive to buy a loaf of bread. People who want to walk out over the moor from the garden gate and like to see muddy, tired dogs lying by the stove in the kitchen.'

'You mean people like us—but with money.'

He nodded, leaning back in his chair. 'Did you really come from London because you fell in love with the photograph?'

She was silent for a moment, afraid of falling into a trap. She'd pretended that her life was still as it had been before Oxford—and she must stick to it.

'I did,' she said lightly. 'I'm getting tired of city life and I want to escape.'

'Forgive me for being personal but could you really afford a house like this if you weren't working in one of the big law firms?'

'Well,' she tried to maintain the casual note, 'the London house is worth quite a lot of money, you know. Perhaps I'd find a job locally.'

'I see.' He was silent for a moment. 'So what now?'

Melissa couldn't quite meet his eyes. Instead she leaned forward, refilling their wine glasses. 'I love it,' she said. 'I really do. But I'd have quite a lot to do before I could make an offer.'

'Perhaps,' he said slowly, diffidently, 'perhaps between us we could manage something.'

She looked at him, then, hating to deceive him, unable to burst the golden bubble. 'It's possible,' she said slowly. 'It's a bit . . . unexpected, that's all.'

'I know,' he said quickly. 'Of course it is. For me too. It's just . . . I seem to be falling in love with you, Melissa.'

'Oh, Rob.' She took his hand. 'It's the same with me. Are we crazy?'

'Probably,' he answered soberly. 'Does it matter?'

She laid her cheek against his hand, suppressing a terrible desire to tell him the truth. The fear of the love and admiration in his eyes being replaced by pity, his tenderness becoming a smothering anxiety, his cheerful, teasing banter smoothing into gentleness, held her back. His normal, natural, healthy love was all that was left to her now and, selfish though it might be, she couldn't bring herself to destroy it.

'No, it doesn't matter,' she said, releasing his hand, raising her glass. 'Let's drink to the routing of all yuppies and moneyed prospectors. You *shall* go to the ball, Cinderella. Your dream shall come true and Moorgate shall be yours.'

'Ours,' he corrected her, raising his glass. 'Thank you, fairy godmother. What did we do with the apple pie?'

'On the shelf in the larder.' She felt a flood of gratitude that he'd been willing to allow the difficult moment to pass. 'With the cream. It seemed the coldest place, out there on the marble slab. I hope the milk doesn't go off.'

'We've got some powdered stuff, just in case.' He cut two generous portions of pie. 'We shall manage, never fear. So tell me about your life in London. New readers start here. No cutting corners, mind. I want to know everything.'

Later, much later, she leaned on an elbow, watching him sleep. He'd flung off the blanket—the room was much too warm for him—and his face, turned upon the pillow, was peaceful.

She thought: I should leave now. What more can we possibly have together? I should slip away, like a thief in the night. He'd grieve for a while but he'll soon forget me. How could such a short time of love make a real difference to his life? Better to go now, before we get too deep.

Gently, carefully, she slid away from him, pushing herself to her feet, feeling for her shawl. He'd left a paraffin lamp burning dimly and in its mellow light she trod on bare feet to the window. At some point during the evening Rob had rigged up a curtain. It hung loosely, unevenly, but it had lent an air of privacy and cosiness to the bare, empty room. Earlier, they had been too preoccupied with each other to take much notice of anything but their deep, urgent need, but now, shivering, Melissa lifted the corner of the curtain and looked outside.

Snow whirled against the window, dancing and twirling in the wind, settling, blowing, drifting. Her gasp of surprise became a soft chuckle. No chance of going anywhere tonight; no hope of a quick flight down to the car and away back to Oxford. The decision had been made for her and she felt almost weak with relief. She could stay with him a little longer, love him for a little while more.

'You'll freeze, standing there.' His voice made her jump. 'Is it still snowing?'

She turned quickly. '*Still* snowing?'

She heard the rumble of his laughter. 'It had just started when I got back with the pick-up. I thought it might when it turned warmer, but I didn't want you deciding that you should rush off back to London while there was still time. Come back to bed, wench. I can hear your teeth chattering.'

She went back to him, laughing helplessly, and they rolled together, holding tightly, forgetting everything but each other.

Chapter Twenty-four

The snow lasted for two days. Rob and Melissa, cut off and isolated, took advantage of every second of it. The snow had drifted from the northwest, piling up against the back of the house, but Rob was able to dig a path to the woodshed and they had enough provisions to keep them from starving.

'Thank goodness we bought plenty of chocolate,' said Melissa, munching happily, leaning against the Esse whilst Rob washed his hands at the sink after ferrying logs into the sitting room. 'I must have had a premonition.'

He came across, reaching for the towel on the rail, smiling down at her. 'You should be as big as a house,' he commented. 'How do you stay so slender?'

She didn't answer, simply shaking her head, and he slipped his arms about her. She rested her cheek against his shoulder, staring out of the window at the snowy landscape. It was beautiful and unreal, a fairytale setting which enabled her to believe in this moment of escapism, this flight from reality.

'Let's go for a walk,' she said suddenly. 'Just a little one. It looks so perfect out there now the sun is setting. Shall we?'

'Why not?' He couldn't resist her. 'The snow is far too deep behind the house but it's not too bad in the lane. We'll see how far we can get.'

In the lane they turned up towards the moor, passing through the gate beside the cattle grid, wading through the snow. Out of the shelter of the trees it was impossible to tell where the road ended and the moor began and they went slowly, pausing to stare about them.

'It's quite magical,' murmured Melissa. 'Everything is transformed'—and her heart ached with the pain of it.

She thought: How can I bear it? How can I face the end, now, knowing what I am losing?

Yet as she stood there, gazing over the moor, she became aware of an unusual sensation of peace; a quiet strength; as if her heart had been touched by a certainty of something so overwhelming, so all-embracing, that it ceased to fret and grieve and was stilled into a steady rhythm. The moor rolled away from beneath her feet, stretching onward to the earth's fiery rim where the sun was dipping into the sea, and long blue shadows reached across the snowy land. In the east a star was hanging, bright as a lantern, and silence wrapped about them both, embracing them in its healing restfulness.

She had no idea how long they'd stood together, touched by these mysteries, before they heard a hoarse, eerie shriek and a barn owl, drifting on blunt wings, passed above their heads and came to rest on a post some way below them. Roused from their reverie they smiled at each other, delighted at such a sight.

'She nests in a barn just below Moorgate,' said Rob. 'Beautiful, isn't she?'

'Beautiful,' agreed Melissa. 'And cruel,' she added, thinking of the sharp talons and strong, hooked beak.

'Well, that's life.' Rob tucked her hand under his arm. 'Owls have to eat too. I have to admit, however, that I wouldn't want to be a part of the food chain. One long struggle for territory, food, or a mate. Living in permanent fear of death.' He misinterpreted the shudder that she gave, pressing her hand closely beneath his arm, dreading the moment that she would leave him. 'Don't go away,' he said foolishly. 'Stay with me at Moorgate.'

Her eyes burned with tears but she hugged his arm, trying to laugh. 'I have to go. You know I do.'

'But you'll come back?'

'Of course. Part of me will never go at all. It will stay here always.'

'I don't want a bit of you,' he grumbled. 'I shan't be satisfied with that.'

'I have to sort things out,' she said. 'But don't worry. Moorgate will be . . . ours.'

He sighed. 'Why can't I believe it?'

'Because you have no faith. I've told you that between us we can raise the deposit. Stop doubting. Once I'm back in London and have made the arrangements you can put in an offer. I'll sort out all the legal side. We've been through all this before, Rob. Stop fussing and let's just enjoy these few days without anxiety.'

'It's only because you won't say when you'll be back. I hate not knowing.'

'I can't tell you. You know I have to go away on this big case I've got. It's simply impossible to give you a date. But I'll stay in touch. I promise. You must get on with buying the house.'

'If Lady Todhunter knows I want to buy it she'll give me time to sort things out, I know she will.'

He sounded more cheerful and Melissa gave a sigh of relief. It was not always easy to head him away from these emotional moments, yet she could not bring herself to tell him the truth; to shatter his happiness. At least he would have Moorgate. The few thousand pounds she'd made out of her London flat would make up the deposit; a small recompense for the joy he'd given her.

'Well then. Let's not worry about the details.'

'I'm a fool but I have this terrible feeling that once you leave I shall never see you again.'

Silence fell between them like a sword, cutting off intimacy. The sun had set and the shadows were deepening. A chill breath of wind moved lightly over the land and the barn owl rose from his post with an unearthly cry. Melissa suddenly remembered that Geoffrey Chaucer had referred to this bird as a 'prophet of woe and mischance' and she shivered.

'I'm sorry.' Rob was remorseful, knowing that he had distressed her but never for a moment guessing that his prophecy was a true one. He wondered if he might have made her fear an accident on the way home—or some such thing—and cursed his clumsiness silently. How to repair the damage? 'I had no idea that falling in love was so devastating. Take no notice of me.' He laughed. 'It's rather humiliating, feeling like an adolescent at my age. Ready to go back?'

'I think so.' She rose to his mood, encouraging him. 'Anyway, I'm getting hungry again.'

'I should have guessed.' He chuckled. 'I must remember in future never to travel any distance from home without supplies of food.' He stopped suddenly and she slithered to a halt beside him, clutching him. Taking her face in his hands, he kissed her tenderly. 'I love you,' he said. 'Just never forget it. You're shivering again. What a wench! Always cold, always hungry.'

'I love you too, Rob,' she said. 'This has been the best thing that ever happened to me. And just you never forget that, either. Promise?'

They stared at each other, serious, intent.

'I won't,' he said gently. 'I promise. Bless you. Come on, my love. Let's go home.'

Maudie sat at the table, the tartan squares ranged before her. Months had passed since the packet had arrived from The Scotch House yet she seemed incapable of making up her mind: MacCallum Ancient, Hunting Fraser, Muted Blue Douglas, Muted Blue Dress Stewart. She liked the muted colours best, especially the Douglas, yet she was incapable of coming to a final decision. There was too much on her mind. Posy had telephoned earlier, sounding faintly anxious.

'Dad phoned,' she'd said, after a few preliminaries. 'He's coming down to see me.'

A pause.

'Ah.' Maudie had tried to be intelligent; to guess at Posy's feelings. 'Well, that's very nice, isn't it? He's seen your house, hasn't he?'

'Mmm.' Posy wasn't giving too much away. 'He and Mum came down to check it out.' She still sounded faintly indignant about it, embarrassed by her parents looking over the accommodation. 'As if I'm just a kid,' she'd said crossly at the time. Maudie knew that Posy was fiercely protective about her personal life and tried to keep it separate from her home life. Knowing Selina's propensity for publicly putting Posy in her place, Maudie was unable to blame her too much, nevertheless she also knew that Posy could be oversensitive about it.

'Well, it should be fun,' she'd said encouragingly. 'You haven't seen much of him lately and you can show him round. I thought you wanted the chance to make up for Christmas.'

'I do. I just wondered if you'd, like, heard anything.'

'If you mean has your mother phoned, the answer is yes, but only about Moorgate. I think it was last weekend. She's still hoping to buy it but I'm afraid that I wasn't very encouraging. Perhaps your father is hoping to sound you out about it. If your mother is pressing him he might feel that it's a way to make restitution. He seems to have made himself generally unpopular and is maybe considering a way of making it up.'

'I don't want him to feel like that,' Posy had mumbled. 'Anyway, I'm not sure anything happened. Hugh says that he might have been helping Mary out and Mum got the wrong end of the stick.'

'That's very likely. So why not just accept that he's coming to Winchester because he loves you and misses you. Does there have to be a hidden agenda?'

'No.' Her voice was none too certain. 'He just sounded a bit odd, that's all.'

'Odd? How?'

'He sounded . . . happy.'

She'd seemed so surprised, so mystified at such a manifestation, that Maudie had burst out laughing. 'Poor Patrick,' she'd gasped. 'Poor, poor Patrick'—and Posy had become defensive.

'I don't mean it like that,' she'd said. 'He was more than just happy. There was something else . . . Perhaps you're right and he thinks that agreeing to buy Moorgate would be exciting for all of us but, unless they sell up and move down, I think it would be awful. They can't afford two houses.'

'Well, between you and me, I've heard that I may have a buyer. Someone's very interested, apparently, so keep your fingers crossed. It would certainly solve that particular problem.'

In the end, Posy had agreed that she must simply wait and see, and had gone off with Jude and Jo, 'clubbing' as she called it, leaving Maudie to brood. She had no wish to raise suspicion or alarm in Posy's mind but the description of Patrick's happiness puzzled her. Her conversation with Selina made her feel quite confident that Patrick had no intention of being party to buying Moorgate—so what else might make him so happy? Could it be that he'd taken up again with Mary? If so, why on earth should he want to tell Posy about it? He must know how she would react.

Maudie fiddled with the squares of wool, thoughtfully. She'd tried never to interfere with the decisions of her stepdaughters, though, when Hector was alive, it had never really been necessary. Selina had often sought his advice and Hector had never been averse to giving it.

'You are so bossy and domineering,' Maudie had told him once, during the early years of Selina's marriage, when Patrick had announced that he was buying a new car and Hector had roundly told him that he couldn't afford it. 'How do *you* know what they can afford?'

'Absolute madness,' he'd snorted. 'Utter extravagance. He should know better.'

'I think he does,' she'd answered coolly. 'He's trying to meet Selina's need to keep up with her smart friends.'

He'd said nothing, shaking out *The Times* and retiring behind the sheets, but he'd been less outspoken after that, more tolerant towards Patrick, and there had been a generous contribution towards the car. Selina had been touchingly grateful—big hugs and a kiss, with a slyly triumphant glance at Maudie—whilst Hector had growled that it was an advance Christmas and birthday present for both of them.

Maudie thought: Why did everything have to be a contest? The trouble was that I was too outspoken. Neither Hector nor Selina was used to it. And now it's too late. Despite my good intentions, Selina and I will never be friends. If only Hector hadn't felt so guilty at the end. He apologised to Selina whenever he saw her and I feel that he regretted ever marrying me. But guilty or not, I'm sure he wouldn't approve of Selina buying Moorgate as a holiday home.

She pushed the pieces of cloth aside and went to sit by the fire, pulling her knitting out of its bag, spreading it across her knees.

'I absolutely agree,' Daphne had said, recently. 'It's crazy. Financial suicide.'

'I feel like an executioner,' Maudie had said. 'We've all had such happy times there, haven't we?'

'We can't hold on to everything,' Daphne had said firmly. 'Part of what we remember is our youth. It's like the people who can never forget the war because it was the happiest time of their lives. Generally it's because they were young and those war years were their youth and because it was such an extreme nothing could ever measure up to it afterwards. For Selina, Moorgate represents her childhood before Hilda died, before her life changed, but it would be ridiculous to attempt to recreate it. Selina needs her feet on a pavement. Do stop ferreting, Maudie. This isn't like you at all. You've always been so pragmatic.'

'Not always,' she'd answered reluctantly. 'I've had my moments too, you know.'

'Oh, Maudie.' Daphne had begun to chuckle. 'Do you remember

when you emptied a jug of cold water over Hector's head and he was so surprised he simply sat there, dripping?'

'He was hectoring.' Maudie was laughing too. 'He could be *so* infuriating and I was hideously menopausal.'

'His face! He looked so hurt and offended and we both shrieked with laughter.'

'And he said, "I'm so pleased to have afforded you amusement . . ." all huffy . . .'

'And you threw the kitchen towel at him and he threw it back in a fit of pique and got up and stomped out. And we simply cried with laughter and opened a bottle.'

'And we were halfway through it when he came back and said "Where's mine, then?" '

There was a short silence.

'He was rather an odd duck, wasn't he?' said Daphne unsteadily.

'There was nothing mean-minded about Hector. I miss him, Daffers.'

'You and me both, love. We had some good times. Don't let Selina get you down . . .'

If only Ned Cruikshank's client made a genuine offer she could accept it thankfully and put the whole thing out of her mind. Tomorrow was Friday, so perhaps he might telephone with good news before he left for London. Maudie counted her stitches carefully, settled herself comfortably and began to knit.

Moonlight poured its cold, white brilliance through the bedroom window—'We can't pull the curtain on a night like this,' Melissa had protested—and laid black bars across the bare floorboards. Curled against the warmth of Rob's back, Melissa dreamed fitfully. The house had come to life about her and she could hear voices: doors slammed and there were running footsteps on the stairs. The boy must have been almost outside the door. 'Hurry up!' He was impatient. 'Miss Morrow helped with the picture but you'll have to colour it in yourself.' The smaller child had reached the landing now. 'I wish I could come to school.' Her voice was wistful. 'You will soon.' The boy attempted comfort. 'Do come on or Daddy will be back and it will spoil the surprise.' In the small nursery room a baby began to cry and the boy swore softly. 'Mummy's coming,' whispered the little girl. 'Let's hide the card . . .'

Melissa shivered, pulling the rug closer about her shoulders, and drifted back into sleep. A Christmas tree was standing at the back of the hall, beside the stairs, its lights twinkling like coloured gems in the twilight of the hall. A young woman came down the stairs behind it, holding a baby, and paused on a level with the highest branches so that the child might see the brightly coloured baubles. She murmured to it, her cheek against its tiny head, and then went on down the stairs and into the kitchen. The front door opened and a man came in, shutting the door behind him, smiling at the sight of the tree. 'Hi, kids!' His voice rang round the hall, echoing up the stairs. 'I'm back.' The girl came out from the kitchen and they hugged, whispering together—and Melissa, pressing close to Rob, smiled in her sleep.

Chapter Twenty-five

Selina stared at herself in the looking-glass. She felt panicky and very angry: even her own face looked unfamiliar to her. She leaned forward a little, studying her image more closely. When had the wrinkles formed? Those grooves which were scored between nose and lips; the discontented lines about the drooping mouth? There were shadows under her eyes and her hair needed restreaking. She was looking her age and was suddenly reminded of photographs of her mother—except that Hilda would have been smiling, always smiling: bravely, determinedly, brightly, even grimly—but always smiling.

Selina thought: Well, she had plenty to smile about. Daddy would never have been unfaithful to *her* and then abandoned her.

For the first time ever, a tinge of resentment crept into her memories of her mother. She'd always been loved, respected, bathed in her husband's honours, lapped in comfort; why the hell shouldn't she smile? Selina leaned both her elbows on the dressing table and sneered into the mirror. She'd perfected this look from an early age—she could date it exactly—from the moment Maudie had arrived on the scene. It was meant to be a look of utter contempt; of despising.

'I've never known anyone,' Posy had once cried furiously, 'who can ruin a good time as quickly as you can!'

Oddly, Selina was able to remember the exact occasion. Chris had brought home his first really serious girlfriend for the weekend and Patrick had suggested that they should drive into Surrey on Sunday morning for a pub lunch. He knew a really good pub, he'd said, near Farnham, so they'd all piled into the car and driven out of London. It had been a bright sunny morning, Sue and Posy were getting along splendidly, Chris was clearly head over heels in love and Patrick was singing to himself as he drove. Why had she felt so irritable, so touchy? Was it Chris's openly displayed adoration for the silly, simpering Sue? After all, *she* had always been first with Chris. He was her eldest child, her firstborn; Chris was special. All his life she'd been able to manipulate him by a word or even a look. Until now *her* happiness had been paramount, *her* comfort and wellbeing his first concern. This morning he was far more anxious about Sue; fussing about where she should sit, so that she could see out of the window, worrying in case she was too hot, quite foolishly bound up in the girl.

Even at this late date, Selina felt her irritation rising. He'd made an absolute fool of himself—and Patrick had been aiding and abetting him: admiring the girl's long hair, teasing her a little, playing up to her. Of course, the girl had been loving every minute of it, bridling and simpering; even Posy had been taken with her—Selina shrugged at her reflection— not that she'd ever expected the least show of loyalty from Posy. Anyway, they'd found the pub at last and, of course, it was packed, heaving wall to wall with people. Patrick had grabbed the only empty table, which seated two, and had told her to sit down, so that at least they had somewhere to put their drinks.

'We don't mind standing for a bit, do we?' Chris had been smiling into Sue's eyes, leaving Selina to grind her teeth in fury, isolated at the table whilst Posy and Patrick fought their way to the bar. She'd stared coldly ahead, shrugging when Patrick had come back to ask her what she'd wanted to drink and to assure her that a table was about to be vacated which would seat them all.

'Gin and tonic?' he'd asked, still cheerful, enjoying the family outing. 'Wine? A spritzer?'

'No thanks.' The sneer was coming into play. 'Just an orange juice.'

'Are you sure?' He'd looked dismayed, his happiness fading a little. 'We'll get a table, honestly, darling. The food's good.'

She looked about her, frowning at a group at the next table who were laughing loudly, shaking her head disgustedly at a dog who was lying beside another family. Her expression conveyed utter disbelief that he should have brought her to such a place. He'd turned, fighting his way back to the bar, and, out of the corner of her eye, she'd seen him exchange a few words with Posy who'd turned to look at her anxiously. She'd enjoyed the power, the ability to spoil their silly, selfish fun, to punish them for forgetting, even for a moment, to put her first. At last, when they'd got a table and were looking at the menus, Patrick had smiled at her hopefully, willing her to be happy.

'Now, what shall we have?' he'd asked, beaming at Sue, winking at Chris. 'What would you like, darling?'

'I'd like to be in a decent restaurant,' she'd said icily, disdainfully, 'with decent people. Can you explain to me, can you just tell me, what on earth made you think that I'd like a place like this?'

She could remember the reaction—Chris's look of fear, Sue's embarrassment, Patrick's misery, Posy's rage—and her own fierce elation, the sense of power. That's when Posy had made her remark and the others had pretended to study their menus, trying to ignore it, but the day was ruined. Yes, she'd always enjoyed being able to subdue her family with a look but it was being borne in relentlessly upon her that soon there would be no one left to be impressed by that practised curl of the lip. The boys were already beyond her influence, their wives had seen to that, and Posy had never been truly cowed by it. Only Patrick had remained affected— until now. Now her power was going, she was losing control, and she was frightened; frightened and angry. She simply couldn't believe that Patrick was serious. This was the most alarming development—that Patrick was utterly unaffected by her. He was unmoved by rage, by contempt, even by a more gentle approach. He remained remote and detached—and unbearably, infuriatingly happy.

'I've given in my notice,' he'd told her jubilantly, 'and it's been accepted. I have the feeling that perhaps I wasn't so discreet as I might have been over Mary and they're pleased to see me go without a fuss. If they can find a replacement I shall leave at Easter.'

'Easter?' She'd goggled at him, her fury at his casual mention of the little tart overborne by shock. 'You're leaving at *Easter*?'

'Why not? Why wait? Don't worry. I shall only take a few books and some clothes. Have you thought what you might do?'

'Is it any of your business?'

'Not really.' He'd shrugged cheerfully. 'I'm sure you'll cope. I'm going down to see Posy on Friday. I guessed from my conversation with her that you haven't told her that I'm leaving. Why not? You were quick enough to tell her that I was an adulterous bastard.'

She'd been speechless. This was a Patrick she'd never known and she had no idea how to handle the situation.

'What should I tell her?' she'd said contemptuously. 'That you've found another little tart in Brecon?'

'If you call people with learning disabilities "tarts" then I suppose that's about the sum of it. You know exactly where I'm going, Selina, and why. You've looked through all my papers and I've made no secret of it.'

'And what will those people think when they find you're abandoning your wife on some selfish, quixotic whim?'

'I've explained my position truthfully and they're prepared to give me a try.'

'You're such a hypocrite,' she'd shouted. 'You're beyond contempt. Pretending to be so holier-than-thou whilst betraying me and then abandoning me after nearly thirty years of marriage. How will you feel when I tell our friends that?'

'How will *you* feel?' he'd asked quietly. 'Happy, content people don't walk out of loving relationships. How will *you* explain it, Selina?'

She'd had no answer for him. Already she'd shied away from telling even her closest girlfriends that Patrick was leaving her—especially for such a cause. How much easier to paint him as a weak philanderer! Almost she wished that she'd let him go to Mary. It would have been so much easier, as the injured wife, to gain sympathy. This was quite different; it was humiliating. Selina stared at herself, panic rising. Furiously, she seized a bottle and began to apply her make-up.

Later on in the morning, the west wind brought warmer weather and the thaw began. Snow fell from the trees in huge slabs, crashing to the ground, dripping from the gutters. A tractor passed up the lane, turning the soft ice to slush, and, on the higher slopes, the drifts melted away into a thousand rivulets of sparkling water.

'I shall be able to go tomorrow, after all,' said Melissa, watching as the moor dazzled in the bright sunshine. 'No excuse now.'

For these few days she'd been able to believe that she might never leave, that the dream would become a reality. She glanced at Rob, who was bravely resisting the urge to persuade her not to go, to sort everything out by telephone, and smiled at him.

'I know,' he said. 'We've been through it all before. I know you have to go. I just don't want to think about this as our last day.'

'No,' she said quickly. 'Oh, no. Neither do I. Oh, Rob, we mustn't be miserable.'

She sounded so suddenly desperate, so unhappy, that he shelved his own feelings and put his arm round her. These four days had been a step out of the world and it would be very hard to go back to the normal everyday.

'We won't be miserable,' he assured her. 'We'll take the pick-up and go and forage. It'll be a bit slippy but a bit of an adventure. If the tractor's managed to come up from the village, we should be able to get down. How about it?'

'Oh, yes.' She rubbed her cheek against his sleeve. 'That sounds fun. I'm nearly out of chocolate.'

'Well, we can't have that. We'll stock up for this evening and cook ourselves a slap-up meal.'

'Great.' She sighed contentedly and then looked at him more seriously, slipping her hand into his. 'Rob, I think you should telephone Ned Cruikshank and make an offer. He's left several messages on your mobile and I think it's only fair. Today is his last day, after all. Tell him you've got the spare keys and that we want to buy Moorgate and then he can phone Lady Todhunter.'

'You're absolutely certain?'

She nodded. 'I've been thinking about it and I'm quite certain. The money won't be a problem, I promise, and I want to be sure that the house is . . . ours.'

He took a deep breath. 'That's fantastic.'

'Once the offer is accepted we'll have time to breathe,' she said, trying to sound casual, hoping to forestall too many questions. 'I'll sort things out quickly when I get back. A girl I was at law school with works at a practice in Truro. I'll get her to do all the legal stuff. OK? And as soon as I know where I am work-wise I'll let you know. We'll stay in touch by mobile, shall we? I may have to stay with friends while I wind up at the practice but you'll always have my number.'

'I suppose so.' He didn't sound too happy. 'But I wish we could be a bit more definite.'

'Ned Cruikshank will be surprised, won't he?' She tried to distract him. 'To hear that you're going to buy Moorgate, I mean.'

'*We're* going to buy it,' he corrected her. 'Not nearly so surprised as Lady Todhunter will be.'

'Do it,' she insisted. 'Telephone him now. It would be too awful if someone who'd seen it earlier pipped us at the post. Go on, Rob.'

'OK.' He kissed her quickly. 'I'll do it now, before we go out.'

'Fine.' She released him. 'I'll go and get my coat.'

Upstairs, she sat down on the window seat for a moment. She felt terribly tired and very weak but quite determined to make certain that Moorgate should be Rob's. Nothing else mattered now. It was all that she had left to give him. He had made her happier than she had ever been, enabled her to forget the horror that lay ahead, given her the opportunity to have some kind of stake in the future that she would never see. Soon, quite soon, he would be able to put these few days aside—to remember them always, yes, but begin to build a new life for himself here at Moorgate. She could give him that, at least: the chance to live in the house he loved more than anything in the world.

Downstairs in the kitchen, waiting for Ned to answer the telephone, Rob was thinking how odd it was that, now that he was able to make an offer on Moorgate, the house mattered less than it had ever done before. Since Melissa had come into his life, so dramatically and unexpectedly, everything else had taken second place. His passion for Moorgate had paled before his love for her. He knew now that, as long as they were together, he wouldn't really mind too much where they lived. She was so special, so rare, so utterly beloved, that he couldn't imagine life without her now. Moorgate was a bonus, no doubt about it, but she was all that mattered.

'Hello, there.' Ned's breathless voice broke into his thoughts. 'I've been trying to get in touch with you. What weather! Are you OK?'

'Very OK.' Rob was smiling. 'Hold on to your hat, Ned, I've got a bit of a surprise for you.'

Maudie kicked off her gumboots at the back door and hurried into the living room to pick up the telephone receiver. As she placed her hand upon it the bell was abruptly silenced.

'Damn,' she said crossly. 'Damn and blast. I do find that so annoying.

Don't you dare come in here, you wretched animal, until I've wiped your paws.'

Whilst Polonius submitted to having his feet dried, Maudie decided that one of the advantages of living with a dog was that you could talk out loud to yourself without being considered odd.

'There,' she said. 'That's that, then. Thank goodness it's warmed up and we can get out for a good walk again. Move over, you great lump. That's it. Now the back ones. Good! There you are. All done.'

She hung the towel to dry and filled the kettle. Just as she was reaching for the teapot the telephone began to ring.

'Curses!' she muttered. 'Don't you dare hang up. Yes? Hello?'

'Lady Todhunter?' Ned Cruikshank sounded quite jubilant. 'It's me. Ned. Terrific news. We've had an offer for Moorgate. A very good one.' He named a figure. 'I think you'll be happy with it.'

'I am indeed. That's wonderful, Ned. Is it the woman you were telling me about?'

He started to laugh. 'You'll never believe this. *I* didn't. It *is* the girl I told you about but it's Rob Abbot, too. They're buying it together.'

'You mean she's an old friend? What an odd arrangement. Of course, I know he loves the house . . .'

'Well, actually, it seems he's only just met her. It was love at first sight and they want to live at Moorgate.'

'Good grief! Isn't that rather sudden? I do hope Rob knows what he's doing. He's so level-headed and . . . well, sane.' Suddenly she remembered her first meeting with Hector, the way they'd looked at one another, and she smiled to herself. 'It sounds wonderful. I hope they'll be very happy. I shall go down to see him and meet her.'

'She's an absolute sweetie.' He sounded confiding, rather breathless as usual, and she felt an absurd surge of affection for him.

'I'm going to miss you, Ned,' she said. 'I hope you do splendidly in London.'

'So do I,' he said. 'I can't tell you how pleased I am to bring this one off, Lady Todhunter. It's the icing on the cake.'

'Bless you,' she said warmly. 'And Ned? Make sure you get that commission.'

'I will.' He was laughing. 'The office will be getting in touch and all the wheels will grind into action but I'll tell Rob you accept his offer, shall I?'

'You certainly may. Tell him I'm delighted. Many thanks, Ned, and good luck.'

She replaced the receiver and stood for a moment, lost in a reverie. The relief was very great but there was a measure of sadness, too. She remembered the summer she'd spent there with Daphne and Emily, and the baby Posy. How happy they'd been. Maudie sighed as she went to make her tea, hoping she'd made the right decision.

She thought: At least it solves the problem for Patrick. Perhaps now Selina can forget Moorgate and she and Patrick will be able to make a new start.

Chapter Twenty-six

It was terrible to leave him, to drive away down the lane, letting him believe that she'd be back soon, waving cheerfully. Only the thought of Mike, waiting for her in Oxford, and all the arrangements yet to be made regarding Moorgate kept her steady. There was still a great deal to do, to be organised, and, as she conned it over in her mind, she was able to maintain some kind of composure. She felt tired—and the further she travelled from Rob and Moorgate so the weariness increased—but she knew that the greatest danger lay in the depression which hovered, which waited to convince her that there was no point in making any effort now; that there was nothing to try for, nothing to keep hope alive. Whilst she'd been with Rob at Moorgate she'd managed, for gloriously happy stretches of time, to believe that a miracle might happen. His love had strengthened her, his need had made her strong. His ignorance of her physical condition had allowed her to imagine that it did not exist. Now, without his vitality to warm her, his happiness to give her courage, the chill in her bones seemed to creep around her heart and weaken her. Even holding on to the steering wheel was an effort.

Nevertheless, she knew that she must not, this time, stop for the night. If once she broke her journey to sleep she feared that she might never find the energy necessary to start off again. No, she must keep going, making do with short breaks for coffee. Mike, she knew, would be angry with her but he would be too relieved to see her to be cross with her for long. She considered turning off the A38 for a break at Bovey Tracey, half wondering if she might see Posy again, but decided against it. This time it would be different: the window table would be occupied by other people and her holiday feeling would be woefully absent. Better to remember things as they had been on that sunny morning. It was dangerous to go back; it invited disappointment. She could hardly believe that only a week had passed since she'd wandered in the town, browsed in the bookshop, and talked to Posy. Melissa wondered if Posy would ever see the message she'd written for her and remembered the odd feeling of warmth and friendship she'd felt for her. How she wished she could turn back the clock and be starting out again on her Moorgate adventure.

She swallowed down the treacherous tears and glanced at her watch. There was no reason why she shouldn't be at home for tea. She decided that when she was very nearly at Oxford she would telephone Mike. By then it would be too late for him to worry about her but he would have a chance to make any preparations he considered necessary for her arrival. It would be wonderful to see him and Luke. Concentrating on this, looking forward to hot coffee at Taunton Deane, Melissa drove on.

Watching her go, Rob felt that his world was going with her. The prospect of life without her was dull and empty and he could hardly remember how he'd managed before her arrival. He knew now that he'd only been half alive. The whole week had been extraordinary; even the weather had conspired. As he went back into the house, alone again, a thousand questions presented themselves. During this last week, buying Moorgate, being together, falling in love, all these things had seemed perfectly reasonable. Now, walking from room to room, staring out at the drizzle, he wondered if he'd been seized by a form of madness. It would be quite easy to believe that he'd dreamed the whole thing; that his obsession with Moorgate had driven him crazy. He longed to speak to her again, needing reassurance, looking about him for some sign of proof, but all evidence of her occupation had been cleared away; the hamper and her rugs packed into her car. She'd promised to telephone him round about lunchtime and he checked—not for the first time—to make certain that his mobile was switched on. Everything they'd used had been washed up or put away and the house felt oddly empty.

Standing in the sitting room, remembering how he'd first seen her standing looking down at his beanbags, he reflected that it was strange that

Melissa—who loved the house so much—had broken Moorgate's spell over him. She had shown him that his passion was as nothing compared with his love for her. She had released him and he was glad of it. The obsession had been a burden and it was a relief to be free from it.

Rob locked the back door and walked round to the yard. Standing beside the pick-up he looked at the house. Now that the fever had left him he could see it clearly again: a solid, well-proportioned farmhouse in a delightful setting. Remembering his behaviour during the last six months he felt rather foolish and he smiled to himself, shaking his head. There was no question but that he'd been temporarily mad. Nevertheless, it would be good to own Moorgate, to live in it with Melissa, to raise their children here on the edge of the moor. Moorgate had brought them together. He stood for a moment watching the rooks, thinking about the events of the last week. There were so many things he'd never asked her, so much still to learn about her. He glanced at his watch. It was possible that in less than an hour he might be speaking to her. The thought raised his spirits, made his heart beat a little faster. Whistling to himself, he climbed into the pick-up and drove out of the yard and down the lane.

Posy, settled at a corner table in the bar of the Wykeham Arms, watched her father at the bar. He looked different but she couldn't immediately decide how. He was talking to the girl behind the bar, laughing with her, hands in his pockets, and, for the first time, Posy was able to see him as other people saw him; not as her father but as a man in his own right. Her critical faculties—naturally sharp—were always on the lookout lest he should behave foolishly, be embarrassing, but she was beginning to realise that this intolerance was a measure of her own insecurity.

'That's how it started with your mother,' Maudie had said, fairly recently, 'but she never grew out of it.'

This remark had given Posy food for thought. She had no wish to be like her mother, whose glance could wither, whose barbed, acid remarks could destroy happiness, yet she had begun to see how easy it might be to use such power over others; to control them. The difficulty was that you needed to feel very safe, very confident, to be unaffected by the behaviour of people for whom you cared. She had a horror of any form of showing off but living with Jude and Jo had gone some way in helping her to be more tolerant.

'After all,' Jude had observed, 'it's not your problem if someone behaves badly, not even if you're related to them. Stay detached. It needn't affect you.'

'But it does,' she'd argued. 'If it's your mother, say, or a friend, it's bound to reflect on you, isn't it? So people could say, "Poor thing, fancy having a mother like that," or whatever.'

He'd smiled at her. 'Come on,' he'd said affectionately. 'Are you so unsure of yourself that you can't cope with the opinion of idiots? No one is perfect, we all know that. My feelings for you don't change just because you know or love somebody who isn't wonderful all the time. I thought that love was about that. You know? Loving people because of what they are, not in spite of it.'

The problem was exactly that: she *was* that unsure of herself. Perhaps it was due to the continual battle with her mother all through her childhood. Selina had made it clear that the unconditional love she poured out on the boys—no matter what they did or said—was not available to Posy. Because of her affection for her step-grandmother, Posy had been punished by a withdrawal of love, made more obvious by the indiscrimination with which it was lavished on the boys. Especially on Chris, who assiduously courted his mother's approval and slyly rejoiced in his small sister's regular falls from grace. Paul had been less affected, remaining as detached as possible, but nevertheless unwilling to stick his neck out.

Watching her father coming towards her, carrying drinks, Posy remembered how often he had championed her cause and defended her. Immediately she was engulfed in guilt. He had always been so loving yet she had been so critical when he'd had his own fall from grace. Where had her loyalty been then? She had rejected him out of hand, not waiting to be certain that he was guilty, unable to be generous.

'The sandwiches will be along in a minute.' He put the glasses on the table and sat down. 'I was just telling the girl behind the bar that this place has hardly changed since I was here thirty years ago, although dear old Miss Sprules has gone.'

'It must feel odd,' said Posy, 'coming back after all these years. Meeting Mum and all that.' She paused, drinking some lager to cover the confusion of how she should proceed. She still didn't quite know why he'd come down alone to see her and it was impossible to ask outright. 'Is Mum OK?'

He frowned, as if puzzled by her question, debating how he should answer it, and Posy felt a twinge of anxiety.

'She's perfectly fit,' he said, 'but not particularly happy.'

It was such an odd answer that Posy began to laugh. 'I'm not sure that Mum is ever particularly happy, is she?' she asked. 'It's not how she works, is it? What's the problem? Is she still going on about Moorgate? Honestly, Dad, it would be really crazy to let her buy it.'

'No, it's not Moorgate. I'm afraid it's me.'

Posy stared at him. 'How d'you mean?'

He looked at her. 'I'm leaving your mother,' he said, quite gently but without any hesitation. 'No, not because of Mary—that's all done with—but because there's nothing left between us. Whatever we had is finished.'

'Finished?'

He sighed. 'This is so difficult because whatever I say is going to sound utterly callous. I'm hoping that you've had enough experience of both of us to try to understand. Your mother doesn't need me as a friend or a lover or a companion. Looking back I wonder if she ever did. I met her when she was anxious to get away from home and marriage was a wonderful escape. Of course it's wrong—if tempting—to imagine that we weren't happy. There have been some very special moments but there's nothing left and I don't want to waste any more time. Sorry. I'm not putting this very well.'

Posy was trying to stem a rising tide of anger. This was her first reaction: anger. She swallowed, her hands twisting together between her knees, and tried to answer calmly.

'So, OK you're bored, fed up, but does that mean you can simply walk out on your marriage? Isn't that a bit extreme? Even irresponsible?'

He looked at her almost humorously. 'Probably. But I'm going to do it anyway. If Selina loved me—oh yes, I know it sounds pathetic—all the humiliations wouldn't matter. But she doesn't. She isn't unhappy that I'm going because she'll miss me. She is losing a possession, not a husband. Her main fear is how she will explain it to her friends because, this time, there is no woman involved, only my own sense of worth and a few last rags of pride. It's embarrassing for her.'

As Posy watched him, she realised that this time there was one very different emotion missing. When he'd tried to talk to her about Mary, there had been the element of guilt; the longing to be understood, forgiven. Now, he was indifferent. He felt she had a right to know, that it would be nice if she could see why he was leaving, but there was no pleading, no requirement for her approval.

Fear began to edge out the anger and Posy thrust her hands through her hair. 'But how can you just walk out on us all? How can you *do* that?'

'I hope that I shan't walk out on you. Just because I shan't be living with Selina in London doesn't mean that I shall stop caring about you.'

'But it's not the same.' She could hear her voice rising in panic and bit her lip, glancing round anxiously lest others had heard her. 'It won't be home without you,' she muttered. 'Anyway, where would you be?'

'I shall be in Brecon.' His voice was light with happiness and she stared at him incredulously. 'I am going as an assistant to help people with learning disabilities.'

'In Brecon?' She tried to sound cool, even faintly amused. To her horror she felt an acute desire to sneer a little. Her mother's sneer. She fought it back. 'So what's in Brecon?'

'One of the L'Arche communities. They are committed to helping such people. It's wonderful. I feel tremendously privileged and I can't wait to get started.'

Looking at his face, alight with anticipation, Posy wondered if she'd ever really seen him before.

'It sounds as if it's all been arranged. So when are you going?'

'Easter.' He took a pull at his pint.

'*Easter?*'

'There was no point in procrastinating,' he said gently, 'once I'd taken the decision. I have to admit that I thought that Selina would have told you before this. I gave her the chance to do it, so that she could tell it to you from her viewpoint, but for some reason she hasn't. I'm sorry it's such a shock but it's impossible for it not to be.'

'So you won't be there when I come home for the holidays?'

He looked at her for a moment and then shook his head. 'No. Selina will keep everything. The house, savings, pensions, everything is hers. From that point of view nothing need change. Hector's money paid off the mortgage so she doesn't have to move although she might need to work. If she downsizes she could be quite comfortable.'

'Does she see it like that?' asked Posy drily.

'Probably not, but those are her decisions not mine.'

'You sound so . . . different.'

'Callous? Selfish? Yes, I know. So your mother has repeatedly told me. Only, I don't care any more, you see. I've done everything I had to do to support her and all of you and now it's at an end. Now I want to do something for other people. Teaching is changing. My ways are old-fashioned and I don't enjoy it any more. I still have it within me to be useful and I don't want to waste the rest of my life pandering to the whims of a selfish woman or dealing with a new generation of children I no longer understand.'

'What about me?'

He smiled tenderly at her. 'You are Posy. I love you. Nothing changes that. I hope we'll still see each other, stay in touch, spend time together.'

'But how? How can we do that if you're not at home any more?'

'There will be ways. Come on, Posy. You're not at home too much these days, are you? I know that I'm removing an aspect of security from your life but I think you're old enough to cope with that. As to the financial aspect, you'll find that the bank has had instructions to take care of you. Fees and allowances and so on have all been dealt with. You won't suffer because I choose to be callous and selfish.'

'It's not a question of the money,' she mumbled, near to tears. 'It's just it won't be the same any more.'

'I can't deny that. I'm sorry, darling. I hate hurting you but I know that if I don't do it now I shall never do it. I'm not abandoning you, Posy, just hoping we can do things differently and be flexible. I hope you'll come to Brecon to see me and I can come here . . .'

'One tuna and one beef?' The waitress stood beside them, holding two plates.

'Oh, yes.' Patrick smiled up at her. 'Thank you. Tuna for my daughter. Beef for me, please.'

Posy sat back in her chair, almost grateful for the interruption, her brain still reeling with the shock. She stared at the sandwich, her appetite ruined, and wondered how on earth she would manage to eat it. Bravely she picked it up—and put it down again.

'So,' she said, almost conversationally, trying to be adult, 'tell me about this L'Arche place.'

Chapter Twenty-seven

On Sunday morning Mike bundled Luke into his clothes, whisked him out of his bedroom and hurried him downstairs. He was hoping that Melissa would be able to sleep as long as was necessary in order to recover from the journey back from Cornwall. She'd arrived just before six o'clock, climbing wearily out of the car and stumbling into the house, her face blurred with exhaustion. He'd been shocked by the way she'd looked but had allowed the words of reproach to die on his lips.

'Oh, Mike,' she'd said. 'I've fallen in love with a farmhouse and with a man called Rob Abbot,' and he'd returned her hug, holding her tightly, a look of mingled compassion and bitterness on his face.

She'd sat beside the fire with Luke in her lap whilst he heated soup and put hot-water bottles into her bed and then she'd talked and talked. He'd wanted to say 'Stop, you're overtired. Tell me tomorrow,' but he'd caught the shadow of her fear; that she might never again have the energy to tell him all she needed him to know. By the time he'd persuaded her into bed she'd made it all clear to him; that she wanted to help Rob buy Moorgate; that Mike must have power of attorney.

'You don't mind?' she'd kept asking. 'Only it was so wonderful. I want to try to repay him. Oh, Mike, it was such heaven. I felt normal and fit and so happy'—and the tears had slid down her cheeks, dropping on to her hands, until she'd brushed them away impatiently.

'Of course I don't mind,' he'd answered. 'If it's what you want . . .'

'If only you could see it,' she'd said, staring dreamily into the fire. 'It's such a lovely house. A family house. You and Luke will have the insurance money after . . . afterwards. But I want to use the money from the flat for Moorgate.'

'Please,' he'd said wretchedly. 'Please, Melissa. I don't care about the money.'

'I know,' she'd said quickly. 'Oh, I know that, Mike, but I need you to understand.'

'I understand,' he'd said reassuringly. 'Honestly, I do. I'm glad for Rob to have Moorgate after all he's given you. It's given you a stake in the future. I understand that.'

'Yes.' She'd looked at him gratefully. 'It's probably foolish but that's how I feel.'

She'd talked on and on, describing, laughing, crying, until she'd been too exhausted to do more than climb the stairs and fall into the warm bed. He'd returned to sit by the fire and think about all that she'd told him.

Now, having fed Luke and settled him with some toys on his tray, Mike began to eat his own breakfast. He felt troubled and his heart was heavy. It seemed to him that Melissa wasn't thinking clearly and that purchasing Moorgate for Rob was going to be much more difficult than she realised. It was unlikely, to begin with, that Rob would remain tamely in Cornwall for as many weeks as it might take to complete the sale. Melissa had been so tired and had looked so fragile that he'd been incapable of bringing her down to earth but he was finding it difficult to see how her dream might be achieved. Even as he wrestled with the problem, murmuring to Luke, his mind preoccupied, the door opened and Melissa came in. She wore a long green wrapper, her feet in espadrilles, a pashmina around her shoulders. Her eyes were enormous, dark-circled in her thin face, but she was smiling cheerfully.

'Good morning,' she said, bending to kiss Luke's rosy cheek, taking the car which he held out to her with crows of pleasure. 'Isn't it a nice one? Look.' She pushed it round his tray whilst he watched, chuckling, and then drove it lightly over his chubby fist and up his arm. 'I wish I had a car like this one.'

'How are you feeling?' Mike stood up to make more coffee. 'I was hoping you'd sleep in.'

'I slept very well,' she assured him. 'I really did. But I wanted to see you and Luke. I've missed you.'

'And we missed you, didn't we, Luke?'

Melissa gave Luke his car and sat down at the table. It was comforting to be back, in these familiar surroundings, without the need to pretend, but her heart ached when she thought of Rob and of the old farmhouse at the moor gate.

'I've been thinking.' Mike turned to face her. 'I'm very happy to help organise this, I really am, but I don't think it's going to be quite as simple as you've imagined.'

'Why not?' She looked alarmed. 'Why shouldn't it be simple?'

'There are all sorts of reasons,' he said gently. 'To begin with, Rob is going to expect to hear from you regularly, isn't he?'

'Oh, that.' Her face cleared. 'Yes, I thought about that. He's got the number of my mobile but he thinks I'm at work, you see. So we leave each other messages and I talk to him quite often. But he knows I've sold my flat and he thinks I'm staying with friends whilst I wind up my work. I've told him I've got a heavy case on so he doesn't expect me to be too available.'

'Right. OK. But it could take weeks to complete on Moorgate.'

'I know.' She was watching him anxiously. 'I want you to have absolute power of attorney, Mike, so if anything happens you'll just carry on dealing with it. You don't mind, do you?'

'No, of course not.' The light on the percolator shone red and he began to pour the coffee. 'Look,' he said, his back to her, 'I'm sure we can work through the legal bits. You're going to speak to Jenny in Truro and you can lodge the money with her for the deposit, and she has limited power of attorney to deal with the sale? Have I got that right?'

'Quite right. It means she can sign all the papers for me and I'm going to ask her to advise Rob to take out a simple repayment mortgage. I know paying the mortgage isn't a problem for him and it lets me out of having to have a medical. Jenny knows the truth, remember. I can absolutely rely on her.'

'That's fine but there's the other side to it.'

'What side?'

'Rob himself.' He put the mugs on the table, picked up Luke's car, which had fallen to the floor, and sat down again. 'Look, Lissy, don't you think all this is a bit tough on him?'

'How do you mean?' She looked puzzled.

'How do you think he's going to feel when he finds out the truth? At what point will you stop taking his calls? Think of the shock it will be for him.'

She was staring at him, huddled into her wrap, eyes wide with anxiety. 'But what else can I do? I don't want him to know, Mike. If I tell him he'll want to come and find me, I know he will. I can't bear the thought of it. Everything will change. There will be all that pity and horror. I can't do that. I want to be free to . . . to just finish peacefully. Please, Mike, don't ask me to tell him.'

'I know how you feel.' He felt utterly miserable, hating to upset her, trying to think of a way which would be right for both of them. 'But we have to think of Rob too. I want to do it your way but I don't want the shock of it to ruin everything for him.'

'Is that likely, do you think?'

'Look, love.' He took a deep breath. 'From what you've told me this has been a really important thing for you both. Not just a light flirtation but something that would have gone on into a permanent relationship. From what I've heard about Rob I think he's going to feel terribly hurt that you couldn't confide in him. No. Wait. This isn't a criticism. I know just how you feel and I quite understand but *he* might not, not unless it's explained to him. After all, this poor guy is down there thinking you're going back to him, that you have a life together. Try to imagine how he'll feel when the letter arrives from the solicitor telling him that he's suddenly the sole owner. I'm sure that he'll be delighted to have Moorgate but I suspect that it's you he wants, not a farmhouse.'

'But what else can I do?' she cried angrily. 'How could I possibly tell him now, even if I wanted to? I can hardly introduce it into light conversation on the telephone, can I?'

'Of course not,' he agreed compassionately, understanding her desperation. 'I absolutely agree that you can't possibly tell him on the telephone.'

Luke was distracted from his game by the tone of their voices and Mike stood up, swung him out of his highchair and sat down again, holding him on his lap. Luke leaned against him drowsily, crooning to himself, and Melissa watched them both, her face softened by love and sorrow.

'I couldn't go back, Mike,' she said quietly. 'Even if I had the stamina, I simply couldn't do it. Fancy walking in and saying, "Hi, Rob. Yes, great to see you too, and by the way . . ." I hear what you're saying but I can't think of a way round it. Oh, I can't bear it. It was all so perfect.'

'I know,' he said quickly. 'I can tell that. And we simply mustn't destroy the memory of all that or ruin Moorgate for Rob but I think he's going to suspect something's wrong and I'd rather be prepared for it.'

'Perhaps I could write to him.' She sounded dejected, all the joy gone, and he cursed himself for spoiling it for her. Why should he care how Rob felt, after all? He'd never met the guy so why should he worry about his reaction? 'I wasn't really thinking. I've been so happy and, selfishly, I wanted to forget everything else except that happiness.'

'There's nothing wrong with that,' he said strongly. 'You were both happy and he's going to have Moorgate. He'll never forget that week, either. I just don't want anything spoiled for either of you.'

'But how could it be done?' she asked wretchedly.

'I have an idea,' Mike said slowly. 'He'll have to know the truth but, because he loves you, he'll understand what it meant to you as long as it's explained properly to him. I just don't want him to have some kind of official letter out of the blue and if you write to him he'll want to see you. So suppose *I* go down to see him and explain exactly how it is?'

She began to look hopeful. 'Would you? But would that work? Suppose he refuses to accept Moorgate once he knows the truth?'

'That is the danger.' They stared at one another.

'Let's see if we can get it through quickly,' Melissa said pleadingly. 'He's expecting me to be tied up for several weeks. Let's hope we can get to completion and then you could go down to see him. That would be wonderful, Mike.'

'OK.' He sighed with relief. 'We'll leave it like that, then. Tomorrow morning you can telephone Jenny and tell her to get her skates on. If she has limited power of attorney it will save weeks. There's no chain, nothing to hold it up. It could be done in a fortnight if we really tried.'

'Bless you, Mike,' she said gratefully. 'And then you'll go down and tell him?'

'Whatever happens,' he said, 'I'll go and see Rob and tell him everything. Drink your coffee and pour me some more, would you? Luke's gone to sleep and I don't want to disturb him.'

Walking back from the station, having seen her father off on the train, Posy was beginning to feel the need of someone to whom she could talk. She couldn't decide what her stance should be. 'Guess what! My dad's going off to do this incredible thing. He's giving everything up for it.

Brave isn't it?' It reminded her of the Indians who left their families and went out with begging bowls. What was it called—sannyasi? She understood it to be some kind of spiritual quest, undertaken late in life, when they had fulfilled their commitments to their families, but it was rather different when it was your own father. Or she might take a different line. 'My dad's walked out on us. Chucked it all in. He couldn't cope any more and he's gone to live in a commune.'

At least Jude would sympathise. His father had walked out when he was hardly more than a baby and he'd had to cope with various men who had lived briefly with his mother before disappearing in due course. Jude had survived. She could talk to Jude. Jude was a bit like Hugh; there was a calmness, a stability, which was odd when you thought about how unstable Jude's life had been.

'Mum loved me,' he'd say. 'That's all you need. One person really loving you and believing in you. Anything else is a bonus.'

He'd said that when she'd been whingeing once about her mother always getting at her and how they'd always argued.

'What about your dad?' he'd asked—and she'd admitted that her father had always been on her side, always defending her and encouraging her.

'Well then.' Jude had shrugged. 'It's more than a lot of people have.'

She'd thought about it afterwards, wondering if it were feeble to want your mother's approval too. After all, she'd always had Maudie. She could telephone Maudie, of course. Maudie was always ready to listen to her problems, although she'd been on Patrick's side over the Mary thing. Maudie always held a rather detached view, which was helpful but not always particularly comforting. She'd once told Posy that too much sympathy could be ruinous, enervating, weakening, and that it was more helpful to look at things with a clear eye, but there were moments when unadulterated sympathy was very pleasant. Now, she felt, was one of those moments. At times like these she longed to ride out on to the moor with Hugh. The combination of Dartmoor and Hugh's brand of companionship always lifted her spirits—but both were too far away on this Sunday afternoon to be of much help.

As she turned into Hyde Abbey Road, Posy found that she was thinking of her mother. What a shock it must have been for her; how humiliating. Posy shrank from thinking about how she must be feeling; how bitter and lonely it would be to face life alone after nearly thirty years of marriage.

Posy thought: She's got the boys. They'll be on her side.

Scrabbling in her bag for her key, Posy felt guilt creeping round her heart. She'd tried not to judge her father nor to feel angry with him, waiting until she could think it through calmly. It was selfish to expect him to stay in an unhappy relationship and an unsatisfying job, simply so that she could have him there on the few occasions when she wanted to go home. At the same time she felt that it was wrong to walk out on a marriage simply because you'd had enough. She felt thoroughly muddled and miserable and longed to talk it through calmly with someone who would understand.

Posy shut the door behind her. She could talk to Jude, if he were around, or Maudie. There was no sign of Jude, however, and Jo was out too. Posy stood for some moments beside the telephone before she dialled the number.

'Hello, Mum,' she said quickly. 'It's me. Posy. Just wanted to see how you are.'

Her mother laughed somewhat mirthlessly. 'You mean that your father has told you his news.'

Posy's heart sank. 'Well, yes. It's a bit of a shock, isn't it?'

'It's not a shock to me to know that your father is a coward. You've always been prejudiced about him, of course, so I can't expect you to understand how I feel.'

'I just wondered if you wanted to talk about it.'

'Why? So that you can gloat?'

'No.' Posy tried to hold on to her temper. 'I don't particularly approve of his going if you want to know the truth.'

'You amaze me. I thought he could do no wrong as far as you're concerned. I thought you'd encourage him to go off and help the disabled. Didn't you tell him how wonderful and noble he is?'

'Actually, no. No, I didn't. Well, never mind. I just thought you might like to know that I'm sorry . . .'

'I'm sure you are. You're going to miss him. It's not nice to be rejected, is it? Perhaps, now, you'll just begin to understand how I've felt about you and Maudie all these years.'

'Right. OK then.' Posy felt disappointment, along with all the old familiar antagonism, burning inside her. 'I'm here if you need me. See you.'

She replaced the receiver, wanting to burst into tears. After a moment or two she dialled another number.

'Hi, babe,' she said. 'It's me. How are you? . . . Great. And Polonius? . . . Well, yes, I do. I'm hoping I might come down again next weekend if that's OK? Brilliant. Thanks, Maudie. Oh, and do you think you could arrange for me to go out with Hugh for an hour or two? . . . Thanks. Yes, I will. I'll be really looking forward to it. So what's been going on down in Devon, then?'

Chapter Twenty-eight

'How are you?' asked Rob eagerly. 'How are things going? I've had a call from someone called Jenny at the solicitor's in Truro. She was really positive. Thinks it can all happen quite quickly.'

'There's no reason why not.' Melissa closed her eyes so as to be able to imagine him more clearly. 'Where are you?'

'Up in our bedroom. I can get the best signal here.'

'Yes. Yes, I know.' It was there she'd telephoned to Mike, sitting on the broad window seat. 'Can you see the rooks?'

'Yes.' She knew he was turning round, looking out of the window, peering upwards. 'See them and hear them. It's a wonder you can't hear them too, the racket they're making.'

Hot tears slipped from beneath her closed lids, sliding down her cheeks. She could see the bulky, twiggy nests, propped in bare branches, silhouetted against a cloudy, windy sky; she could hear the acrimonious argy-bargy, punctuated by the high, plaintive cries of the lambs on the moor below.

'Are you still there?' His voice was anxious.

'Yes.' It was barely more than a sigh. The pain in her heart was suffocating. 'Yes, I'm here. Wishing I was there with you.'

'Oh, Melissa.' His voice was strong with happiness. 'It won't be long now. I'm arranging for the building society to do a valuation. You're sure you're happy to leave it all to me?'

'Of course I am. You're on the spot. Only . . . Rob. Don't waste any time, will you?'

'I promise I won't.' He rejected such a foolish idea cheerfully. 'But don't worry. We won't lose Moorgate now. Lady Todhunter was delighted. She telephoned and wished us every happiness. Wasn't that nice of her? She wants to meet you.'

'That's . . . very friendly.' She felt exhausted. 'Rob. I have to dash. This was just a quick one. I wanted to say "hello".'

'It's wonderful to hear your voice. I love you, Melissa. I know it seems as if the whole thing was a dream but it won't be long before we're here together.'

'No.' She made a tremendous effort. 'Of course it won't. I love you too, Rob.'

She switched off her mobile, her mouth trembling with grief.

'Lissy,' said Mike from the doorway. 'Lissy. Should you be doing this?'

She stared at him, her eyes dark with pain. 'I have to speak to him,' she said. 'I have to, Mike. Whilst there's still time.'

He went across to her, crouching beside her, holding her tightly. 'I'm just afraid that it's making it worse for you,' he murmured. 'It's so unutterably bloody.'

She leaned against him. 'It's odd, isn't it, that I can visualise it all so clearly? I can hear the rooks quarrelling and the sound of the lambs crying for their mothers. I was only there five days, yet it seems like a lifetime. He'll be all right, won't he, Mike?'

'Yes, he'll be all right.' He rocked her, feeling her bones beneath his hand, the lightness of her. 'Of course he will. He'll need a bit of time but he'll recover.'

'And you'll see him?'

'I shall see him. Perhaps, later, I'll go and stay with him. Luke and I might go together, for a weekend.'

He spoke hesitantly, unwilling to describe a future in which she could have no share, but when she raised her head to look at him her face was full of wonder.

'Oh, that would be good, Mike. I had so many dreams when I was there, at Moorgate. Such strange dreams about lots of people all there with me. I'd like to think that you might go to Moorgate—you and Luke.'

'Rob might find it a comfort too. I'm sure we'll be friends.' He wanted to weep, to scream, to vent his rage. Instead he loosened his hold, helping her up. 'You're cold. Come on. Hot coffee and chocolate time.'

'Jenny's already been in touch with him, bless her. And Rob's getting the building society's valuation organised. At least he doesn't need an independent survey. No one could know more about the house than Rob.'

She followed him into the kitchen, steadier now, concentrating on what needed to be done. As he filled the percolator he watched her covertly. She was thinner; the marks of suffering were drawn lightly but ineradicably on her face. The drive to Cornwall, the whole Moorgate experience had taken a greater toll even than he had feared. She sat at the table, wrapped in her long woollen bouclé coat, breaking some chocolate into squares and eating it thoughtfully.

'Mike, how would it be if I were to write a letter to Rob?'

He frowned consideringly. 'How do you mean? What kind of letter?'

'Well.' She paused, thinking it through. 'I know that you'll go to see him, once the sale is finalised, but supposing I wrote it all out. The whole bit. Why I went to Moorgate in the first place and how I feel about him. And why I couldn't bring myself to tell him the truth. I could explain it to him, couldn't I, and tell him what it's all meant? I want him to know just what he did for me, Mike. It's been like a miracle. Something to hold on to when things are . . . difficult. In some ways it's made it worse. You know what I mean, don't you? Ever since Rob, it's made it much harder to let go. To know all that I shall be missing is simply agonising but, at the same time, I can relive it all and lose myself in it. I had one glorious week when I thought that there was nothing left but waiting. I want him to know all that.'

'I think it's a brilliant idea.' He began to fiddle with the mugs lest she should see the heartbreak in his eyes. 'I can tell him, of course, but it will be much better coming from you. Your own words will mean a lot to him and he'll be able to keep the letter. In his place I should be really glad of it.'

'Well then.' Her face was bright with contemplation. 'I think I'll do it. I should like to. Not anything morbid or self-indulgent, just saying how it was.'

'That's right.' He stood the mug of coffee beside her. 'I can give it to him when I see him.'

'OK.' She smiled at him, comforted by this new sense of purpose. 'I'll get on with it. Are you managing to get any work done on your new book?'

'The page proofs of the last one arrived when you were away last week.' He grimaced. 'Just when I was beginning to feel really involved with my new characters.'

'How irritating.' She could sense his frustration. 'Listen. Why don't I check the proofs for you? I'd be very careful. I am a lawyer, after all. I'm used to reading small print and contracts.'

'That would be great.' He was genuinely grateful. 'If you think you could manage it. But don't distract yourself from Rob's letter.'

'No, I won't do that. I need to think about it for a while. How I intend to approach it and things like that but I could get on with the proofs straight away.'

'Fantastic. Could you work here at the table? I'll get them down from my study and you can see how you manage.'

'I'll make a start while Luke's still asleep,' she promised. 'It will be a very welcome distraction from thinking about how things are going down in Cornwall. Oh, Mike, I shall be so pleased to know that all the documents have been signed and sealed and that Moorgate is Rob's.'

Maudie finished drying up the lunch things, put them away and went into the living room. She'd been putting off the moment when she should telephone Selina and tell her about the offer on Moorgate. It had crossed her mind to tell Posy when she'd spoken to her on Sunday evening but in her heart she knew that it was not the right thing to do. Selina must hear the news from Maudie herself. Anything else would be cowardly. Nevertheless, she'd allowed herself to procrastinate and, even now, she was picking up Daphne's letter and glancing through it; anything to postpone the moment. With a sigh of irritation and a twinge of apprehension, she dialled the London number. Selina answered so listlessly that Maudie's anxiety increased.

'Hello,' she said, with an attempt at cheerfulness. 'Hello, Selina. It's Maudie.'

'Good heavens!' Selina laughed, an artificial cackle which upset Maudie further. 'The vultures are gathering. Who told you? Posy? Don't tell me Patrick had the courage to telephone?'

'Told me what?' Surprise lent an added crispness to Maudie's voice. 'What are you talking about? I've phoned to give you some news. Not very good, I'm afraid, from your point of view.'

'That's par for the course, then.' Selina laughed again. 'So what now? Come along, Maudie, dear. Spit it out. Tell me this news. Is Polonius dead? Oh, no, of course not. You said the news wasn't very good, didn't you?'

'Whatever is wrong, Selina?' Maudie stared in perplexity at the recumbent Polonius. 'Why should Polonius be dead?' A thought occurred to her. 'Have you been drinking?'

'Yes.' She was giggling now. 'Ten out of ten, dear stepmama. And what business is it of yours if I have?'

'None at all.' Maudie employed the old trick of disinterest. 'It just seems rather early in the day for it. But why not, after all?'

'Why shouldn't I?' Selina sounded rather sullen now. 'I've enough to drive me to drink. So Posy didn't tell you?'

Maudie sighed. 'I have no idea what you're talking about, Selina. This is clearly a bad moment. Perhaps we should try again later.'

'Patrick's leaving me.'

Maudie was silent. The trick had worked but she felt no triumph; she was too surprised. Posy had been so certain that the affair with Mary was over.

'Are you still there?' Selina asked peevishly. 'Of course, I suppose it's too much to expect sympathy from you?'

'Why should he leave you?'

'You tell me! Probably because I intervened between him and his little tart last year and he's still sulking.'

'Do you mean he's going away with her?'

'Oh, no. No, it's nothing to do with *her*. He's giving everything up to go off and work with the poor. He's going to live in a commune in Wales.'

'You're drunk, Selina,' said Maudie coldly. 'I've never heard such nonsense.'

'Well then, for once we agree, dear stepmother. But it's the truth. He's tired of being boring old Patrick Stone and he's decided that he wants to do something worthwhile. So he's leaving me and the children for good works.'

Maudie thought: So that's why Posy is coming down again so soon.

Aloud, she said, 'Isn't it rather drastic?'

'Rather drastic?' Selina's shrill tones indicated that she was finding Maudie's cool reaction irritating. 'Rather drastic? It's bloody disgusting. After thirty years he's walking out just because he's bored. Bored!'

'I simply can't believe it.'

'Well try, dear. He's given in his notice and he's leaving at Easter. It's all arranged.'

Maudie was silent: too startled to speak. She heard a clink of glass and a gurgling of liquid.

'Are you still there? Did you hear what I said? He's like a child with a new toy and I simply can't get through to him. So. What was your news, stepmother?'

'It's not good, Selina. I'm sorry to have to tell you this now. I have an offer on Moorgate.'

'Oh God!' There was a louder crash of glass, followed by the sound of sudden, noisy weeping. 'Oh, I can't stand this. Not now. Oh, Christ! This is just too much.'

'Selina,' said Maudie desperately, 'please listen to me. Moorgate would never have worked. You must know that, in your heart. With or without Patrick, Moorgate was not right for you.'

'I've got nothing now,' sobbed Selina. 'Mummy and Daddy have gone. Patricia's so far away she might as well be dead. I hardly see the boys any more. And now dear old Moorgate . . . Oh, God, I hate you, Maudie!'

The receiver was slammed down and Maudie replaced her own handset more slowly. She felt old and shaken, distressed by Selina's outburst, shocked by her news. It was so improbable that it had the ring of truth about it—and how typical of Patrick to be prepared to give everything up for an ideal. It sounded as if he had simply come to the end of his tether and, unable to cope with his wife and his job any longer, had switched off. She picked up her address book and looked for the number Patrick had once given her for emergencies. She dialled it, her hand trembling a little. His secretary answered and presently she heard Patrick's voice.

'Maudie?' He sounded concerned. 'What's the problem?'

'It's Selina.' She decided not to beat about the bush. 'I just phoned to tell her that I've accepted an offer on Moorgate. She's taken it very badly. She sounded very odd, Patrick, as if she'd been drinking, and she hung up in a terrible state.'

'I see.' He sounded noncommittal.

'I'm sure you can't speak openly at the moment but I was hoping you could perhaps find an excuse for going home. You know I wouldn't be making a fuss about nothing, Patrick.'

'Yes, Maudie.' His voice was warm. 'I know you well enough for that. I'll attend to it.'

'Thank heaven! If you could telephone later just to put my mind at rest I'd be very grateful.'

'I'll do that too.'

'And Patrick? Don't tell her I called you.'

Maudie hung up and sat staring out into the garden. The warm weather, which had swept away the snow, had left a soft grey dampness in its wake and the afternoon wore a muted, dun-coloured mantle. A black-bird was building in the high thick hedge, pausing briefly in the bare branches of the lilac tree, before plunging into the privet with her beak full of nesting material. A male bullfinch struck a note of pure bright colour as he perched on the bird table and a rabble of sparrows squabbled below him on the grass.

She thought: Why? Why can't I be nice to Selina? Why can't I manage it even for a few seconds? I didn't *have* to tell her about Moorgate when she was so upset.

Maudie picked up the *Cottage* magazine, read an article about Teign-bridge District Council's plans to introduce Pay and Display charges in Bovey Tracey's free car park, and put it down again without having taken in a single word of it. Was it really true that Patrick had given in his notice and was leaving Selina? And, even if he had, surely she, Maudie, could have managed a genuine word of sympathy or shown some compassion? The trouble was that she'd never quite understood how Patrick had man-aged to live with Selina for nearly thirty years in the first place. It was only because he was so utterly self-effacing, so blessed with humility, that he'd been able to cope with her at all.

'It would be a mistake,' Daphne had once said, 'to believe that Selina is a strong character. Her aggressiveness and desire to control is rooted in fear. My anxiety is that Patrick will not help her to grow. He will simply acquiesce whilst protecting her from herself.'

Maudie groaned aloud. It seemed as if all that were about to change.

Chapter Twenty-nine

The café in the Mill was quiet on this cold, wet Saturday afternoon. Thick grey cloud obscured the higher slopes of the moor and the rain drummed relentlessly in the valleys. Riding was out of the question but Hugh had suggested tea, instead.

Posy thought: He probably heard the desperation in my voice. Dear Hugh. He is so kind.

Maudie had dropped her at the Mill before going on to have tea with her friend, Jean Serjeant.

'Of course I don't mind,' she'd said. 'I'd assumed you'd be riding, anyway.'

For some reason Posy had been quite unable to bring herself to relate to Maudie this latest instalment in her parents' drama. She'd found it impossible to tell anyone, yet; probably because she couldn't sort out her own feelings. She edged her way along, looking at each step carefully, from all angles, lest she should be unjust or selfish. Sometimes, briefly, she allowed herself to be both at once but it was surprisingly difficult to come to a mature conclusion. What might seem reasonable from her father's point of view looked quite different through her mother's eyes. Her thought processes described frustrating circles until she thought she might scream aloud.

Hugh was watching her.

'I met a really nice girl in here a couple of weeks ago,' she said quickly, randomly. 'We sat by the window and talked about the birds . . .' And about being married for thirty-five years with five children, she might have added—but she could not bring herself to say that out loud to Hugh. Suddenly she was bathed in a hot tide of self-consciousness and she remembered how she'd felt like this years before when she'd imagined herself in love with him. She buttered her scone with great deliberation but it remained uneaten on her plate.

'So how are things at home?'

Posy heaved a huge, silent sigh of relief. In her anxiety she'd begun to feel it impossible to talk even to Hugh about it.

'Terrible,' she said—and fell silent.

'Were we wrong about your father?'

'Yes. No.' She pushed her hands through her hair, straining it back from her face. 'Sorry. I mean that the affair, if it was one, doesn't matter any more. Dad's decided that he's had enough. He's giving up his job and leaving Mum and he's going to work with an organisation called L'Arche. They have houses, communities, all over the world and they help people who have learning disabilities and have been marginalised by society. You get your board and lodging and a bit of pocket money, from what I can gather . . .'

'Yes, I've heard about L'Arche. A friend of mine put in a year after university. Wonderful places.'

She stared at him. 'But you don't think it's a bit bizarre? Like, giving up your job and abandoning your family at fifty? I agree, it's great if you're just out of university, but don't you think it's a touch weird when you're middle-aged? Not to say irresponsible?'

'You're angry with him?'

Posy closed her eyes—and then she laughed. 'Yes. *Yes.* I am angry with him. I admit it. I've been trying to be very fair and sensible about it but I can't get my head round it.'

'Perhaps you should do the angry bit first? Get it out of your system? Then you can be very cool afterwards.'

'It's not funny,' she said crossly.

'Who said it was?' Hugh drank some tea. 'But it's always best to allow yourself to react. No good pushing it down so that it can erupt later.'

'But what I feel doesn't really matter, does it? As Dad says, I'm grown up now, I'm hardly ever at home. Why shouldn't he do what he wants for a change? He's done all the right things for thirty years and Mum's made his life hell. Now it's his turn.'

'Sounds reasonable. How does your mother feel about it?'

'She won't talk to me,' said Posy moodily. 'She thinks I'll be on his side and she's just sarcastic all the time. I tried to say that I thought it was a bit much but she wouldn't let me get a word in.'

'It sounds as if he's just come to the end of everything, doesn't it? Perhaps the girl was a kind of catalyst. Whether he had an affair or not, she was the one that brought things to a head.'

'Mum probably wishes he'd had an affair after all. It would have fizzled out and things would have gone back to normal.'

'You think your mother would rather have an adulterer for a husband than one who gives up everything to help disadvantaged people?'

'Well . . .' Posy hesitated, frowning. 'I don't know. Sounds a bit crass when you put it like that. Either way it's selfish, isn't it? Leaving someone after nearly thirty years.'

'It *sounds* selfish. But I think it depends on what's gone on during those thirty years. If your mother's been the selfish one then perhaps it's time your father had a turn. How will she manage without him?'

'There's not a financial problem. He's leaving everything for her—the house and their savings and stuff. She'll be OK. He's suggested that she sells the house and downsizes, which won't have pleased her, but she won't starve.'

'Perhaps it might even be good for her.'

'*Good* for her?'

Hugh shrugged. 'You can never tell. Life ought to be about growing. Letting people walk all over you isn't good for them. It might be a blessing in disguise.'

'And I thought you were going to be sympathetic.'

He smiled at her. 'Do you need sympathy?'

'Yes,' she said firmly. 'I needed tea and sympathy and you've been . . . realistic.'

'Sorry.' He poured more tea. 'Shall we start again?'

'No.' She pushed her cup over to be refilled. 'No, it's OK. I can hack it.'

'After all,' he said, 'you'll still be seeing him, won't you? He hasn't stopped caring about you.'

'No,' she agreed. 'I know all that. It's just that there are special family moments . . .' She paused again. Times like weddings, she wanted to say, and when babies are born—but she couldn't bring herself to say the words to him. 'Just moments,' she finished lamely. 'Moments when you want them there, being a proper family.'

'Well, of course, in an ideal world that's what we'd all like. Unfortunately we don't live in an ideal world. Our expectations are not always attainable. People don't live up to our requirements. Siblings are selfish and quarrelsome. Parents are argumentative and tiresome and get ill and need to be looked after. Sometimes they even die, usually at inconvenient moments.'

'Oh, shut up,' she said—but she was laughing now. 'I wanted to have a good whinge not a lecture.'

'Well, that just proves my point,' he said comfortably, starting on his cake. 'Your expectation was unattainable. To begin with, you don't even know whose side you're on. Or was that what you wanted to whinge about?'

'I don't know what I wanted,' she admitted. 'I still don't, really. But I feel better about it.'

'Good,' said Hugh. 'Splendid. I have to say that this cake has absolutely lived up to my expectation of it and I intend to have some more. Want to try some?'

'Why not? Thanks.'

Feeling happier she began to eat her scone. The couple at the window table began to gather up their belongings and Posy wondered whether to make a dash for her favourite seat. The rain was slanting down, the sky heavy and dark, and she decided that it wasn't worth the effort, but as she ate her scone she remembered the girl and how she'd told her about Hugh. There had been something special about her, something indefinable.

Posy thought: I wonder where she is now?

Rob drove into the yard, climbed out of the pick-up and felt in his pocket for the keys. It was odd that, now everything was in train, survey done, mortgage agreed but documents yet to be signed, he had no desire to continue his clandestine visits to Moorgate. Ever since Melissa left, it had seemed rather pointless; in fact he sometimes wondered whatever had possessed him in the first place. Even thinking about it could make him feel rather foolish until he remembered Melissa saying, 'I would have done exactly the same myself.' She had understood his obsession; had been ready to behave in the same reckless way. What a week it had been!

Letting himself into the kitchen Rob was aware of the now-familiar secret warmth. That fusion of chemistry was so incredible, so unlikely, that he longed to telephone her; to hear her voice and confirm her existence. She was such an extraordinary girl, so beautiful, so funny, so vulnerable, yet so brave, that he was not yet quite able to believe his luck. He needed regular contact. Trying to resist the urge to telephone her he went from room to room, checking that all was well. Now that the weather was warmer he'd stopped trying to keep the sitting-room fire alight but trusted to the Esse and the woodburner to hold the damp at bay.

Upstairs in the big bedroom he sat down on the window seat. He often telephoned her from this vantage point; listening to the rooks, recalling how they'd made love. In his mind's eye he saw her standing at the window watching the snow; asleep, dreaming, with the moonlight on her face; her passion for chocolate and the way she wrapped herself in shawls, always cold. Unable to resist, he took his mobile telephone from his jacket pocket and pressed the buttons. Her voice was slow, dreamy, preoccupied.

'How are you?' He always asked this question.

'Busy.' He could hear that she was smiling. 'I'm checking proofs. Concentrating.'

'Proofs?'

A little pause. 'Yes. You know. Contracts and things. Where are you?' She always asked this question.

'In the bedroom.' He chuckled. 'It's true. It *is* the best place for a signal inside the house.'

'Oh, Rob.' She was laughing now. 'Our lovely air bed and those wonderful hot-water bottles.'

'I was thinking about that, too. We'll keep it and use it on every anniversary.' A much longer silence. 'It won't be long now,' he said urgently. 'We're getting on, aren't we? The mortgage's arranged and Jenny's being fantastic. I had no idea things could be moved along so quickly.'

'There are no chains. Nothing to hold it up.' Her voice sounded as if she were tired.

'Are you OK?' he asked anxiously. 'Not overworking?'

'Probably, but never mind.'

'I wish I could see you. Are you sure I couldn't come up, even for the day?'

'No, honestly, Rob. It would be such a muddle. Now the flat's sold I haven't anywhere to put you up. It's horrid being homeless and having to stay with friends. And I don't want us to be roaming the streets in the rain. I know it sounds crazy but I want to think of you there. At Moorgate. It won't be for much longer.'

'I know. I'm just being selfish, really. We had so little time together.'

'Oh, Rob, I know. I love you so much. Look, I really must go.'

'Sorry to distract you. I just needed to hear your voice. What's that noise? Sounds like a baby?'

'What? Oh, yes. A colleague's brought her new baby in to show us. Take care, Rob. I'll phone this evening. About eight? Love.'

He thrust the mobile back into his pocket. He felt all the frustration of their separation, yet the brief contact had comforted him and there was the evening call to anticipate, to hold as a talisman throughout the day. He went downstairs, planning a message to send to her later, hoping she might send him one. Now he was never parted from his mobile and it was never switched off, just in case. Whistling quietly to himself, Rob began to feed logs into the woodburner. He'd spoken to his mother the previous evening, told her that he was buying a house. She'd sounded quite pleased in her usual laconic manner.

'That's good then. So what's it like, this house?' And when he'd told her, described Moorgate, 'Not taking on more than you can chew?' she'd asked shrewdly. He'd felt the age-old antagonism rising but had been quite unable to tell her about Melissa. He knew that it would be impossible to explain to his canny, pragmatic mother the effects of that magic week or how he felt. She would be horrified to hear that he was buying a house with a girl he'd known for barely five days. The thought of her reaction made him nervous—though he hated to admit it to himself—made him wonder if he'd taken leave of his senses. At these times he absolutely required contact with Melissa. Only the sound of her voice could restore his confidence.

'I'm thirty-five,' he'd tell himself, irritated by his weakness. 'I don't need my mother's approval.'

He'd told her that he knew what he was doing, had everything under control, and she'd replied—brightly—that she was glad to hear it. Afterwards he wondered why, since they were not particularly close, she still had the power to get under his skin. No, he had not been able to talk to her about Melissa. She would have asked searching questions, demanded to know the date of the wedding. It was odd that he and Melissa never actually talked about commitment. It seemed implicit in all that they were planning that their lives were bound together. He imagined that this was why he no longer needed to camp at Moorgate. Soon they would be here together, doing it for real; there was no need, now, for pretence.

Melissa pushed back her chair and went to Luke, where he lay sobbing quietly to himself in his playpen. He'd managed to pull himself up, so as to fling one of his toys over the bar, and then had tumbled backwards. He was surprised rather than hurt, wanting the toy which now lay beyond his reach, and Melissa leaned over to lift him out so as to comfort him. She staggered a little beneath his weight, feeling suddenly weak, and was glad to fall into the roomy armchair beside the French window. Luke stretched out his hand, yearning towards the toy, a plush golden lion, which lay nearby on the floor, and she bent down to pick it up.

'Boh, boh, boh, ba,' he murmured contentedly, taking it in both chubby hands, and she lulled him with a wordless little tune, rocking him.

She thought: He must have put on weight. Or maybe it was the way I picked him up.

Fear plucked at her heart and her throat and she held Luke closer, willing away her private terror with the comfort of his warmth. As Luke became sleepy she concentrated on thoughts of Rob, of Moorgate. Closing her eyes, she saw again the sweep of moorland and Rob, climbing the slope in the shadow of the thorn. She relived their first supper; Rob in the deckchair eating the steak and kidney pie; talking about furnishing the kitchen, buying china for the dresser.

'Treasured pieces that go together,' she'd said, 'because they're loved and because you simply couldn't live without having them. Do you know what I mean?' she'd asked and he'd said, 'I'm beginning to think I do,' and had raised his glass to her. How hard it had been to hide her confusion, to pretend that she had the right to embark on this magic, incredible affair. Holding Luke tightly she wrestled with the guilt which threatened to diminish her happiness. Was it merely delusion to imagine that Rob would forgive her deceit; would understand once he knew the truth? She must write the letter before it was too late; too late for the memories to be clear, to explain exactly why she'd misled him. And he would have Moorgate . . .

Luke's warm, heavy body, his regular breathing, relaxed her and presently she, too, slept, her cheek turned against his soft hair and small round head.

Mike found them thus when he came down for lunch. He stood inside the door watching them, painfully aware of Melissa's thin cheeks, the dark shadows beneath her eyes, the terrible transparency and frailness of her slender form. In contrast the child seemed to bloom, exuding vital, sturdy life, even in sleep. Despair seized him; the powerlessness and inevitability of it, numbing and weakening him. Melissa smiled and murmured in her sleep.

'Can you hear the lambs?' she asked.

He turned away, then, going out into the shadowy hall where his tears might not be seen, standing for a moment, leaning against the wall. After a moment he went back, noisily enough to disturb her, to give her time to collect herself.

'Lunchtime,' he said. 'How have you been getting on with the proofs?'

He took the heavy child from her and they smiled at one another, each knowing the effort the other was making; the knowledge making it possible to endure what lay ahead.

Chapter Thirty

'Mum?' said Posy. 'Are you there, Mum? Look, I know you don't really want to discuss this with me but I want to know what you're going to do?'

'Do?' Selina, still smarting from the embarrassment of overindulgence, sounded frostier than usual. 'I suppose you mean about your father? Why should I do anything?'

'So you're just going to carry on like nothing's happened?' Posy tried not to let irritation creep into her voice.

'I don't have much choice. I'm certainly not going round telling everyone, if that's what you mean, and I'd be pleased if you could make an attempt at discretion.'

'You know, it's really amazing how many people here don't have the least bit of interest in our family life. What you and Dad do isn't exactly of global significance, if you know what I mean.' Posy grabbed at her temper and bit her lip. 'Sorry . . .'

'Oh, don't bother to apologise. I don't expect anyone to empathise with me.'

'Oh, *please*. Can we just have a normal conversation? Dad says he's leaving a few days before Easter and I thought I'd tell you that I'll be home for the holidays then. If it's any help—'

'I might not be here,' said Selina airily. 'I'm thinking of visiting Patricia.'

'You're going to Australia for Easter?'

'I might. Why not? There's nothing to keep me here, is there?'

'No,' said Posy, after a moment. 'No, I suppose there isn't.'

'I have tried to reason with your father.' Selina shuddered as she remembered her weak, drunken weeping when Patrick had arrived home early and found her well into the second bottle of wine. How could she have abandoned her pride and self-respect so far? Begging him to stay, clinging to him . . . 'He is completely selfish,' cried Selina angrily, 'and I am not only resigned to his going, I positively welcome it.'

'Right,' said Posy. 'Fine.'

'I have no doubt that he'll be back,' said Selina viciously, 'with his tail between his legs. Your father is an idealist'—if she'd called him a serial murderer she could have hardly sounded more disgusted—'and it won't be the first time that I have been asked to pay the price for his flights of fancy. One of us has to hold things together.'

'OK,' said Posy. 'Well then. As long as you're happy.'

Selina laughed. 'When have you ever worried about that?'

'Look,' shouted Posy. 'It's not just you. He's leaving all of us. You, me, the boys. We're all feeling pretty shaken up about it. He's my *father*—'

'Well, perhaps you should have thought about that sooner. If you'd behaved like a normal natural daughter instead of rushing off to Maudie whenever you could—'

'Oh, it was bound to come back to Maudie, wasn't it? It's all my fault because I happened to want a perfectly ordinary relationship with my grandmother.'

'*Step*-grandmother,' hissed Selina. 'She is no relation to us whatever. She is a cold, calculating cow.'

'Grandfather didn't think so, did he? He adored her.'

There was a click and a buzzing noise. Posy took a deep breath and put down the telephone receiver.

'Sod off, then!' she muttered and felt a foolish, childish desire to burst into noisy, luxurious weeping. She went upstairs, into her room, and sat down on the bed, pushing her hands through her hair.

'I will not feel guilty,' she told herself. 'I won't.'

She stood up and wandered over to the table which was littered with books, papers and other evidence of study. She stood for a while, staring down, picking up sheets of paper, glancing at one or two textbooks. After some moments, she sat down on the small upright chair, pulled a book towards her and tried to concentrate on her work.

———

Shopping in Bovey Tracey, buying some Sharpham cheese at Mann's, chatting with David Pedrick about the price of lamb, Maudie was thinking about her conversation with Patrick.

'Thanks for phoning,' he'd said. 'She'd got herself a bit worked up. Everything's fine now.'

'Is it?' Maudie had chuckled a little. 'Really? Are you sure?'

'Well,' he'd sounded somewhat embarrassed. 'Given the circumstances.'

'Ah, I see.' Maudie had taken him up on it at once. 'Given that you're leaving her, you mean?'

'Maudie,' he'd said warningly, 'don't push your luck. I came home and sorted things out and I'm glad you telephoned. Selina shouldn't have been alone, I agree, but I'm not open to emotional blackmail. I've been there, done it and I have a whole wardrobe of T-shirts.'

She'd raised her eyebrows, surprised by his cool, calm determination. 'Fair enough. So when are you off?'

'Just before Easter.'

It was clear from his brevity that he'd had no intention of confiding in her, nor had he allowed any room for cross-questioning. He'd also wisely refrained from requesting her to look out for Selina—thus opening himself up to criticism. Maudie had wished him luck and hung up. All the same, she couldn't simply forget about Selina.

'The G-word,' she muttered as she drove home; turning out on to Monk's Way, diving off to the left by the thatched cottage and bumping down the narrow lane. 'The G-word is raising its ugly head again. Selina has always made it painfully clear that she's never accepted me as a member of her family, so why should I care what happens to her?'

She thought: Is it because Selina is Hector's daughter? Or because she is Posy's mother? Or is it simply because I could have made more of an effort to reach her when she was a child? I couldn't understand what all the fuss was about and it was terribly difficult to love someone who disliked me as blatantly as Selina did. But she was a child. I shouldn't have expected her to make all the running. I was old enough to know better. The truth of it is that I was jealous. I can see that now. Trying to compete with the perfect Hilda, crazily in love with Hector, resenting anything that came between us. I still do. I still hate it that he apologised to Selina at the end for loving me. She had the last laugh. Oh, hell and damnation, shan't I ever be rid of it?

She passed between the two stone plinths which had once supported the railway bridge, feeling depressed and old, trying not to hate both Hilda and Selina. Quite suddenly she recalled a conversation with Daphne, years before. They'd been talking about shoes; discussing Maudie's long, narrow feet and the difficulty about finding anything that fitted really comfortably.

'Hector always said that Hilda didn't have toes,' Daphne had said, chuckling. 'He said that she simply had serrated edges to her feet.'

'Really?' Maudie had felt the usual unworthy delight in any disloyal confidence about Hilda. 'When did he say that? Was it in front of Hilda? Did she mind?'

'Oh.' Daphne had looked nonplussed for a moment, probably feeling rather guilty. 'I can't remember. No, Hilda didn't mind. At least, I don't think so. You know Hector. He likes a joke. Better not remind him, though. He's a touch oversensitive about her now.'

'Of course I won't,' Maudie had agreed—but she'd felt complacent, after that, about her long elegant feet.

Now, passing over Wilford bridge, turning into the drive, she felt a huge sense of relief at the thought of Daphne's impending visit. She needed Daphne; a detached but loving spectator who would sort them all out, bringing her humorous, calm wisdom to bear on this emotional muddle. As Maudie lifted out her shopping she called to Polonius, who was baying a delighted greeting on the other side of the gate. She'd considered it too warm, on this sunny spring morning, to cram him into the car but as soon as she'd put away the shopping she would take him for a walk through the woods. The prospect filled her with pleasure and her depression receded a little. The sun was almost hot, there was delicious cheese for lunch, and, in a few weeks' time, Daphne would be here.

The kitchen was deserted. Mike yawned, rubbing his hands over his unshaven jaw, noting that it was nearly nine o'clock. He'd worked well, today, and he felt weary but at peace—and terribly hungry. A note was propped on top of the tidily stacked pile of proof pages: 'Feel too tired to eat. Gone off to bed.'

Fear jolted him out of his other, imaginary, world back into the present. He stood for a moment, indecisively, and then went quietly upstairs. Luke slept peacefully, tidily, his thumb still half in his mouth, and Mike stared down at him thoughtfully. They'd both taken a break at Luke's teatime and had given him a bath before feeding him and putting him to bed. Mike had noticed that lately Melissa was having great difficulty in lifting the child and he'd realised that he must be on his guard to protect her. Crossing the small landing, he gently opened her bedroom door. The light streamed across her bed and he saw that she was lying on her back, so flat and light that she seemed to make no impression on the bed, no shape beneath the quilt. Silently he raged against the pervasive, cruel, relentless disease, impotent with helpless fury.

They'd heard earlier that completion should take place within the next few days and Mike had realised, by the look on Melissa's face, that she was simply waiting. Ever since she'd returned from Moorgate it was as if she were being sustained by the need to see the sale through. Once it was accomplished she would feel able to let go. And then what? It was difficult to imagine life without Melissa. She inhabited his earliest memories; how would it be without her fun, her determination, her undemanding companionship? Without her love and support?

His attention was caught by a pale oblong shape, lying on the table beside her bed. He stepped forward cautiously and picked it up, holding it angled towards the light. 'For Rob' was written on the front of the bulky envelope. So she'd managed it. In the last few days she'd found the strength—and the courage—to write to him; to explain the reasons for the deception and to assure him of her love.

Mike thought: I said I'd go down to see him but how will I be able to leave her now? She's deteriorating so fast. How could I leave her? I'd have to take Luke with me.

He replaced the letter gently on top of *The Golden Treasury* and went out. As he made some supper he wondered what he should do. Should he telephone Rob after completion and talk to him? Mike shook his head despairingly. What a shock it was going to be for the poor fellow; how would he deal with it? He might want to refuse to accept Melissa's part of the house, reject her bequest, and then what? Rob sounded a resourceful, determined man. Once he knew the truth it would be almost impossible to refuse to allow him to come to Oxford, yet Mike knew that this would ruin everything for his sister. She wanted Rob to remember her as she had been in Cornwall and it would be cruel to weight her last days with the responsibility of comforting him, or the guilt of admitting that she'd misled him. The whole thing was quite mad; wildly, crazily impossibly foolish.

Yet it still might be achieved. His head aching with ideas and plans, Mike sat down to his supper.

Yet, when the end came, it was so quick that Mike found himself travelling down to Cornwall in the dawn light of a wild March day, speeding along wet deserted roads, his whole mind concentrated upon the interview which lay ahead. Exactly six days after the keys of Moorgate had been officially handed to Rob, Mike found himself standing outside the gate, staring up at the house. The wind roared across the moor from the northwest, battering at the rooks' nests high in the trees, screaming round the house. The rain had cleared away and the sun was bright, casting sharp shadows, and daffodils gleamed gold in the borders beneath the windows. It was all exactly as Melissa had described it to him.

The front door opened and Rob stood, hands in pockets, watching him. Mike's heart thumped against his side and he gasped, a deep steadying breath.

He opened the gate and walked slowly along the path, pinned by Rob's unwavering stare.

'I'm Mike,' he said awkwardly, praying desperately for some kind of guidance. 'I'm Melissa's brother.'

'Yes,' said Rob, almost grimly. 'I thought you might be. I've been expecting . . . something.'

'Expecting . . . ?'

Rob shrugged. He looked angry, even threatening, and Mike felt a tiny stab of fear. After a moment, however, Rob stood aside and indicated that Mike should enter. They stood together, in the hall, until Rob closed the front door and turned to him.

'I knew something was wrong when I couldn't get an answer from her mobile and there were no more messages. She's changed her mind, hasn't she? Doesn't want to go through with it?'

His misery was palpable and Mike's fear dissolved in sympathy. In his overwhelming need to disabuse Rob of such terrible suspicions, he spoke baldly.

'She never changed her mind for a moment. It's not that, Rob. Melissa is dead.'

'Dead?' His lips formed the word but did not utter it and he seemed to stagger slightly, as if from a physical blow. He put out an arm, as if to steady himself, and Mike caught him, horrified by his thoughtlessness. Yet how else could he have done it?

'Rob. I'm so sorry. Forgive me for being so brutal. She'd been ill for some time but the end was quick. Oh, *hell*! Look, can we go somewhere?'

Rob stumbled ahead of him through the hallway, into the kitchen. A small table stood by the stove, with some chairs, but Rob went to the sink and stood staring out, gripping the edge, his back to Mike.

'Why did nobody tell me she was ill?'

Mike looked compassionately at the straight back and clenched muscles, sharing the man's furious unhappiness. 'She left you a letter.' He took it from his pocket. 'Would you . . . ? Do you think you could read it, Rob? She'll have explained it all so much better than I could and then we can talk. I'll tell you anything you want to know. She loved you, Rob. Please read the letter.'

After some moments, Rob turned and took the envelope which Mike held out to him. He nodded, made to leave the kitchen, hesitated.

'There's coffee and sugar under the sink,' he mumbled. 'Milk's in the larder,' and went away, shutting the door behind him.

'Shit!' muttered Mike, near to tears. 'Oh God.'

Shaken with grief, weary from the drive from Oxford after long days and nights of vigil, he stumbled about, pushing the kettle on to the hot-plate, opening and shutting cupboards, dropping things in his clumsy distress. Presently he stood at the window, holding the mug of coffee, staring out at the wild, majestic landscape. It was as if Melissa leaned at his shoulder, wrapped in her ruana, gazing out eagerly.

'Listen,' he could hear her saying, 'can you hear the lambs?'

Hot tears ran down his cheeks. His own loss was so new, so raw, yet how to comfort Rob? He had no idea how long he stood, waiting, watching the changing colours of the moor, gold, indigo, lavender, as the clouds raced before the wind, but at length he heard the door open behind him. He turned eagerly—but glanced hastily away from the red eyes and ravaged face. At a loss for words he began to make more coffee, his hands trembling.

'When?' asked Rob.

'Yesterday morning. It was just getting light.' His own voice wavered. He swallowed, gaining a measure of control. 'In the last few days she seemed to think that she was here. You were always in her mind. You and Moorgate. She was so happy.' He spooned coffee into the mugs, his face screwed up like a child's, and it was Rob who came to comfort him, dropping an arm along his shoulder. 'Don't blame her,' Mike muttered. 'She loved you but she couldn't bear for it to be spoiled.'

'It's a very . . . wonderful letter,' said Rob gently. 'I can't believe you came so quickly. It's . . . extraordinarily brave of you.'

'She wanted you to have the letter earlier.' Mike wiped away his tears. 'But the end came so fast, I couldn't leave her. I hoped that you might come back with me to the funeral. I . . . She . . .' He bent his head and Rob tightened his grip on Mike's shoulder. 'We thought it would be right to scatter her ashes here at Moorgate. Where she longed to be.'

For a moment there was only the wild crying of the wind; then Rob spoke sadly, his eyes on the moor beyond the window.

'Yes, please, Mike. I'd like to come back with you. We'll have our own little ceremony here later.'

Mike nodded and Rob hugged him briefly and let his arm drop away. They stood together, each comforted by the other's presence and by the hot, sweet coffee. Neither felt the need for conversation, wrapped as they were in their own thoughts, grateful for this moment of shared silence.

'When you're ready,' Rob said, at last, 'we'll get going. I think that we'll talk later, perhaps on the journey, if you're up to it. There will be plenty of time for talking.'

Mike looked at him gratefully. 'I'd like to get back. There's Luke . . .'

'Oh, yes, your little boy. It was good of you to come, Mike.'

'I promised Melissa.' Mike stood his mug on the draining board and rubbed his eyes. 'I'm so tired. I feel I could sleep for a week.'

'Would you like to grab a quick nap?'

'No,' said Mike quickly. 'Thanks. I probably should but I'd rather get straight on. I . . . don't want to be away longer than I need. There will be plenty of time for rest afterwards.'

'Would you let me drive?' offered Rob. 'Just to give you a bit of a rest? I'm insured. I have to be in my kind of work.'

'Thanks. I'd like that. I'm not certain I should be driving, if I'm honest. If you'll drive I can sleep on the journey.'

'I'll throw a few things in a bag and be right down.'

Mike felt a brief lightening of spirits at the thought of companionship on the long drive back, relief that the worst was over. He opened the back door and stood, braced against the gale, letting it blow over him, cold and fresh and cleansing. A parliament of rooks argued in some trees somewhere out of sight and, borne on the wind as it fled over the moor, he heard the high plaintive crying of the lambs.

Part Three

Chapter Thirty-one

It was hot. Spears of sunshine pierced the leafy canopies and thrust downwards into the water. In the cool, shadowy depths dark fish hung; a flick of a tail, a flash of gold, a sliding, glancing, silvery arrow. Tall yellow flag irises shone bright as flame whilst below, reflections of white and purple cloud, solid as a wall, moved slowly across the trembling surface. Tiny wild strawberries, sweet and ripe, trailed across the slate flags, and pansies, delicate, silken tapestries of colour, edged the mossy paths. A jackdaw sidled round the chimneypot, head cocked, listening to two swallows gossiping busily on the telephone wire.

In the deep shade of the veranda, Polonius lay; head on paws, utterly relaxed. Yet a watchful eye gleamed and his ears were pricked attentively. He was not allowed into this part of the garden and he was waiting for Maudie to return from her weeding. Some excitement was afoot, he knew that quite well, but wasn't certain yet as to what it might be. It had involved a great deal of busyness in the spare bedroom, several trips to Bovey—from which he'd been excluded—and a stocking up of the shelves in the storeroom. He followed Maudie about, faintly anxious, inquisitive, interested, sensing her suppressed anticipation. Now, with the onset of this hot sunny spell, this busyness had extended itself to the garden. Polonius yawned massively, snapping at a passing fly, stretching himself upon the sun-warmed wooden planks.

Maudie, pottering happily with the sun on her back, was in high spirits.

In little more than a week, Daphne would be here. She was staying for a month.

'But not with you, love, don't panic,' she'd said. 'Not for all of it.'

Maudie had protested but Daphne had been quite determined.

'I shall be with you for most of it,' she'd promised, 'but I shall come and go. Leave you time to breathe and have a rest. You're used to being alone, Maudie, and a month is a very long time.'

Part of Maudie knew that this was true; nevertheless she'd felt ridiculously hurt—almost jealous—that Daphne had other friends to see. She knew how silly this was, how childish she was being, but she couldn't quite help herself. Daphne was a popular and well-loved woman who made a point of keeping in contact with her friends. Naturally she would want to see them, as well as the few remaining members of her family. It was quite unreasonable to expect to have her all to herself for a whole month and Maudie consoled herself with the knowledge that she was having the lion's share of Daphne's company.

'Just over a week to begin with,' she'd said, 'if you can cope with me that long, and then I shall go off for a few days to see an old cousin of mine and Philip's brother. Oh, Maudie, we're going to have such fun!'

It was nearly two years since they'd been together last; at Hector's funeral. They'd stood together—two tall, elderly women, with a wealth of shared memories—straight-backed, dry-eyed. Theirs was not a generation who'd known the luxury of easy tears or the indulgence of indiscriminately or publicly displayed emotion. They'd said their farewells to Hector with dignity and it was only after the door had shut behind the last guests that they'd kicked off their shoes and allowed themselves the relaxation of grief. On that occasion Daphne had stayed for barely a week; this was to be a real holiday.

'And then I shall come out to see all of you,' Maudie had said. 'That's what I planned to do once Moorgate was sold. This has only postponed it, you know. I long to see darling Emily and the children. *Do* bring some photographs with you, won't you?'

Maudie, kneeling beside the border beneath the hedge, prepared herself for the painful act of rising. The garden was looking delightful, the house was spring-cleaned, all was ready; but first, before Daphne was due to arrive, Posy was coming for the weekend. Posy was longing to see Daphne again, always interested in everything that Emily was doing. She had a special fondness for Emily, although she hadn't seen her for many years, and still liked to talk about the holidays at Moorgate, insisting that she could remember those far-off happy days. Perhaps the three of them might make a visit to Moorgate, to see Rob and the girl whose name she'd forgotten. Maudie had sent a card once the house was finally, legally, his but in the ensuing two months, what with Patrick's departure and the need to prepare the house for Daphne's arrival, she'd had little time to spare for Rob. Somehow, the knowledge that Rob was there made her feel that Moorgate was still accessible; that it was not lost to the family for ever.

As she kicked off her shoes, and stepped over the rope which prevented Polonius from going into the garden, the telephone began to ring.

'Damn,' she muttered, 'damn and blast. *Don't* hang up!' and, abandoning the search for her espadrilles, she fled barefoot through the French doors into the living room and snatched up the receiver.

'Lady Todhunter? Hello. It's Rob Abbot. How are you?'

Maudie sat down, took a deep breath and began to laugh. 'Rob, how good to hear from you. You must have second sight. I was just thinking about you and wondering if I might come down and see you. Just a quick one, you know, to say hello.' A short silence. 'Not if it's difficult, though,' she added quickly. 'I certainly don't want to be a nuisance. It would simply be nice to see you—both of you—settled in.'

'That would be good.' Rob sounded as if he'd made up his mind about something. 'Yes. You do that. Only, could you come this weekend?'

'This weekend?' Maudie was rather taken aback. 'Well, I could. I'd have my granddaughter with me, if you can cope with that?'

'Of course. Bring her along. Would Saturday or Sunday be best?'

'I'd prefer Saturday. She travels back to Winchester on Sunday.'

'Saturday it is, then. About coffee time?'

'Excellent. I shall look forward to it. Goodbye, Rob.'

Polonius came padding in and sat down beside her chair. 'That was rather sudden,' she told him. 'But it should be fun. Perhaps I can go again later, with Daphne. I hope Posy won't object to being dragged down to Cornwall. Well, never mind. Saturday it is. If it's not too hot we might take you with us but don't count on it.'

Polonius sighed heavily, as one who was continually and cruelly exposed to disappointment, and Maudie patted him consolingly. She knew how much he hated being left alone; she also knew that Posy would be loath to leave him. Posy had spent most of the Easter holidays with Maudie, although Selina had not gone to Australia after all. Chris and his wife had arranged to take a holiday and had invited Selina to go with them to Edinburgh. Selina had accepted with alacrity and Posy had felt free to travel to Devon without feeling guilty.

'Trust Chris,' she'd said rancorously. 'Chris always does the right thing. It makes you sick. I wish you could have seen Mum doing the wistful abandoned wife bit. She was like, "Oh, however shall I manage?" with her handkerchief at the ready and Chris doing his filial stuff and saying what a bastard Dad is. I wouldn't mind but when Chris went she was back to her normal sarky self before he'd got outside the gate.'

'Never mind. At least she's being looked after and you can relax.'

'I know.' Posy had still looked cross. She'd frowned, dragging her hands through her hair. 'I know it's silly but it hurts. *I* offered to spend the holidays with her and she just chucked the offer back in my face and said she was going out to see Auntie Pat. But the minute Chris steps in she changes her mind and goes off with him and Sarah.' She sniffed. 'I can't think why I'm surprised. Chris has always been her favourite. I suppose I can understand it but she's so . . . so *blatant* about it.'

'Perhaps Patricia didn't want her.'

It had been a naughty and provocative thing to say but it had distracted Posy from her woes.

'I never thought of that,' she'd said, shocked. 'Oh dear. You could be right. Poor old Mum . . .'

Maudie pushed Polonius's heavy head off her knee and stood up. It might be tactless to take Posy down to Cornwall so as to see Rob and his partner happily settled into the house she'd always loved so much. On the other hand, they might all become friends. Either way it was too late now to worry about it. Maudie went into the kitchen to wash her hands. Her knees and back ached from weeding and stooping, and she longed for a cup of tea.

'I'm an old, old woman,' she told Polonius, who had followed her and was now staring hopefully at the biscuit tin. 'And much you care. Oh, very well then. One biscuit and that's all and now go away. I'm going to sit down with my cup of tea and read the paper.'

It was only much later that she'd realised that she hadn't asked Rob why he'd telephoned.

Rob stood at the kitchen window, hands in pockets, gazing at nothing. He did a lot of this these days: walking from room to room, staring out of windows. Fortunately he had a great deal of work at the moment, and for most of the time he was occupied, but during those other empty hours he was apathetic, unfocused and lonely. The odd thing was that, before Melissa, he had never been lonely. He'd been self-sufficient, quite content with his own company if none other was forthcoming. It was as if she'd shown him how delightful life could be with the right companion and then departed, leaving him alone, dissatisfied and miserable. Only his friendship with Mike had kept him going. The shock of her death had momentarily unbalanced him but Mike's need had steadied him, giving him something which enabled him to think his existence was worth preserving.

It seemed so utterly extraordinary that five short days could have changed his life, given it new, sweet meaning, whilst now the slowly passing hours were flat, empty, wearisome. Even the possession of Moorgate could not comfort him. It was ironic that Melissa should have supplanted Moorgate in his heart and then left both heart and house untenanted. Without her the house simply underlined all that he had lost. He saw her everywhere; expected to hear her voice. Missing her was a permanent physical ache. Yet he was not bitter; he utterly understood why she had allowed herself those five days of fun and love and he did not begrudge her a minute of them. So many things had become clear once he'd read her letter and talked to Mike, but he wished that she had not wanted him to have Moorgate. He knew quite well that this was her offering to him, the only thing she could leave to him, but she hadn't foreseen that without her it kept his grief and loss at the forefront of his mind.

'I don't think I can go on here alone,' he'd said to Mike, one evening on the telephone. 'I keep expecting to find her, sitting by the fire or looking out at the moor or watching the rooks. I think I can hear her voice. It should be comforting, to be here where we were so happy, but it isn't. It's agonising.'

'It's early days.' Mike had sounded almost as desperate as he was himself, and Rob had been struck by remorse.

'I know it is,' he'd answered quickly. 'How are you managing? How's Luke?'

'He misses her. He looks for her and grizzles to himself. I don't quite know how to deal with it.'

'Why don't you come down?' Rob had suggested eagerly. 'You and Luke. Just for a weekend or something. It would distract him.' And me, he might have added. 'Or would it disrupt your work?'

Mike had laughed rather mirthlessly. 'I'm not getting much done. It sounds a great idea, Rob. Are you sure? Luke's a bit of a handful.'

'Just tell me what you need.' Rob had sounded almost buoyant. 'I can buy some secondhand bits and pieces. After all, I'm hoping you might consider this to be a second home.'

'Well.' Mike had hesitated. 'He still needs to sleep in a cot. And a playpen is an absolute necessity if we want a few moments of peace and quiet. Honestly, Rob, I can't put you to all that trouble.'

'It's no trouble.' Rob had sounded almost happy. 'I might have been his uncle if . . . if . . .'

'You *are* his uncle,' Mike had said quickly. 'Definitely. His only uncle. OK, I accept your offer with gratitude. Maybe a few days in the peace and quiet of the Cornish countryside will unblock my thought processes.'

So it was that Mike and Luke had made their first visit to Moorgate together. Once they'd settled in, joking at the makeshift arrangements, jollying each other along, Rob, and Mike—with Luke slung papoose-like across his chest—had walked across the moor as far as Rough Tor. It had been a calm, mild day and Mike had visibly relaxed in the soft air and warm sunshine.

'I can see why Melissa loved it here,' he'd said. 'It's a different world. It meant so much to her, Rob. That glorious week of freedom coming out of nowhere when there was nothing left to look forward to.'

Out there on the moor they'd talked naturally, easing their pain, sharing their grief. Even Luke had been soothed by the peace and had slept soundly in the old, white-painted cot.

'Melissa wanted this to be the nursery,' Rob had said. 'She'd have guessed that Luke would probably be the first to use it.'

A few weeks later Mike and Luke had made another visit. It was clear that Mike was puzzled by the continuing scarcity of furniture although he said nothing.

'I can't bring myself to get on with it.' Rob had answered his quick glance around the kitchen, still furnished only with the gate-leg table and two chairs. 'I had very little down in the caravan so it means a special shopping trip and I simply can't bring myself to make it. Melissa was so sure about what the house needed. She had such positive ideas . . . and so did I. It's just not the same without her.'

For a brief moment he'd feared that Mike might offer to go with him, to jolly him along, but Mike had remained silent. Luke's playpen sat proudly in the middle of the huge floor space and it was almost a relief when the usual detritus that gathers about small children began to spread around the house. When they'd gone Rob left the playpen where it was; it was company for him.

Now, as he stared out of the kitchen window, he realised that he hadn't given Lady Todhunter a reason for telephoning. It was just as well that she'd jumped into the breach. He had no idea why he'd needed to speak to her; a sudden requirement to hear her crisp old voice had possessed him. He'd remembered those conversations with her, and cheerful pub lunches, her sharp humour and charming smile, and he'd simply picked up his mobile and dialled her number. He'd had no opportunity to explain about Melissa and he could foresee difficulties there but—Rob shrugged—he had to get it over sometime. Maybe it would be easier with a granddaughter about but, anyway, he'd had little choice. Mike and Luke were coming down again the following weekend and he preferred to see Lady Todhunter without that added complication.

Rob frowned. He had the oddest sensation that Melissa was sitting at the table behind him, her ruana clutched about her, eating chocolate, smiling at him. He wouldn't turn round. He'd done it before and had always been disappointed. Yet, today, he'd felt her presence keenly. Whilst he'd been thinking about Lady Todhunter she'd been there, in the shadows of his mind. He clenched his teeth, tears starting in his eyes, his body aching for her.

. . . You can't imagine what you gave to me, Rob, *she'd written.* The best and most precious gift, ever. Love and life when I'd thought it was all over. Forgive me, won't you? I shall always love you. Think of me when you see the rooks building and hear the new lambs each spring . . .

He crossed his arms tightly over his chest and allowed the tears to fall.

Chapter Thirty-two

Mike sat at the kitchen table looking through his post. He still occasionally received letters of condolence, as the sad news filtered outward through close friends to acquaintances, but this morning he was studying the latest details sent from estate agents. There were photographs of beautiful cottages, in idyllic Oxfordshire villages, and larger rectories and vicarages in Wiltshire and Gloucestershire. Mike studied them thoughtfully whilst Luke chuntered cheerfully in his highchair. He had no plans for taking out a large mortgage—as a writer he felt that his income was too uncertain to justify such a risk—but he had a very respectable sum at his disposal. The proceeds from the life assurance policy that Melissa had taken out against the mortgage of her London flat were now his. The flat had been a modest little affair and, comforting though it was to know that the money was there, it seemed a small sum compared with the prices of these houses. Mike and Melissa had both used the twenty thousand pounds, given to each of them by their father, as deposits to buy flats but Mike still had a mortgage to pay. His real hope, now, was to buy outright, to take this opportunity to free himself from debt and begin to build a stable future for himself and Luke. It seemed that, if he wished to realise this hope, he might have to move further afield than these expensive counties of middle England. The buzz of the doorbell disturbed his reflections and he piled the house details aside and went out into the hall.

He opened the front door and hid his dismay behind a smile.

'Rebecca. How nice . . .'

'No, honestly, I shan't stay a minute. I'm sure you're much too busy to be disturbed.' Her expression—rueful, flirtatious, intimate—was a masterpiece. 'Just to say—what about supper on Saturday evening? We've got a little party going . . .'

'Come in,' he said, trying to keep the despair from his voice. 'Don't stand on the pavement.'

'Only for a tiny second, then. Promise. I know you writers.' She preceded him into the kitchen. 'Oh, the little darling. Good morning, Luke. Do you know, I think he recognises me.'

Mike thought: I'm not surprised. We see enough of you. Aloud he said: 'It's possible. Coffee?'

'Oh, *well* . . .' She clasped her hands together, a girlish gesture which sat uncomfortably with her years. 'Now there's an offer I can't refuse. Can I, Lukey?'

Mike grimaced horribly at the percolator: Lukey! *Lukey!* 'How are the girls?' he asked politely.

'Don't ask. Just don't ask!' She rolled her eyes humorously. 'Thank God, for a wealthy ex and boarding school. Now! Don't go putting that in your book, will you? My friends are just so impressed that I know you. "He'll be putting you in one of his books," they say to me. Honestly!'

Resisting the urge to observe that he never wrote about the commonplace or banal, Mike smiled noncommittally. 'Black?'

'Fancy you remembering. No sugar. I'm desperately trying to lose weight.' Another of her expressions—an agonised grin of bravery. 'How do you manage to stay so lean?'

Mike refused to be drawn into the weight debate. Perhaps she was hoping he might tell her that she had no need to diet; if so she was destined for disappointment.

'It's Luke who keeps me in training,' he answered lightly.

'Well, I must say,' leaning towards him, suddenly serious, voice pitched low with emotion, 'I have to say I think you are *so* brave. Not only about your sister. No'—a hand raised—'I know you don't want to talk about it, don't worry. No, I mean managing all on your own. Honestly. Me and my chums are all just *so* impressed.'

'I can't imagine why.' Mike put the mugs on the table and sat down, swallowing down a huge yawn. Rebecca's company invariably induced a frightful apathy and excruciating boredom. 'I expect you looked after your children, didn't you?'

'Well, yes. I did. But it's different somehow, isn't it?'

'Is it?'

He had a sudden vision of Melissa, appearing in the study doorway, grinning, finger to her lips. 'It's that frightful woman from round the corner. I told her that it was more than my life is worth to disturb you but I'm going to have to give her coffee. I'll tell you when she's gone.' The sudden wave of loss made it impossible to make another effort. He drank some coffee and remained silent.

'I think it is. Quite different. I hope you'll forgive me saying that you look tired.'

Mike looked at her. He thought that her impertinence was breathtaking but he managed to smile. 'So what was this about a party?'

She had no idea that she'd been snubbed. Excitement kindled in her again. 'Just a little group of chums coming in for some supper on Saturday evening. They'd be *so* thrilled to meet you. We've all seen *Changing Places*, of course. Brilliant production! And we can't wait for the next book. Now *do* say you'll come.'

'This Saturday?' He pretended disappointment. 'Oh, I can't, I'm afraid.'

Her face fell ludicrously. 'But why not? It's not darling Lukey, is it? We can easily put him to bed upstairs.'

'No, no,' Mike said quickly. 'Nothing to do with Luke. The truth is,' his eye fell on the calendar pinned to the notice board behind her head, saw the thick green circle drawn around the date of the following weekend, 'we're going down to Cornwall for the weekend.'

'Oh, that's too bad.' She actually looked quite put out but managed to pull herself together, smiling quickly. 'We shall all be so disappointed.'

'Me, too.' In his relief he sounded almost genuine. 'Another time perhaps.'

She was not so easily consoled. He was not to know that she'd let it be understood that Mike Clayton was more than just a neighbour, had hinted that he was more, even, than just a friend. Oh, there was nothing definite, nothing that could be repeated with confidence, only little remarks left unfinished, an air of being in the know, of being someone who was rather special to the Claytons. Rebecca knew that, without Melissa, it would be much more difficult to gain access. She might never have got further than the kitchen, had rarely seen Mike, but Melissa had been unable to withstand such a determined attack of neighbourliness, and Rebecca had gained a tiny, precarious foothold. Now she needed to secure Mike's friendship or that foothold would be lost. How humiliating to have to admit that she'd been unable to persuade Mike to come to her party. However, if he were indeed going away for the weekend it was, at least, a sensible excuse. She rehearsed it mentally whilst Mike gave Luke some milk.

Oh, such a bore! He's away in Cornwall, again. Yes, with that chap Melissa knew. Rob Something. He's seriously upset, apparently. I think there was something going on there. Oh, definitely. Mike's such a sweetie. It's a long way to go to simply be supportive and he has his own grief to contend with. Oh, very cut up about it. They were very close, you know, and she was such a darling. Utterly tragic. Poor Mike. What with the ghastly Camilla leaving him literally, but literally, holding the baby, and now poor Melissa. He's so brave. We have these little chats together. Oh yes, only on Wednesday morning we were having a heart-to-heart . . .
She brightened a little.

'Well, never mind. Another time. I'll be certain to give you more notice.'

'You do that.' He remained on his feet. 'Look, sorry to break it up but it's time for Luke's nap and then I have to get on.'

'Absolutely. I quite understand.' She leaned across the table, her expression a mixture of sympathy, admiration, coyness. 'Isn't there anything I can do to help? Put Luke to bed? Wash up? Anything at all? You must miss Melissa so much. Can't I be useful?'

'No.' The repugnance which filled him sharpened his voice and he bent over Luke, giving himself a moment to regain control. 'No, thanks.' He straightened up, smiling at her. 'It's really very kind. I promise I'll ask if I have a real problem. Writers are grumpy, selfish people, you know. We have to have our space or we bark and bite and become intolerable. I've lost too many friends already.'

'Now you know much better than that where *I'm* concerned . . .' She was arch now, smiling with an intolerable intimacy. 'You can trust me, Mike.'

'I know I can.' He was herding her towards the door like a collie with a distracted sheep. 'Bless you, Rebecca. Give me a buzz sometime. Yes, when I'm back from Cornwall. That'll be great . . .'

He closed the door on her promises and leaned against it, his eyes shut. Luke shouted and he hauled himself upright and went back to the kitchen, wondering how he and Luke could hide for a whole weekend. Murmuring to Luke, picking up his lion, he reached for the telephone and dialled.

'Rob? Hi! It's Mike. How are you? . . . Good . . . Yes, I'm OK but I've got a problem. Could Luke and I come down to Moorgate this weekend instead of next? . . . You don't sound too certain . . . Oh, right. I'd rather like to meet her, actually, but not if it's going to be difficult for you . . . Really? I must say I'd be truly grateful . . . Thanks, mate . . . Oh, Friday, about teatime? . . . No, don't worry about that. I've got some keys, remember . . . You've saved my life. Yes, I'll tell you later. I can hear you're pushed for time. Great. See you.'

He hung up and lifted Luke out of his chair, blowing raspberries into his soft neck, holding him high in the air.

'We're going to see your Uncle Rob,' he told him. 'Good, isn't it? And now you're going to bed and I'm going to work. Here's Leo, don't panic. There you are. Now, up we go.'

He carried him up the stairs, singing to him, looking forward to the unexpected bonus of the weekend.

'I know. Isn't it just too tiresome?' Rebecca was already on the telephone. 'Yes, we've just been having coffee together . . . Oh, I know. He makes me feel *so* special . . . Yes, just the two of us and darling little Lukey. I'm such a lucky girl, aren't I? . . . Don't worry, sweetie, you'll meet him sometime . . . Well, he's just a *tad* reserved but too sexy for words.' A light laugh. 'How sweet of you. Well, I *was* very close to poor, darling Melissa, of course . . . Oh, honestly! You're very naughty! Now, I'm not saying a single word more. Not a word . . .'

Selina opened the cupboard door and stared at the line of clothes: suits, flannels hung neatly beneath jackets, shirts. She longed for the courage to drag them out; to fling them on the floor and mutilate them; or at the very least bundle them up and take them to the local charity shop.

'You know what I think?' Chris's wife, Sarah, had asked. 'I think that Patrick intends to come back. I think that this leaving all his belongings hasn't got anything to do with seeing the light or whatever. I think it's his subconscious at work. Deep down, although he's not admitting it to himself, he knows he'll be back.'

Pride had required a sharp answer here and Selina had not been at a loss for one. She'd retorted that she had no intention of taking Patrick back— and made several pithy observations about his character—but Sarah's remark had taken root. As the days passed, and anger was replaced by a dull depression, she realised just how much she missed him. Despite his gentleness, his dislike of confrontation, Patrick had a quiet strength and Selina was beginning to realise how much she'd leaned on it. She missed other things, too: the early cup of tea in bed; the washing-up unobtrusively completed whilst she watched a favourite television programme; the ready sympathy when one of her migraines took possession of her. He came of a generation of men who carried heavy objects, opened doors and put up shelves and she knew now how much she'd taken for granted.

Selina fingered the blue shirt which Paul had given his father for his fiftieth birthday present. It was a James Meade shirt, thick twill with a Prince of Wales check, and Patrick had been delighted. She remembered that he'd worn it proudly to school the next morning, along with the silk tie which had been Posy's present, smiling agreeably at her suggestion that the effect would be more impressive if he got a haircut and bought himself a new suit. She closed the cupboard door abruptly, carefully keeping her eyes away from the photograph he'd put on the shelf on his side of the bed. It was a family group; the two boys crowding beside him with Posy as a baby in his arms and Selina standing slightly to the left. It was surprising, and rather hurtful, that he had not even taken a photograph.

'You don't know that he hasn't,' Posy had pointed out. 'There are millions of photographs stuck in envelopes lying about. He might have taken some of those.'

'He's rejecting something,' Sarah had said importantly. 'He needs to work through it,' and Selina, somewhat acidly, had asked if she'd ever thought of taking up counselling as a career.

As she went downstairs she felt moody and irritable. The holiday in Edinburgh had not been an overwhelming success. Chris was far too easygoing with Sarah; her lightest whim was his command and he was quite foolishly concerned about her now that she was pregnant. And as for Sarah's mother, a bossy old woman who wanted them to move nearer to Edinburgh so as to support her in her old age—well, Selina had made no bones about her opinion regarding that idea.

'But, Mum,' Chris had said pacifically, 'it's quite reasonable. She only has Sarah, after all, and now with the baby coming—'

'You're not seriously suggesting that you intend to give up your job and move to Scotland?'

Rage, jealousy and fear had battled together in her breast whilst Chris had shuffled about, embarrassed, anxious, looking just like his father.

'The company has a branch in Newcastle,' he'd mumbled. 'It's a kind of compromise. There's some beautiful countryside round there and the houses are cheaper than London. It would be a good move now that we're starting a family.'

Selina had made some sharp observations which embraced genetics, loyalty and weakness of character but Chris had merely listened, shrugged and gone away. Paul, who worked in Bristol, was sympathetic—from a safe distance—whilst refusing to be drawn into taking sides and as for Posy . . . Well, Posy had always been a broken reed when it came to loyalty. The only good thing, for which she gave daily thanks, was that her friends had never been selected from Patrick's colleagues. As far as they were concerned, Patrick had decided to give up teaching—'Couldn't agree more, darling. So sensible with all this wretched OFSTED'—and was away on some kind of course. She simply could not bring herself to tell them the truth. So far she'd managed very nicely with a blend of long-suffering vagueness: yes she was managing quite well on her own; no he didn't get much time off but she dashed up to see him whenever she could. Oh, it was something to do with helping disabled people with learning difficulties.

'How brave!' they cried, studying their score cards. 'Darling old Patrick. So typical. Always doing something for somebody else.'

Occasionally, just occasionally, Selina looked at their well-maquillaged, complacent faces and felt a surge of antipathy. She longed to slam down her hand and storm out—but the thought of the empty house kept her in her seat. At these moments, surrounded by her friends, she felt terribly alone.

Selina reached the bottom of the stairs and picked up the letters from the mat. A telephone bill—she must really make up her mind what she intended to do about selling the house—a circular offering her yet another credit card, and a postcard. It was a scene of rolling Welsh moorland and she turned it over, her heart bumping unsteadily.

'It's great here. Terrific challenge. Hope all is well with you.'

The sight of Patrick's looping generous signature engulfed her in a kaleidoscopic lifetime of memories. She swallowed painfully. Presently she went into the kitchen and filled the kettle. Whilst she waited for it to boil she continued to look at the card. Even now, with all of the novelty and excitement of his new life, he had not quite forgotten her. She propped the card against the fruit bowl, made some tea and sat down, still staring at it.

Chapter Thirty-three

'I'm feeling rather a fool,' admitted Maudie as they bowled along the A39, between the sea and the moor. 'I wish I'd asked Rob why he'd telephoned, instead of just butting in. After all, there's no real reason why I should go to see him now that he owns Moorgate. It's not the norm, is it? Going back to visit the new owners?'

Posy stared out at the grey granite mass of Rough Tor. 'But you and Rob have become friends, haven't you? So it's a bit different. So what? I think it's nice of him to invite us.'

'That's the problem. I have this feeling that I invited myself.'

'You're feeling guilty again,' accused Posy. 'We'll have to have a G-word box. What's his girlfriend's name?'

'I didn't even ask him,' wailed Maudie. 'I feel so . . . so idiotic.'

'I think it's going to be fun,' said Posy contentedly. 'I wasn't certain at first that I'd want to see Moorgate, now it's not ours any longer, but I have this feeling that it's going to be good. If we can be friends with them it won't seem as if we've really lost it.'

Deep inside, Maudie felt quite wretched. Despite her plans for the money, to invest some for Posy, have the roof of The Hermitage mended and to buy a more reliable—though not new—car, she still had misgivings about selling Moorgate. Being in the position of fairy godmother had seemed so promising; she'd wondered whether she might buy Posy a little car and had spent many happy hours looking through the local paper at the prices of second-hand hatchbacks. It was extraordinarily pleasant to have the means to contemplate such a purchase but, at the back of her mind, she'd wondered what Selina might have to say about it. The phrase 'He who pays the piper calls the tune' had come to mind again, but, defiance aside, she was concerned that it might not be good for Posy to have such a luxury. Of course, these days nearly all young people owned cars—just as in her own youth they'd owned bicycles—but, once the seeds of doubt were sown, she was unable to approach the proposition with unmixed pleasure.

'I love it here,' Posy was saying dreamily. 'It's so wild and rugged. It has everything. There's only a few miles between the coast and the moors and yet the cottage gardens are full of flowers and that lovely sandy beach at Rock is so sheltered.'

Maudie struggled from beneath another crushing stab of guilt. 'Perhaps you should have trained for an outdoor kind of career,' she suggested. 'Something like Hugh does, for instance. You love horses and riding.'

Posy shifted a little in her seat. 'Mmm,' she murmured evasively. 'Are we nearly there?'

'Not far now. What a day! It's quite hot. I'm sorry Polonius couldn't come but if this girlfriend is anti-dog he might have had to stay in the car all morning.'

'I know. Don't worry.' Posy seemed almost drowsy. 'I gave him a good walk in the woods. He'll be fine. Don't we turn off soon?'

'Quite soon.' She peered at a fingerpost. 'Here we are.' She swung the car off the main road into the network of narrow lanes, so dim and secret after the bright, high, open road. Earlier, Posy had been all agog at the news of the unexpected trip to Moorgate; ready to discuss at length, yet again, the romantic story of Rob's sudden decision to buy the house with his new love. She'd been fascinated by it, the surprise of it outweighing her sadness that the sale was completed and Moorgate no longer a part of the family. This morning, however, as they drew closer, this rather fey, dreamy state had come upon her and Maudie was beginning to dread the actual moment of arrival. She changed down into a lower gear. 'Not long now.'

Posy sat up straighter, watching and waiting as they passed through the small hamlet with its cottages set about the grassy triangle with its stone cross. The deep lane curved sharply left, uphill, and there was the house. Set back from the lane, washed a deep, warm cream with its window frames and gutters painted a dark red, Moorgate looked well settled in, comfortable, solid. Posy sat quite still, staring, suddenly speechless. As she gazed, the front door opened and Rob came out. He came swiftly down the path and out into the lane. Maudie wound down her window but before she could speak, Rob was talking, quite urgently, so that they both leaned to look at him, surprised, intent.

'I'm sorry I have to break this news so abruptly, Lady Todhunter, but the situation is a bit tricky. I should have told you when I telephoned but . . . Look, I think you know that I was buying Moorgate with my partner. Well.' He paused, swallowed, glanced back at the house. 'The terrible fact is that she died quite suddenly two months ago. Yes, I know.' He nodded in response to the shock on their faces. 'I wanted to tell you in a more . . . acceptable way but the truth of it is that I have her brother staying with me unexpectedly. He was due next weekend but the situation changed and I don't really want to talk about this in front of him.'

'My dear fellow, of course not.' Maudie shook her head understandingly. 'Rob, I am so terribly sorry. Why don't we disappear and come back another time?'

'No, no. It's fine. Honestly.'

'But surely we shall be terribly in the way? Why on earth didn't you simply ring and put us off?'

Rob frowned. 'I tried to but I never got an answer or the line was engaged. Mike only let me know on Wednesday. I *did* try to telephone but . . . Look, it's OK. I just don't want to talk about it in front of him. They were very close. His wife left him with a small boy to look after, they're divorced, and now this. So it's all a bit dire. Never mind. I'll open the gate and you can put the car inside.'

'Hell and damnation,' muttered Maudie as she turned the car in through the gateway. 'This is going to be dreadful.'

'No it won't.' Posy seemed quite composed. 'It's going to be OK. Not about the girl, of course—that's simply awful—but it'll be all right.'

Rob was opening her door, smiling at her, and she stepped out, smiling back at him.

'I'm Posy,' she said. 'Hello. I'm just so sorry about all this.'

He nodded gratefully. 'It's been . . . rather fraught. I just don't want Mike more upset than is necessary.' He raised his voice. 'It's good to see you again, Lady Todhunter.'

'You, too, Rob, even in these unhappy circumstances. I wanted Posy to see the miracles you'd performed on dear old Moorgate.'

'It's brilliant.' Posy looked about her, at the charming little stable with its half-door and the restored barns. 'I love the colour you've painted the walls. It's so warm and mellow. Almost Mediterranean.'

'I know.' They stood together, studying the house. 'Oddly, it works. Perhaps it should have been left as bare granite, more in keeping, but this seemed right.'

'It *is* right,' she said confidently. 'I know it can be cold here but it's a place of contrasts, isn't it? The bleak open moor on one side and fuchsia and escallonia flowering on the other.'

He laughed. 'That's Cornwall for you. I'm glad you approve. Come and see what I've done inside.' He opened the front door and stood back to let them enter. 'Come and meet Mike,' he said.

Hearing their voices in the hall, Mike sat Luke in the playpen with his toys and put his hands in his pockets. Feeling unusually nervous he waited, leaning against the sink, ankles crossed, feigning indifference. Lady Todhunter came in first and he looked at her critically. She was a tall woman with a feathery cap of grey hair and large grey eyes. A blue chambray shirt hung loosely over her comfortably fitting jeans, her feet were thrust into tan leather deck shoes and a navy blue pashmina was draped casually about her shoulders. She looked stylish, interesting—and formidable. She paused for a moment in the doorway, still turned away from him, talking to Rob, and Mike was able to see the younger woman behind them. She was gazing eagerly about her, her small pointed face alive with curiosity. Shining dark hair was gathered loosely up into a knot from which long wisps had escaped and warm, honey-brown eyes darted hither and thither until they finally rested on Luke. Her face lit, then, with delight and she gave a small cry which moved the whole party forward into the kitchen.

'How do you do?' He straightened, holding out his hand. 'I'm Mike Clayton and this is Luke.'

'So what did you think of her?' asked Rob, casually, as they stood in the lane watching the car jolt away.

'I thought that they were both quite delightful,' answered Mike carefully, jogging Luke upon his hip.

Rob glanced at him sharply. 'Mmm. They are, aren't they? And Posy approved of everything? Of course Lady Todhunter has seen it all before.

I hope you didn't mind showing Posy round? I thought it might be easier than leaving you with Lady Todhunter. She and I are old friends.'

'So I gather. No, I didn't mind. In fact it was rather the other way round. Posy was very enthusiastic, and she loves the things you've done, but she can remember it from when she was a child.'

'Lady Todhunter was worried about that. She was upset about having to sell it.'

'It's always upsetting,' said Mike, as they wandered back into the house, 'to lose a family home.'

'They never actually lived in it.' Rob sounded faintly defensive. 'It was always let out. But they spent family holidays in it.'

'She could remember odd things.' Mike sounded amused. 'Atmosphere as much as anything else. I wondered if her memories were more to do with what she'd been told about it, you know what I mean? Family stories and so on. But she was very determined that it was her own memory.'

Rob smiled almost affectionately. 'I think Posy is a rather determined character. A chip off the old block, I'd say. Lady Todhunter certainly knows her own mind.'

'Actually, she's her step-grandmother.' Mike sounded thoughtful, absent. 'But she's extraordinarily fond of her.'

Rob raised his eyebrows. 'I didn't know that. That she was her step-grandmother, I mean. Shall we have a beer?'

'Why not? Luke's ready for a sleep after all the excitement so I'll tuck him up for a bit. Shan't be long.'

Rob fetched two cans from the larder and looked for some glasses. It had been a good day, in the end, but tiring. The clearly defined no-go zone had initially put a strain on conversation, nevertheless it had been fun. The two women had stopped in Camelford and bought some delicious pasties which they'd produced only when Rob had insisted that they stay for lunch. It was so warm that they'd been able to eat outside, in the sunshine on the lawn, in the shelter of the escallonia hedge. Luke had enjoyed himself immensely and, briefly, Rob had been able to put aside his own pain. Yet, oddly, he'd been keenly aware of Melissa all day. He'd felt her friendly presence presiding, as it were, over the party. He shook his head, wondering if he might be crazy, and smiled at Mike as he came into the kitchen.

'Is he OK?' He held out a glass of beer. 'Good. Was Posy surprised at the sparseness of the furnishing?'

Mike was taken aback at this direct reference to a subject which was generally avoided. 'She didn't mention it. Did Lady Todhunter remark on it?'

'Much too polite.' Rob chuckled a little. 'She was the mistress of tact, for once.' He swallowed some beer, becoming serious again. 'But I want to talk to you about it. It's no good, you know, Mike. It isn't going to work. I can't stay here without Melissa.'

Mike stood his glass carefully on the table. 'Rob—'

'No.' Rob shook his head. 'We've been through it all before. I know it's early days. I know I'll come to terms with it. But I can't stay here. I can't make a new start here at Moorgate. It should be wonderful to be here, where I'm so conscious of her, where we were so happy together, but it isn't. It's as if I'm waiting for her all the time, like I'm in a kind of vacuum. It's not that I want to forget her—I don't—but I have to get on with my life. If we'd been here together for years it would be different but we weren't. It'll be OK. I shall cope with it but I can't do it here.'

'She thought that it was what you wanted. More than anything else in the world.'

Rob sighed. 'Until I met her that was true. I was obsessed with Moorgate. You know how I camped here, pretended it was mine, put off prospective buyers. But when I met Melissa I realised that I didn't give a damn where I lived as long as we were together. Ironic, isn't it?'

'Oh, Rob, I'm so sorry . . .'

'Don't be.' Rob was upset by Mike's evident distress but he knew he must remain firm. 'Melissa freed me from that obsession but if I stay here I shall go under. I can see what she was trying to do, bless her, but it isn't going to work.'

'But what will you do?'

'I don't know. Sometimes I've thought of moving right away.' He looked directly at Mike. 'Of course, Melissa made a generous financial contribution to the house—'

'Forget all that,' said Mike abruptly. 'It's yours. She'd want that. And if it will help you get another place then that's great. Oh, Rob. This is . . . sad. But I want you to do what's right for you.' He glanced round the kitchen. 'It's just all so bloody. It's such a fantastic house. I can understand how you feel but, after all you've done to it and all you've been through here, won't you find it hard to leave it?'

'After losing Melissa this will be bad but not tragic. I know now about real loss. But the thing I wanted to say, Mike, was this. I wonder whether you might consider buying Moorgate.'

Mike stared at him. His shock was so great that Rob smiled a little.

'After all,' he said gently, 'that was the original intention, wasn't it? That's why Melissa came in the first place.'

'Well, yes.' Mike looked confused. 'Except that I always thought it was too far from London. But . . . Good God, Rob! You're not serious?'

'Absolutely serious. Why not? It's perfect for you and Luke. Peace and quiet. Glorious countryside. If you were to agree to it, I might buy a little cottage in Camelford or Boscastle and . . . well.' He shrugged. 'Will you think about it?'

Mike stared round the kitchen again, as if he were seeing it for the first time. 'I . . . simply don't know.'

'It needs thinking about,' Rob said reassuringly. 'Give yourself time to get used to the idea. Drink up and we'll have another. I think we need it.'

'So what do you think of him?' asked Maudie, casually, turning out of the lanes on to the A39.

'I think they're really great,' answered Posy carefully, taking a suddenly intent interest in the passing countryside. 'All three of them.'

Maudie glanced at her sharply. 'They are, aren't they? Luke's a sweetie. And do you approve of what Rob has done to Moorgate?'

'It's perfect,' she said dreamily. 'Exactly right. Mike thinks so too.'

'I was rather impressed by Mike,' said Maudie. 'He coped very well with us, I thought. I admire the way he's looking after Luke himself. It must be a full-time job, I should think.'

'He works when Luke's asleep, so he says, but he admits that it's getting more difficult now that Luke's growing older.'

'I must read his book,' said Maudie. 'Rob says it's very good. It must be a great comfort for Rob to have him there.'

'It's so cruel. You can see by the way he's restored it that he must really love Moorgate, can't you?'

'Odd that he hasn't furnished it yet, though,' mused Maudie. 'Rather as if he's still camping in it.'

'Well, it must have come as a terrible shock for him.' Posy's face had a brooding look. 'It's thrown him into a kind of limbo. Poor, poor Rob. He reminds me of Hugh. He's attractive, isn't he? And he's so nice.'

'Yes,' said Maudie, after a moment. 'He's very nice indeed. And resilient, I should imagine. He'll soon recover, wouldn't you say?'

'Mmm,' said Posy absently. Suddenly she shook off her contemplative mood and looked about her. 'I hope Polonius is OK. I'll take him for a long walk through the woods when we get back.'

'Good idea,' said Maudie, with the strangest feeling that she'd been warned off. 'He'll enjoy that. I don't know why but suddenly I feel very tired. Shall we have a tape on?'

'Why not?' Posy sorted through the selection and presently the cheerful strains of Haydn's trumpet concerto filled the car.

They drove for some while in silence, listening to the dazzling performance by Wynton Marsalis, and, the next time Maudie glanced at her, Posy appeared to be fast asleep.

Chapter Thirty-four

There was no time for Maudie to think too much about the visit to Moorgate. Later that week, giving thanks that the fine weather was still holding, she was driving to Exeter St David's to meet Daphne. The train was on time and Maudie, stationed near the exit, watched the doors as they swung open, aware of a sudden nervous terror that she might not recognise her old friend. As soon as she saw her, however, she realised how foolish such a fear had been: the short fair hair, the small square jaw, those pansy-blue eyes had all been delightfully translated into old age. It was typical, too, that Daphne should be attended by a male. Not that there was anything helpless about Daphne, Maudie reminded herself, watching the scene, simply that even in her mid-seventies, Daphne was still irresistible. Clearly the young man thought so; helping her with her case, laughing at her observations, refusing to be thanked. He stood by with an almost proprietorial air whilst the two old friends exchanged greetings.

'Maudie, this is Russell.' Daphne smiled upon him charmingly. 'Russell, this is my friend, Lady Todhunter. I've been telling him all about you on the journey. We've had such fun. Do get back on the train or it will go without you. Goodbye, Russell. Thank you for your company.'

'You're hopeless,' chuckled Maudie, taking the case whilst Daphne slung herself about with smaller bags. 'No man is safe from you. Not even a schoolboy.'

'My dear,' Daphne took Maudie's free arm, her voice lowered confidentially, 'he's a married man with a child of two. Can you believe it? I was about to ask him if he were on his way home for half term. Such a shock!'

They laughed together, pausing to watch the train pull away, waving to Russell who had waited by the door, and then went out to the car. The luggage loaded in, they stood and looked at one another.

Maudie shook her head. 'I can't believe that you're really here. You look terrific.'

'Now that's very kind of you, Maudie. I happen to know that I look as if I've just been dug up and given a quick paint job. I feel as if I've been travelling for light years. Is it appallingly old-fashioned to say that I would kill for a cup of tea?'

'Not a bit. Can you wait until we get home? It will probably be quicker than fighting our way into the city centre. Or we could have one here?'

Daphne closed her eyes. 'No,' she said quickly. 'No more rail company liquid masquerading as tea or coffee, thank you. I can wait.'

'It'll only be twenty minutes,' promised Maudie. 'Let's get going.'

The journey was occupied with an exchange of news but they were both relieved to pull into Maudie's drive, glad to be home.

'It's so peaceful,' remarked Daphne, stretching luxuriously, looking up at the trees. 'I'd quite forgotten how beautiful it is here. Oh, Maudie! It's been much too long.'

Maudie smiled at her across the top of the car. 'Much too long,' she agreed. 'Aha! The kraken wakes. Here's Polonius to meet you.'

Polonius, who had been taking a long and refreshing nap in the wood-shed, came yawning into the sunshine and was brought up short by the sight of a stranger on the other side of the fence. Daphne stared at him for a moment and then turned to Maudie.

'I feel very slightly overawed,' she admitted. 'He's rather impressive, isn't he? He reminds me of Georgio Bartolucci. Remember him, Maudie? He was the Italian Ambassador when we were all in Rome. Polonius has that same cynical and disillusioned eye combined with the gravitas of an elder statesman. Does he mind strangers on his patch?'

'He's learning,' answered Maudie grimly. 'The hard way. He's not barking, which is a start.'

'Dear old boy,' said Daphne caressingly, approaching the fence. 'What *is* she saying about you?'

Polonius immediately flattened his ears, assuming a rather cowed appearance. He wagged his tail, his wrinkled face bearing a sad, yet noble, expression.

'Does he have a melancholic disposition?' asked Daphne, stretching out a tentative hand and stroking his head. 'Or is that impression inevitable when your skin's too big for your face?'

'My skin's been too big for my face for some years now,' said Maudie, hauling out the suitcase, 'but nobody has accused me of being melancholy. Not yet. Don't be taken in by him, that's all. Come on in and we'll have that cup of tea.'

Daphne began to gather up her belongings. 'There's so much to catch up on. I'm longing to hear about Selina and Patrick,' she said, following Maudie inside and pausing for a proper greeting with Polonius. 'Where am I? In here? Oh, it's so pretty, Maudie. I shall be very comfortable here.'

'Are you longing for a bath?' asked Maudie, putting down the suitcase, lingering in the doorway. 'Or shall I make the tea?'

'Tea first,' said Daphne at once. 'A bath would be wonderful but tea must come first.'

'Well, I'll leave you to get yourself sorted out while I get the kettle on. Shout if you need anything.'

The door closed behind her and Daphne sat down on the bed and stared at the vase of hawthorn blossom. Alone for the first time for several hours, her body relaxed and her expression grew thoughtful. This visit was not simply a holiday; there was another far more serious purpose behind it. How to approach it without damaging the relationship she had with Maudie? How to solve one problem without creating others? Instinctively she recoiled from the thought of it. Surely there was time for some fun, first; a few days, at the very least, to see exactly how things stood with Maudie? There was so much to remember, to share. Perhaps a right moment would come: a time for confidences and explanations which could be accepted and understood.

'Tea!'

Maudie's cry echoed along the passage and round the bedroom. With a conscious effort at relaxation Daphne took a deep breath. She stood up and went out, closing the door behind her. Polonius was waiting for her, tail wagging, and she bent to stroke him.

'You are a very handsome fellow,' she told him. 'How my Emily would love you.'

Polonius sighed deeply. He was convinced that a great many people would love him if only they were given the chance. It wasn't his fault that he was extraordinarily large and had a tendency to enthusiasm on first acquaintance. He felt that this stranger within the gates understood and appreciated his position and he padded after her, wondering if her sympathy might be matched by a generosity with cake.

The table was set by the open French doors and Daphne exclaimed with pleasure. Whilst Maudie poured the tea, Daphne wandered out on to the veranda. Afternoon sun slanted across the lawn so that the still, dark water glinted, and secret, shadowy corners were briefly lit. Pretty 'Nelly Moser' flowered riotously over the small toolshed, her flowers big as tea plates, and the heady scent of lilac drifted in the warm air. Beyond the hedge, in the wood, the yaffle was laughing. Daphne stretched luxuriously.

'This is perfect,' she sighed. 'It's so quiet. Like the secret garden in the book. I could never really like Mary Lennox, could you? Nor the spoiled Colin. Such a tiresome child. But the garden itself was something else. No wonder you left London for this, Maudie. I really can't blame you.'

'Most of the gang think I've gone quite potty but I was never a London person. Especially not without Hector.'

'No,' said Daphne, after a moment. 'No, I quite see that.'

'Hector was so good at all those things: exhibitions, concerts, first nights, the best restaurants. He had a kind of instinct which led him to the best seats, the best bars. Oh, I don't know. It was just Hector's way. *You* know what I mean.'

'Yes, love. Very well indeed. He had a knack of making people feel pleased to oblige him.' Daphne came back into the living room and sat down at the table. 'But it wasn't a heartless thing. He didn't use people, did he? Hector was naturally generous. He liked people to be happy.'

'Yes, that's true.' Maudie smiled reminiscently. 'He certainly had a huge capacity for fun.'

'Exactly,' said Daphne. 'Just that. Dear old boy!'

'Oh, it's good to have you here,' said Maudie impulsively. 'I've got things out of proportion lately and I've sometimes wondered if I'm going quite mad. You'll get me back on the rails again. I've been so bitter, Daphne.'

'Yes,' said Daphne quietly. 'Yes, I know you have, love. It hasn't been easy for you since Hector died.'

'I'm a jealous cantankerous old woman,' said Maudie remorsefully. 'We were so happy together, Hector and I. We enjoyed some truly blissful times and we were very good friends. Yet I could never quite get the wretched Hilda out of my system. I had long spells of peace but at the end all the bitterness came back. When Selina used to come to see him and he used to apologise to her over and over again for marrying me I thought I'd kill him. And her. Of course, it wasn't her fault. He thought she was Hilda—Selina looks just like Hilda from what I can gather from the photographs of her—and he'd hold her hand and drone on and on. "I'm so sorry. I'm so sorry." Selina loved it, of course. And then there was the business of his stocks and shares. Oh, hell and damnation, Daphne. I didn't mean to start on all this so soon. Let's forget it. Have some scones and some jam and clotted cream. A proper Devon tea.'

'It sounds delicious. Yes, please.' Daphne hesitated but Maudie had clearly decided to change the subject.

'And now there's been the great drama with Patrick,' she continued, ladling cream on to her scone. 'I cannot imagine what Selina is going to do without him.'

'It's quite extraordinary.' Daphne decided to accept the change of direction, not without a certain relief. 'I know you've kept me informed but it's not the same by telephone. Start from the beginning and tell me again properly.'

In Winchester, Posy lay on her bed, staring at the ceiling, her work forgotten.

'I don't suppose you get back to London very often,' he'd said casually and she'd answered that, just now, she went home quite often. She'd said that her mother wasn't too good at present, that there were a few problems and that she needed company. She'd been kneeling on the broad window-seat on the landing, looking out over the moor, whilst he'd leaned beside her.

'I'm going up next weekend,' he'd said. 'I have to see my agent. Maybe we could meet up?'

She'd felt a tiny shock of surprise at the invitation—even anxiety—but rather flattered, too.

'That would be good,' she'd replied, very calm, very cool.

'Well, then.' He'd shifted his weight. 'Perhaps I'd better have your telephone number.'

'Oh yes.' She'd turned quite naturally, frowning a little. 'I think I can remember it. Or do you mean the London number?'

'I mean both.' He was smiling. 'Hold on a moment.'

He'd gone into the room he was using as a bedroom and returned after a minute with a pad and a pencil. She'd been able to give him both numbers and had watched whilst he tore out the page and tucked it into his wallet.

'Great,' he'd said. 'Thanks. We'll talk, then. I don't like to leave Luke overnight if I can help it but perhaps we could have lunch?'—and she'd nodded, suddenly shy.

It was odd how, from the beginning, she'd had a special feeling about the day, a certainty that something really good might happen, but this was rather beyond her experience. After all, this was Mike Clayton, the playwright and novelist who had caused a sensation with *Changing Places*. She'd been given tickets for her eighteenth birthday, when she was deciding that her future lay within the theatre. His wife, a beautiful, dazzling, sophisticated woman, had been playing the leading role and Posy had been utterly enraptured by the play. It seemed unbelievable that this was the same man, who'd joked with Maudie and was so sweet with his baby son.

He'd telephoned on Tuesday afternoon at about three o'clock—a time which she'd suggested. She couldn't have borne hanging about downstairs, dashing out every time the phone rang, making a spectacle of herself. She had no lectures on Tuesday afternoon and knew that she'd have the house to herself. He'd telephoned just after the hour and she'd willed herself to let it ring twice, thrice, before suddenly snatching up the receiver in a panic lest he should ring off.

He'd been jokey, happy, amusing, and she'd fallen in with his mood, talking, listening, utterly happy until he'd had to go because Luke had woken from his after-lunch nap.

'See you on Saturday, then,' he'd said.

She closed her eyes, imagining him, frowning slightly. He reminded her of someone; someone she'd met recently. Ever since last Saturday she'd been racking her brains, cudgelling her memory, but it eluded her. She shook her head, suddenly seized by a mixture of anxiety and anticipation, and, rolling off her bed, turned her mind deliberately to her work.

Chapter Thirty-five

Rob washed up his supper things, rinsing them, setting them on the draining board. He performed the task mechanically, his thoughts elsewhere, the slow almost rhythmical movements bringing a small measure of peace to his unquiet mind. The serene beauty of the evening beyond the window for once had no power to soothe. The deep, overarching bowl of blue trailing the last flaming banners of a glorious sunset, the golden flowering furze, the evening shadows stealing along deep-sided coombs, all these things merely increased his melancholy. Here, looking across the huddled grey roofs, over neatly parcelled fields towards the sea, he was aware of his isolation. Before Melissa he'd sought out this seclusion; happy to be alone after a busy day, glad to go apart. This had been part of Moorgate's charm: set on its own, looking over the surrounding countryside, splendidly detached. Climbing up from the field below, he'd pause to gaze up at the house, rooted, secure. Once inside, closing the shutters, lighting the fires, he'd felt a strangely peaceful contentment. Perhaps this contentment was the first temptation to which the recluse succumbed. Others would follow: a growing unwillingness to communicate, to make an effort; the inability to become involved.

He'd been aware of these tendencies growing in him: a relief when the working day was over, a reluctance to join his friends down at the pub, an indifference to the affairs of the world beyond his gate. Solitude had begun to be an ideal to be sought, worked for, treasured—and then Melissa had arrived, demolishing the illusion with her vital presence. Strange that she, who was so near death, had been so full of life. Her absolute need for warmth, her passion for chocolate, her amazed delight at the small miracles—the rooks building their nests and the lambs crying at their mothers' heels—had shocked him back to life. Love had unfolded, flowering, growing, bursting out of him, smashing the protective shell which had been gently but ineluctably enclosing his heart.

Rob removed the plug, letting the water rush away, and reached for the tea cloth. He knew that this love, which now included Mike and Luke in its embrace, must not be forced back. It should not be labelled 'Remembrance' and pressed down into a small space, cold and narrow as a grave. He could not understand why he should have discovered this loosening of love, this new awareness, a greater capacity for compassion, only to be left without the one upon whom he longed to shower it, yet some instinct warned him that he must let Moorgate go. He knew he must resist the gentle path of melancholy, the tempting comfort of retrospection, the dulling, numbing company of self-pity. Even the sharper, more painful emotion of bitterness was more welcome than the indulgence of self-pity.

As he put away the plates he considered the possibility of Mike buying Moorgate. He had no fears for Mike. The solitude would be a balm to Mike after the company of the characters who filled his imagination and with whom he spent so many hours. Mike needed privacy and peace but, once refreshed, he would seek out company with a friendly ease which would guarantee him companions. And then there was Luke. Luke, as he grew, would keep Mike in touch with his own small world. Rob pushed the kettle on to the hotplate, wondering if he'd imagined the attraction which had flared between Mike and Posy last Saturday. His own heightened emotions had made him unusually aware and he'd felt that the whole day was building towards some climax which was yet to be fulfilled.

Now, as he made some coffee, he was visited by an odd sense of wellbeing although his heart was heavy. He was waiting for something; some word or sign. Perhaps it would be Mike's agreement to buy Moorgate, perhaps something else which would release the weight of the pent-up pain in his breast into simple, ordinary grief.

'Hi.' Posy stood awkwardly in the sitting-room doorway looking across at Selina. 'I was just wondering . . .'

Selina did not remove her gaze from the flickering screen of the television. 'Wondering what?' she asked indifferently.

Posy tried to quell a faint irritation. Since her arrival earlier she'd felt a distinct lack of enthusiasm for company on her mother's part but she was determined to try to create a cheerful atmosphere.

'I was wondering about supper,' she said brightly, too brightly—rather as though Selina were half-witted or senile, 'and thought we might go round to the pub.'

At last Selina turned to look at her. 'To the *pub*?'

She sounded so incredulous that Posy was seized by a nervous desire to burst out laughing.

'Why not?' she asked. 'It would save us having to cook and stuff. I'll pay. Come on, Mum,' she said, almost pleadingly. 'It'll be fun. It'll stop you moping.'

Even as she said the words she knew she'd made a terrible mistake.

Selina stiffened. 'I happen to be watching television,' she said icily. 'What makes you think that I should be moping?'

Posy sighed and rolled her eyes impatiently. 'OK, so you're not moping. It's just difficult to imagine anyone watching reruns of *Steptoe and Son* if they've got anything better to do. But perhaps you're actually enjoying it. So if you don't want to go to the pub what are we going to eat? There doesn't seem to be much in the fridge.'

'There's plenty to eat,' snapped Selina. 'I'm not running a hotel, you know. You think that just because you suddenly deign to grace the house with your presence I should be killing the fatted calf.'

'No,' said Posy wearily. 'No, actually, I don't think that. I just thought we might try to have a fun evening together. Never mind. I'll make us an omelette.'

'Not for me, thanks,' said Selina. 'I'm not hungry.'

Posy stood for a moment, holding the door handle, possessed by an urge to scream loudly.

'Mum,' she said. 'Mum, why does it have to be like this? I thought we might spend some time together. I've got tomorrow off and we could go shopping or something, and have lunch.'

Selina sat quite still whilst her pride, which had always made it so difficult for her to give in, to accept favours, to suffer indignity or criticism, battled with a desire to break down and admit her loneliness. But how could she admit such a thing to her daughter; to Posy who had shamed her by taking Maudie's side and, from babyhood, had wilfully flouted her mother's authority? This was nothing more than pity that Posy was offering; humiliating, degrading pity. She'd probably tell Maudie about it, later. And here was another grievance. Maudie had Daphne staying with her. It was disgraceful that Daphne, Selina's mother's oldest and best friend, should have passed through London without coming to see her. She had gone directly to Devon without so much as a telephone call. Oh, she'd called earlier that evening from Maudie's, said that she'd be in London in a fortnight and would love to see her, but by then Maudie would have told her all about Patrick's defection. How they would enjoy it! All this passed through Selina's mind as Posy waited for an answer.

'Strange as it may seem,' she said bitterly, 'I have other plans for tomorrow. I do *have* a life, you know, although you might find it difficult to imagine. I can't just drop everything because you suddenly decide to come home for a long weekend. Why should I?'

'Why indeed?' asked Posy. 'I can't think of a good reason. Great. I'll do my own thing, then. See you around.'

The door closed and Selina sat on, her hands clenched in her lap, staring at the flickering screen. Harold Steptoe and his father were playing badminton and the studio audience were shrieking with laughter. Now Harold was missing the shuttlecock, falling over, getting cross, and the laughter was increasing, growing louder whilst, all the while, Selina, locked in the prison of her insecurity and pride, was regretting her lost opportunity, swallowing down her misery, the tears trickling down her cheeks.

All the way from Oxford, travelling on the Circle Line to Embankment, walking up The Strand and along William IVth Street to The Chandos, Mike was thinking about Posy. Ever since last Saturday, she'd occupied his thoughts, coming between him and his work, distracting him and puzzling him. Camilla had been beautiful, amusing, desirable and a boost to his ego but Posy was the stuff of every day: interesting, funny, kind, bossy, inquisitive, enthusiastic. There was a *durability* about her that was enormously attractive. For one so young she'd handled the situation at Moorgate with great tact. It hadn't been easy for either of the women, given that there were so many sensitive areas, but he'd been impressed by

Posy's ability to deal with it without either descending into sentimentality or creating an atmosphere of false jollity. He was too experienced to be unaware of her interest, yet even the chemistry which had tingled between them had not rendered her tongue-tied or coy.

As he went up the steps and into the upstairs bar of The Chandos he was prey to a sudden attack of nerves. Perhaps, today, she might be different; perhaps his judgement had been clouded by the extraordinary circumstances. He was early, so he bought himself a pint and went to sit in one of the window seats, thinking about Melissa. No doubt there were many sensible explanations for that strange, magical influence which had informed the whole day at Moorgate. He'd wondered if his creative instinct, the novelist's sense of the dramatic, had provided that happy, peace-pervading quality. Melissa had been so much in his mind that it had been a terrific shock when Rob had announced that he didn't want to stay at Moorgate. His own reaction had been one of anxiety lest Melissa should be hurt. It had been her great consolation, that Rob should have Moorgate; it had been her way of making restitution for misleading him. Yet, on reflection, it was easy to understand how he must be feeling. To be at Moorgate alone, to attempt to create, on his own, the home they might both have shared, was a heartbreaking concept. Melissa had not taken into consideration the essential fact that, without her, Moorgate would be a reminder of all that Rob had lost. That brief week in winter was not enough on which to build sustaining memories, yet her impact had been too great for him to be able to start a new life at Moorgate.

So far, Mike was in agreement—yet to buy Moorgate himself was a big step to take. It was a large house, fairly isolated, and a long way from London and Oxford and his friends. On the other hand, it was exactly what he'd been considering: a place in the country where Luke might grow up in a rural community. As he'd walked over the moor with Rob his own creative juices had begun to flow freely, excitingly, and he'd felt rejuvenated. After all, he need not fear isolation. His friends would be delighted to spend weekends in Cornwall and he'd have Rob nearby to ease him into the community.

Once he'd adjusted to Rob's announcement, one level of his consciousness was telling him that this was quite right, that all the pieces were falling into place. Perhaps this was what had been intended all along. Given Rob's decision, surely Melissa would have been delighted to think that Mike and Luke were at Moorgate, with Rob near at hand. As for

Posy . . . He was convinced that Melissa would have approved of Posy. In some ways they were alike: enthusiasm, inquisitiveness, an easy companion, these were qualities they both shared. Yes, Melissa would have liked Posy . . .

He turned, sighing, and saw her standing in the doorway, looking faintly anxious. As he stood up he saw her expression warm into eagerness and instinctively he held out his hand to her. She came quickly towards him and took it in her own, beaming at him, noticing his half-empty glass.

'You're early.'

'Oh, that was quite deliberate.' He grinned down at her, releasing her hand, pulling out a chair for her. 'I needed to get a quick pint in to steady my nerves.'

'Excellent,' she said, pleased. 'I like to see myself as a scary character. How's Luke?'

'Fine. I have a very motherly lady next door who comes round for the day if I really need her. She's great.'

'And does she mother you too?'

'If I let her. I'm not really the mothered kind. Now what will you have to drink?'

She watched him go to the bar, his fair hair gleaming under the bar lights, his easy stance, the way he laughed at something the barman said. Once more a teasing memory flickered at the back of her mind; his resemblance to someone who had laughed just like that, with that same relaxed posture and in-built confidence. He came across to her with her glass and the menu and went back for his own drink.

'This is fun,' he said. 'Now, what shall we have to eat?'

Chapter Thirty-six

'So now,' said Maudie, on the Tuesday evening after Daphne's arrival. 'What about these photographs? We've been meaning to look at them ever since you arrived.'

'The time has flown so fast,' said Daphne, 'and it's been such fun,' but she looked suddenly tired.

'It seemed such a pity to waste the weather,' said Maudie cheerfully. 'I think we're in for a wet spell now, though, and it's quite chilly again. I think I was right to light the stove up only it seems such a luxury when it's nearly June.'

'Polonius is enjoying it,' said Daphne, looking with affection at the recumbent figure. 'He must be exhausted after that long walk this morning. I know I am.'

'Exactly,' agreed Maudie, 'which is why a nice, quiet evening looking at photographs is just what we need.'

There was a silence. After a moment, when Daphne had made no move, Maudie glanced at her in surprise. Daphne's eyes were closed and her face wore a concentrated look, as though she might be praying. Maudie felt a spasm of fear. She leaned forward and touched her friend's knee.

'Are you all right?'

Daphne opened her eyes and smiled but her face was strained. 'Yes,' she said, but with a kind of sadness. 'Quite all right. I'll get them, then.'

'Shall I go?' Maudie was still concerned. 'I can fetch them if you tell me where they are? Or would you rather leave it?'

'No,' she answered, quite firmly. 'No, I think you're right. The time has come. It's been put off quite long enough.'

She got up and went out leaving Maudie staring into the fire, puzzled. Daphne's choice of words held an almost ominous tone and Maudie was still frowning when Daphne came back holding several folders. She sat down again, holding them on her lap, looking preoccupied. Maudie watched her curiously. Presently Daphne shook her head and sighed.

'Very well,' she said, as though she had come to a decision. 'Where shall we start?'

'With young Tim,' said Maudie unhesitatingly. 'I've been saying for ages that I never see a decent photograph of him. He's always blurred or has his back to the camera. I hope you've brought some good ones, Daffers.'

Quite spontaneously, Daphne began to laugh. She laughed so much that Maudie began to feel uneasy. It reminded her of another occasion when Daphne had laughed like that, years and years ago . . . after something Maudie had said about trusting her although she'd been Hilda's oldest friend . . .

'Sorry,' Daphne was saying. 'It's simply so typical of you, Maudie. You always did go straight for the weak spot. It's what makes you so formidable. Very well.' She shuffled through the photographs, found one, held it for a brief moment and then offered it to Maudie. 'That's young Tim.'

Reaching for it eagerly, Maudie did not see the almost anguished expression on Daphne's face. She scanned the photograph, looking intently at the young face which stared out at her.

'What a nice-looking boy,' she said approvingly. 'How dark he is! Not a bit like the other two, is he?' She frowned a little. 'He reminds me of someone. Not Emily, certainly . . . Oh, I've got it. How extraordinary.' She peered more closely, turning it to the light. 'It's Posy. He looks just like Posy when she was this age. She was so like Hector. In fact this reminds me of a photograph taken of him at just about this age. Isn't that amazing?'

She glanced briefly at Daphne, still absorbed by her discovery, not taking in the consequences, until her friend's silence, her utter lack of reaction, caught her attention. Still holding the photograph, Maudie looked again at Daphne. Her words seemed to hang deafeningly in the silence. Daphne raised her head at last and their eyes met in a long look: Maudie's frightened, questioning; Daphne's compassionate, desperate. Silence stretched between them. Polonius yawned and shifted, settling himself more comfortably, and the clock wheezed out eight tinny chimes.

'Hector?' whispered Maudie. The fears and doubts of the last year crystallised into terrible certainties. Suddenly she was an old, old woman. 'Hector and *Emily*?'

'No!' cried Daphne strongly. 'Good God, Maudie. No, of *course* not Emily. Forgive me, Maudie. It was me.'

'You had an affair with Hector,' said Maudie slowly, painfully. 'And Emily is his child.'

'It had finished long before he met you,' said Daphne quickly. 'I swear to you, Maudie. There was nothing between us then. It happened after Selina had scarlet fever. She took a long time getting over it and Hilda and both girls went home to Hilda's mother for a while. Hector was alone and . . . Well, it just seemed to happen.'

Maudie watched her bleakly. 'You were in love with him.'

'Yes,' said Daphne, after a moment. 'Yes, I was in love with him. Philip was a dear but he was so terribly dull. And then, you see, we couldn't have children. Philip never wanted to discuss it. He was afraid it might be his fault, although I never accused him. After all, it might just as easily have been mine. I simply didn't know although, by then, I'd quite given up hope of a baby. We both had. He was so delighted when I became pregnant. Hector was furious when I told him. I pretended that it might be Philip's child but I knew it wasn't and Hector knew it too. But I was so happy, you see, and Philip thought it was some kind of miracle, so we agreed to take the chance. I was terrified it might be a boy and look like Hector but I couldn't have done anything else. A baby, after all those years of longing! But Hector was never in love with me, Maudie. He never pretended to be. We'd known each other for years, I was Hilda's best friend, and there was an easy, careless intimacy between us. But just that once it toppled over into something more. It was crazy, a sudden madness. We both needed it, if you can understand what I mean. Hilda and Philip were good, upstanding people but oh, the joy of being with someone who liked to laugh and have fun!'

'And that was why you were so passionate about Emily.' It was a statement. The pieces were fitting slowly into place.

'I was so relieved that she was a girl, you see. I can't tell you the strain it was, with Hilda being so thrilled about it and giving me advice. And Hec-

tor and I pretending that everything was just the same between us. I felt so
guilty. It was agony and Hector was so worried. He regretted it always but
at the time he was simply terrified that I would have a boy that looked like
him. His dark colouring was so distinctive and Philip and I were both fair.
But darling Emily never let me down. Not until Tim. Even so, I wasn't
sure until he was three or four years old but then I could see quite clearly
that he was beginning to look just like his grandfather.'

'Which is why I never had photographs of Tim, only of the girls.'

'I knew you'd spot the likeness, you see.' Daphne shook her head. 'I
couldn't risk it. I picked the ones which weren't too clear but I suspected
that one day I'd have to tell you.'

'Why now?' Maudie tried to control her hurt, to bring all her powers of
detachment to bear. Later, she would allow herself the luxury of feelings.

'Oh, love.' Daphne looked at her sadly. 'I couldn't stand it any longer.
You see, he never loved me. I really faced that when I met you. For the
first time in his life Hector was really in love and it simply shone out of
him, so much so that I knew that the small piece of him that I'd had, our
moment together, couldn't possibly hurt you. We became friends, you
and I, and that was precious to me. Each time Emily became pregnant the
old terror reappeared but I might never have had to tell you if it hadn't
been for the way you've suffered since he died.'

'I don't understand.'

'You can't come to terms with Hector's death because of two things.
The first is the way that he apologised to Selina, thinking she was Hilda,
for marrying you. But that wasn't what he was apologising for, Maudie.
He was apologising for betraying her with me. I told you, Hector never
forgave himself for that lapse. He might have been fun-loving, happy-go-
lucky, but he wasn't by nature an adulterer. I got him at a low moment
and he succumbed to it. He was horrified that I was pregnant, that I carried his child and that he couldn't acknowledge her. His guilt was tremendous and, manlike, he couldn't quite forgive me either. I think he lived in
terror that I might spill the beans to you. He told me that he would never
forgive me if I hurt you, Maudie. But I didn't want to hurt you, which is
why I've kept silent. But I can't go on any longer. I can't see you tearing
yourself apart with suspicion. The other thing is the money. Hector's
stocks and shares. When Tim was killed in that car accident Emily was left
practically penniless. There were all sorts of complications. It was a terrible
time. Hector came to me to see if there was any way he could help.'

'The money went to Emily and the children?' Maudie sounded as if a mystery had been finally solved, as if the last piece of the puzzle had slipped into place.

Daphne sighed heavily. 'He felt that it was the least he could do although I hoped it wouldn't be necessary. "She's my daughter," he said, "and they are my grandchildren. You *must* allow me to do this." He was convinced that you wouldn't suffer financially and, you see, he'd always felt it so keenly that he could never acknowledge them. I always tried to show him the joy we'd had, Philip and I, because of Emily, but he was eaten up by guilt on both counts. Because of Hilda and because of Emily. I can't tell you, Maudie, how glad I was that he married you. You made him laugh. With you he grew young again.'

'I was often cruel to him.' There were tears in Maudie's eyes: tears of pain and tears of relief. 'I was often such a cow.'

'And Hector was often domineering and tiresome.' Daphne looked exhausted. 'But he loved you. There was never a moment's question of that. Try to remember how it was.'

'Does Emily know?'

Daphne rested her head against a cushion and closed her eyes. 'Yes, she knows. I didn't tell her until after Philip died but I was afraid that she might begin to guess. Tim is so like Posy and Emily started to talk of coming over and seeing you all. She and Posy stay in touch and I began to be afraid that it was only a matter of time. I wanted her to hear it from me.'

'How did she take it?'

Daphne smiled. 'She was terribly sweet about it. She was always very fond of Hector, you know. She told me to tell you that she's always looked on you as her second mother and that now you can be step-grandmum to the children. She was so worried that you might be hurt.'

'Darling Emily,' said Maudie unsteadily. 'She belonged to all of us.'

'I'm so sorry about the money, Maudie.'

'It doesn't matter about the money,' cried Maudie impatiently. 'Not as *money*, if you see what I mean. It was just not knowing, thinking that Hector had kept things hidden from me.'

'I know,' said Daphne remorsefully. 'But you wouldn't have had to sell Moorgate if you'd had it. I've felt so guilty.'

'The G-word,' said Maudie. 'We all carry so much guilt. Poor Hector. I wish he'd told me at the beginning.'

'Do you?' Daphne raised her eyebrows. 'Are you sure?'

'No.' Maudie smiled reluctantly. 'No, I'm glad I didn't know. I might not have been able to feel so safe with you. It was Hilda's power over Hector that I feared. What a fool I was, now I come to think of it, to trust you as I did.'

'No, you weren't.' Daphne shook her head. 'Your instincts were quite sound. You had nothing to fear from me.'

'Poor Daphne.' Maudie looked at her affectionately. 'How lonely you must have been. I can't believe that you didn't hate me.'

'I thought I was going to. Hector wrote to tell me, to warn me, and that was the final blow to any hope I had. After Hilda died, you see, I thought that I might have a little bit of him to myself. It was madness, of course. With Philip still alive, Hector would never have crossed the line again, but there's always a tiny foolish dream we nurture, isn't there? Once I had his letter I knew my dream was just so much dust.'

'Oh, Daphne, I am sorry. And you were so generous, so kind. I've depended on you so much.'

Daphne stretched out a hand, her eyes filled with memories. 'It was odd. I dreaded meeting you and yet, when I saw you, I felt a great liking for you. It was so strange. I knew that you were utterly right for him and that you would make him happy. It was very clever of Hector to find you. And, you know, despite my unhappiness, gradually things began to work even better. We were all such friends and, through you, I seemed to regain Hector's friendship and trust. That was very precious to me.'

'But what a weight you've carried.' Maudie held her hand tightly. 'And you came all this way knowing that you were going to have to tell me.'

'You've been wonderful. I thought it would be so much worse.'

Maudie knitted her brows. 'I suppose it's rather peculiar but I feel in some way that we've shared him. I couldn't have borne it if it had happened after I'd met him but, as it is, somehow I feel that it simply doesn't matter. The other things are far more important. I can believe now that he didn't regret marrying me and that he didn't lie to me. That's what matters to me. You and Emily were to do with Hilda, not me. I can go on loving you just as I always have.'

Daphne took a deep breath. 'It was how I prayed you might feel but I couldn't rely on it. Bless you, Maudie. Now, do you really want to look at photographs or shall we have a good stiff drink?'

'I can't see why we shouldn't do both.' Maudie got to her feet rather shakily. 'We've both sustained a shock and we need something to revive us. But you've kept this young man from me for quite long enough and I want to see more of him.'

Later, as they sat comfortably, a bottle on the table between them, Maudie asked suddenly, 'And what about Selina? Does she know she has a half-sister, two nieces and a nephew?'

Daphne laid down the photograph she'd been studying and picked up her glass.

'No,' she said, 'she doesn't. And I've decided that she's happier in ignorance.'

' "Where ignorance is bliss, 'tis folly to be wise"?'

'Something like that. Emily is one of the few people that Selina hasn't fallen out with. Oh, I know that the three thousand miles between them might have something to do with it, but nevertheless I've always thought that it would be simply cruel to tell her the truth. She found it difficult enough to cope with Hector remarrying. To know that he was unfaithful to her mother with me would be the last straw.'

'Yes, I think I agree with that.' Maudie smiled at the photograph she was holding. 'You know, this child is incredibly like Posy. It's rather nice to think that there's another little bit of Hector growing up, don't you think?'

'Oh, I do.' Daphne sighed with relief. 'Every time I see him I think so. He has a few little tricks that make my heart turn over. I long for you to see him, Maudie.'

'So do I. But supposing, later on, Selina or Posy guess? I imagine they might meet Tim, one day?'

'Emily and I have talked it over endlessly. We hope that Posy might not be particularly affected if she ever finds out. After all, it's a couple of generations back and she and Selina aren't particularly close. We'll have to hope she understands and forgives us. As for Selina . . .' She shrugged, shaking her head. 'Am I right, I wonder? It's so difficult to decide what is right for other people. I'd hate to alienate her. It sounds as if she has enough problems at the moment.'

'You're going to see her next week?'

Daphne nodded. 'I'm staying a couple of nights with her before I go north to see Philip's brother. To tell you the truth, I'm rather dreading it now.'

Maudie stared reflectively into her glass. 'She's alienated her own family. The boys flee at the sight of her and Chris's wife can't stand her. Selina can't forgive Posy for loving me or me for loving Hector, and it must be years since she saw Patricia and her family. And now, on top of all that, Patrick's left her. I wish I could help her but we invariably rub each other up the wrong way. I'm ashamed of myself, to tell the truth. I've failed miserably with Selina.'

Daphne shifted uneasily. 'What are you saying?'

'I'm not too sure. It just occurred to me, while we were speaking, that Emily might be able to help her. I can't imagine how, mind. Perhaps you should take the photograph with you, after all.'

'She'd turn me out of the house.'

'Join the club. We've all been turned out, why not you? Seriously, I'm probably talking nonsense. Too much whisky and the enormous relief of knowing about Hector. I'm abrogating my responsibilities. I can't help Selina and I'd be grateful if someone else would. I'd feel less guilty about her. Anyway, let's not worry about it any more. Come on, Daffers. Fill up the glasses and pass some more photographs. I'm just beginning to enjoy myself.'

Later, alone again in bed, Daphne lay propped against her pillows, her eyes closed. She was exhausted by her ordeal. Deeply thankful though she was that Maudie's relief, her release from tormenting doubt, had outweighed any feelings of anger at Hector's deception, yet her own confession had been much more gruelling than she'd allowed it to appear. It had been necessary to confirm, to insist on the fact that Hector had never loved her, but it had hurt her to do it. It had reminded her of the pain of those years, seeing him with Hilda and his daughters, watching him lavish affection on those who were legally entitled to his love and protection. How painful it had been, excluded from his care, their brief passion unacknowledged, regretted even, on his part.

She was glad that Maudie had been unaware of the real cost of her confession; glad that she'd taken it so well. Maudie's love for her and for Emily had carried them over the worst of it—and she'd been quite right. With Maudie she'd been able to have a share in Hector's love in a way that had been impossible with Hilda. And she'd had Emily, his child, to ease the pain—Emily and the girls and now Tim . . .

Daphne turned out her light and settled her pillows, preparing herself for sleep, but, as she lay staring into the dark, her thoughts were of Selina.

Chapter Thirty-seven

Rob stood the bags of shopping on the kitchen table, and opened the kitchen windows. After a short cold spell of rain, a brief regression into winter, summer had arrived, overtaking the tender, cool green spring and rushing nature into a more generous and luxuriant growth. Below the house red and white blossom lay thick along the thorn, and the bracken, tight-curled as a question mark, was springing from the peaty earth. He opened a can of beer and drank deeply, thinking about Mike.

He'd telephoned last evening, his voice charged with some kind of suppressed excitement mixed with another, different, emotion.

'I've been thinking,' he'd said. 'I've thought it through and I think you might be right about me buying Moorgate.'

Rob had felt almost weak with joy and relief. 'Oh, that's great, Mike,' he'd said. 'I can't tell you how pleased I am.'

'It feels right, somehow.' He'd hesitated briefly, then—'I'm going for it,' he'd said firmly. 'Get it valued, Rob, will you?'

'Oh, surely—' he'd begun to protest—but Mike had overridden him.

'It's got to be done properly, I insist on that, although at least we can cut out agents, but get started on it. We'll talk about it properly when I come down.'

'And when will that be?'

A tiny pause. 'To be honest, I'm hoping you can put me up this week.'

'This week? But that's great. When?'

'I'd like to come down midweek if you can cope. I'm busy next weekend. The thing is, Rob, I'd like us to inter Melissa's ashes. I think the time has come, don't you? She wanted them to be with you at Moorgate, and I think it's a wonderful idea but I know you were cautious about it—'

'Not because I didn't want them here,' Rob had interrupted quickly. 'It was only that I didn't know whether I'd stay and I didn't want her to be left with . . . strangers.'

'I know. I'm sorry, Rob.' Mike had known immediately that Rob was near to tears. 'It's just that I think the time has come, don't you? While you're still there but knowing we shall be there soon.'

'You're absolutely right.' He'd been unable to swallow down his grief which seemed to stick, like a lump in his throat. 'It's a nice idea, Mike. So when will you come?'

'I thought Wednesday. Just me, by the way. Best to leave Luke here, this time. I'll leave early and be down mid-morning. Is it a problem for you? You don't have to take time off.'

'Oh, an afternoon won't do any harm. I'll try and get back for lunch. Will you go back the same day?'

'No. I'll stay over and leave on Thursday morning. If you want me to, that is. Let's play it by ear.'

Rob had smiled, then, knowing that Mike was trying to gauge how Rob might feel: whether he'd need company or whether he'd prefer to be alone.

'Fair enough,' he'd agreed. 'See you Wednesday, then.'

Rob finished his beer and began to unpack the shopping. His relief that Mike would buy Moorgate was very great. Any other solution would have felt as if he were betraying Melissa.

'I'm sorry, my love,' he murmured, as he went to and fro between the kitchen and the larder. 'I know what you tried to do. Forgive me that I can't cope here without you.'

He wondered if he would continue to feel so close to her in the small cottage he'd seen for sale in Tintagel. Perhaps it was only at Moorgate that he would be aware of her presence and hear the echoes of her voice but at least he would still be able to come here, to visit Mike and Luke. He would not be leaving her or denying her dream. He kept his thoughts deliberately turned away from the idea of interring her ashes. It was unthinkable that such a vital, human, vivid person could be reduced to a handful of dust. Rob closed the larder door, fear, misery, loneliness, rising in him at such a reminder of his own mortality. He thrust away his morbid thoughts, consigning them, with his grief, to some distant part of his mind, but unable to subdue the pain in his heart. It would be such a comfort to have Mike at hand. Only Mike knew his situation. In a way, it was a relief that none of his acquaintances, or the men with whom he worked, knew about Melissa. Their ignorance allowed a kind of freedom; he need not suffer their sympathy or explain his feelings. In their company it was easier to keep his pain at a bearable level. With Mike, however, there was the companionable comfort of shared loss; each helped the other. Grief could put a man into exile, shutting him away from the humour, irritation and rough-edged living of the day-to-day. People were careful of you; either shunning you from sheer embarrassment or being supersensitive about your condition. Both reactions kept you permanently aware, rendering mental escape impossible. You were an outcast, your pain and grief a constant, unpleasant reminder to them of their own frailty. Their own feelings were expressed in anxious grimaces to warn the unwary of your presence, lest they make some thoughtless observation, and relief once you were safely out of the room. Only with Mike could he relax into his true self and yet, even with Mike, he could not allow himself the luxury of real grief.

Rob threw the empty can into the rubbish bin. He would have a shower, put on some clean clothes and then make up Mike's bed. Keeping busy was the answer. It didn't do to have too much time to think. After making Mike's bed he'd mow the lawn. The small, sheltered garden was beginning to blossom into lushness and needed tidying. With this thought, the question of where to inter the ashes presented itself and he thrust it hastily away. One thing at a time. Shower; make Mike's bed; mow the lawn. By then it would be suppertime. Concentrating on this necessary itinerary Rob went out of the kitchen and ran quickly up the stairs.

Maudie sat at the table, the French windows open to the garden, some photographs spread before her. Yesterday afternoon, she'd driven Daphne up to Exeter to catch the train to London and she was now enjoying the prospect of a few days alone. Since Daphne had shown her the photograph of Tim and told her the truth, Maudie had looked forward to a period of time when she could ponder these things more carefully. The relief had been so overwhelming, so liberating, that it was only now that she'd begun to realise how painful such a confession must have been for

Daphne. She had, in part, acknowledged it at the time but her own feelings had been paramount. The strength of her reaction—that huge, glorious swamping relief—had been the measure of her fear: the fear that Hector had never really loved her, had always missed Hilda, had kept something important hidden from her. During the two years since his death these suspicions and doubts had grown out of all proportion, forcing out confidence and peace of mind, distorting the truth and corroding her memories.

Daphne's revelations, though startling, had destroyed the enemy within and restored her. Yet it was a shock to know that Daphne and Hector had been lovers. To begin with, to have her suspicions and doubts explained away was enough, nothing else had mattered; later, a rather horrid mental picture of Hector and Daphne, intimately together, had threatened to destroy her present calm. Was it really true that he had never loved Daphne? Could she really believe that there had never been other such moments after she herself had met him? A rather unworthy sensation of triumph had manifested itself at the thought of Hector being unfaithful to the perfect Hilda; a sensation quickly superseded by the horrid possibility that if he'd betrayed Hilda he might also have betrayed her, Maudie. Was it Daphne who had been the threat after all?

She remembered that there had been a wariness on Hector's part at the beginning; a wariness which Maudie had put down to the fact that Hilda and Daphne had been lifelong friends and that Daphne might resent Maudie on Hilda's behalf. Now she saw that this wariness had sprung from a very different cause. Yet her instinct had been to trust Daphne although, looking back, many things were now clear that had seemed puzzling at the time. It was hard to be unaffected by the thought of intimacy between Hector and Daphne but she was determined not to replace one set of suspicions with another. Without quite knowing why she'd rooted out the photograph albums, along with the manila envelopes full of ancient snapshots, and settled herself at the table. Perhaps the evidence of the past could help settle her mind.

The afternoon sun was too high to penetrate the shade of the veranda, and Polonius lay, peacefully asleep, insensible to the birdsong which filled the sunny garden. Maudie reached for her spectacles and opened the first album. Selina had commandeered the earliest records of her life with her parents and, apart from the framed studio portraits, very few records remained of Hector's early married life. A few had slipped through the net and Maudie studied these black-and-white snapshots of the young Hilda with her two small children: sitting in a deckchair, a daughter on either side, laughing at the camera; standing alone, wearing a voluminously skirted sundress with big patch pockets, eyes shaded by a straw hat; posed beside Hector, who stood easily, his hands in his pockets, her smile rather self-conscious as she held the girls' hands. Her fair hair was carefully set, always tidy; her face subtly made up. Maudie stared curiously at this woman whom she had feared. Even given the formality of the fifties she was so like Selina it was rather unsettling but there was nothing else to give rise to anxiety or jealousy. A rather ordinary young woman, whose life had been cut short, yet she had been the cause of so much pain.

Maudie held the album closer, examining Hector now. There was no way that he could be described as ordinary: dark, dashing, confident, he must have caused many a flutter in hearts other than Hilda's—or Daphne's. Maudie turned the pages slowly, studying these records of the past. Some of the photographs had simply been put in loosely between the pages and it was one of these which attracted her attention. The camera had caught Daphne unaware. Her whole concentration was centred on Hector, who was laughing, head thrown back, hands on hips, unconscious of anything apart from whatever it was that was causing him so much amusement. Hilda was there too, glancing at the person behind the camera, but it was Daphne's expression which riveted Maudie's attention. Her smile was wistful, tender, loving—oh! such a wealth of feeling was expressed in that smile. Maudie felt tears pricking at the back of her eyes and it was some while before, putting the photograph to one side, she continued to turn the pages.

At last she found what she had been subconsciously hoping for: a photograph of herself with Hector. There were plenty of these, Selina had no desire to look at them, but this one was special. Although she could not remember seeing it before, Maudie could clearly remember when it had been taken. Staring at it, it seemed that she could hear the creak and flap of the sails, the gentle slap of the water against the hull, the seagulls screaming overhead. She was leaning back against Hector's shoulder, her legs stretched along the thwart, dreamy and relaxed. They'd been swimming from the boat and she wore his jersey but her long brown legs were bare. His arm was round her and she held his hand in both of hers. He was looking down at her with a brooding, passionate intensity which even now, more than thirty years later, had the power to make her feel quite weak. How well she could remember that look—and yet, she had forgotten it; forgotten so many things about Hector that now came flooding back to remind her of his love.

Daphne was right: she'd had nothing to fear. Gently, Maudie held the two photographs together, comparing the way Daphne looked at Hector with Hector's expression as she, Maudie, lay in his arms on the boat. Presently she had an idea. Fetching some scissors, she very carefully cut Hilda out of the first photograph, trimming it so that it showed only Daphne and Hector. Next she searched for the envelope containing the photographs of Hector as a boy. Finding the copy of one she had framed—the one that looked like Tim—Maudie trimmed it to the same size as the photograph of Daphne and Hector. She held them together, matching them, smiling at the boy who gazed out, almost proudly, in his cord shorts and collared jersey. Alert and confident, he looked almost eagerly into the camera, just as Tim looked, nearly seventy years later. Keeping aside the third photograph, Maudie bundled the rest away into their carrier bags.

It was after she'd found a leather folder and was carefully inserting the first of the two photographs that the telephone rang.

'Hi, babe,' said Posy. 'How are things?'

'Things are splendid.' Maudie laid aside the folder. 'How are you?'

'Great. I thought I might come down at the weekend. Aunt Daphne's gone to see Mum, hasn't she?'

'She has indeed. She'll be with Selina for the weekend and back at the end of next week. I shall be delighted to see you.'

'Fab. I'll bring my sleeping bag so you haven't got to worry about sheets.'

'That would be helpful. Usual train?'

'Yes.' A slight hesitation. 'I've got something to tell you, Maudie.'

'Oh?'

'Mmmm. You know Mike?'

Maudie frowned, searching her memory. 'Mike?'

'You know. We met him at Moorgate with Rob.'

'Oh, *Mike*. Of course I remember him. Sorry.'

'Well, the thing is . . .' a longer pause. 'It's just . . . I think it's getting a bit serious between us.'

Maudie was shocked into complete silence, which was, perhaps, fortunate.

'I know it seems sudden,' Posy was saying breathlessly, 'but I've actually been seeing him a lot. He's been up to London several times and I went to Oxford last weekend. It's just . . . well, I'm begining to think I love him.'

Maudie's gaze fell distractedly on the photographs: Hector's look of love, Daphne's longing smile.

'Well,' she said weakly, 'well, my darling . . . of course, you haven't known him long but if you're sure . . .'

'Bless you, Maudie,' said Posy. 'I knew I could rely on you. Mum's making a dreadful fuss, flapping about like a chicken with its head off about Mike being divorced and having a child. As if it matters. And Maudie, you'll never guess what?'

'What?' asked Maudie predictably.

'Mike's going to buy Moorgate from Rob. Rob doesn't want to be there without Melissa, you see, so Mike's buying it.'

'That sounds . . . wonderful.'

'Do you think you could talk Mum round a bit?' asked Posy anxiously. 'About Mike being divorced and having Luke and stuff? I think this might be really serious, Maudie, and I can't bear all the hassle. She's having fits about me even going out with him. Look, I'll see you at the weekend, Maudie. I'll explain everything then and we'll decide how to deal with Mum. And I want you to meet Mike again, properly. There's so much to talk about. If Mum phones tell her how much you like Mike, won't you? If I don't phone again, I'll see you on Friday at the station. Love you lots. 'Byeee.'

Maudie put down the telephone receiver and picked up the photographs, hands trembling a little, her head rocking. Hector looked back at her with Posy's eyes. Posy: her baby, her child, her darling. Might Posy, too, become a second wife, a stepmother? Poor Selina. What a shock, coming so soon after Patrick's departure! And poor Daphne, her mind fixed firmly on Hector and Emily, quite unaware of the drama awaiting her in London. Anxiously, Maudie tried to remember the name of the friend with whom Daphne was spending a few days—but with no success. No chance, then, of warning her.

There was nothing to be done. She must wait patiently until the weekend and then find out as much as she could. It was quite possible, after all, that Posy and Mike were genuinely in love, just as she and Hector had been in love after one meeting at a snowed-in airport. Maudie picked up the third photograph and tucked it into the back of her wallet. Perhaps, one day, she might show it to Posy.

Chapter Thirty-eight

Mike was relieved to see that the pick-up was not in the yard when he arrived at Moorgate. He needed a little time alone, to collect his thoughts. It was odd to approach the house, knowing that it was to be his. He stood in the lane, staring round him, in an emotional confusion. An exciting sense of ownership was infused by a Posy-induced joyfulness, yet he was aware of an overall sadness, the familiar weight of loss. He'd come to terms with these conflicting emotions. His knowledge of Melissa enabled him to reject guilt, quite certain that she would be at one with him in his new-found happiness, yet he missed her painfully. He was confident that she would understand Rob's reason for leaving Moorgate—in her condition she'd had no chance to think it through coolly—and she'd be delighted to know that her brother and Luke were to live there; he and Luke and Posy.

As he opened the gate and put the car away, Mike was remembering the astonishing scene in Oxford last weekend. He'd fetched Posy from the station and taken her home, with Luke belted into his seat behind them. Her shyness had quickly dissolved into her natural friendliness but a vestigial awareness remained. He'd felt it too. It meant that they hadn't quite been at ease. An accidental touch, a glance that lingered into a longer look, a casual phrase—all these things found a nervous, quivering response which meant that the earlier intimacy had to be re-established. He'd known it would be more difficult here, in Oxford, than on neutral ground in London but he had an unexpected ally in his small son.

Luke was missing Melissa too, and, having already created a rapport with Posy in Cornwall, he'd greeted her with an enthusiasm which was both gratifying and a welcome diversion from their own immediate problem. Carrying Luke in from the car, Posy perching with him at the table while Mike had made tea, making themselves heard above Luke's delighted roars, had made it impossible for them to remain self-conscious. When at last Luke had been persuaded to be separated from Posy to the extent of being put into his highchair, and she'd settled herself more comfortably, her attention had been riveted by a photograph standing on the shelf. She'd frowned, about to speak, then paused, and he'd glanced in the same direction, immediately understanding her caution.

'That's Melissa,' he'd said at once, putting down the teapot, lifting the photograph and handing it to her. 'Taken a few years ago, just after she'd graduated.'

Posy had taken it, still frowning. 'This is so bizarre,' she'd said slowly, 'but I feel I know her. Or perhaps she reminds me of someone.'

'People say we're alike,' he'd offered diffidently. 'Could it simply be a family resemblance?'

'I don't know.' She'd shaken her head. 'It might be. I've felt the same with you once or twice. It's like a kind of fleeting memory of something. I expect it will come back. She's so beautiful.'

'Yes,' he said. He took the photograph, looking at the bright, laughing face, the thick bronze-coloured hair, remembering that happy, triumphant day. 'She was . . . lovely.'

'Oh, Mike.' Posy had stood up, putting an arm about him sympathetically, and suddenly they'd been in each other's arms, everything else forgotten. It was Luke who had brought them back to the present, hammering on his tray, shouting for his tea, and they'd broken apart, laughing rather breathlessly.

It was the next day, when the weekend was nearly over, that he'd talked to her about Rob, about being together, living at Moorgate—'Oh, this is so amazing,' Posy had cried, her eyes brilliant. 'I can't believe this can be happening!'—and had talked for hours about their feelings, their hopes.

'I'm not easy to live with,' he'd told her. 'I get utterly absorbed with what I'm writing and you'll probably feel neglected. The trouble is that most people think that writers are only at work when they have a pen in their hands or they're sitting at a word processor but it isn't true. It goes on and on in their minds and they become withdrawn and preoccupied and touchy if they're distracted. Moorgate is rather isolated and I don't want you to be lonely.'

'I shan't be lonely,' she'd assured him. 'I like my own company and there will be Luke. Perhaps I'll get involved with the local playgroup when he starts going. Things like that. I shan't sit about watching the grass grow.'

'No,' he'd said, 'no, I'm sure you won't. But it's all happened rather quickly. What will your parents say?'

She'd shrugged impatiently. 'Who cares? It's my life and I want to be with you. What's the point of waiting?'

'If you're certain . . .' He'd still sounded anxious and she'd grinned at him.

'Trying to get rid of me before we've even started?'

'Of course not. I just don't want to be the cause of you missing out on anything. What will your grandmother say? She's a daunting lady, if I'm a judge.'

'Maudie? Maudie will want me to be happy. It's Mum who's the daunting one.'

'Yes,' he'd said uncomfortably. 'So you keep saying. I'm not looking forward to meeting your mother.'

'Neither am I,' she'd agreed frankly. 'But we can do it now that we've really made up our own minds. You have to be absolutely determined or she'll undermine you. Look.' Suddenly she'd become very serious. 'We don't want to waste time, do we? We know how precious it is and we know that you can't take it for granted.'

It was as if Melissa had materialised beside them, encouraging them, and his eyes had filled with tears.

'No,' he'd mumbled. 'You can't take it for granted.'

Posy had held his hand tightly and, once he'd recovered, he'd begun to talk about his next visit to Moorgate.

'I was wondering,' he'd said, 'about giving Rob a keepsake. Melissa didn't want anything that might be a tie, if you know what I mean. Moorgate was something else but she didn't want him surrounded by things which might prevent him from forming new relationships. She had no idea, of course, that she'd made such an imprint on the house itself as far as he's concerned. Anyway, she couldn't think of anything that might not, ultimately, be a kind of reproach, if you see what I mean.'

'I think so.' Posy had looked thoughtful. 'I can understand how she felt. She'd had that wonderful week with him knowing that she had to leave him and she would have hated him feeling a kind of on-going allegiance. Things that would have constantly reminded him and tied him to her memory.'

'Exactly.' He'd been grateful for her insight. 'But I think that when we've . . . dealt with the ashes, he might suddenly feel bereft. Moorgate gone. Melissa gone. Perhaps I'm being fanciful. Anyway, I've framed this photograph, a recent one of her, which is how he knew her. What do you think?'

He'd taken the leather case out of the drawer and shown it to her. Her response had been electrifying.

'Oh, my God!' She'd clutched the case with one hand, the other pressed to her mouth. 'I don't believe it! I know her. I met her.' She stared at him, her eyes almost wild with shock. 'Oh, Mike. I met her.'

'But where?' He'd felt almost angry with the surprise of it. 'Are you sure? Was it in London?'

'No.' Posy had stared down at the photograph and her eyes had filled with tears. 'It was in Bovey.'

'In *Bovey*?'

'We had coffee in the Mill.' She'd looked at him, her lips shaking. 'We talked about the birds. She was so lovely. I remember thinking how elegant and confident she was and wishing that I was like her. I imagined that she was terribly successful and sought after. She said that she was on her way to look at a house in Cornwall and we talked . . .'

Posy had lapsed into silence, sitting quite still, hearing Melissa saying, 'Perhaps you want five children and a husband that writes nice things about you when you're sixty.' This recollection, her remembrance of an odd feeling of kinship, suddenly brought home the reality of Melissa's death; it had made the loss personal, and very real, and the tears had poured down her cheeks.

Mike had tried to comfort her, still trying to come to terms with this revelation.

'We'll go there together,' Posy had said later, drying her tears. 'I'll show you. Oh, I simply can't believe this . . .'

Now, with the photograph and Melissa's ashes in his bag, Mike let himself into Moorgate, dreading the ordeal that lay ahead.

It was early evening, however, before either of them had the courage to take the small box and go out into the garden. After lunch, they'd gone for a walk across the moor, allowing the bleak majestic beauty to creep into their souls, preparing themselves. The exercise and the invigorating air had made them ready for an early supper although, after the first few mouthfuls, they'd suddenly lost their appetites. Each had struggled on, however, lest the other should be affected.

At length conversation had begun to lag; silences stretched longer and the atmosphere grew heavy with suspense.

'Come on,' said Mike gently, at last. 'Shall we go into the garden, Rob, and . . . do this last thing?'

Rob nodded, pushing back his chair, his face grim, and Mike picked up the small casket from his bag and followed him outside. He was waiting on the lawn and Mike could see that the ground beneath the escallonia hedge had been freshly turned.

'Where do you think?' muttered Rob. 'I thought that . . . it would be . . . safe there. But I don't really know . . .'

Mike held the casket tightly, staring down at the dark, peaty earth. He had an impression of Melissa, standing behind him, shivering, clasping her ruana tightly about her; heard her voice in the wind.

> 'Still wouldst thou sing, and I have ears in vain—
> To thy high requiem become a sod.
> Thou wast not born for death, immortal Bird!'

'No,' he said desperately, with a kind of revulsion. 'No. I can't put her there. Not in the cold and wet. Not Melissa.'

Rob stared at him. 'Let her go where she likes,' he said suddenly. 'Let her be free. That's how she was, wasn't she? Not tied down and constrained.'

On an impulse, Mike opened the lid, holding up the casket, letting the contents be taken by the wind which streamed, cold and cleansing, over the moor from the west. They stood together until the casket was quite empty and Rob took Mike's arm.

'What shall we do?' he muttered. 'We can't just leave it like that.' He was shuddering with reaction and Mike took a deep breath, steadying himself. The sun had disappeared beneath the horizon, the garden was washed in the golden light of evening and, in the east, a star was twinkling. In his confused mind some lines from a prayer formed; the prayer which he and Melissa had said each evening at school, before bed. Slowly, haltingly he began to speak the lines.

'O Lord, support us all the day long of this troublous life, until the shades lengthen, and the evening comes, and the busy world is hushed, the fever of life is over, and our work is done. Then, Lord, in thy mercy, grant us safe lodging, a holy rest, and peace at the last; through Jesus Christ our Lord.'

Wrenchingly, Rob began to weep, almost doubling up, his body racked with sobs. Keeping control of his own reactions, Mike led him into the house and pushed him into a chair at the kitchen table. Without thinking he dragged a rug from his bag, Melissa's rug, placing it round Rob's shoulders.

'There's nothing left now,' Rob said, raising his head to look pitifully at Mike. 'Nothing at all. How shall I manage?'

Mike took the photograph from his bag and placed it wordlessly before him, tucking the rug more closely over his shaking shoulders, before going to push the kettle on to the hotplate. Rob stared down at Melissa's face, his hand unconsciously smoothing the soft, comforting wool. Presently, as if growing aware of his unconscious action, he glanced at the rug. His face changed as a thousand memories possessed him and he began to cry in earnest, allowing, at last, the agonising weight of grief to dissolve in healing tears.

At the same hour, Posy was standing in the hall at Hyde Abbey Road talking to Selina.

'I know it's sudden,' she was saying. 'Of course it is. It's a sudden sort of thing, isn't it?'

'But you're talking about *marrying* this . . . Mike.' Selina's voice sounded strained. 'That's certainly sudden. I can imagine you falling in love with someone suddenly—I'm not quite stupid—but marrying them after . . . how long is it? And what about your own career?'

'I'll think about that later.' In her anxiety Posy managed to sound cock-
ily defiant. 'After all, you were never terribly impressed by the thought of
my having a career in the theatre, were you?'

'That's not the point.' Selina wanted to burst into tears, to scream. She
was tired, lonely, unhappy and she wanted to be made much of, to be cos-
seted and looked after. This was simply too much; she hadn't the strength
for it. 'You're only twenty-two, Posy, and did you say this man is
divorced? With a child?'

'I did say that.' Posy was on the defensive. 'So what? It's not his fault
that his wife became famous and chose a career instead of motherhood.'

'Please, Posy.' Selina, remembering long ago yoga classes, took a few
deep, calming breaths. 'Please can we discuss this sensibly? Must we do it
on the telephone?'

Various sarcastic answers presented themselves but, seized by an unexpected fit of maturity, Posy rejected them.

'I can't get home in the middle of the week,' she said, quite reasonably,
'and you've got Aunt Daphne staying the weekend, haven't you? Not
much point me coming home while she's there. We wouldn't be able to
talk properly. I just wanted you to know about me and Mike getting really
serious. I'll come home the following weekend if you like.'

'Yes,' said Selina, with a gasp of relief. 'Yes, do that . . .'

'And I'll bring Mike to meet you.'

'Bring Mike?' cried Selina, alarmed. 'But isn't that rather premature?
Can't we talk about this first, Posy?'

'We've already talked about it.' She paused, steeling herself. 'There's
something else, Mum.'

'Oh God, you're pregnant, aren't you?' said Selina flatly. 'I might have
guessed. That's what all this urgency is about, isn't it?'

'No,' shouted Posy crossly. 'No, it bloody isn't. I'm not pregnant. I just
wanted to tell you that Mike's buying Moorgate. The man who bought it
doesn't want it any more because . . . well, it's a long story and I'll explain
when I see you. But . . .' She laughed almost hysterically. 'Isn't it amazing,
Mum? I'll be living at Moorgate. You'll be able to come and stay with us.
Aren't you pleased?'

'Buying Moorgate?' Selina sounded as if she'd been temporarily
stunned by a blunt instrument. 'What on earth are you talking about?'

'Mike's buying Moorgate,' explained Posy patiently. 'He knows the

man who bought it from Maudie. He was engaged to Mike's sister
but . . . well, she died. It's really sad. Rob doesn't want to be there without her so Mike's buying it. Oh, Mum, I'm just so happy. Can't you be
pleased for me?'

Selina sought for words; her brain reeled. For once the usual cutting
remarks and cruel observations deserted her. She felt bone-tired,
exhausted, beyond all rational thought.

'Yes,' she said faintly. 'Yes, of course I'm pleased. We'll talk later, next
weekend. Bring Mike. I shall be pleased to see him if he'd like to come.'

The line went dead and Posy stood for some time, eyebrows raised,
staring at nothing in particular. After a moment she dialled another number and was eventually put through to Patrick.

'Hello, love,' he said cheerfully. 'I've had your letter. It's great news,
isn't it?'

'Oh, Dad,' she said, gratefully. 'Do you think so? You're not . . . well,
upset or anything?'

'Upset?' He sounded surprised. 'Why should I be upset?'

'Well, it's a bit sudden, isn't it?'

'Falling in love is a sudden business,' he answered. 'What else would
you expect?'

'Nothing,' she said, pulling herself together. 'I mean I'm being stupid.
I've just been talking to Mum.'

'Ah.' His voice was guarded. 'Problems?'

Posy began to laugh. 'Not really. That's the point. She took it quite
well and invited Mike home to meet her the weekend after next. But she
sounded a bit odd.'

'In what way odd?'

'Tired,' said Posy after a moment's thought. 'Like she was too
exhausted to care much, really. Dad?'

'Mmm?'

'I wish you were going to be there next weekend.'

'Oh, Posy, so do I. Well, in a way. I'm sorry, darling.'

'It's OK. But I want you to meet him.'

'So do I. Of course I do. Just tell me when he's got some time spare and
I'll be there. He sounds a nice chap and a very interesting one. I've bought
his book.'

'Thanks, Dad.' Posy was near to tears. 'Thanks for . . . understanding.'

'Forget it,' he said. 'Don't forget to let me know when we can all get together.'

'Of course I will. Thanks, Dad.'

She replaced the receiver, pushing back her hair, sighing with relief. Climbing the stairs to her room, she wondered how Rob and Mike were coping at Moorgate.

Chapter Thirty-nine

Selina wandered round the house, checking for the twentieth time that all was in order for Daphne's visit. So lonely was she that she was longing for the older woman's arrival, despite her own bitterness at Daphne's faithlessness. After ten days with Maudie it was only to be expected that Daphne knew all about Patrick and the situation which had led up to his departure. It was humiliating to think about it: Daphne and Maudie, sitting together, discussing her private life and, no doubt, enjoying themselves at her expense. Yet she needed company. It was so difficult being with her friends, keeping up appearances, pretending that Patrick was simply on a long course—she'd said that it was for a year, so as to give herself space—and acting as if nothing had changed.

She'd heard nothing more from him after the postcard and she swung between hoping that he might suddenly telephone to say that he was coming home and deciding that she must do something positive: get a job or sell the house. The problem was that these last initiatives needed energy, they required enthusiasm, and she was so tired. She slept the heavy, dreamless sleep of the depressed person, waking unrefreshed, dreading the prospect of another day ahead. Her stomach churned with terror for no apparent reason and she was beginning to feel the stirrings of panic at the least thing—the telephone ringing or the sight of the letters lying on the mat. It was a major task deciding what to wear and the ordinary household jobs were a dreary drudgery.

She knew that she must make an effort to pull herself together, but she did not know how, and now Posy's news was yet another anxiety for her to bear alone. She'd hardly been able to take it in and, after a while, her brain had refused to function properly. It was easier to give in and agree to meet this Mike; less effort to agree to it than to fight it. Nevertheless, it was another addition to her load; another terrible worry. Her only daughter thinking about marrying a divorced man with a small child! And what on earth did Posy mean when she said that he'd bought Moorgate? Surely the child was raving? Selina groaned aloud. She needed a drink. Since Patrick had gone, she tried not to start drinking before seven o'clock in the evening, but just lately it had been very hard to stick to her rule. She glanced hopefully at her watch and, as she did so, the doorbell rang.

Hurrying out into the hall, she flung open the door and stood staring. In all the years she'd known her mother's old friend, Daphne seemed hardly to have changed: tall, fair, pretty, she smiled at Selina as she'd smiled at her when she was a little girl, when Mummy was alive and Daddy had been there, handsome and strong and devoted.

'Selina, darling,' said Daphne, holding out her arms. 'My very dear child. How are you?'

Forgetting her accusations of duplicity, her fears of betrayal, Selina flung herself upon the tall figure and burst into a noisy fit of weeping. Taken by surprise, her own terrors temporarily put to one side, Daphne led the howling Selina inside and closed the door firmly on the surprised and interested looks of a passer-by. Her instinct leading her unerringly to the kitchen, Daphne dropped her bag on the floor, her other arm still about Selina, and saw the bottle waiting invitingly on the dresser.

'A drink,' she said, relieved. 'We both need a drink. Now sit down while I forage.'

Still sobbing, Selina allowed herself to be lowered on to a chair and Daphne hastened to find glasses and to pour the wine—a very nice Australian red, she noticed—which had been open and waiting for some time.

'Now that's what I call thoughtful,' said Daphne approvingly, pouring cheerfully. 'We'll feel better after one of these.'

Selina took her glass, her sobs gradually diminishing, and smiled feebly through her tears.

'Sorry,' she said. 'It was just seeing you there like that. Time swung backwards.' Her face creased up again. 'It was as if I was a child again.'

'Poor darling,' said Daphne, somewhat insincerely but ready to encourage this softened, malleable Selina for her own ends, 'what a terrible time you've had.'

Selina groped for her handkerchief, her sense of injustice renewed by Daphne's ready sympathy.

'It's been awful,' she agreed, a tissue to her eyes. 'I expect Maudie told you . . . ?' She began to cry again, remembering her fears of humiliation.

'Only a little,' lied Daphne diplomatically. 'She felt that it was better that you should tell me yourself.'

'Oh.' Surprise dried Selina's tears. She hadn't expected such consideration from her stepmother. 'I imagined she'd tell you all about it.'

A sulky note had crept into her voice and Daphne made haste to discourage it.

'No, no. We had rather a lot of other things to talk about. Anyway, I want to hear it from you.'

'I'm absolutely desperate.' Tears were threatening again. 'And now, on top of everything else, Posy's dropped this bombshell.'

'Posy?' Daphne's surprise was quite genuine. 'What's Posy been up to?'

Selina took a large swig of wine. She was beginning to feel very slightly better.

'Don't tell me Maudie doesn't know? She's fallen in love with a divorced man with a child of nine months. He's some kind of writer. She phoned again just now to say that she's thinking of marrying him and says that they'll be living at Moorgate.'

Daphne was silenced for a moment. She glanced round the kitchen, wondering how many empty bottles might be lying about, and took a firm grip on the situation.

'I simply can't believe it,' she said, with the air of one who was only too ready to be convinced. 'But I want to hear about everything. Now, I'm going to take off my coat, put my bag in my room—no, no, don't get up, I'm sure I'll find it—and then we'll have a good old session. I shan't be long.'

Selina finished her wine and poured another generous glassful. By the time Daphne returned a second bottle was waiting temptingly beside the first.

'Excellent,' said Daphne. 'Now where shall we start?'

'I don't know what I'm going to do,' Selina said, nearly two hours later. The second bottle of wine was half empty, supper had been hastily assembled and disposed of, and Daphne was still trying to decide if Selina should know the truth. So far the conversation had related mainly to Patrick, his affair with Mary and his ultimate defection, with diversions into Posy's ingratitude and disloyalty which inevitably included Maudie's insensitivity and selfishness. As she watched and listened, Daphne was struck by Selina's likeness to Hilda and, as she nodded, sympathised, expressed disbelief, she was trying to remember how she'd felt towards Hilda after the affair with Hector. Surely she must have been consumed with guilt? She knew that finding herself pregnant had tended to absorb her utterly but it was difficult to recall her feelings at the time. There had been an impregnability about Hilda, a smiling, unemotional façade. Discussions about events, whether disasters or celebrations, seemed to slide and drift about her, neither denting her consciousness nor evoking her compassion. Nothing seemed capable of jolting her out of a serenity which appeared to be rooted in indifference rather than achieved by any hard-won personal discipline or spiritual awareness.

Now, as she listened to Selina, Daphne began to recognise the same symptoms. Nothing was Selina's fault, this much was clear. The irritation, aroused in the past by the mother, was beginning to be created by the daughter and Daphne stirred restlessly. Advice, here, was pointless. Selina would stare at her blankly and immediately return to her first standpoint. The best she could do—and she owed this much to Hilda, surely—was to attempt to help Selina out of the maze of her apathy.

'Had you thought of anything that you might do?' she asked lightly. They were still in the kitchen—the women's workplace being from time immemorial the room for confessions and the sharing of secrets—sitting comfortably at the table, the bottle between them.

Selina looked helplessly at her. 'I'm feeling so tired, you see. It's simply not like me to be doing nothing. I've always been the organiser in this family. Patrick's useless, of course.'

'So you haven't had any ideas.'

It was a statement, as if Daphne were drawing up a debit sheet, and Selina frowned defensively.

'I wouldn't say that. It's just my options are a bit extreme.'

'Are they?' Daphne looked interested.

'Well, the obvious one is to sell the house.' Selina paused, waiting for

Daphne to protest, to say how unfair it was that she should have to consider such a step, but Daphne merely refilled her glass and waited. 'I could move to a smaller place,' she said rather sulkily, 'and invest the money. When Daddy died we had enough to pay off the mortgage so I could do quite well, I suppose.'

'And would you move out of London?'

'I don't want to move anywhere,' snapped Selina, resentful at Daphne's lack of sympathy.

Daphne pursed her lips. 'That sounds reasonable. So what are the other options? Can you afford to stay here?'

'Probably not. I'm living on savings at the moment but when they've gone I'll have to do something drastic.'

'Like what?'

'Get a job, I suppose.'

Daphne did not look horrified at this proposal, there were no cries of 'At your age? Oh, how unfair, it shouldn't be expected of you!' She simply straightened in her chair, her face alert.

'What could you do?' she asked brightly.

Selina stared at her. That first impulse to throw herself upon Daphne, to become a child again, seeking comfort and reassurance, was passing. Pride was reasserting itself.

'I don't know,' she answered coldly. 'It's nearly thirty years since I was in the marketplace. I can't imagine that there would be many openings for a woman of my age.'

'Oh, nonsense,' said Daphne, with an almost offensive heartiness. 'Emily works, you know. She had to when Tim died. She had no choice.'

'Emily's younger than I am,' said Selina sullenly.

'She was when she started,' agreed Daphne thoughtfully. 'But she enjoys her work. The children are older, now, which makes it easier, but it was very difficult with the girls so young and Tim a baby.'

'But she cooks, doesn't she?' Selina was reluctant to admire Emily too openly lest it invited unfavourable comparison. 'She works from home.'

'She started like that,' said Daphne, 'but she's out much more these days, doing lunches and dinners and all sorts. She loves it but then Emily always got on very well with people.'

'Of course it's almost easier if your husband dies than if he leaves you, isn't it?'

Daphne was silent. How like Hilda this was: it must always be easier for the other person, whatever their situation. *Their* terrors, disasters, anxieties must always be less dire, *their* triumphs less praiseworthy. Only Hilda—and now Selina—ever truly suffered. 'Isn't it typical!' was their cry. 'Isn't it just my luck!'

'I can't quite see why,' she answered at last, 'unless you're talking about pride. Naturally it's embarrassing to admit that your husband—or wife—has left you, isn't it? It suggests an inadequacy on your part. Is that what you mean?'

'Inadequacy?'

Daphne raised her eyebrows in surprise. 'Wouldn't you say so? Why else should he—or she—go? Nobody walks out of a happy, loving relationship voluntarily.'

'Are you suggesting that it's my fault that Patrick's gone?'

'Well, isn't it?'

'But I told you about Mary. That's when all this started.'

'Yes, you told me. But why was he attracted to her in the first place? What was missing in his relationship with you that he needed to look for it elsewhere?'

'It was simply Patrick's pathetic need for gratitude. His ego has to be bolstered up by being told he's wonderful.'

'Sounds like the rest of us,' murmured Daphne. 'And I gather that you resented supplying that need?'

'Why should I?' demanded Selina. 'I've given him thirty years of support and he betrays me with a little tart and then leaves me. After everything I've done for him.'

'What have you done for him?'

Selina shook her head with an expression which asked if Daphne was in her right mind. 'I've supported him, brought up his children, run the home, taken all the responsibility. Patrick never had to think about anything but his job. Such as it was.' Selina was flushed with righteous indignation. 'And, even then, if it hadn't been for Daddy's generosity I'm not sure how we'd have survived.'

'Sounds very businesslike,' Daphne said judiciously. 'The perfect wife and mother. Rather like a job description, isn't it? But it tends to leave out the messy, human bits.'

'What's wrong with that? It works for decent people. It worked for my parents.'

'Not altogether.' Daphne's calm voice belied her inward terror.

'What do you mean?'

'You are very like your mother, Selina. You keep to the letter of the law but it leaves out all the warmth and frailty and fun. Hilda was the same and, although your father was devoted to her, he needed some of that fun. Hilda rarely condemned or criticised, she was always correct, but her forgiveness was cold as charity; it could freeze sea water. Hector was different. He was infuriating, tiresome, overbearing, but he had a generosity and a kind of humility which made him great. Even he, honourable though he was, needed to breathe the ordinary air of the lesser mortals.'

'If you mean Daddy was unfaithful to Mummy I don't believe a word of it. He wasn't like that.'

'I don't know what "like that" implies. There are so many areas of grey in a relationship. Your father certainly wasn't promiscuous, he was like most of us are—human—and, like Patrick, he had a lapse.'

'How would you know?' asked Selina contemptuously.

'Because he had it with me,' said Daphne wearily.

They stared at each other across the table. Daphne held her trembling hands clenched in her lap but she kept her eyes fixed bravely on Selina's.

'I don't believe you.' But she did. Her face showed it.

'He always regretted it.' Daphne felt a compulsion to comfort. 'It was at a bad time and he needed simple affection, uncomplicated fun. He wanted to be seen as Hector, not just as a provider.' She was pleading now, wondering how she could have destroyed Selina's trust so cruelly. 'Hilda never knew.'

'How could he do it to her?'

'It wasn't like that. Not premeditated. It just flared up out of nothing—'

'And how could *you* do it? You were her best friend. Oh!' She covered her face with her hands. 'I can't believe this.'

'I loved him, you see.' Daphne spoke quietly, rather as if she were talking to herself. 'I loved him so much. Philip was rather like Hilda—punctilious, proper, kind, but there was no warmth, no hugs and silliness and ordinary fun. Hector and I were rather like brother and sister. No.' She shook her head. 'More like cousins. We could hug and joke and be silly but occasionally there was a flash of something else. I loved him, Selina.'

Selina raised her head. Her eyes were puzzled and Daphne was seized with guilt.

'But you loved Mummy too. Didn't it bother you at all?'

'Oh, my dear child.' Daphne almost laughed. 'Have you never known that kind of passion? That mindlessness that sweeps everything before it? The kind of need that you'd sacrifice everything for gladly? No, clearly not. Well, it's a sort of madness that possesses you and that's the only excuse I can offer you. For a few days your father and I were mad together. If it's any comfort, he never forgave himself. That's what he was apologising for at the end. It was nothing to do with Maudie. It was me he was apologising for.'

Selina sat in silence, staring back into the past, adjusting her ideas.

'And Mummy never knew?' Daphne shook her head. 'And how did you deal with it afterwards? Weren't you tempted again?'

'I was too busy having Emily,' she said almost bitterly, 'and Hector was too angry with me for it to happen again.'

Selina leaned forward. 'What do you mean?' she cried fearfully. 'Do you mean Emily is Daddy's child?'

Daphne looked at her compassionately. 'She's your half-sister,' she said. 'Your father was unable to acknowledge her. At least you know that. You can believe that because you know it to be true, Selina. Nobody ever guessed.'

Selina looked so shocked that Daphne filled up her glass for her. She took it mechanically and drank but she seemed dazed.

'I'm sorry,' said Daphne at last. 'I simply didn't know if I should tell you. It's just that Emily is hoping that you'll come out and stay with us. She was always very fond of you, Selina, as you know, but young Tim looks just like Posy did at that age, just like Hector, and I think it's only fair that you should know.'

'Emily knows, then?'

'I told her when Philip died.'

'What did she say?'

'I wondered if she'd suspected something. She took it so calmly. Philip never guessed, of course, and she loved him very much, but she was always very fond of Hector and of you and Patricia.'

Selina's eyes filled with tears. 'Emily was like a little sister,' she said. 'I loved Emily . . .'

'I hope you'll go on doing it,' said Daphne gently. 'I can understand that you might not be able to forgive me but none of it was Emily's fault.'

They sat in silence for a while. Selina felt as if she'd drifted from some safe, quiet mooring into a busy waterway and she was trying to take a bearing on her present position. Her head was dizzy with wine and shock, and presently she looked at Daphne.

'I was thinking,' Daphne said carefully, 'if a visit to see us all might be good for you.'

Selina shook her head helplessly. How would she feel, visiting Emily, knowing her to be her half-sister, remembering what Daphne had said about her father; *their* father? How would she deal with it? Pride wearily raised its head.

She thought: But I was first. Daddy loved me. Emily never had that.

Somehow, though, she felt that, with Emily, it needn't be important.

'I keep wondering,' she said, dully, too tired to think clearly, 'whether Patrick might come home.'

'I think he might.' Daphne smiled encouragingly at her. 'I think Patrick needed to feel useful. The Mary thing isn't important—try to forget about it if you can—but this was a challenge, a crusade. After a year or so he might feel he'd like to come back. If you could cope with it. But wouldn't it be better if you weren't sitting and waiting? Don't you think you'd feel more positive if you'd been getting on with your own life while he's sorting himself out?'

'What life?'

'For a start you could come out to Canada. You could meet your nieces and nephew and you could see how Emily runs her business. After that delicious supper I must say that I think you could do worse than start your own little outfit.'

Selina stared at her. 'Cooking, you mean?'

'Why not? There must be a tremendous demand for lunches and supper-parties in London. It's quite a smart thing to do, isn't it? And rather fun. Emily meets all sorts of famous people. You could see for yourself. She'd love it.'

'I'd need to think about it.'

'Well, naturally. We'll talk about it again, over the weekend. That's if you want me to stay.'

Selina took a deep breath in and let it out very slowly. 'Yes, of course I do. I'm just rather . . . overwhelmed.'

'Of course you are. I'm sorry, Selina.'

'I think I'll go to bed. My head is beginning to pound. Do you think you can find your own way around?'

She stood up, glancing about the kitchen as though puzzled that everything was still the same.

'Go to bed,' said Daphne gently. 'I'll clear up. Tomorrow is another day.'

'Thanks. Good night then.'

She went out and Daphne poured herself another glass of wine. It was done and the bond had not broken; strained, weakened, but not broken.

She thought: I must warn Emily that I've told her and that I've invited her to stay. I'm sure it was the right thing to do. Oh God, I am so tired.

She stood up, stiff after sitting for so long, and, moving slowly and painfully about the kitchen, began the process of clearing up.

Chapter Forty

'The thing is,' said Posy, as though it were the only thing in the world that could matter, 'I love him.'

She stared at Maudie anxiously but with a determination which Maudie did not for a moment underestimate. She knew that she'd let Posy down, that Posy had counted on her total sympathy and support. Yet her desire to be at one with this beloved child, her fear of risking her love, struggled with a requirement to show Posy the whole picture.

'Don't misunderstand me,' she said gently. 'I'm not suggesting that you shouldn't marry him. It's simply that you'll be sacrificing your own career to his.'

'That's what Mum said,' Posy sighed. 'The thing is that I want to be with Mike and Luke. It's been fun hanging out with Jude and Jo and stuff but now I want to get on with my life, Maudie. I've never had any clear idea as to quite what I'd do once I've graduated. The theatre is a difficult world to break into and it's not the kind of degree that gives you an automatic entry into one of the professions. I know what you're all thinking. You want me to have some career of my own in case things go wrong later and Mike and I split up.'

'Something like that,' admitted Maudie. 'You mustn't be too hard on us for wanting to protect you.'

'I'm not.' Posy's face softened. 'I know that you're only thinking about what's best for me. But Mum's certificate from Miss Sprules thirty years ago isn't much help to her now, is it?'

Maudie sighed. 'I expect you're right. Technology changes so quickly these days. Things are out of date before you even start on them but at least you'll have your degree. It shows you've reached a level of application and learning.'

'I'll have my degree,' agreed Posy. 'And, anyway, I think that being with Mike and looking after Luke will be pretty useful job experience. I could always get a job as a nanny. Look at it like that.'

'Has Luke's mother completely abandoned him?'

Posy nodded, her face sombre. 'She's got this really brilliant Hollywood career now, and she doesn't want to know. It's been sorted out legally, though. Mike didn't want her turning up suddenly five years on, deciding that she'd have Luke back. It's complicated but Mike seems quite certain that there won't be problems.'

Maudie sighed inwardly. How confident the young were, how self-assured.

'You don't mind being a stepmother?' She had to ask the question. 'It doesn't worry you?'

'I don't mind a bit.' Posy smiled at her comfortingly. 'It's not like it was for you, Maudie. Luke can't remember his mother. He's not even twelve months old. It's a bit different from two teenage girls.'

'I know it is.' Maudie smiled back at her, trying to relax. 'You must be patient. It's all rather sudden and I'm having to adjust my ideas.'

'But you liked Mike,' said Posy, 'didn't you? You thought he was really nice. You said so.'

'I liked Mike very much,' agreed Maudie, 'but I didn't look at him in the light of being your husband. It makes a bit of a difference.'

'I want you to meet him properly,' said Posy. 'Could he come down? He could stay in Bovey. If you got to know him I know you'd be much happier.'

'I'd like that,' said Maudie gratefully. She knew she had no right to demand such a favour. At moments like these she never forgot that Posy was no blood relation at all and that only out of love might Posy grant her such a privilege. 'That would be wonderful—if Mike agrees to it.'

'Oh, Mike's looking forward to meeting you again,' said Posy cheerfully. 'He's just as worried as you are. He knows that a divorced man with a small child isn't everyone's idea of a good catch and he doesn't want me to miss out. The trouble is, I know that my heart just wouldn't be in a career now. It would be down at Moorgate with Mike and Luke. If you love someone you want to be with them, don't you? Just because you're young doesn't necessarily mean that you have forty years ahead of you. Look at Melissa.'

'Yes,' said Maudie, after a moment. 'Yes, that's quite true.' She was remembering how she'd felt when she'd met Hector and their absolute need to be together. She knew that many of his friends had been shocked when they'd married as soon as his year of mourning for Hilda was completed, yet they couldn't have helped themselves, even if they'd wanted to; being together was all that had mattered.

She thought: And we were adults. Middle-aged and supposedly sensible.

'Mike really misses her,' Posy was saying. 'Luke does, too. Isn't it really bizarre that I met her, Maudie? I can't get over it. I want to take Mike into the Mill when he comes down, to show him where we had coffee together. It's really weird, like it was meant. She was so pretty and such fun. I can't believe she was dying. Oh, Maudie.' She shivered. 'It just makes you want to grab at life with both hands, doesn't it? Oh, I know that's what's worrying you, that I'm just going into this with my eyes shut, but it's not *like* that.'

'No,' said Maudie with an effort. 'I'm sure it isn't. We're all being too interfering. Bring Mike down by all means. And Luke too. It will be good to be able to spend some time with him. Don't be too hard on us, Posy. It's too trite for words to say that we only want your happiness. It's hubristic too. Who are we to suppose that we can ordain happiness for other people when we can't organise our own lives?'

'Dad said something like that,' said Posy. 'He wrote to me after I'd telephoned him. It's a really nice letter. Actually, I think he and Mike will get on really well together.'

'I wouldn't be at all surprised. How's Selina taking it?'

Posy made a face. 'Dramatically. I'm hoping Aunt Daphne will take her mind off it this weekend. Do you think that's likely?'

Maudie, still in a state of shock at Daphne's revelations, wondered whether Selina also knew by now that Emily was her half-sister.

'Yes,' she said thoughtfully. 'I wouldn't be at all surprised if that should be the case.'

Selina watched Daphne climb into the taxi, waved again and then closed the front door. Her overwhelming reaction was one of weariness;

she felt too tired even to think properly. It would have been better, once Daphne had told her this devastating truth, if she'd left at once. The most difficult thing had been to sustain a polite exterior through the whole of Saturday. It had been difficult for Daphne too, that was obvious, yet good manners had prevailed and they'd managed to get through the day somehow without sacrificing any of the rules of hospitality. Selina had been determined that she would not break down. Looking back, she could congratulate herself that she'd acquitted herself without too much loss of pride and she intended to keep it that way.

Once or twice Daphne had attempted to broach the subject again but Selina had managed to maintain a calm attitude which enabled them to discuss certain aspects, such as going out to Canada, as if it were nothing out of the ordinary. It had been important to retain her sense of dignity. She'd made such a fool of herself at the outset. The sight of Daphne, hardly changed, standing on the doorstep had taken her off balance and she'd bawled like a child. Not that she should blame herself: what with Patrick, and now Posy, she'd had more than enough to upset her. Nevertheless, she wished that she'd been more controlled. It was simply that it had undermined her; Daphne had reminded her of those halcyon years of childhood and the unexpected jolt into the past had weakened her.

Selina went into the kitchen and sat down at the table, staring at the remains of their breakfast. Now that she was alone she could give her thoughts free rein, letting them run hither and thither, remembering, rejecting, pondering. Chin in hands, Selina frowned as she tried to create some kind of order out of the chaos. What was odd was that, terrible though Daphne's revelations had been, her observations about darling Mummy seemed even more shocking. Of course, Daphne was bound to try to shift the blame. She'd as good as confessed that she'd tempted Daddy when he was alone and feeling down, and she'd admitted that he'd always felt guilty about it, even when he'd been dying. Remembering, Selina felt a twinge of remorse. She'd been so sure that it was Maudie he was regretting and now it seemed that it was an affair with Daphne for which he'd been asking forgiveness. How terrible for him to have carried such guilt all those years but he'd only had himself to blame. It was ridiculous to hint that it was Mummy's fault. Mummy had been wonderful; always so goodtempered, so available, so . . . so *motherly*.

Selina shifted, folding her arms beneath her breast. It was so typical of men to want you to have their babies but expect you to go on behaving like some kind of sex symbol. They should try looking after children all day long! Mummy had done wonderfully well; the house was always run beautifully, spotlessly clean, meals on time, everything orderly.

'Sounds very businesslike,' Daphne had said. 'The perfect wife and mother. Rather like a job description, isn't it? But it tends to leave out the messy, human bits.'

Was this why Patrick had turned to Mary—because she, Selina, had been unable to fulfil some essential need? Could it possibly be true that, through some lack on her part, Patrick had looked elsewhere for comfort? Surely the lack was on Patrick's part. If there had been inadequacy it was his, not hers. Yet Daphne's words stuck like a burr beneath the skin.

'Nobody walks out of a happy, loving relationship voluntarily.'

The words 'happy, loving' were, even she was forced to admit, not ones that she'd necessarily apply to her marriage. She'd never been a one for all that lovey-dovey business and it had been *necessary* to keep Patrick in line, to make him aware of the sacrifices she was continually making. Being cheerful and happy was all fine and good but pretty soon people took you for granted and you got no gratitude. A tiny memory struck into her mind. Despite Mummy's good-temper there had, on reflection, been the tiniest air of long-suffering about her; little sighs escaping and a partic- ular expression of . . . what? Of patience, of private suffering, nobly borne . . .

Selina got to her feet; the sudden movement instinctively rejecting such heretical thoughts. If Mummy *had* been long-suffering she'd probably had plenty to be patient about. It couldn't have been easy, moving from pillar to post, all that entertaining, two children to look after, whilst Daddy at the first opportunity was unfaithful with her best friend and remarried barely a year after she'd died.

Clearing the table, preparing to wash up, Selina wondered what Emily had felt, suddenly discovering that Philip wasn't her father after all; finding that her real father had never acknowledged her. At least Daddy had not been prepared to break up his own family for his illegitimate child. He'd loved Emily—everyone had loved Emily—but she, Selina, and Patricia had come first. She was able to feel sorry for Emily, able to go on loving her. Emily had been the victim and could not be blamed. Yesterday, Daphne had shown her the photograph of Emily's little boy, Tim. It had been a shock to see him looking so like Posy; so like Daddy in the photos taken when he was small. Any comfort she might have taken in believing that Daphne might be lying was destroyed in that moment. It was odd how that photograph had moved her: it might have been of her own child.

'Come out and see us,' Daphne had said, then. 'Come and meet Tim. Emily would love to see you again. Won't you think about it?'

And, still staring at the photograph, Selina had said that she would.

As she plunged her hands into the hot, soapy water the telephone rang. Cursing, she snatched a tea towel and went to answer it, still wearing her rubber gloves. It was Patrick.

'I wondered if you might want to talk about Posy,' he said, after a rather awkward greeting. 'It must have come as a bit of a shock.'

Hastily Selina gathered her rags of pride about her.

'Obviously,' she answered coolly. 'I'm really concerned that she seems intent on abandoning any ideas of a career. But then some members of this family don't have much staying power.'

'Well, it was just a thought.'

There was so much resignation and finality in his voice that she clutched the receiver tighter, regretting her sharp remark . . . 'Philip was rather like Hilda. Punctilious, proper, but there was no warmth . . .' Had she ever been warm or loving to Patrick?

'Daphne's been staying with me.' She spoke at random; anything to keep him from hanging up on her. Suddenly she knew that she could not possibly admit her father's indiscretions to Patrick; it would almost be as if she were condoning his own behaviour. 'She's invited me out to Canada.'

'Really?' His voice was warm with the acknowledgement of Daphne's generosity. 'And are you going?'

'Yes, I think so.' She managed a nice casual note. 'I don't see why not. I haven't seen Emily for years. Apparently she's running this very successful cooking business and I thought I might pick up a few tips.'

'She was such a sweetie.' He sounded so affectionately reminiscent that Selina was brought up short. Clearly remembering Emily was more important, more pleasurable, than asking why she should require any tips. If she thought that he might show an interest she was disappointed. 'Sounds like a great idea, Selina. Anyway, Posy is arranging for me to meet Mike. Have you met him yet?'

'No.' How she wished that she could have said 'yes', been the first. 'Not yet. I'd rather she wasn't marrying a divorced man with a child, but you know Posy. I'm sure my point of view will be ignored.'

'She sounds very much in love. That's how it was with us, remember? Luckily you were within a month or two of finishing your course at Miss Sprules'. I'm not sure we'd have wanted to be sensible and wait, are you?'

She swallowed. How underhand of him to speak of such a thing now; to make her remember . . .

'Daddy wouldn't have allowed us to marry if you'd been divorced with a child.'

She spoke with difficulty and he laughed softly.

'Oh, I don't think old Hector would have stopped us. He was a big man, Hector. There was a generosity about him and he knew all about passion. Hector wasn't the sort who forgot what it was like to be young.'

She was breathless with surprise and indignation. She did not need Patrick to explain her father to her—and in such terms.

'He liked things to be done sensibly . . .' Even as she spoke, she faltered. Had her father behaved sensibly with Daphne, leaving his child to be raised by Philip?

'Perhaps. Anyway, Posy's twenty-two and Hector's granddaughter. I think we may have to give in gracefully. Aren't you pleased about Moorgate? You were so miserable about it going out of the family.' He chuckled. 'It all sounds quite extraordinary to me. However, I can see that I have forfeited all rights to comment so I just feel very lucky that Posy wants me to meet Mike. Poor Selina. You must be feeling just the least bit gob-smacked.'

She longed to reject his pity yet she needed it.

'I'm managing.'

'I'm sure you are. Let me know if you need anything—'

'I was wondering,' she broke in quickly, 'if we might have a chat after we've both met Mike. After all, you *are* her father. I should be glad of your input.'

'Thank you,' he said, after a short pause. 'That's very . . . generous of you, Selina. I should appreciate it.'

'Well, then.' She felt almost ridiculously light-hearted, as if some great point had been gained, some unselfish action achieved. 'We'll stay in touch then, shall we? I don't quite know when she's bringing him to stay.'

'Me neither. If I haven't heard from you in a few days I'll give you a buzz. How does that sound?'

'It sounds fine. And thanks for phoning, Patrick. How . . . how are things with you?'

'It's tremendously hard work but terribly satisfying. It's being a real eye-opener. So what's this about professional cooking, then?'

She felt a strange desire to burst into tears. 'Oh, just an idea I had. I don't want to sit about being useless. We'll be in touch then. 'Bye.'

She replaced the receiver and went back to the kitchen, feeling quite strangely happy. The washing-up water was cold and greasy but somehow it didn't really matter after all.

Chapter Forty-one

Several weeks later, Posy and Mike sat at the window table in the Mill. They were on their way to Cornwall and Mike had spent the night at The Dolphin and renewed his acquaintance with Maudie.

'You were right,' he said, as he stirred his coffee. 'Your mother was much more intimidating. Maudie's a sweetie. I really like her.'

'It's weird, actually,' said Posy thoughtfully. 'Mum wasn't too bad, after all. I thought she'd be much worse. She was kind of muted, I thought. Having Aunt Daphne to stay must have loosened her up.'

'Then please give my thanks to Aunt Daphne. I'm sorry I missed her.'

'She's gone back to Canada, now, but it was great to see her. She's really cool. One day we'll go out and see them all. Or better still, they can come and stay with us at Moorgate. That would be brilliant. Just like when we were all little. I can't believe Mum's going out to stay with them. I know she always had a soft spot for Emily but it was a real surprise. Poor old Mum. I feel a bit guilty now she's been quite good about it. And Dad's given us his blessing. No backing out now.'

Mike smiled at her. 'Your father was really nice. I rather admire what he's doing but I hope he'll come and visit us too. But not while I'm writing. They'll all have to wait until I'm between books.'

'We'll have big parties.' Posy sighed contentedly. 'Lots of quiet and then big celebrations. It's going to be so good.'

'I can hardly believe that you sat here with Melissa.' Mike looked out across the river, over the thatched roof of the pub, to the high slopes of the moor beyond. 'She didn't want to break her journey but I insisted. We chose Bovey Tracey because it is the gateway to the moor. It's quite incredible.'

Posy watched him. 'It was a busy morning,' she said. 'This was the only table left. She watched the birds and I showed her the book. People write down what they've seen and some make funny remarks.' She paused, reaching for the diary. 'There's a nice entry a man wrote about his wife and I showed it to her. I wonder if I can find it.' She turned the pages and, after a moment or two, gave a cry of triumph. 'Here it is.'

She passed the book across the table and sat back, looking about her. She remembered how she'd had tea with Hugh here, weeks ago, and told him about her father. How kind he'd been then. She knew now that her feelings for Hugh had been a young girl's infatuation: a trying of the wings, a testing of the water, but she was still very fond of him. She'd gone riding with him a few weekends back and told him about Mike. She'd been fearing family opposition then, afraid that there would be a fuss about her giving up all idea of a career of her own. He'd listened with his usual attention and then he'd laughed.

'You've come to the right person this time,' he'd said. 'I had a terrible fight on my hands when I wanted to give up university and join Max. My parents were furious, especially my mother. I stuck it out, though. I was just twenty-one and I dug my heels in. I knew it was right and I went for it and I've never regretted it.'

'I'm twenty-two,' she'd said. 'I'm old enough to know what I want. I won't let them get me down.'

He'd smiled at her. 'That's my girl,' he'd said. '*Omnia vincit amor.* Believe it.'

'What does it mean?' she'd asked—and he'd laughed.

'You sound just like Max,' he'd said. 'It means "Love conquers all things".'

He'd looked rather sad suddenly and she remembered that his girl-friend, Lucinda, hadn't loved him enough to live with him on the moor and then she'd felt guilty because she was so happy. She'd hugged him just before she'd left.

'You'll come and stay with us, won't you, Hugh? I'm going to keep a horse, maybe two. Please come and we can go riding together. We'll stay friends, won't we?'

He'd held her tightly, just for a moment, and given her a quick kiss.

'Try and stop me,' he'd said—and she'd turned to wave to him as she'd run up the track to where Maudie waited in the car. He was still leaning on the gate, watching, when she'd turned round for the last time, the old dog, Mutt, sitting patiently at his feet.

She came out of her reverie with a start as Mike gave an exclamation.

'Good God!' he said. 'Look at this. Melissa wrote in the book, Posy. Did you know?'

'She put some birds in. A nuthatch, I think one of them was. Do you know, I'd quite forgotten.'

'But she wrote something about you. It must have been after you'd gone. You said you went first, didn't you? Here it is. Look.'

'Maudie came for me.' Posy took the book and stared at the entry. 'Met a great chick called Posy.'

When she looked up she had tears in her eyes. 'I don't believe it.'

'You met each other and she wrote about you.' Mike shook his head, near to tears himself. 'It's like a little message to us, isn't it?'

Posy nodded, hardly trusting herself to speak. 'There's something else. A quotation, is it? "Thou wast not born for death, immortal Bird!"'

Mike was silent, shaken by a thousand memories. 'It's Keats,' he said at last. 'One of Melissa's favourites, especially . . . towards the end. I think your meeting was very important to her.'

He took the book and, after one long, last glance, put it back on the window seat.

'Come on,' he said. 'Let's get going, shall we? I can't wait for us to be at Moorgate. Just the two of us for the first time. It's silly, I know, but it's like we've been given a special blessing. How like Melissa, the immortal Bird, to be able to reach beyond time and space and touch us with her love.'

Rob shook the quilt into its clean cover and laid it on the air bed. He stood back to study the effect and glanced about the room. Soon Moorgate would be furnished properly, lived in, alive, just as it should be. Its months of waiting were nearly over. Meanwhile he would be very snug and comfortable in the small cottage with its tiny courtyard down in Tintagel. The purchase had gone through very quickly and he was busy making it very much his own. He didn't need too much in the way of furnishings: a kitchen and big living room downstairs; a bedroom, box room and bathroom upstairs. It was quite big enough for him and he intended to build a barbecue in the sunny courtyard and add a few tubs of flowers to liven it up.

As he passed through the house, he was able to remember his obsession with a smile. It was bound to be special to him—how could it be otherwise?—but the terrible ache of desire, the desperation to own, had ebbed away, leaving him at peace. He looked in at the downstairs rooms, as clean and ready as empty rooms could be, a fire laid ready in the fireplace, and went on into the kitchen. There were provisions in the larder and the Esse ensured that there would be hot water when they needed it.

He placed a note with the word 'Welcome' written on the outside against a bottle of champagne which stood on the kitchen table and gave one last look round.

'So,' he said—and picked up the photograph of Melissa and the rug which Mike had given him. 'Come on, my love,' he murmured. 'Let's go home.'

They arrived at about teatime. Posy jumped out so as to open the gate and Mike drove in, parking in the open-fronted barn. They stood together, looking about them, revelling in their sense of belonging.

'Rob said he'd leave milk and stuff,' said Posy. 'I'm dying for a cup of tea, aren't you?'

They let themselves in through the front door, enjoying every second, longing to explore the old house inch by inch now they could do so alone.

'Tea first, though,' said Posy. 'And then we can really savour it. Oh!'

'What is it?' He followed her into the kitchen, looking over her shoulder. 'Champagne!' He began to laugh. 'What a terrific thing to do. I'll give him a buzz later.'

'We're going down to see him tomorrow,' Posy told him. 'To see how he's getting on at the cottage. He's trying not to be too thrilled about it but he's dead pleased, really.'

'It's such a relief,' said Mike, pushing the kettle on to the hotplate whilst Posy fetched the milk. 'I couldn't have felt really happy about Moorgate if Rob wasn't happy, too.'

'He'll be able to come whenever he likes,' said Posy. 'It'll be his second home. You know, I don't think I'll ever get used to that view.'

They drank their tea, talking quietly together, making plans, and presently, arm-in-arm, they went out to look around the house, murmuring to one another.

'Huge, comfortable sofas . . .' said Mike, in the sitting room.

'Oh, yes, but not too smart. No fussing if the dogs climb on them.'

'Or the children?' He was smiling at her.

'Of course not,' she said indignantly. 'It's their home, isn't it?'

They crossed the hall to the other room.

'So what about this as my study, then?'

'It would make a wonderful playroom.' Her voice was wistful. 'A really terrific living room for everyone. And it's so sunny.'

'Perhaps you'd like me to work in the loosebox?'

'The pony wouldn't like that.'

They laughed together, softly, intimately, and, as they climbed the stairs, Posy glanced behind her. She'd had the oddest idea that someone was following them.

'It's such a lovely room.' They were standing together at the window of the big bedroom. 'We'll have the bed facing the window so that we can see the trees.'

'This is the nursery.' She was very confident about it. 'Isn't it perfect? With the room next door, and the small bathroom, it makes it the children's quarters.'

'I must put up a swing on the lawn.'

'Under the escallonia hedge.'

They paused on the landing to look out across the moor and Mike slipped his arm about her.

'Don't you think old Rob made the bed look inviting?' he murmured.

She chuckled, holding him tightly. 'I don't remember,' she answered teasingly.

'Then let's go and have another look,' he said.

Maudie poured herself some coffee, sliced the top neatly from her egg, and settled herself to look at her letters. It was a promising selection: a letter from Daphne, a card from Posy and the autumn catalogue from the Scotch House. She slit open Daphne's letter and began to read it as she ate her egg.

'It's being such a success,' she'd written. 'Emily and Selina get on so well and Selina has really fallen for Tim. He adores her. It's such a relief I can't tell you, but then I don't have to, do I?'

Maudie laid down the thin blue sheets for a moment. She'd been shocked to see how much Daphne had aged when she'd returned from London. They'd spoken on the telephone, and Maudie had realised that it had been a great ordeal for both of them, but she'd been quite frightened at the haggard appearance of her old friend.

'It's worth it,' Daphne had said, relaxing in an armchair, sipping hot tea. 'I cheated and said some brutal things but we've worked our way through it and she's coming to terms with it. She's not giving away too much too soon, but at least she's still speaking to me. If we can get her out to Canada we shall be home and dry. Emily will see to that. Emily and Tim.'

'It was very brave of you,' Maudie had said, 'and now you must relax for your last week. We'll have a wonderful time.'

'Have you forgiven me, Maudie?' she'd asked. 'For deceiving you and making you worry?'

'It's all over,' she'd answered. 'In fact, I wondered if you might like these.'

She'd opened the drawer and offered her friend the leather folder. Daphne had taken it wonderingly, opening it cautiously. She'd given a little gasp when she saw the photograph of the young Hector—looking so like Tim—but as her gaze fell on the other photograph of Hector and herself, her face turned pale. She'd sat immovably, studying it, and then she'd closed her eyes.

'Where on earth did you find it?' she'd asked faintly, pressing the folder to her breast. 'Oh, Hector . . .'

Maudie had kneeled beside her, putting an arm about her. 'I just found it,' she'd said, 'and I thought you might like to have it.'

They'd looked at one another for a long moment, two elderly ladies remembering days and nights of love, until Daphne had leaned forward and kissed her.

'Now I know that you've forgiven me,' she'd said. 'Oh, Maudie, how foolish we are.'

'It's certainly foolish to kneel down at my age,' grumbled Maudie, getting up painfully. 'So tell me what you think about Posy's bombshell and how did Selina take it? If only I could have warned you . . .'

With the mysteries solved and secrets shared and forgiven, the last week had been such a happy one.

'I shall come out to see you,' Maudie had promised, as they'd said goodbye at St David's. 'Perhaps for Christmas. Kiss Emily and the children for me . . .'

It had been hard to watch her go, Maudie's link with Hector and the past.

'I miss her,' she said aloud—and Polonius stirred and wagged his tail sympathetically, sitting up to look hopefully at the toast rack. Maudie frowned at him severely. 'Don't think you'll get round me that easily,' she said. 'You're still in disgrace.'

Yesterday, whilst Maudie had been examining her new car, checking the switches, learning her way round it, she'd left the gate open and Polonius had sneaked out. Once he was safely clear, no raised voices or whistle blowing, he'd padded along happily, down to the bridge. Having pursued several interesting scents, he'd set off again, along the lane to Lustleigh. He'd gone some way before he'd come upon the car, pulled in tight to the hedge, the driver fast asleep. It was a warm and sunny morning and the occupant had left his window open. His seat was tilted back and he was snoring a little; a rep taking a breather between calls. Polonius had paused to look at him. Usually, at his approach, there was some kind of disturbance, a reaction—generally involving rapid movement and a lot of noise—but this man had slept on, unaware of Polonius watching him. Polonius had come closer, right up to the window, interested by the noise issuing from the man's open mouth. Receiving no response, he'd put his head into the car with a loud and throaty 'woof' and, as the man came blearily awake, he'd licked him generously and wetly around the face.

With a startled cry, the man had shot upright, grappling clumsily with the seat lever. Pleased by this attention, Polonius had barked loudly, prancing a little before thrusting his head through the window again. Shouting, gesticulating, the man had attempted to start the car, whilst also trying to close the window, and Polonius, thinking that this was some kind of new game, had barked himself hoarse before the driver had managed to gain control and the car had shot off down the lane. He'd followed it, rather puzzled, until, above the receding noise of the engine, he'd heard the whistle being blown.

Maudie had missed him fairly soon and, having hunted about the house and garden, had followed him into the lane blowing furiously on her whistle. The car had nearly knocked her over.

'If that's your dog, lady,' the driver had yelled, braking violently for a moment, 'he should be properly controlled. I've a good mind to report you,' and he'd rocketed off again. A few moments later Polonius had trotted into sight, pleased with his morning's work, refusing to be cowed by her remonstrances.

Now, seeing that no toast was to be forthcoming, he yawned contemptuously and stretched himself out again on the veranda.

'I'm not surprised that Posy doesn't want you,' muttered Maudie. 'We're stuck with each other, you and me.'

'It's not that we don't want him,' Posy had protested. 'It's because I'm not sure that he'll be able to adapt to Mike and a baby. He's just got used to you and it seems mean to ask him to start all over again. And he's so big and boisterous. Poor Luke will never learn to walk. He'll be knocked over every time he stands up. Do you really mind, Maudie? He can come to us if you ever want to go away.'

Maudie had grumbled, pretending that she'd known how it would be all along, but secretly she was relieved. She'd become surprisingly attached to Polonius and had been rather dreading being alone again. As for Polonius, he regarded Maudie as his own property and had settled so happily at The Hermitage that she, too, wondered if he were rather too old to cope with yet another change in his life.

She opened Posy's card, smiling at the familiar spiky writing, the little pictures drawn round the margins.

Only another week, *she'd written*, and I shall be finished here and can start organising the wedding. I can't believe it, Maudie. In three months' time I shall be married and living at Moorgate. Mike's decided to use the old office as his study. He says that, with the loo and storeroom, it makes splendid quarters for him and he can lock himself in! Hugh's found a horse that he thinks might be right for me. Is it OK if I come down the weekend after next . . . ?

Maudie stood the card against the marmalade with a little sigh. How strange that first Rob and Melissa, and then Mike and Posy, should meet and fall in love at Moorgate. It was extraordinary—and yet somehow so terribly right: that the brief week in winter for Rob and Melissa had resolved itself into a happy future stretching ahead for Mike and Posy and little Luke. As for herself, after September there would be no more week-ends . . .

'Don't start that,' she told herself sternly. 'I shall go and see them at Moorgate and there's my trip to Canada to plan. Perhaps I'll build an extension so that Posy and Mike and Luke can come and stay. And Emily and Tim . . .'

She spread some butter on her toast and opened the catalogue. The glossy pictures of rich tartans and supple tweed jogged at her memory. What had happened to the letter and samples that Miss Grey had sent last autumn? She felt a spasm of guilt, remembering that she had never replied to the letter, and, pushing back her chair, she went to look in the desk drawer. There it was, the thick envelope, put away until she had the time to think about it. She sat down again, eating her toast, looking at the soft squares of tartan, recalling the day that they'd arrived. That was the morning she'd had a card from Posy, asking her if she'd give Polonius a home, and the letter from Ned Cruikshank, telling her that Moorgate was nearly finished and wondering about the missing keys. How long ago it seemed; how much had happened since.

Maudie finished the coffee in her big blue and white cup and picked up the samples. No reason, now, why she should not order something special; something, perhaps, for the trip to Canada at Christmas. She caressed the fine woollen squares, letting them slide over her fingers: Muted Blue Douglas, Ancient Campbell, Hunting Fraser, Dress Mackenzie. It was difficult to decide, impossible to choose. Suddenly, from nowhere, a memory slipped into her mind: Hector talking to someone at a party.

'Of course, my mother was a Douglas,' he was saying, 'descended from the Bruce, she used to say. It's a very pretty tartan. Subtle and understated.' He'd smiled down at her, sending her a tiny, private wink, a pressure of his elbow pressing her hand close against his side. 'Just the thing for you,' he'd said. 'We must buy some and have something made up for you . . .'

Maudie closed her eyes for a moment, the better to remember that little wink, so intimate, so gut churning, his heart-warming smile.

'Darling Hector,' she murmured. 'How I miss you.'

She removed her spectacles, selected the square marked 'Muted Blue Douglas' and, rising from the breakfast table, went to make a telephone call.

Epilogue

The lone walker on the hill paused to remove his jersey. The late afternoon sun slanted from the west, touching the slopes with fire, warming
the grey, rough granite outcrops. He was looking forward to a cold drink,
his own bottle of water long since finished up. The early spring day had
been unseasonably hot, the blue air still, the distant view hazy. Below him
the deep lanes would be cool and dim, twisting and descending beside icy
moorland streams, their steep, dark, rocky sides streaked with fern and
mosses. As he tied the sleeves of his jersey about his waist he watched the
small figures in the garden below him. It was several years since he'd
walked these hills but the farmhouse was a familiar sight; a landmark. The
cream-washed walls glowed warmly in the sunshine and, in the open-
fronted barn, a man was piling logs into a barrow.

The last time he'd been here the house had been for sale but now it was
clearly occupied. Washing hung on a line stretched across the yard and,
once again, he could hear children's voices as they clambered on to the
swing beside the tall escallonia hedge. A young woman was encouraging
them, her laughter mingling with their cries, pushing them gently as they
clung together on the swing, shrieking with delight.

The schoolmaster smiled in sympathy, touched by the simplicity of the
scene, and then paused, staring intently. It seemed that another woman,
tall and slender, was standing in the shadow of the escallonia, watching the
happy group by the swing. Yet, as he watched, a rippling breeze shook the
branches so that the sunlight danced and trembled and he saw that, after

all, the figure was simply a delicate fusion of light and shade. The house, built at the moor gate, in the shadow of the hills, always reminded him of some verse he'd known from childhood. As he set off, descending rapidly, his face to the west, the lines were clear in his mind.

> From quiet homes and first beginning,
> Out to the undiscovered ends,
> There's nothing worth the wear of winning,
> But laughter and the love of friends.

The sun was dipping towards the sea and smoke was rising, drifting up from the chimneys of the cottages which huddled in the village in the valley. Long shadows, indigo and purple, crept upon the slopes and now, in the quiet spring evening, he could hear the rooks, quarrelling in the wood below, and the high, plaintive cries of the lambs.